The Heart
of a Lie

MEG NORTH

Black Rose Press
PORTLAND ME

Copyright © 2012 by Meg North

Cover design by Meg North
Book design by Meg North
Cover image: *Mignon*, by William-Adolphe Bouguereau (1869)

All rights reserved.
No part of this book may be reproduced in any form or by any electronic or mechanical means including information storage and retrieval systems, without permission in writing from the author. The only exception is by a reviewer, who may quote short excerpts in a review.

The Heart of a Lie, by Meg North

Printed in the U.S.A.

ISBN: 978-1466281660

The Heart of a Lie

A Novel

Also by Meg North:

NOVELS
Daniel's Garden
The Heart of a Lie
The Curtain Falls

SHORT STORIES
September Sunlight: A Civil War Short Story
The Slave Block: A Civil War Short Story

NONFICTION
The 9 Master Plots for Bestsellers & Blockbusters

For my sister Lisa, the first listener of my stories.

* * *

And Erik, whose humor and love
make me a better writer.

Prologue: An Evening's Entertainments

"Why, yes," Jane said. "Miss Perry has boasted long enough about her ability. Let us hear it at last."

With this encouragement, I walked over to the piano.

The keys shone with a creamy luster beneath the gaslight chandelier. I ran my hand along its shiny top, the wood warm and smooth beneath my fingertip.

Mr. Jakes pulled out the bench. I smiled, a deep glow alighting within me. As I took my seat, for the first time since arriving at the Curtis house I felt truly comfortable. My feet found the pedals, pressing first the left foot and then the right foot. It was like a little dance with the piano before the music began.

I opened the sheet music folio, past the *Pathetique* I had last played at the farm and to a Johann Sebastian Bach sonata, the *French Suite Number Five*. The steady tempo and evenness of the Baroque period was suitably light for my intended audience. The Romantic pieces were for myself when I was alone.

I began the first movement, the *Allemande*, its dance-like gracefulness and elegance complementing the gentility of the Vallencourt guests. I played it slower than the suggested tempo, but as I had never heard it played by any other than myself, it more than sufficed. It was a rather short piece and I soon came to the final chord.

A polite applause accompanied my completion.

"Your technique is sound," Mrs. Vallencourt said. "You would only need a few lessons from Mr. Lambson and then the overall impression would be complete. Polished, I daresay."

Mr. Vallencourt patted his wife's knee. "My dear, you cannot hope to have an ear for music you have never attempted."

"Thank you, Mr. and Mrs. Vallencourt," I said. "I appreciate all listeners."

Henry Vallencourt rose from his seat beside Jane and approached the piano. From over my shoulder, he scrutinized the Bach piece with great interest. It took me a bit by surprise, for I didn't think he had paid attention to me.

"A good start. Played rather well. Yet, I believe you mistake the composer." He came around to my side, pointing to the notation above the first measure. "You think it should have been played legato rather than adagio?"

"I mistake no one sir," I said quietly, "least of all the composer. Have you been schooled in music?"

He laughed and I felt prickled with annoyance. Why could he not entertain my cousin, rather than nitpick my piano playing?

"Mother started me in voice lessons when I was three." A mocking grin still played at his lips. "So, yes Miss Perry, I have been schooled in music."

"I see. But as you are not going to demonstrate your instrument, let me kindly play mine."

His grin turned from scorn to genuine amusement. I would have none of his opinions anymore. Wasn't Jane going to play for us this evening?

"I say, Esther," Elliot said as he came over to the piano. He tossed back the rest of his drink. "Lara says she requested a song for us to dance to!"

Henry suddenly reached out and plucked the sheet music folio. He flipped through the pages with a polite but intrigued quickness, until he at last came to a piece he preferred and set it back upon the stand. It was a Strauss waltz.

"It seems you have a piano version of the *Morning Papers Waltz*." Henry gave me a pat on the shoulder as patronizing as if I was five years old. "Please begin as soon as the dancers have assembled with their partners."

I positioned my feet above the pedals and my hands above the keys. "Miss Curtis is in want of a partner, sir. Not I."

1

As soft and lovely as the opening notes of a sonata, morning sunlight washed over my farm. Alighting the green front fields with golden tips. Bouncing over the ripples in the duck pond, splaying across the wide gray barn. The white farmhouse emerged from night's shadow. Already a light clucking sounded from the henhouse, and a moo or two groaned from the barn.

Before the day's tasks beckoned me, I paused by the parlor windows. I gazed through the thick wavy glass, arms rubbing my shoulders, feeling a bit of the morning's chill and also the warmth I felt whenever I looked upon my farm.

My home.

"Esther! Biscuits are done!"

Sarah's hearty fare awaited me at the breakfast table. Lara was already placing sausage links on her plate. I ate absentmindedly, thinking of the things I had yet to do, while my younger sister kept up a stream of chatter about Jacob Hodges, the neighbor's boy, being so kind and cordial to her yesterday.

"He's even offered to help with the harvest, Esther. Now, don't you look so dreary about it. We could always use an extra hand. Nick and Wesley can't do it all by themselves."

I spooned baked beans onto a biscuit half. "They don't, Lara, for we are helping with the harvest as well. Starting this morning after the feeding, we'll be apple-picking."

"Lara, you ride Sarge every day." I paused. "It's already the fourteenth of September. I have put it off as long as I can, but we must begin."

"Oh, all right." She played with a twist of her golden hair. "Then I am having Jacob come over, whatever you say."

"Fine." I tried to give her a cross look, but she turned her bright blue eyes to me, and I chuckled. It was impossible to be mad at my sister for longer than a moment.

I finished the last of the breakfast and stood from the table. "I'm going to feed the cows. Please take tea up to Mother before you go out on your ride. You may have a carrot for Sarge, if you wish."

"He likes apples more."

"Then I guess you have found a reason to help with the apple-picking, haven't you?" I gathered the plates. "Come to the orchard at ten o'clock. Jacob better be on time."

She grinned. "Thank you, Esther."

She hopped up out of her seat and gave me a quick kiss on the cheek before skipping out of the dining room to the kitchen. I shook my head. Some days it was hard to remember my sister was nineteen, for all the girlishness she displayed. She had been a wondrous help with Mother's care this summer, though. I took on the majority of the responsibility for the farm and we had taken turns nursing her. She fell ill with the most dreadful cough in June, and her fragile health clung to life like the last blossom before winter.

Perry Farm had little recovered from losing Mother's guidance and help. I picked up the reins and directed the farm-hands as best I could, but some days I felt I was out on a branch in a storm, waiting to crash to earth. It was my home, and I'd do what I could to save it. Never mind the rumors about town it was failing. Never mind Jacob Hodges' greedy father who desired my land like my own father desired drink. Never mind that Father had been killed in the war and we were three women alone. It was Lara, Mother and I. We had none to protect us.

Yet, somehow, our burdens had strengthened me. Like I was slowly being forged from raw metal into iron. The more I led Perry Farm, the better I became. The more I saw it not as a hardship, but as my rightful position. It was what I wanted, and I accepted it with complete conviction.

All I needed now was to have someone by my side. The strength and protection of a husband would provide me and my farm with strength, stability, leadership and direction. I could run Perry Farm, but I was ill-equipped for its more masculine duties. Someone for me. Someone like … Caleb Randolph.

I remembered the day he was hired to be our newest farm-hand. He'd come into the parlor to speak to Mother, his cheeks and nose a burnished red from the late winter cold. I was bringing laundry down from upstairs and at first sight of him, a rush whooshed up from my knees like a chimney blast.

It was time for the chores. I paused by the parlor mirror on my way down the back hall. My hair was the deepest brown, like an oak tree at night. Its length and weight kept it pinned in a heavy roll at my neck. I continued down the hall and stopped at the back door for my apron and bonnet. After I'd tied my homespun apron over my dress, I pressed the back of my hand to my cheek. Oh, it was not the warming September morning that brought such heat to my face.

But thoughts of Caleb were not needed to feed and milk the cows. I met Nick and Wesley, my other two farm-hands, at the door, and gave them the morning instructions - start the turnip and squash harvest in the kitchen garden.

"Where's Mr. Randolph?" I asked, as quietly and steadily as I could.

Nick spit in the grass. "Ah, you know Caleb, Miss Perry. Shows up when he wants to."

"I see." My jaw tightened. "Jacob Hodges will be helping with the apple harvest."

Wesley laughed. "I'll bet he will. Scopin' out the place for his father, no doubt."

"It is my farm. Not his," I muttered. "Time to get to work."

Oh, how I hated Mr. Hodges. Jacob seemed amiable towards Lara, but it would not surprise me if he picked up a handful of my black soil and squeezed it between his fingers.

Most of Bayview's shore and soil were littered with rocks like currants in a scone. Perry Farm was on the choicest land in Knox County and a prize for any farmer. Thanks to the towering pines and the giant bulk of the Camden hills, the soil was rich and fertile and the wind not quite as fierce as the farms closer to the sea. After Father left for war seven years ago, the townspeople started asking questions about my farm. My brusque answers left little doubt that neither Mother nor I would sell.

But it did not stop Mr. Hodges. The horrid man lived just down Pine Street and leered at my place like a lecherous sailor. It raised my hackles just to think about it. I picked up the tin milking pail and stomped off towards the barn.

If only Father had stayed. If only Mother was well. I could do little for these circumstances. As for marrying ... it was something I could do. With Caleb by my side, Mr. Hodges had no chance and his pestering would cease.

Like a queen with her king, I would stand by his side and be the mistress of my home.

2

After rolling the sleeves of my dress up to my elbows, I put a hand to my eyes and gazed up the trunk of the apple tree.

"You must have a dozen by now!" I called. "Toss them down, Lara!"

Glimpses of her golden hair peeped through the leafy apple tree branches, but she was giggling too much to pay attention to me. Between Jacob and her desire to ride Sarge, Lara had seemingly forgotten we were here to work. Meanwhile, my apple basket sat empty at my feet and we had been out in the orchard for almost an hour. The September day was hot and dry, and a trickle of sweat snaked down the back of my neck.

"Lara? Did you hear me?"

"I think Jacob Hodges has her attention, Miss Perry."

So, my third farm-hand had at last decided to make his appearance. Caleb Randolph, browned and handsome from a summer working the hayfield, approached the apple tree. He set down the two-wheeled cart and picked up a bushel basket.

"That he does, Mr. Randolph," I said, thinking that Caleb certainly had my attention.

Caleb planted his foot against the apple tree trunk, his shadow stretching across the bark like a crooked wishbone. His hands reminded me of my father's, and for once, I felt comforted by the memory. Dirt creased along his knuckles and gathered into each fingernail curve like a black crescent beach.

"Mr. Randolph?" he chuckled. "How long we known each other?"

I half-smiled. "Since March."

"Then it's high time you called me Caleb."

Warm brown eyes, an easy smile. When he looked at me like that, it was easy to forget my burdens. And it was easy to think of him as mine.

Caleb pushed back the brim of his straw hat, squinting up at the tree's occupants. His chest and thick shoulders were covered by a baggy linen shirt. Brown work pants, a strip of leather as a belt. He cupped his hands about his mouth.

"Helllooo there, Miss Lara!"

"Is that Caleb Randolph?" my sister called. "Goodness, it's about time you're here. Come up and I'll go ride Sarge. If Esther lets me, that is."

"Toss down the apples first and then you can go." I looked at Caleb. "Caleb and I will finish the apple-picking."

"Oh, goody! Hurry up, Jacob!"

Both Caleb and I chuckled at my sister's antics as she tossed down her apples into my basket. The fruit bounced off branches and thudded into the basket. Then Lara hurriedly scrambled out of the tree and landed in a heap of petticoats and calico on the grass beside me. Jacob jumped down beside her, wiping his hands free of sap.

"Thank you, Esther," Lara said. "Jacob can take Ace, then?"

"Yes," I said, for Ace was my horse. "You get until luncheon, and I'll be wanting you back here afterward."

"I will!"

She gave me a quick embrace, and then grabbed up her skirts, challenging Jacob to a foot-race over to the stables. The boy barely had time to acquiesce before she took off, her blond braids flying out behind her.

I laughed. "My sister was practically born in the saddle. She'd rather ride than do just about anything."

"Why, Miss Perry," Caleb grinned, "that's the first time I've heard you laugh in a month."

He was probably right, which gave me pause. Did he think I was too serious? I'd fancied myself level-headed.

"Lara cheers me," I admitted, "though I am not too keen on her choice of company today."

Caleb balanced an apple basket on his hip. "Can you blame Jacob? Or his father? You've got the best land in Bayview."

My fingers tightened on the rim of the bushel basket. "Enough about this topic, Mr. Randolph. I have plenty to do today."

"How much is it?" Caleb asked. "The farm, Esther. What's the asking price?"

I scoffed, disgusted that he would even ask such a question. "It is not for sale."

"Ah." He nodded, standing at the base of the tree and looking up into its branches. "Well, I guess it's time to get this apple harvest started."

"Yes. We have a lot of work to do."

With his hands on his hips, he turned back to look at me. We were alone, and I suddenly felt nervous. My level-headed mind seemed to turn blank. I tried to tell him I'd stay on the ground and he could toss down the apples to me, but my mouth had gone dry. So, I stepped over to him until we were side by side, breathing in the crisp scent of the ripe apples. His eyes bore into mine, his sweat-streaked face close.

"I can help you, but you've got to let me, Esther."

He slowly turned his body until he was facing me, the sunlight bright behind him, the apples and branches surrounding us like a fragrant embrace.

"You'll not have to worry anymore. You'll have your farm. And me."

He reached down and took my hand. He was strong and steady, cupping my dream in his hands. I'd never leave my home and he would be beside me like he had all summer. A lifetime like this.

"Yes, Caleb," I murmured. "Yes, it is what I want."

His fingers untied my bonnet strings and it tumbled down my back. He bent and touched his warm forehead to mine and my eyes closed as I breathed in his scent of leather and musky sweat. All silenced in my head. My heart spread warmth through me and I was succumbing and soaring at the same time.

"Esther? ESTHER!"

Good heavens, who was that? My tender warm moment shattered and Caleb grunted as he straightened. His hands dropped and my face felt cold.

"Mrs. Perry," Caleb was saying.

I steadied my breathing, trying to focus through the foggy haze of my brain. My feelings had me in such a crazy whirl that for a moment I didn't even know where I was and was confused about what was happening.

But my world came sharply into focus as I noticed my mother striding through the trees.

Caleb abruptly stepped away from me, returning to the two-wheeled cart. I was still clutching the apple basket and looked down at it as if I'd never seen it before. My bonnet lay rumpled on the ground and I hastily picked it up.

Mother stopped at the edge of the orchard row, hands on hips, her mouth twisted into a snarling frown.

"What in God's name were you doing with my daughter?"

"Mother, you should be in bed," I said calmly. "Please go rest. I'm sorry to have you troubled. Caleb -"

"Caleb?" Mother queried. "Take the wagon to town, Mr. Randolph. I have an order at the store. Ask Mr. Warren about the cider press."

He knew better than to argue. He touched the brim of his hat, and without looking at me, hurried away.

"Look at you," Mother hissed after he had gone. "Straighten your hair."

My stomach slid lower into my belly, and the sunlight bore down on me. I wearily put my bonnet back on and wiped my forehead, swatting wisps of hair from my eyes.

Mother was so angry she was shaking. "What are you doing? You want be known as the town hussy? You are not to be with Caleb Randolph."

"He wants me to marry him, Mother." I enjoyed a fleeting remembrance of his warm hand. "I would make him a fine farmer's wife, and we'll stay here. I'll take care of you."

She crossed her arms, her face suddenly years older. She was tired of this, too, I realized. Tired of the arguing, tired of keeping promises made too long ago. Promises that didn't apply to my life any more now than they applied to my life then.

"Esther, you must be sensible. Caleb Randolph shirks his duties. I can't depend on him! You can't either, you know."

I didn't care. He wouldn't be like that to me.

"I am not afraid, Mother. I am not afraid of struggle."

Her eyes crinkled at the corners. "But haven't we struggled enough since your father left? Wouldn't you like to ease this heavy yoke that we bear?"

She had thought our troubles would end with the war. Yet every day for the past three years, I had thanked God that He does not provide us with a clear view of the future. For if we had known that our troubles were just beginning, that yoke may have broken us.

I sighed. Mother was scared. She'd been scared for the three of us, three women alone. Without Father and owning the farm that everybody wanted. I wiped my hands on my apron and went over to her, sliding a hand around her shoulder.

"It is because Father is gone that I am not afraid."

I still wanted Perry Farm as my own and I still wanted to marry Caleb. My school-friends were already wed to the fishermen and farmers of Bayview. Patsy found a storekeeper and Caroline helped her husband at the sawmill. I was twenty-two years old and didn't feel like a foolish girl any longer.

But my thoughts about Caleb suddenly vanished. Mother should be in bed, and I had to take care of her. Her eyes were widening and she had begun to cough. Its grating rasping shook her and bent her.

"Mother?"

I gripped her shoulders and tried to walk with her back to the house. But she was coughing and coughing. The hoarse barking echoed through the apple trees and carried like the wind above the farm. I felt myself losing her, losing my grip until she slipped into the grass.

"Mother?" I knelt beside her, gripping her hands. "Stay here, you'll be all right. I'm going to get help."

She nodded weakly, coughing and coughing. I turned and ran across the yard towards the stable and paddocks. Lara was walking Sarge around the paddock, keeping up a conversation with Jacob. At the first sight of me she nearly let go of the bridle.

"Esther?"

"Help me with Mother, Lara. She's collapsed near the apple tree."

"Oh God!" Her hand flew to her mouth. "I'll take Sarge in. What do you want me to do?"

"Have Sarah make her broth. Jacob, go fetch Nick and Wesley. I need your help getting her to bed."

Jacob hopped off the fence and bolted towards the pastures. Lara led her stallion towards the stable. I returned to Mother, soothing her as best I could with my murmurings and my handkerchief. Her coughing subsided, but the handkerchief was thick with a foul-smelling mucus. I held my stomach and concentrated on keeping her calm.

At last, the three young men came from the pastures. Jacob held her head while the two farm-hands supported her with their arms forming a chair. I followed behind as we hurried across the yard and into the house.

Lara met us at the door. "Mother? Mother! Sarah's making the broth. Will she be all right?"

She was wringing her hands and looking so distraught I clasped her shoulders and made her look at me.

"Bring a bowl of cool water and a towel upstairs. Can you do that, dearest?"

She nodded and departed for the kitchen. I took off my bonnet and wiped the grime from my forehead. Oh, why did she leave her bed? She had been ill for months and this was the worst attack I'd ever seen.

Lara brought the bowl and the towel. I gave my sister a kiss on the cheek, picked up my skirts, and hurried upstairs. We met Jacob at the top of the stairs. The two farm-hands mumbled something about trying to make her comfortable, then departed down the stairs.

Jacob took Lara's hand. I felt grateful he was with her, though it didn't make my relations with his nasty father any easier.

"Keep her occupied today, Jacob," I said as I walked past them. "You may dine with us, if you like."

"Thank you, Esther." He tipped his straw hat. "Anything else I can do for Mrs. Perry?"

I shook my head. Lara whimpered, but allowed herself to be led downstairs. I would check on her later and make sure she was all right.

I continued down the hall and went into Mother's bedchamber. She lay propped up on pillows, her lungs heaving, her throat raspy. I set the bowl on the bedside table and seated myself on the bed.

"Es ... Esther," she wheezed. "I ... I can't ... breathe."

Fear constricted my throat, and I swallowed hard to keep my voice steady.

"I've brought water."

I dipped the towel in the bowl to soak it, and touched the wet fabric to her lips. The moist drops soothed her, and she was able to draw in a deep breath. As she exhaled through her parched lips, I felt my heartbeat slow down.

"A good girl," she whispered, still clearing her throat. "Let us not ... bear ill will against one another."

I kissed her wet fingers. "I won't, Mother."

"You ... you have a home here."

With you and with Caleb, I thought. I hoped the exertion during our quarrel hadn't caused her coughing. I rose to my feet, then bent and kissed Mother's forehead.

"Sarah is making a broth. I will bring it up later."

"Thank you." She looked at me, then her head sank into the pillow. "You are like your father. So kind ... "

She slipped into sleep. I reached up to close the bed counterpanes against the bright sunlight. Darkness swept over her face and she closed her eyes.

My father, George Perry, was a large man with huge shoulders where he would hoist me up. A shock of blond hair the same bright corn silk as Lara, the same merry blue eyes. But his eyes clouded like the sea in a storm when he returned from the Sloop Tavern. He smelled of leather and ale, his hands wet from cold pewter mugs, his breath rank with hops and barley. The day he left for war, he was so soused he could barely sit upright in the saddle.

Kind he may have been to Lara, lifting her onto Sarge's back for a ride. Kind he may have been to his friends at the Sloop, playing whist and faro long into the night.

But he was nothing like me. And long ago, I had decided never to be like him.

3

After closing Mother's bedchamber door, I left her resting and went downstairs. I stopped before the hall looking-glass. My hair roll was askew, my forehead swiped with dirt, a grimy smudge on my neck. I made myself look more presentable, but I needed a wash.

In the back kitchen, Sarah had a copper soup pot of invalid broth bubbling on the range. Her forehead glowed pink in the heat, and she sang a wordless tune as she reached into a gigantic yellow bowl on the kitchen work table and pulled out a great mound of bread dough. Slapping the dough onto the bread board, she shoved her chunky fists into its gooey center.

"Hey honey girl," she greeted as she worked. "How's your mum?"

I made my way to the pump sink. "As well as she can be."

Sarah patted my wrist and got back to kneading. After splashing water onto my face and hands, I took down an old silver tray and fetched a bowl from the built-in hutch.

"I fear for Mother's health," I began while taking out clean teacups and saucers. "This is her second coughing fit in less than a week. And this time was the worst I've ever seen."

Sarah kept her eyes on her bread. She wiped her hands on her apron and then wiped down the yellow bowl. I took a kerchief from the peg rack by the door and tied it about my head.

"She may be unable to rise from her bed for quite some time."

"And what about the harvest, Esther?" Sarah asked.

She slapped the dough into a round shape and plopped it inside the bowl to rise. I took out the sugar bowl and a sack of sugar. It was nearly empty. A last bag of sugar, a last dozen eggs. I took a deep breath, quieting my inner panic. When at last I answered Sarah, my voice was steady.

"I can manage it, with Lara's help. We have the three farm-hands and Jacob Hodges could be spared from his father's farm."

"Then that is what you will do."

I felt better after I heard her say that, for it felt like she had confidence in me. I was nigh on a grown woman. Becoming mistress of Perry Farm had been a definite for my future. It was the right time to assume its duties.

Sarah tended to the broth, poking at the coals in the range. She reached for a ladle, and I held a bowl while she scooped broth into it.

"I have some remedies for her lungs, Esther. I'll make up the recipes tonight."

I spooned tea leaves into the teapot. "Thank you. I suppose that is the best we can do. Mr. Randolph returns from town this evening, so the wagon will be available for the doctor should her condition worsens."

She poured water in the pot. I watched the small leaves dance amidst their hot bath, and inhaled the sweet earthy aroma.

"Don't you worry none, girl. She's stronger than she looks."

"I hope so."

I kissed her warm cheek and gave her shoulder a loving pat. Then I took the broth and the tea up to Mother. She was still resting when I brought it into the bedchamber, so I set it on the side table and went back downstairs. Sarah's broth was soothing and had always helped Mother before. It made me feel a little better to be able to do something for her. I ducked out the back door and into the garden shed for a bucket, tools and gloves. The shed was ringed in beautiful sunflowers, their smiling yellow faces nodding in the Indian summer breeze. As I headed across the farmyard, the brimming apple trees in the orchard brought him to mind.

Caleb.

For a moment, the anxiety about Mother's illness vanished and I was once again collapsing into his strength. I was once again the only thing his brown eyes beheld as he cradled me in warmth. Never had I thought about a boy like this.

Lara had many suitors and courters, some young and foolish, others more serious like Jacob. Nervously asking if I could deliver flowers or a letter, peering around me to catch a glimpse of her from the carriageway, their voices cracking. Had she said whether she would attend? Was she available?

At last, this summer I had someone asking about me. Someone wondering if they could speak to me, someone seeking my opinion other than to ask how much to feed a calf or when to bring the horses in. Mother's poor opinion about Caleb wasn't going to deter me from enjoying his company. How could his intentions not be clear, when he had passionately swept me up that morning? It would be foolish to doubt him.

Would ... would he ask me? When he got back from town? Would today be the day? Oh, I hoped it would!

My heart grew lighter and so did my steps. But as I passed the horse pasture on my way to the vegetable garden, a worried voice shook me from my pleasant daydreams.

"Esther!" Lara left the fence and hurried towards me, followed by Jacob. "How is Mother? Is she all right?"

"Yes, she is resting." I smiled, trying to cheer her furrowed brow. "Sarah also thinks she will recover."

"You see?" Jacob reached out and took Lara's hand, but she didn't seem to notice. "She will be fine."

"I don't know," Lara fretted. "I don't feel right. Can you not fetch the doctor, Esther?"

"Caleb could," I began, then stopped, feeling hot in the cheeks.

"One of the farm-hands has taken the wagon to town. Sarah said she would make a remedy."

"Once he gets back, please go to the doctor." Lara shrugged off Jacob's protesting. "I'm sorry, Jacob. Goodbye."

He gave up, throwing his hands up in frustration, and started across the grass towards the carriageway. I shook my head, but Lara still looked so concerned, I gave her a kiss on the cheek.

"Dearest, don't worry. There is much work to be done and we're one hand short. I'll take the wagon tomorrow."

"Oh, Esther." She embraced me and I soothed her frustrated tears. "We should have gone on Monday when she was sick the first time."

"We did not know she would cough again. Dry your tears. I need your help with the harvest, too."

She nodded in agreement and walked off towards the farm house, still sniffling. Though Lara was nineteen, her spoiled nature and her sorrow at losing Father at such a young age had made her prone to moodiness and sentiment. I petted her, too, though not as much as Father had. She was his golden-haired angel.

Sighing, I picked up my gardening supplies again and headed towards the kitchen garden. Besides a short dinner break for cold beef cuts and cheese, I worked alongside Nick and Wesley harvesting squash and turnips for the rest of the day.

As I worked, I found myself glancing towards the carriageway with such frequency Nick asked if my neck hurt. I blushed, mumbled some excuse about the sun in my eyes, and kept my gaze away from the direction that the wagon - and Caleb - would arrive.

At last, shadows began to lengthen. We had baskets and barrels full of squash and turnip ready to be loaded onto the two-wheeled cart and taken down to the root cellar. It had been an exhausting day, though the work kept my hands busy and I loved the smell of the warm earth. Suddenly, the sound of crunching wheels on the gravel carriageway snapped me to attention, and I was more than secretly delighted.

Caleb had returned.

I removed my gloves and started towards the garden shed. Caleb pulled the wagon up the carriageway into the farmyard. He circled around, then slowed our old mare and swung down. He was dusty from the trip and slapped his hat against his knee to rid it from the dust.

I stood by the garden shed, watching him. My heart was doing strange twists and turns in my chest. He was handsome, he worked hard, he was what I wanted. No matter what Mother said. I frowned as I looked up towards her bedroom. How did she know what I wanted? She thought I should be careful, but I'd always been careful.

"Did you have a fine trip to town, Caleb?" I called.

He looked around the farmyard for the source of my voice, so I stepped from the shade of the sunflowers. Soon I would be in the warmth of his arms again, soon I would feel that strong chest under his thin cotton shirt. The thought made my cheeks flame.

"Miss Perry." His voice was stiff, his manner courteous and yet distant.

I slowed my steps. I could not think what had occurred in a few short hours to make him restrain his feelings. Perhaps he was tired from the journey.

"Mr. Randolph," I said quietly.

I stopped a few feet from him. He turned from me and reached into the wagon. He drew out a small leather satchel, and I watched wordlessly as he opened it and took out a piece of paper.

"Mr. Hodges was at the store," he said. "He was looking for a farmhand. Pay is twice what it is here."

I couldn't have been more shocked than if he'd said he was going to the moon. "You wish to join the Hodges farm?"

Thanks to my nasty neighbor's greed, Caleb wouldn't be the first to be lured away by promises of a good pay.

I just hadn't expected him to be the next.

"You cannot be serious," I went on. "What of Nick and Wesley? And the harvest? You are needed here."

"Miss Perry." He held up a hand, cutting me off. "It's done. I signed this afternoon."

"You cannot trust Mr. Hodges," I said severely. "You can trust us."

I crossed my arms about my chest. Though anger flared hotly in my throat, I could not help the sorrow surging through me. To lose him, when I had wanted everything he offered. Every promise of a future.

"Trust got nothing to do with it, Miss Perry." He would not use my first name. It hurt even more than him leaving. "I mean, you were there in the orchard. Your mother doesn't want me here, unless ..."

"Unless what?" I snapped.

"Well, I'm not marrying you."

He had no intention. He felt nothing. Nothing for me, nothing for us, nothing for anything I wanted. I felt as if the ground was opening, as if I would drop into the dark bowels of the earth.

"Then I'm better off without you," I said as steadily as I could. "We all are. I want you gone within an hour."

He scowled. "I wouldn't have to leave if this place paid better."

My sadness dissipated and anger stiffened me. I felt stronger, as if I were being carved from stone on the inside. I stormed up to him.

"That's not the reason and you know it. You thought you could do what you wanted with me, and there would be no consequences."

He huffed. "You don't get it, do you, Esther?"

Before a reply tumbled from my lips, my body went cold. My knees felt weak and I could have crumpled to the dust. I was nothing to him. Not only was I nothing, but I never had been something.

I reached my hand back and slapped him. My palm tingled from the impact with his grizzled cheek. For a few seconds he stood motionless, staring open-mouthed at me. But then his look of shock turned to a grimacing smile and his brown eyes mocked me.

"I should have listened to what the other fellers said about you."

"No, Caleb," I said coldly. "You should have done the right thing."

He turned and stomped up the carriageway towards the Hodges farm. I leaned against the garden shed under the shade of the sunflowers and watched him without remorse or wanting him to return.

I didn't know whether I slapped him because he played with my feelings. Or because Mother was right. I had looked in vain for something that wasn't there.

A mistake I vowed not to make again.

I looked out of the window at the rain. It painted the farm in such drab-ness I could hardly tell where the gray barn ended and the dawning gray sky began.

The rain fell, and I thought of the piano downstairs in the parlor. One of my deepest joys was to sit and play a song from my old leather music folio. My fingers flitting along the smooth keys, notes pattering like the rain pattered Mother's window. How a song would begin slow and soft and haunting, and then a quiet steady crescendo, like walking up the stairs. At the end, in a cupped and perfect moment, it would bloom like a flower and it was as if I was playing morning sunlight.

Mother murmured from her bed. She was stirring, awakening, after a fitful night's rest. The rush of seeing to her throughout the night had long faded, and intense weariness overcame me. She'd been awake every few hours, coughing fits wracking her body. Water to her forehead, as much of Sarah's broth as she could take, soothing honey drops for her throat.

Doc Wilson came earlier that night, but with no look of comfort. He shook his head and placed a sympathetic hand on my shoulder. Nothing he could do, nothing anyone could do. The hours stretched long. Lara and I kept the broth warm and made cups of tea, but Mother slipped from us like water through a cracked vessel. Eventually, Lara dragged herself to bed. I stayed.

I stayed and I waited.

"Esther …"

Her voice was faint. I left the window and crossed over to her, pushing back a bed curtain to allow some of the dawn's light. She turned onto her back, her dark hair spread about her pillow like a fan. I leaned over and smoothed the strands away from her forehead, tucked them behind her ear.

"I'm going to go get Lara," I said. "She will want to know you're awake."

"No. Let her rest." Tears came to her eyes. "Look after her for me. Take care of her. She is such a good girl."

"I will." I grasped her hand and kissed her pale knuckles. "I won't let anything happen to her."

"Esther, you are strong." She breathed with great difficulty. "You must also do something for me. It is … of the utmost importance."

I nodded, for I could not speak.

"Announce my death in Portland. In the newspaper … it must be. You will do this, won't you?"

I would do anything for her, and I squeezed her fingers.

"Yes, Mother. Don't think of it now. I will."

She sighed, and smiled sadly. It was a great relief to her that I would take care of Lara, that I would be the one to carry on the farm. I did not fear the responsibility. I was ready for it, and it was my rightful place.

"Do not worry about us or the farm any longer." I held her hand against my cheek. "We will be all right."

"Esther, forgive me." Her voice was faint, quiet and weak under the sound of the rain. "I'm sorry to not tell you, when you do not know."

I leaned forward and kissed her cooling brow. Her voice was whispery and eerie, fingers closing slightly over mine. Skin papery, thin, stretched taut over her knuckles.

"I kept my heart for him. My love ... did not forget ..."

She turned her head to the side, deeper into the pillow. Her skin was growing colder, her hand a cold fragment in mine. I scraped my teeth across my lips, my heart as full as a moon. I put my hands on her shoulders and bent to her breast, sobbing quietly into the covers.

Mother, don't leave. Don't leave me alone. I pressed my cheek against her face, feeling her slight weight turn towards mine. A last quiet sigh, like the closing of a door.

"Mother?"

Her fingers turned limp in my hands, her shoulder slipping back upon the pillow. I clung to her in the bed, willing my warmth to seep into her sunken cheeks. The dusky shaft of light crept from her face, and I breathed, the only sound in the room. My heart eased and was still. She was gone, her unresting soul in peaceful arms.

For a long time I lay upon her, breathing in and out, listening to the rain. I was so tired, as if all her weight had floated from her body and pulled down on me.

When I at last rose to a sitting position, the heaviness shrouded me, pressing against my chest, enveloping my being. Some part of my mind began to think of all I had to do, but I struggled through the heaviness and could not bear to stand. Could not bear to leave her.

I promised I would watch over Lara, that I would carry out her final wish. I'd take an announcement out in the Portland Press Herald and let the city know of her passing. I took in a deep breath, gave Mother one last sad smile, and drew the bed curtains closed.

Rain beat against the roof with soft and soothing hands. I quietly turned the doorknob and stepped out into the hallway, closing the bed-chamber door. Sarah was snoring in the guest room. She had taken up quarters there when Mother became ill. Lara's room was down the hall, next to mine. It was time to wake her.

But I didn't know how to tell her. I didn't know how to protect her from what she had to know. I wanted to keep her safe, to let her sleep as long as she could.

I pushed open the door. My younger sister slept well, her golden curls tied up in ragged strips. Turned on her side, old brown bunny rabbit tucked under her arm. I had to smile, tears coming to my eyes. What would the boys of Bayview think to see nineteen-year-old Lara Perry with her beloved toy?

I knelt by her bed, rubbing her upper back. She murmured and stirred sleepily.

"Esther? Is Mother all right?"

I didn't know what to say, so I just held her hand. Her eyes, a deep navy in the dark, brimmed with sadness and her throat caught.

"Mother? No!"

She pushed past me and sprang up from the bed. In one swift gesture, she'd grabbed her woolen robe, yanked open the door and run down the hall. I stayed by the bed, sobbing quietly into her bedclothes as her wrenching cries fill my ears.

Yes Mother, I will keep her safe. I would do this even if you hadn't asked me to. I promise you.

Nothing will ever separate us.

5

"A shame."

Mr. Hodges stepped near me and wrapped an arm about my shoulder. His touch was repulsive. As discreetly as I could, I removed my greedy neighbor's arm from my shoulder. He didn't seem to notice my thin-lipped gaze as I stared straight ahead.

The September breeze rustled through the pine forest at the edge of the graveyard. The church bell clanged ominously, casting a metallic lull over our small group. Lara's face was white with shock and she said nothing. Her eyes were fixed upon the gravestone.

"A real shame," Mr. Hodges repeated, louder since the minister had finished his closing reading.

Nick, Wesley, Caleb, and Jacob stepped forth. They lifted the simple wooden coffin from its sawhorse and lowered it into the ground with ropes. Nobody said a word and the men sweated with the effort, though the fall breeze was slightly chilled. A swirl of freshly fallen leaves was the only merry sight, catching the September wind and cavorting at our feet. The minister closed his Bible, crossed himself, and gave the final "Amen."

"Amen," I said, but Lara said nothing. She was trembling and I reached over to grip her shoulders. She stared straight ahead, still saying nothing. What was there to say?

"Mother," I heard her whisper.

Only once, and then she was quiet. Her silence made me sadder than our sorrowful morning. Lara's golden cheeriness had vanished. She was no more than an empty shell beside me, devoid of her sunny merriment. I wanted Lara to smile again, for her to not let this deep sadness eat away at her natural girlish charm. She had often teased me for being too serious, but I had to be. I had to take care of Mother and the farm.

One by one, the members of our small funeral added final gifts to Mother's grave. I had saved a pressed lilac, her favorite flower, in a book over the summer. I placed the fragile and faintly perfumed blossom on the coffin. Lara had clutched her sunflower bouquet stiffly and tossed the sunny blooms into the grave. Our friends and acquaintances of Bayview squeezed my shoulder, murmured condolences and walked away.

As the farm-hands picked up shovels to fill the grave, Mr. Hodges put his hat back on and cracked his knuckles. I clutched Lara's shoulder, shielding her fragility with my body. Her face was concealed behind her black bonnet, golden curls resting against her shoulder.

"If you please, Mr. Hodges," I said. "We need peace on this day."

"Why, whatever do you mean, Miss Perry?" he asked in a mocking display of sympathy. "It is the twentieth and there are less than two weeks until the end of the month."

"I will come to Mr. Greene's office at ten o'clock tomorrow morning."

He looked pleased, as if he had not expected me to keep my appointments. "You have remembered, that is good. However, Silas has a client to see at that time."

"Then the day after," I said through gritted teeth. The foul reptile wanted to see me right after my own mother's funeral? The indecency was almost incomprehensible.

Mr. Hodges summoned his carriage over. "I expressly brought a carriage to convey you, free of charge. Jacob can accompany you ladies."

Lara trembled beneath my touch. The poor thing.

"Let me take my sister home first, sir. She is not well."

"Both signatures are needed for the transaction. You do understand?"

Horrible man. To make it worse, Jacob stood by the carriage door, in complete compliance with his greedy father. I steeled myself and refused to let either of them dictate to me. I needed to be strong. Lara was under my exclusive care, and we were alone. There was no one else anymore. Squaring my shoulders, I looked Mr. Hodges straight into his eyes and said in a tone that removed all doubt of my meaning:

"Conduct your business."

He smiled an infuriating half-smile. I gripped Lara's shoulders and bent to murmur in her ear.

"One last goodbye for Mother, dear. We have to go."

She whimpered, but a moment later obediently walked with me to the carriage. I assisted her up onto the seat, and then climbed in next to her. When Jacob started to get in, Lara stared at him.

"Our business does not concern you, Jacob. Go away."

He looked hurt for a moment, and my wretched heart felt a stab of regret. Scarcely a week ago I had been watching their friendship grow. His hurt expression changed to a cold mask, eerily reminiscent of his father.

"The Perry Farm will be my inheritance some day," he said without feeling or remorse. "It is my business."

With that, he settled in the carriage seat opposite us. Lara folded her arms and concealed her face with her bonnet as she looked out the window. I reached for her left hand and held her fingers.

We rode to town in silence. Bayview looked pretty in the September afternoon, maples and oaks changing color. Here and there a flash of bright scarlet, a streak of golden yellow. In the distance, by the creek, I could hear the steady splashing of the cider mill waterwheel. We passed several wagons heaped with apples heading towards the mill.

As I sat in the carriage watching the familiar faces going about their daily lives in Bayview, the tune I'd played last night came to my mind. For one lovely and exquisite moment, my sorrows subsided and it was enough to sit and remember how I'd felt when I played. The parlor fireplace flames dancing across the burnished cherry surface of the piano, flickering on the ivory keys, washing the sheet music with golden light.

But then the Silas Greene Law Office sign came into view and my reverie vanished, leaving me with a cold feeling for the errand I was about to run. Lara's bonnet pressed tightly against the carriage window.

"We're almost there, dear," I whispered. "Please let me do the talking."

She didn't say anything, but I knew she heard me. My poor sister. I missed her laughter so dearly it ached.

At last, the carriage came to a stop in the street outside the law office. Mr. Hodges jumped down from the driver's seat and Jacob made ready to open the carriage door. Lara was reluctant to move, so I grasped her about the waist. Jacob opened the door as soon as the carriage stopped and held it for us.

I descended from the carriage, half-carrying Lara along with me. Her numbed sorrow had spread to her limbs, for she could barely walk across the remainder of the street and over to the office door. Her weakness and deep exhaustion threatened to pull us both into the churned mud and rutted dirt at our feet. I kept her upright and was secretly grateful when Jacob opened the office door.

The entrance room was dark, save for an oil lamp casting dim shadows on the wall. The heavy paneling and thickly carved furniture looked repressive rather than cozy. I helped Lara and myself inside, Mr. Hodges uncomfortably close behind us. Lara gave another whimper. I murmured more comforting words into her ear, but her weak health was alarming.

"Ah, cheer up girlie," Mr. Hodges said to Lara. "It will be over soon."

I speared him with a look of ferocious anger. "Do not speak to her, sir. She is unwell. Where is Mr. Greene?"

"Here I am thinking you don't want to sell, and you hurry things along!" He gave a coarse laugh. "Patience, Miss Perry."

I guided the both of us to a pair of chairs, where Lara collapsed. I perched on the edge of my seat, back ramrod straight, ready to rise again.

"We're going to look over Phoebe Perry's will," Mr. Hodges began, but I was in no mood for conversation and cut him off.

"I discuss this matter only with Mr. Greene present."

"Then perhaps Miss Lara would?"

But Lara turned her head away from him and I sought his gaze no more, either. I sat stone-faced, staring at a framed document on the wall from Bowdoin College.

After a long moment of stifling anxiety, the office door opened. Mr. Warren, Bayview's general store proprietor, tipped his hat to Lara and I before leaving. His daughter Caroline was my age, and we'd been friends for several years.

Mr. Greene then appeared in the doorway, motioning us inside. He was as thin as a string bean, with a thick droopy mustache. But his large blue eyes darted like a rat's, and he didn't miss the slightest detail about the goings-on in Bayview. He put Mr. Warren's gossipy wife Bertha to shame.

"Good afternoon," he said airily, as if this were any other day.

I rose from the chair. "It is a shame you could not see us tomorrow."

He shrugged, but the look he gave Mr. Hodges told me everything I needed to know. Mr. Greene's schedule was purposefully booked this week. My neighbor wanted my farm so badly he was willing to do almost anything. I swallowed, my throat dry. Mother warned me this summer that Mr. Hodges was ruthless. I thought I had more time. It was hard to believe she was gone.

I took Lara's hand and led her into the inner office. A large window looked out on Bayview's pretty harbor, misty and gray. Boats bobbed gracefully on the waves and fishermen brought the day's catch in from the sea. In the center of the room was a large old oval table with chairs. I helped Lara into hers, making sure she was far from the lawyer and our neighbor, and took another.

Mr. Greene reached into a cabinet, pulled out some papers and proceeded to spread them about the table while Mr. Hodges lounged in the chair opposite me. He tucked his chin in his hand and smoked his pipe as if he was sitting at a dinner table.

"Ah, here." Mr. Greene pulled a document from a large envelope and laid it on the table in front of me. At the top were the cold black words:

Last Will & Testament

My eyes fell upon my father's signature and my heart gave a sudden leap. George Perry. His great large hand looped across the document's ragged yellow surface. The date was quite significant: October 18, 1861. He left for war two days later, never to return.

Then I saw my mother's name, written smaller and with practiced penmanship. Phoebe Perry. Lara bowed her head. Her shoulders shook as she tried to suppress her weeping. I reached beneath the table and took her hand.

"This is the last will and testament of Mr. George Perry and Mrs. Phoebe Perry, dated almost seven years ago." Mr. Greene reached into the envelope again. "In the event of George Perry's death, all lands, property holdings and financial accounts passed directly to Mrs. Perry as his sole benefactor."

He brought out a second document, and my heart lurched. Good God. I remembered how this simple sheet of paper had changed our lives. In one crushing blow, we were fatherless and alone.

It was a war death certificate, plain and with no embellishment.

Captain George Perry. 1st Maine Vol. Cavalry Reg't.
Served October 23, 1861 to May 31, 1864.
Killed in action at the Battle of Cold Harbor.

I was concerned for Lara, but she held her own and did not succumb.

She was his favored daughter, his little golden goddess. My father, who could hold his own in any tavern brawl, put frilly hats on dolls and poured imaginary tea. Hoisting her up onto her first pony. His death shadowed her, and she took to riding his favorite horse, Sarge.

"Proceeding with the amendments," Mr. Greene continued as his hand reached in the envelope again.

"Pardon me, Silas," Mr. Hodges leered. "You've forgotten the death certificate."

"No, I have not," Mr. Greene said shortly. He looked at me. "Neither have Miss Esther or Miss Lara Perry. We proceed."

Thank goodness for his ounce of kindness. Mr. Hodges still looked smug, especially when a third document joined the other two.

"Upon May 11th, 1868, Mrs. Phoebe Perry made amendments to her will."

It was the day after my twenty-second birthday. I remembered thinking it was odd for Mother to venture into town alone, but she insisted. I was gathering a bouquet of lilacs when she returned, and when asked, she would not speak of her errand. Now, I was to find out why.

"George Perry had accrued a large amount of debts before he went to war. Upon his death, it fell on Phoebe Perry to keep the farm from financial ruin. She was saddened to hear that her efforts were failing, so she came to me and requested help."

"She knew she was ill," Lara said. "She knew she didn't have much time."

She pressed a handkerchief to her eyes. I held her about her shoulders and rocked her.

"She should have come to me," Mr. Hodges said. "I'd have helped!"

"Ebeneezer." Mr. Greene silenced him. Then he looked at me, and when he spoke, his voice was almost kindly.

"Due to its severity, the accounts on the farm were shared only between your mother and myself. No other in Bayview knows."

Knows what? My stomach was starting to slide lower in my belly. I forced myself to remain stoic, looking right into Mr. Greene's eyes. Let

Lara be strong too, I prayed. Let us both summon from inside ourselves the strength we need.

"Miss Esther, it is with deep respect for your mother that I must inform you of the current financial situation with Perry Farm."

Before he even told me, I knew. As if I pushed off from shore with no oars, I was adrift. There was no solidity, there was no anchor. My deepest fears surfaced from murky depths.

"The debt on the farm is forty thousand dollars."

Forty thousand. My mind went blank. I couldn't think. Forty thousand. How could it be that much?

"Due to this staggering amount, your mother's will amendment states that the Maine Bank owns the Perry Farm in full. The amendment also includes a twenty percent reduction in mortgage if a new buyer is found within twenty-one days. Whomever purchases the property will assume all debts and be responsible for them thereafter."

"Esther. Esther?"

Lara was pulling on my arm, pulling me from the depths of drowning. My face burned with an intense heat and my throat was so full I couldn't answer her.

"What does he mean?" Lara's eyes sought mine. "I don't understand."

"The farm is bankrupt." My voice sounded distant, as if someone else spoke through me. "We can't afford to keep it going. We have to sell."

"What? No." She was breaking inside, as I was. Small fragments of hope splintering and cutting like wood shards. "Esther, no. Do something. There must be something!"

"Please, dearest. Mother tried to help, but she couldn't. This must be what she wanted."

"No, you are wrong! This is not what she wanted!" Lara looked at Mr. Hodges. "You, sir! You forced her to do this. You had to!"

"Miss Lara," Mr. Greene started, but his client's face was crimson.

"You put this on me?" Mr. Hodges roared. "It's your damn father's fault!"

He stabbed his finger at the war certificate, his dirty hand covering my father's name.

"He was a worthless tippler! It all went to his cronies at the Sloop Tavern. He racked up all that money and then ran away to war! George Perry deserved what he got."

Lara burst into wrenching sobs. I'd never seen Mr. Greene move so fast as he stood and descended upon Mr. Hodges. I comforted my sister as best I could, but my words were hollow with shock and grief. The two men at last calmed down and settled in their chairs. I clung to Lara. I couldn't think. I didn't know what to do.

"There will be no more outbursts, from either party," Mr. Greene said firmly. "What's done is done. It is useless to blame each other. Let the Perrys rest in peace with their sins and their virtues. We are not here to judge them."

Lara meekly nodded, her pale lips pressed so tightly her chin jutted. I took a deep breath. My father was a man of more clay than divine reasoning. He made and lost fortunes so rapidly the men in town sang a ditty about the rich man/poor man of Perry Farm. I had wanted to believe his ill luck didn't spread its poison after his death, but I was wrong. We were bankrupt and soon to be homeless.

Mr. Greene produced a final document. He handed pens to both my sister and me. All feeling had drained from me and I sat numbly, as if I was made of flat stone.

"This is the deed to the Perry Farm and the transference of ownership. Miss Esther and Miss Lara, you must sign the farm over to Mr. Hodges. He is the new buyer and assumes complete ownership of the house in twenty-one days."

"On the ninth of October," Mr. Hodges said.

"Yes. Upon October 9th, 1868, Ebeneezer Hodges of 23 Pine Street will assume property of the Perry Farm and estate, et al of 24 Pine Street, Bayview, Maine."

How cold and official his words sounded, like a toneless chime. Lara's gestures were like an automaton as she took the pen, dipped it in ink and signed her name upon the line. There was nothing she could do, and she seemed to acquiesce to it.

I, however, was not willing to concede my home and all of my possessions without first believing I had fought for them.

"What of another buyer?" I said. Mr. Hodges looked surprised; clearly, he thought this final act would go smoothly. "Mr. Hodges is not the only person in Bayview who wants Perry Farm. It is the choicest land in the county. The fact it is now for sale has not been made public."

Mr. Hodges' face blackened to a scowling frown, but Mr. Greene appeared amused. He laced his fingers and laid his elbows upon the table. He seemed to be thinking intently, but I had a feeling he knew exactly what he wanted to say.

"Miss Esther is an astute young lady. And you are correct, since Phoebe did not wish it advertised. However, as the current owner of the farm, you do have that power."

"Then I exercise it. Effective today." Like a distant storm, I felt my strength gather. I may have to give up my home, but I could choose someone other than the scum of Bayview to live there. "Notice is made to all eligible buyers of Knox County, as well as advertisements for both Portland and Bangor. The Perry Farm is available. Those who purchase it by October ninth will receive their twenty percent reduction."

Lara stared at me. I put the pen down and pushed the mortgage deed towards Mr. Greene. Mr. Hodges wiped his mouth, sneering.

"You want to air your family's dirty laundry to everyone in the state? I think you are not so smart as your mother."

I had made my point and I stood up. "I am not concerned with your opinion."

Lara had found her strength as well, for she got to her feet without help. I extended a hand to the lawyer.

"Mr. Greene, thank you for your time. Our business is finished for today. Post any news to the farm."

"Yes, Miss Esther. Good day to you and Miss Lara."

He dropped my hand, and I headed straight to the door, but my neighbor hadn't concluded his business.

"Not so fast," he snapped. "Esther, that farm is mine. Don't you think for a minute I'm letting it go. I've wanted it ever since your mother arrived with you as a squalling brat all those years ago."

I had my hand on the doorknob, but stopped. What he had said caused a stirring in me.

"My mother came to the farm by herself?"

"Saw it with my own two eyes," he said. "George didn't arrive for weeks."

"Thank you, Mr. Hodges," Mr. Greene cut in. "The ladies have personal business to attend to this day."

But as Lara and I left the inner office and crossed the entrance room to the front door, my thoughts were an echo of what Mr. Hodges had said. Mother told me I was born at Perry Farm, so I couldn't have arrived there the way Mr. Hodges described. It was puzzling, but my exhaustion, confusion and mix of emotions tormented me.

If Mother had hid the truth, then what was her reason?

Jacob drove us home in his father's carriage. I dozed in the seat, my face pressed against the glass window, while Lara sat opposite me. We said nothing to one another, though so much could be said. I felt numb and stripped clean inside, like a bare room freshly whitewashed. As we turned from Pine Street down the carriageway, I lifted my head from the glass. The sun was about to set and long purple rays of twilight painted the large stretch of sky over the horse pastures. I didn't know a day like today could end.

Forty thousand dollars. It was like counting the water drops in the pond at the end of the carriageway, the straws in a field of hay bales or how many seeds scattered over the kitchen garden rows. Forty thousand.

My mind had been as numb as dry wood in the law office, but now sprang to life with incredible zest. Maybe we could scrape together some money. There was the fruit and vegetable harvest, of course, but could I afford to hire more farm-hands? Milk, butter and cheese from our dairy cattle herd had earned a few dollars over the years. But how much in three weeks?

Not enough, I thought gloomily as the carriage pulled up to the large columned side porch. Nothing would be enough.

Lara reached over and squeezed my hand. Touched, I smiled tenderly. Our horrendous office visit hadn't broken her spirit.

Jacob slowed the horses and the carriage creaked to a halt. Lara pushed open the door, stepped out and strode towards the stables with more vigor than she'd had in days. Her obvious ignoring had Jacob taken aback, and he stared at her while reaching for my hand. But I also declined his help and descended from the carriage by myself.

"Come on, Esther," he said. "I couldn't have prevented this."

"You could have done something," I said. "Yet you choose to remain bound to your father's greed."

"Esther," he began again, but was at a loss for words.

I pulled off my black gloves, sighing. The setting sun cast peach and gold rays upon the side of the house.

"It's best that you not associate with us, Jacob. I have a lot of work to do and this -" I gestured to the farm - "is about to be yours. Let my sister and I spend our final days at home in peace."

"Well, if you need help," he offered, "I guess I could send our farmhands over."

Even in my exhausted state, it did no good to let righteous pride burden me.

"We are on our own, Jacob. We need all the help we can get."

6

I untied the bonnet ribbon beneath my chin, hung it on the peg by the front door, and walked into the parlor. When Sarah had greeted me at the door, I simply shook my head and asked for a cup of tea. The poor dear knew not to question, so she gave me a soothing embrace and left me alone.

The parlor was dark. I stood quietly by the window, looking out on my farm. Horses' hooves steadily clopped outside in the pasture. Lara was riding. The piano was behind me, hidden in the shadows. Silent.

For a long while, I stood and I felt nothing. It was like there was nothing to feel. I couldn't weep. I couldn't create a plan. My farm. I had lost my farm today.

Mother.

An angered rush stiffened my back. My arms crossed tighter over my black mourning dress. How could she have never told me? All those times we talked about me owning the farm. It was like she had stepped out of a locked cage and put me in it. Concealing my father's horrific actions and her own weak love for him. Telling me in her final moments that he was kind, when the whole time she knew I'd end up in Silas

Greene's office and all would be revealed.

Why didn't she tell me?

Sarah entered the parlor with a tea tray and set it on the table. After lighting a few candles, she came over to me.

"So Mr. Hodges is taking the old place?"

I wiped my eyes. "You knew."

"Not everything, honey. A bit here, a bit there. The way Phoebe fretted at times. An old hen like me knows what's going on."

"Why didn't she tell me, Sarah?"

"Ah, Esther, don't you understand?" She began untwisting my braid, running her fingers through my hair. "You'll be a mother someday. Then you'll do what you can to keep the truth from hurting the ones you love."

I sighed. "I woke up this morning, and this was my farm. It was my dream to live here. What are we going to do?"

"Esther, home isn't a place. You'll be all right."

I tucked my head on her shoulder. "Oh, Sarah, I hope we will be. When Lara comes in, try to get her to eat."

"I'll take stock of the household goods, don't you worry none. We'll get a leg up on all of this in the morning."

Her arms wrapped about my shoulders in a comforting hug. She kissed my cheek and twirled a strand of my hair like she'd done when I was a child. Then she was gone, bustling down the hallway to the kitchen.

My farm. Unbearable sorrow overtook me, and I sank onto the piano bench, tears streaming like rivers. A week ago I had stood in sunlight with my love by my side, looking over my farm like a benevolent queen. It would be another's now. I couldn't take anything. There was nothing. I had nothing.

Father stared down at me from his portrait above the piano. Yes, not even you are mine anymore. I would be lucky to have the clothes on my back and my leather sheet music folio.

The ivory piano keys were like a lover's cheek beneath my fingertips. It was too wrenching, and I felt numb with grief. Not to have the piano, the hours I'd sat here. I'd played for Father and Mother, I'd played for parties, I'd played by myself. Sunlight or candlelight dancing on the keys. My feet tapping away at the foot pedals.

I opened the music folio, its old leather buttery soft. Turning it to a Beethoven sonata, the *Pathetique*. Its second movement was my favorite piece. The quiet beginning soft, sad and yet hopeful. My left hand tilting, my right playing the delicate ascending scale. Back down again, until they touched, then separated as the right hand climbed to higher notes and the left hand to lower notes. As the opening melody again slipped into the song, I played louder, the energy making my wrists taut. Softer again, then louder, my fingertips tripping along.

The final echo of the opening melody resounded from beneath my hands. I played it tenderly, as if each key was a soft velvet I didn't want to stop touching. A few light trills, a quiet toning deep and then I played the last chord. It warmed me, as if its three harmonious notes were a kind embrace. I lifted my hands and the notes faded into silence. I took my feet off the pedals and sat for a long time looking down at the keys.

The back kitchen door closed and heavy footsteps trudged up the hall. It was Lara, for I could hear her sniffling. She turned and ascended the staircase. I'd look in on her before bed.

I rose from the bench and poured a cup of tea, then settled on the sofa and watched candlelight flicker on the fireplace mantel. Mother's illness and Father's absence had given me such clear direction for my future. I was mistress of Perry Farm. My friends from school pitied me and mocked my calloused fingers, but the work felt good. I could stand in the barn doorway at the end of the evening, vivid orange and pink rays alighting the hills, and survey what I had done.

But now my work was worthy of mockery. I had been so sorely disadvantaged against the jagged gray mountain of debt. It wasn't a fair position to continue working. The pride and deep satisfaction I'd felt for the past five years seemed dim and idealistic. I'd been naive, foolishly unaware of how futile my efforts were.

I set the teacup on the tray and walked over to the writing desk in the corner of the parlor. Sighing, I sat down with a fresh sheet of paper and a pen. How could I write this? I felt like I barely knew my mother, like she had kept so much concealed. I was losing my farm and if she'd only told me the truth ... it could still be mine. My shoulders sagged and I slumped forward onto the desk. Sobs escaped into my arms.

"Esther?"

Wiping my eyes, I lifted my head. "Oh, Lara."

She hurried over to me and wrapped her arms about my shoulders. I clasped her hands and felt my spirits gradually lift. With her by my side, I could do this. I could find a way to help us, no matter how bleak our circumstances appeared to be.

She knelt down and kissed my cheek. "I miss Mother."

"Me, too," I said as a well of fresh tears wetted my eyes. "Lara, we have a lot to do. Bring up a chair."

She pulled over one of the chairs by the fire and sat down, her lower lip trembling. "I heard you playing from upstairs. It sounded beautiful and sad."

"I can't tell you how hard it will be to leave the piano. I will miss it very much."

"What do you mean? Why will you miss it?"

From her surprised look, I realized she didn't understand. She hadn't begun to fathom our situation and what had happened to us. I reached over and took her hands.

"Lara, we have three weeks to find another home. The farm is no longer ours. Not the barn, not the furniture, not the animals. None of it belongs to us anymore. It's owned by the bank."

She looked down at her lap. "Esther, I don't really remember what Mr. Greene said or what happened at the law office. I don't want to leave. I'm scared."

"We will be all right." I kissed her hand. "But there is a lot of work. The apples need picking and the vegetables need harvesting."

The thought of work to be done made me feel somewhat better. I could not stop my snaky neighbor from trying his damnedest to take my home, but I could keep it going for the little time I had. I could sell some of our possessions and buy time to come up with some sort of plan.

"What can I do?" she said.

"Jacob Hodges offered to be an extra farm-hand, so you can go fetch him tomorrow." The thought of Caleb's eyes made my heart pang. "Bring Mr. Randolph as well. They can both pitch in with the harvest."

I looked down at the obituary. Lara indicated it and asked what it was about.

"Mother made a request that her obituary be printed in a Portland newspaper. I'm writing it this evening."

"Write that she was a good mother," Lara said sadly. "Then I guess we have to find a place we could go."

"Caroline or Patsy could take us," I said. "Mr. Greene has a spare bedroom since his son died in the war."

She wrinkled her nose. "I couldn't stay with him, Esther. I'll write to my friends and acquaintances. I'll help find a place."

"We must also begin packing. We can take only what is necessary and what we can carry."

Her eyes went to Father's portrait, and she looked at it for a long while. I sat at the desk, my hand on my forehead, listening to my sister's quiet sniffling. Finally, I leaned over and helped her to rise to her feet. She pressed against me in a tight embrace, and I smoothed her blond waves.

"We'll be all right, Lara."

"As long as we have each other."

I nodded. "Yes. I'm going to finish writing. Try and get something to eat before bed, if you can."

She shrugged. "I'm not hungry, Esther. Good-night."

"Good-night."

On her way out of the parlor, she paused before the portrait one last time. She kissed her fingertips and touched the picture frame. Then she left the room and walked slowly upstairs. So much we had to leave, so much to say good-bye to. My heart was so full of sorrowful farewell I couldn't even look at the piano.

Mother grasped at our lives with desperation, trying to hold our last remnants together like a tattered quilt. One shift of weight and I was the one left with a scrap basket of patchwork to sort and sift through, looking for anything worth saving. I could find work giving piano lessons. Lara was bright and cheerful and good with people. We could earn money.

What of the love Mother had thought about in her last moments? I kept my heart for him. For who? My father? Another she had known? No man in Bayview paid undue attention to her. She kept mostly to herself and was quiet at parties, balls or other social gatherings. After Father left for war, she did not seek out anyone. In fact, she discouraged Lara and I from seeking affection. I had no difficulty following her wishes.

Until Caleb, that is.

Mother had never spoken of her family, so I knew of no relatives we could rely upon. Father mentioned once that his own father died many years ago. His brother William left for war with him and never came home. Lara and I had no family.

Only each other and our memories.

7

Lara's bedroom was empty. Sarah had opened the windows and a crisp breeze played with the muslin curtains. I breathed slowly and deeply. In and out. In and out. Tomorrow was the ninth of October. Mr. Hodges would have my farm, and Lara and I had nowhere to go.

But on this final full day at home, familiar scents and sounds comforted me. Warm apple and cinnamon fragrances drifted up from the kitchen, for Sarah was baking pies on her last day with us. Chickens clucked in the yard, a horse nickered from the pasture, and the old iron weathervane on top of the barn creaked. I'd let Nick and Wesley go yesterday, leaving unharvested vegetables in the kitchen garden and ripe apples in the orchard. Empty buckets sat on the back stoop and saddles gathered dust in the barn tack room.

I walked through the upstairs bedrooms. Trunks and boxes and bags burst with papers, clothes, dressing table items, books and mementos. Sheets were draped over tables and chairs, bed coverings had been stripped clean, and all the paintings and portraits lay stacked on the floor. Bureaus stood gaping with opened drawers, and linens were folded in tipping piles.

I paused in the guest bedroom doorway. Propped against the guest bed, sagging into its own folds, was a large tapestry carpet-bag. It must have lain in the attic for years, for I couldn't remember ever seeing it. I knelt and peered inside, but it was empty. The threadbare tapestry still retained its richness of design, a burgundy and forest green paisley. It smelled faintly of lilacs. If only this bag and I could leave my emptying house and cross the oceans to another land. Then I could begin to fathom a new future.

I took the carpet-bag into my room and set it on the bed. It was as long as my arm and as wide as my hips. Plenty of room for my clothing and my leather music folio. Wherever Lara and I went, this bag would contain all I had left of our home here in Bayview.

"Esther? Esther!"

Startled, I closed the carpet-bag, went out into the hall and hurried down the stairs. Lara was standing at the parlor window, her face pressed to the glass. She sounded so insistent, but there didn't seem to be an alarming situation.

"What, Lara?"

"Someone is coming. Oh, and in such a fancy carriage! I can see its gilding from here."

"Goodness, you silly thing." I chuckled. "You gave me a fright."

I glanced out the window at the hastily arriving newcomer. The carriage was large and ornate, with a driver sitting up top directing the horses up the carriageway.

"Perhaps they need directions or are turning around." I grasped Lara's shoulders, steering her from the window. "I thought you were packing your things."

"I've finished already." She wriggled out of my grasp, enthralled by the carriage's arrival. "Esther, I don't think they're turning around. I wonder who it could be!"

A thought came to mind. "They must be here about purchasing the farm. We won't have to sell it to Mr. Hodges after all."

"With a carriage like that, they'd have the money." Lara looked down at her black mourning dress. "Thank goodness I didn't get my skirts dirty this morning."

My own black and gray striped dress was plainer than Lara's mourning wear, but I also looked presentable enough even for fashionable visitors. The carriage had come to a stop, and the driver descended from his top perch.

"All right," I said. "They are coming in. Our best ladylike manners, please. Go tell Sarah we have a guest and they may want refreshments."

She stuck out her lower lip in a pout. "Oh, I want to meet them."

"Lara, we are on our own. We must be cautious."

The thought that we were penniless and rather helpless must not have dawned on her at first, but it did then. She left the window and went down the hall to the kitchen. I smoothed my dress and hair while on my way to the front hall.

Three brusque knocks rapped upon the door. No sooner had I opened it than a lady in exquisitely fine attire swept inside. Her feathered hat tilted as she surveyed the entry of the house. She carried herself with such airs and self-assured importance I knew at once she was not from around here.

Her dress was of the most fashionable cut, a rich bittersweet hue that perfectly mimicked the October leaves around the farm. Her silvery hair looked like it had been blonde at one time, a shade lighter than Lara's. Her face was wide and smooth, with cold clear blue eyes that bored into me.

"May I help you, ma'am?" I said.

"I have come on a business errand."

So she was here to purchase the farm. "Regarding my sister Lara and myself?"

"Of course, girl."

I closed the front door and gestured into the parlor. "Please have a seat, ma'am. My housekeeper is bringing refreshments."

"Good. A bit of manners, I see."

She bustled past me and into the parlor. I was both curious and startled by her abrupt manner. I was about to join her when the kitchen door opened and Lara tiptoed up the hall.

"Who is it? A lady?" She straightened her hair and smoothed her dress, then approached the parlor door.

"Wait, Lara," I whispered. "Stay in the dining room, if you would."

"Why? You can't make me."

"I can try," I said through gritted teeth.

But it was no use. My sister stuck her chin up, brushed past me, and waltzed into the parlor. If this mysterious visitor thought my manners uncouth, then she'd be even less pleased with my sister.

I cautiously entered the parlor in time to see a sneer curve the woman's lip into a condescending arch. She sat straight on the camel back sofa, both hands clutching the head of her expensive rosewood cane. Lara did a quick curtsey, then greeted in a tumbling rush of a voice:

"Good morning, ma'am! Thank you for visiting us! How can we be of service?"

"You speak plainly, young lady," the woman replied in such a harsh and quiet tone the hairs on the back of my neck stood up. "Tell me, what is your name?"

"Lara Perry," she said, as sweetly as could be. I made ready to shoo her out of the room, but the woman was regarding her in a less icy manner.

"Indeed."

Lara's exuberance left my cheeks hot with embarrassment, but our visitor didn't draw attention to it. She looked at me as if I belonged in the stables with Sarge.

"And you girl? Are you Esther Perry?"

"I am, ma'am."

"And your age is twenty-two?"

What an odd question. "Yes, ma'am."

"With a birthday of May 10th, 1846, I presume."

I nodded, too curious to speak. My mind ran in dizzying circles trying to figure out where I'd met her. I would certainly have remembered.

"That is what I expected," she said, as if she were my physician. "You are, indeed, whom I thought you were. Both of you sit, while I speak frankly."

Ever more confused by her arrival and her questions, I perched in Father's old leather chair. Lara sat in a chair by the fire, neatly arranging her dress. The woman cocked her head, peering at me from beneath her hat's wide brown brim.

"My name is Mrs. Lucia Curtis. I am your mother's elder sister."

Lara and I looked at each other. Mother had a sister? In my entire life, she had never spoken of her family. I was at a loss, since we hadn't known about a sister's existence at all.

"I'm sorry, ma'am," I said, "but there must be a mistake. My mother was Phoebe Perry, and she did not have a sister."

"I'm quite sure she did." Mrs. Curtis nodded smartly, removing her gloves. "There is no doubt of our relation. Three weeks ago, I read of Phoebe's passing in the Portland Press Herald. She and I have not spoken for over twenty years. I was unaware she lived in Bayview, nor did I have any knowledge of family here. My father died five years ago, and I am the last living relative. Did my sister marry? Where is the husband?"

I was so stunned to silence I couldn't answer her. Lara was equally amazed. She looked like somebody had just told her Sarge could fly.

"Well?" Mrs. Curtis said. "Can you tell me?"

"Father is dead," Lara said softly. She indicated the portrait over the piano. "He went to fight in the war."

"I see." She scrutinized Father's portrait. "George Perry. A farmer, then. Well, you resemble him, Miss Lara. So, Mr. Perry is deceased and Phoebe passed away on September eighteenth. What was the cause of death?"

Lara sat still, her hands folded in her lap. She was no longer smiling or exuberant. I gave her a comforting look and answered for the both of us.

"Mother had the lung sickness. There was little we could do."

"She was a sickly child as well." She tapped her fingernails against the cane, looking sharply about the parlor. "You have little furnishings here. I also did not see anyone working the fields, and the apple trees are full of fruit. Tell me about your current situation."

Lara bowed her head, too ashamed and sorrowed to answer. I took a deep breath. This woman fired questions at us like a gun.

"Upon our mother's passing, we were informed that our situation at the Perry Farm has become critical. Consequently, I have been seeking a buyer. None have come forth, so our neighbor Mr. Hodges will assume ownership tomorrow."

Sarah brought a tray of tea, biscuits and the last of the summer's blackberry jam into the parlor. Lara and I waited while Mrs. Curtis helped herself to the refreshments. Neither of us had an appetite, nor wished to carry on this conversation.

"I may not have corresponded with Phoebe, but her faults were well known to me. In truth, I am not surprised to find two young daughters with not a penny to their names."

"We have been seeking new quarters, ma'am." Lara at last had found her voice, but she trembled as she spoke. "Esther said we would find a good place."

"Oh, she did?" Mrs. Curtis looked at me. "If it had been up to me, I would not have come. But, at my husband's insistence, I am here with an offer. I have a spare bedroom at Curtis House in Portland. It has been arranged that you may stay six months with no rent, which will give you time to find employment and a suitable apartment of your own."

Could it be? She was offering us a place to live? My throat became full and I could not speak. It was extraordinarily generous ... but I didn't know her. I did not even know if she was my mother's sister, or if this was all some terrible falsehood.

"You're taking us in?" Lara began to brighten. "I don't know how to thank you. It is so kind."

"Kindness is irrelevant. I am not extending charity for charity's sake. I expect the utmost in politeness, respect, and decorum. No suitors and no frivolous entertainments. This is a temporary situation until a new home is secured."

"Do you have horses?" Lara was almost smiling, she looked so relieved. "And a piano for Esther to play?"

Our visitor looked taken aback at Lara's forwardness, but the requests were made in such a girlish and sweet manner she appeared to soften.

"I own two horses and a parlor square grand piano."

It didn't matter if she had ten pianos. I still felt uneasy. "We understand the offer you have provided. But I am unsure as to the validity of it. Mother never spoke of a sister."

"Ah, I see what she's asking." Mrs. Curtis set her tea cup down with a clang. "You want proof, Miss Perry, is that it?"

I met her gaze. "Yes, ma'am, I do."

"Very well. I do not see how you feel you are in a position to question me, but I shall comply."

She reached into a brown velvet bag and drew out several letters and an old faded daguerreotype. She handed these items to me, and Lara got up from her chair to take a closer look. The letters were addressed to Mrs. Curtis and dated 1844, two years before I was born. At the sight of my mother's handwriting, an unexpected shiver sped up my spine.

The daguerreotype was even more startling. It was an image of my mother and Mrs. Curtis sitting on a straight-backed parlor sofa. Mother was quite young, perhaps twelve or thirteen. Her dark curls were black and she had a bouquet of lilacs in her lap.

"I'd believe me if I were you, Miss Perry," Mrs. Curtis said. "I am your aunt and sister to your mother."

"Oh, Esther, she was so young." Lara studied the daguerreotype and then her quizzical gaze focused on her aunt. "I always thought I looked like Father, but there is family resemblance between you and myself as well."

"Yes, I was the loveliest amongst the ladies of my age. You will hand them back to me."

As we passed the documents back to her, I didn't know what to say. Lara seemed to be embracing this strange turn of events, though it was a move too quickly to my liking. There was little doubt that our visitor was our aunt. To become acquainted with a relative we had never known and for her to come offer a place for us in such a crisis, was both fortuitous and alarming.

"Thank you, Mrs. Curtis, for showing us these documents. Yet, I must request a day to make a decision about your offer."

"A day?" she huffed. "I rescue you from certain destitution and you ask for time, Miss Perry? That would be unthinkable if you comprehended your situation."

"I have business to settle with our neighbor, and we must pack for the journey."

She glanced at the mantel clock. "I will be here at seven o'clock tomorrow morning. If your business is not settled and you are not ready, I return to Portland without you. No further help will be offered. You do accept?"

I didn't move. It was already two o'clock, and the day suddenly seemed horribly short. But Lara got up out of the chair and approached our aunt.

"We do accept, Mrs. Curtis. Thank you for the opportunity."

To say goodbye to our lives here in a matter of hours. I reluctantly got to my feet and thanked our visitor as well.

"If you wish to visit Mother," I added, "she is in the Perry family plot in the First Parish churchyard. It's on Willow Lane."

"You think I will visit a cemetery?" She shook her head as she put her gloves on. "Good day, Miss Perry."

"Good day, Mrs. Curtis."

I walked her to the door, and she departed without another word. Lara and I went to the parlor window to watch her leave. She boarded her lovely carriage and pulled from the farmyard. Somehow I'd known she would not visit Mother's grave. What happened between them for such a lengthy estrangement?

"Oh, Esther!" Lara grabbed me from behind, giving me a huge hug. "She has horses and a parlor grand piano. We have a place to stay! I bet there will be cousins, too!"

She let me go and dashed upstairs, whistling a contented tune. The dust in the carriageway settled, and I thought of Mr. Hodges's greedy smile. Lara, I hope you will be happy. But I do not think I can be, not when I am saying good-bye to my home and my future. Would I ever see Perry Farm again?

I went to the piano and lifted the lid. But even the keys seemed dull and dead. It wasn't mine, and I was standing in someone else's parlor. I could never welcome this new life, at an aunt's strange home in Portland. I didn't want to get to know a new family.

And if they shunned Mother, they couldn't possibly want to know me, either.

8

"Why good mornin', Esther Perry."

Mr. Hodges tipped his hat and bowed so low his back cracked. This caused him some pain, for he rose again with stiffness.

I stood in the front doorway, blocking him from entering. Lara was coming down the stairs behind me, bringing the last of her boxes. After our short breakfast, Sarah rushed to the kitchen for the wash-up. The sound of clanging pots and pans resounded down the hall.

While propping the door with my foot, I reached over to a side table and retrieved a document folder. My neighbor's watery eyes crinkled at the corners and his thin grizzled lips parted to reveal teeth the color of pond algae. I reluctantly thrust the folder at him.

"I've signed it this morning."

"There's a good missy."

He opened the folder and took a ridiculously long time inspecting each page of the mortgage deed. My leg cramped from holding the door open.

At last, he was satisfied. A good thing too, for the large ornate carriage appeared from the pine trees. Aunt Curtis would be here in a few minutes, and her low opinion of our situation would not be improved by this character on my doorstep.

"She's coming, Lara," I called to the parlor.

"Who is?" said Mr. Hodges.

I ignored his question. "My sister and I depart from the farm today. Sarah will leave within an hour afterward, to call upon you with the keys. The farm buildings are unlocked."

He stepped back from the porch. His eyes roamed the farm buildings in such an indecent manner I felt nauseous. Then both of us looked to the carriageway, for my aunt's large vehicle was riding up in a flurry of dust.

"Whooee, that's some fancy visitor."

"I'd be more interested in the autumn harvest if I were you. I have completed as much of it as I can."

"Pshaw," he said, waving his hand. "You barely touched that ripe plump fruit, Esther. Seems you didn't work hard enough."

I could have struck him across the face and not regretted it in the least.

"Speaking of ripe fruit," he said languidly. He turned that indecent gaze towards me and when he spoke his eyes roved up and down my body. "There is a way you can keep this farm."

"Mr. Hodges, my guest is arriving. I do not have the time -"

"Marry me."

It was the most disgusting utterance I'd ever heard. Even if Lara and I had to live as Portland whores I would not allow such a thing. I shot him the coldest look I could give.

"No."

"What, you want more than that?" He opened the folder and held out the mortgage document. "I could rip this to shreds. All it takes is one little word."

My heart wrenched, squeezed by the sight of the mortgage. I promised Mother I would take care of us. But by God, I could not sacrifice my future happiness in marriage. No matter how bleak.

"My final answer is no. I will never see or speak to you again."

Sarah bustled up the hall, summoned by the carriage's arrival. Aunt Curtis's horses slowed.

"The lady's come, then?" Sarah came up behind me, then spotted Mr. Hodges on the porch. "I'll be callin' in an hour, Ebeneezer!"

He kept his grotesque smile, but stiffened at the sight of the grand carriage pulling into the farmyard. The horses circled and at last came to rest before the front walkway.

"Right you are, Miss Wicklow," he said to Sarah. "Be seeing you."

I didn't acknowledge his departure. Sarah rolled her eyes and muttered a string of curses upon him. At least he was gone and the mortgage document with him. At the thought of him living in this house, I couldn't help but shudder.

Aunt Curtis stepped out of the carriage, gave a few words to the driver, and came up the walkway.

Lara joined me on the porch and we greeted our visitor, shielding our eyes from the brilliant fall sunshine. It was unusual for October to be so beautifully warm. Lara gave Aunt Curtis a curtsey and I bowed my head in acknowledgment.

"I see you are ready," she said. "My driver will fetch your things. We stop at an inn in Brunswick tonight and arrive in Portland for supper tomorrow evening."

The driver stepped past me and disappeared into the parlor. My carpet-bag sat on the sofa in the parlor. Lara had a wicker trunk and a hatbox. All we owned.

"Is this all, miss?" he called.

I nodded, unable to speak. Aunt Curtis answered the driver.

"Yes, Murton."

As the driver packed our things in the carriage, Sarah shuffled out to say good-bye. Her eyes were wet. She gave Lara a small basket with hot biscuits wrapped in a pretty tea towel.

"For the road. I have something for you, Esther."

She reached in her pocket and drew out a beautiful fabric cover for my sheet music folio. She had embroidered a white farm house with cows in the pasture.

"Now you can take Perry Farm with you."

"Sarah ..." I fingered the tiny, perfect stitches. "Your fancy work is exquisite. Thank you so much."

She embraced me, and then reached in her pocket and drew out a beautiful hair comb with pearls and scrolls.

"For you, Miss Lara. I bought it for you when you was born, to give on your wedding day. Don't know if I'll be able to make that, so here you are."

"Oh, Sarah!" Lara threw her arms around the old lady's neck. "I'll write to you!"

"You'll be in our hearts, dear Sarah."

I kissed her soft cheek, then bowed my head to keep from openly weeping. Aunt Curtis kept checking her lady's watch, impatient to leave. The driver opened the door.

I sighed and turned from Sarah, turned my back on the farm. It was lost to me. It was not my home any longer. I could not stand in the barn door entrance and feel the wind brush my petticoats. I could not walk in the evening sunlight across the pasture to bring in the last of the cows. I could not pluck lavender lilacs or big-faced sunflowers, or wheel the barrow out to the kitchen garden.

By the time I sat upon the carriage seat, the plush velvet cushion and fine interior didn't comfort my sorrow. I'd have rather been in the crudest of hay wagons than be borne from my home.

Lara's gloved hand slipped into mine. "Esther."

I tried to give her a smile. Her eyes were compassionate, but her smile turned her lips upwards and she sat up straight on the soft cushion. Lara was happy, I realized. She was happy to go to a new place.

"Good-bye Sarge," she said cheerfully, as if she'd be back to ride him tomorrow.

My old carpet-bag sat at my feet, leather music folio tucked inside. Aunt Curtis opened the carriage door and her driver assisted her in. Her voluminous traveling skirts took up the entire opposite seat cushion, and she carefully adjusted her hoops, sitting up as straight as if her back was made of iron. She peered at me from behind her ivory fan, then her gaze passed to Lara.

"When we arrive in Portland tomorrow evening, you will meet my children."

"How many cousins do we have?" Lara asked brightly.

Aunt Curtis tapped the roof of the carriage with her cane. "Two, Miss Perry. Jane is my daughter and Elliot is my son."

The carriage creaked as the driver climbed up to his perch, then a sharp whip crack as he awakened the horses. The whole luxurious conveyance turned about in the farmyard, and then we began up the long gravel carriageway to the road. I kept my face pressed to the cool glass, looking at the farm for as long as I could. The sky was a lovely blue and early morning sunlight splayed across the side of the house, the weathered barn boards, the pastures and fields, the lovely still pond at the end of the carriageway. Butterflies flitted about the wildflowers, and swallows lazily dipped over the lawn.

But then we pulled into the road and Perry Farm was gone, obscured by the dark fir trees. The great Camden Hills cast imposing rocky shadows upon us, and I could no longer see the farm or the carriageway.

"I've never been to Brunswick," Lara said. "What is it like, Aunt Curtis?"

"Never been?" My aunt looked at her, then at me. "Neither of you?"

"The farthest south we have traveled is the village of Waldoboro," I said. "Our nearest town is Camden, which borders Bayview on the north side."

"What is Bayview's population?"

I thought for a moment. "There are about thirty families I know personally."

"My goodness." She reached within her brown velvet purse and drew out a small glass bottle. "Then you have not visited Portland."

Lara shook her head. "No, ma'am."

"The population numbers thirty thousand, if not more."

"Thirty thousand?" Lara laughed. "I couldn't imagine so many people."

Aunt Curtis dabbed the contents of the bottle onto her embroidered handkerchief, then patted her neck. It smelled like violet water. Bored already with the New England autumn scenery, Lara leaned forward in her seat, far more interested in our new relative.

"Can you tell us more about Mother? Like when she was a young girl in the daguerreotype?"

Aunt Curtis took the handkerchief down from her face. Though Lara's request was reasonable to me, my aunt's reaction was as if my sister asked her to describe acts of indecency. She pursed her lips and spoke, her words chosen carefully.

"I will say what I can. But you must understand that she is not to be discussed once we reach the house."

Lara and I exchanged confused glances.

"Why not?" said Lara.

"I have my reasons. Phoebe is not respectable enough to be a topic of discussion in my household."

I could tell Lara was about to ask why again, so I laid a hand upon her wrist.

"We must be content with what our aunt can tell us, Lara."

Yet I felt anything but content. There was something amiss about the relations between my mother and her sister. Perhaps a falling out tore their friendship apart. Something must have happened, but Aunt Curtis would not be the one to reveal it. Though I had known her less than a day, I sensed her values lay along the general view of society's opinion. It was not a viewpoint I shared, but it would be impossible to shake her from the perch of propriety.

All I could do was welcome anything Aunt Curtis decided to reveal about my mother. It made me relish my kinship with Lara, since obviously my mother had not shared it with Lucia.

"I am the eldest by two years," Aunt Curtis began. "Our father, Philip Sullivan, served as mayor of Bangor. We lived in a fine house with six servants and two carriages. My mother died a few days after Phoebe was born. I married my husband when I was twenty-three and moved to Portland shortly thereafter."

"And what of this Phillip Sullivan, our grandfather?" Lara asked.

"He passed years ago."

So much we did not know, had never known. I had no idea my grandfather was so fine a gentleman as to be mayor of Bangor. And my mother had been born there? She grew up motherless, but what was her father like? Why had she married George Perry and become a farmer's wife? Did she meet him in Bangor? It was extraordinarily tempting to bombard my aunt with questions.

"Mother never spoke of her childhood," I said quietly. "Thank you for letting us know."

That was all she would tell. The subject came to a definite close, never to be opened again. As if to illustrate this point, Aunt Curtis snapped her fan shut.

"No more will be spoken of that subject, ladies. Rather, it is time to discuss your future. As I mentioned yesterday during my visit, you each have six months to gainfully learn employment. I trust you have adequate skills to turn into financial endeavors."

"I can make articles for the lady's toilette," Lara said.

"Mr. Grombey of the druggist's shop may be interested in soaps, perfumes, and the like. I will take you there. He also offers supplies at a wholesale cost."

"That sounds ideal," Lara said. "Esther plays piano."

Aunt Curtis looked pointedly at me, as if expecting me to demonstrate my expertise on a carriage ride. "How many years have you been taking lessons?"

"None," I said. "I taught myself."

She laughed. "Miss Perry, only a musically trained lady of talent can gain employment from the piano."

"I have been playing since I was five years old. I can teach others."

"She's quite good, Aunt Curtis," Lara said. "Do you play, ma'am?"

"Yes, of course. My daughter Jane was professionally taught by Mr. Lambson, the finest music teacher in Portland."

"You should play a duet with her then," Lara said to me.

"Perhaps." Aunt Curtis tapped her fan against her hand. "But you shall play for us tomorrow evening. Then I will determine if your talent warrants employment. Do you possess any other skills?"

She didn't believe I had musical talent because I had no way of procuring Mr. Lambson's mentorship. Well, formal training or not, I could play and play well.

As for other skills, the only one I possessed was the ability to be mistress of Perry Farm. But the thought was too painful to bear. Mr. Hodges had the key to the front door and was no doubt walking through the rooms wearing that horrid lecherous grin. By now, he was probably entering my old bedchamber or running his hands over Sarge's neck. Aunt Curtis was still waiting for my reply.

"I have plenty of expertise in nursing invalids and the sick."

My aunt didn't look like she expected my answer.

"Mr. Ambrose Curtis, my husband, is a doctor." Her eyes were proud, but her upper lip curled in a sneer. "The best physician in the city."

That was where the money came from. My mother married a farmer. My aunt married a doctor. And thus two lives diverged. I was catching glimpses of a reason to explain the separation. Though was it the entire story? My heart ached to know.

"How wonderful," Lara said. "Esther might assist him."

"Dr. Curtis does not require assistance," Aunt Curtis said flatly. "You will need to discover other ways to secure a living for yourself, Miss Perry."

"I will."

She had yet to hear my piano playing. I was sure I could make a go of teaching music. This Mr. Lambson who taught my cousin might assist me in finding pupils.

"My charity extends six months," my aunt reminded me. "It is not enough time to become expert at something new."

"Please do not concern yourself with it, Mrs. Curtis," I said politely but firmly. "I shall not be a burden to you in that way."

"This goes for both of you," she continued, as if she had not heard my reassurance. "Today is Friday, October ninth. You have until April ninth of next year to secure your own living quarters."

Even if she had heard my reassurance, she was set on having us out of her house in the spring. Lara's smile disappeared and my own disappointment held itself in a thin-lipped frown. We were dependent on charity, no better than Dickensian orphans. Yet, did we have to be reminded of it at every turn?

Lara reached over and squeezed my hand. With my sister by my side, this would be bearable. Not ideal, but had it ever been ideal? Not since Father left, not since the telegram from the War Department, not since Mother had begun coughing earlier this year. It occurred to me how bleak my life had been.

Without the farm, I felt my future was just as bleak. It was an internal struggle to feel grateful for new quarters, in a city I'd never seen. But every clop of the horses' hooves and every creaky sway of the carriage took me from what I wanted most. What I loved most.

Lara and Aunt Curtis spoke of toiletries and dressing table articles for some time. I grew tired of conversation, so I leaned against the carriage window and watched Maine's little seaside towns roll past.

When I closed my eyes, I thought of Caleb. Warm strong arms beneath me, a massive calloused hand brushing my hair from my face. His chiseled jaw, the way the sunlight caught his eyes. Grinning while we stood beneath the apple tree, boot-heels making great impressions in the dusty carriageway.

And then the final day, the way he looked after my palm slapped his cheek. Oh, Caleb, I murmured in my head. Why couldn't you have done the right thing?

We were both fools. Him for playing with me, and me for stringing along. I thought my love wouldn't do that to me. He seemed different.

But he wasn't. And I would never see him again. Though the staggering farm debt blocked the sun out of my life, the constant house cleaning prevented me from thinking about him. It was easier to focus on dusting, sweeping, rug beating, wiping, wrapping, polishing, folding.

My sister chatted happily beside me about perfumes, and my aunt firmly guided her towards the mercantile profession. But my emotions about Caleb and Mother overwhelmed me. I thought I might faint from the sheer pressing weight of it.

I didn't realize I'd fallen into an exhausted doze until I felt Lara's hand on mine. I sleepily rose from the window, a pang in my shoulder from the awkward position. My stomach rumbled in hunger.

"A stop for dinner," Lara was saying. "We are in Wiscasset, Esther."

"Oh," I said, not quite knowing where Wiscasset was in relation to Brunswick. I squeezed my shoulder, uncramping the muscle, then slid down the length of the carriage seat and out into the dusty street.

We were parked before an old lodging tavern, its painted sign swinging in the October breeze. It seemed around noon-time. A boy came out of the tavern's stables and Aunt Curtis gave directions for the horses' care.

"How long will we be here?" I asked Lara.

She shrugged. "Don't know."

"Not long," Aunt Curtis answered. "It is inexpensive here, but women are discouraged from entering. I have sent Murton in for foodstuffs."

She stood near the carriage, so Lara and I huddled together, tightening our shawls about our bodies as the sun began to disappear and the sky turned gray. I could feel the first wintry kiss in the air and became chilled. I thought of Mother, of how she would feel knowing we were standing by the side of the road with her estranged sister, three dollars in my purse.

Mr. Murton emerged from the tavern with a small wooden box containing three steaming fisherman's pies. Lara and I ate ours with borrowed silver forks from Aunt Curtis, drinking from a canteen borrowed from Mr. Murton.

Then we got back into the carriage and continued on our way. Lara resumed her conversation with Aunt Curtis. She chattered about the farm, about growing up in Bayview, about Jacob and Mr. Hodges. Occasionally she would mention me and I'd lift my head from the carriage window, add an observation, and then resume my silence. Lara also talked a lot about Father, how he would play dolls with her or the day he gave her Sarge after he had enlisted in town.

Aunt Curtis listened, but said little other than to remind Lara to sit up straighter, keep her voice from becoming too loud, cross her wrists over one another, use less wide hand gestures, not kick the carriage seat, and similar criticisms.

"Father was gone after that. We got a few letters, but not as many as we liked, of course. Other men left Bayview, too, and we'd see their names in the papers."

"Miss Lara, the word is newspapers, not papers. Do not use slang or plain talk abbreviations."

Lara sniffed in annoyance. "Oh, Aunt Curtis. I talk the way I like. I didn't grow up in some fancy city, you know."

"You are right, you did not. But as your new guardian, I will not have this rudeness continue. I have gained a respectable position in Portland, and it shall not be sullied by crudeness."

For all her winsome ways and inherent cheeriness, Lara could be as stubborn as a spooked horse when she wanted to be.

"I'm sorry, ma'am, but I am who I am. I am not cruder because I like to use big hand gestures or talk loudly."

"Miss Lara." Her voice made the hairs on the back of my neck prickle. "Must I remind you how greatly you owe me for my charitable offering? I am not bound by law or obligation to take you in. Neither of you have a penny to your names, and you'd be destitute without my assistance. I will train you both the way proper ladies are trained. My Jane would never speak to me the way you have, young lady. I will not tolerate it."

As petulant as the child at heart that she was, Lara's lip turned down in a pout. She rode in silence for another few minutes, but she knew well enough to try and stay in someone's good graces. After a heavy sigh and a firm clasp of her hands, she once again flashed a smile.

"Well, you won't have to worry about Esther on that account, Aunt Curtis. She's more of a proper lady than me."

Aunt Curtis's gaze shifted to meet mine. "Is she? We will see."

Yes, Aunt Curtis, you will see. Neither of us may have a penny, but we are not lesser beings. I was ready to occupy a demanding and mature role at Perry Farm. No matter what new role I was to occupy, I would perform it to the best of my abilities.

Whether she thought I was a lady or not.

9

Aunt Curtis's cutting remarks and the physical exertion spent preparing Perry Farm made me utterly exhausted. I dozed the rest of the way to Brunswick. Lara woke me again later that evening. The sky was already dark, a harbinger of the winter days ahead.

Brunswick was a pretty town lit with gas lamps. We passed brick factory buildings, a central green, a beautiful white church, and the campus of Bowdoin College. Mr. Greene had gone to school here, for I remembered seeing his diploma on the wall of his law office.

We came to a halt in front of an inn that resembled a comfortably large home. Aunt Curtis took her own quarters, so Lara and I shared a bed together in a second room. I built up a fire while Lara rinsed her face in the wash-bowl and dried her hands upon the towel. She pulled up a chair to the fire, unbraiding her long blond hair.

"Aunt Curtis said that next week, we'll visit Grombey and Sons druggist for perfume supplies. She has an entire book of lady's recipes to make. I cannot wait to get started!"

I felt quite comfortable, hands in my lap, staring into the comforting orange flames. Had I left Perry Farm that morning? Kissing Sarah's warm cheek and gazing for the last time upon the wide fields and peeling clapboards. It was half a lifetime ago.

"Esther?"

"Hmm?"

Lara tossed her head, letting her hair fall loose over her shoulders. "What is the matter?"

I gave a snorting laugh. "What do you mean, what is the matter? Lara, it's good to be excited about violet waters and lavender sachets. But we are homeless. We have nothing."

She reached over for a hairbrush and passed it over her hair. "Why do you have to be so dreary about everything? Our situation is not so bad as you put it."

"Yes, it is." I sighed. "It falls on my shoulders to make sure we even have a situation."

"But we do. At least for the next six months."

"Six months goes by a lot faster than you think."

"I will have my perfumes, and you have your music." She shrugged. "The Curtis piano sounds like a fine instrument."

"It does," I admitted. "Though Aunt Curtis seems to have little faith in my talents."

"Oh, rich ladies are fussy. You need to be accomplished with all the right accomplishments. But those who love what they do acquire all the accomplishments they need."

"You are quite determined to cheer me, aren't you?"

She giggled, for she did think I was being morose. But after we'd gotten into bed and blown out the candle, she sought my hand under the covers and squeezed my fingers.

"Esther, I'm sorry you miss the farm. I hope you're happy at the Curtis House. As long as we're together, our situation will be all right."

Tears came to my eyes. She was right, as only Lara could be. As long as we were together, we would be all right.

I slept better than I thought I would and donned my black mourning dress the next day. Lara did not like arriving at the Curtis home in such a "dreary" color, but it was out of respect for Mother. After a filling breakfast of sausages and eggs at the inn, we were on our way again. The day was sunny and cool, a windy breeze blowing from the nearby coast.

The carriage wound up and down the twisty roads. The October leaves made a blending tapestry of yellows, reds and oranges that passed by. We drove by a number of farms, and one farm had the most beautiful brown horses. Lara pressed her nose against the glass until they were completely out of sight.

"I miss Sarge," she admitted.

I wished I could tell her that she'd see him soon. But I had no idea when or whether she could even ride horses in the city.

"If I don't make lady's toilette articles," she said to Aunt Curtis, "then I shall become a saddle and tack merchant."

I laughed, for the thought was rather absurd. Women didn't do such things. Aunt Curtis's scowl spoke volumes of her disapproval. Then I received a similar frown.

"Miss Perry, you should discourage your sister's idea. Horsemanship is not suitable for city ladies."

Why was she blaming me for what Lara had said? I had little say over my sister's blurting, though I did what I could to prevent it.

"Aunt Curtis," I began, "Lara is well suited to take part in any profession with horses. She is quite their equal and can tame any of them."

"I do not think you grasp my full meaning," came the retort. "Miss Lara will be under your supervision while you are in my house. Any ill behavior on her part is reflected upon you. Due recourse will be given."

Punished. Punished for Lara's behavior. I didn't know what to say and sat silently, my hands clasped in my lap and my head aching. I couldn't bring myself to acquiesce to this.

As for Lara, she was trying not to be cross or argumentative. She bit down on her lip so hard it was turning white. She looked at me with a strange sympathy.

"I will watch my behavior, Esther. Do not worry."

It was hard not to worry, especially about this new development in our situation. I had no idea what recourse would be given if she was rude, but I didn't want to find out. I was looking forward to seeing Portland and the Curtis home, if only to distract myself from this growing unpleasantness.

"Do either cousin Jane or cousin Elliot ride horses?" Lara wasn't letting the equine topic rest.

"I do not let my daughter near those stable beasts. However, Elliot has been trained should he have a need for riding."

"Have our cousins ever been to the country?"

"No, they have not."

"Not even for a picnic? Or a day by the seaside?" Lara cocked her head. "There are beaches near Portland, are there not?"

"Neither of my children have vacated the city premises for any reason other than train voyages to Boston and New York."

"Oh! A train ride." I had to smile at Lara's wondrous look as she imagined boarding the iron horse. "Neither of us have been on a train before."

"I would imagine not, given your rural location."

"Someday we shall accompany you to Boston or New York," Lara said. "I should like that."

"Perhaps." Though it sounded like another "No" to me.

"What is a train ride like?"

Aunt Curtis entertained Lara up until the noon-time hour with stories about train trips. Large Pullman cars with cushioned seats, sleeping arrangements and meals served in plush dining cars. By the time we reached Falmouth, Lara was enthralled with train travel and wanted to sell plenty of lady's toilette articles to afford such a journey. Despite a bombardment of unladylike manners, Aunt Curtis seemed to enjoy her rapt pupil.

The carriage stopped at a hotel, and we dined in the restaurant, a place of incredible luxury. Fisherman's pies and thick stews had been replaced with terrines and oyster soup. There were snowy damask linens, real silver candlesticks, and fine china. We were entering a different world, on all levels.

Lara could not get past the upscale dining experience, so she and Aunt Curtis talked about menu choices and plate settings as we continued. But after a few minutes, the topic shifted to our new location.

"Portland is placed on a peninsula surrounded by Casco Bay," Aunt Curtis said. "The Curtis House is number one hundred and eleven High Street and it overlooks Portland harbor."

"That sounds lovely," I said.

"It was a lovely view," Aunt Curtis said, "before the fire. Now, most the city is involved in architectural construction."

"What a terrible disaster for Portland," Lara said. "We heard of the tragedy up in Bayview."

I remembered reading of it in the newspaper. "You must have taken part in it, then ma'am?"

"I did what was required of me. My husband was more intimately involved, as he is a physician."

Lara gave such a visible and exaggerated shudder, I smiled. "Ooh, it gives me the willies thinking of the people who needed medical attention after so great a fire."

"Elliot was of assistance as well. But Miss Lara," she began in that reminding tone, "you must not dwell upon such unladylike thoughts. It is unbecoming for a girl to be excited by violence or tragedy."

Lara plopped her head on her gloved hand and stared out the window. I was chuckling inwardly, for I recognized that pouty look. She was as wild and untamed as the stallion she missed. I wanted to help her adjust to the confines of city life, but I had little idea on how to advise her.

"You are a girl of few words," Aunt Curtis said to me.

I smiled. "And Lara is a girl of many."

My sister smirked, then her gaze returned to the window. She strained to catch a glimpse of the half-burnt city and revel in it before Aunt Curtis deterred her.

"Miss Lara will need to rein in her tongue," my aunt continued, "but you should be encouraged to engage in conversation. A silent presence is unsuitable for social interaction."

If she expected me to say I was sorry or amiss, then I wasn't going to give her the satisfaction.

"The reason is exhaustion and nothing else. No disrespect was meant."

"Exhaustion?" Aunt Curtis sat back. "The weather has been agreeable and the roads dry. What tires you?"

What indeed. Was she overlooking the fact that I had packed up my entire home for sale and was still grieving my mother? Thankfully, I was saved from making a curt reply.

"Esther has had to take care of everything since Mother's passing," Lara said.

"Well, you will be excused for a day. But I am inviting the Vallencourts to dine with us and I expect proper conversation. Understood?"

We both nodded, our renewed thoughts of Mother discoloring anticipation about meeting the grand Vallencourts. The name sounded like a royal family. Our journey relapsed into silence for some time, until Lara's excited voice shook me from my reverie.

"Esther! Esther, we've arrived. We're here in Portland!"

Clang. Clang.

A rich metallic pounding resounded from far off, like I was standing in a cast iron room while someone banged on the walls. Lara grabbed my hand and pulled my arm.

"Miss Lara!" Aunt Curtis said. "Calm yourself, child."

"Please forgive her, ma'am," I said before I could think of something else to say. "What is that noise?"

"Progress," my aunt said with a satisfying smile.

I slid down the carriage seat to the window. We drove along a wide yellow road beside a watery bank. I smelled the ocean's pleasant saltiness and watched gulls dip and glide over the little cove.

We ascended a hill and I viewed the city in full. Its large tree-covered embankment crested and rolled between picturesque saltwater coves. Giant wooden skeletons of scaffolding were erected throughout the streets, swarming with carpenters, stonemasons and bricklayers. Red and gray dust tinged the air as massive amounts of bricks and stone were laid in place. Occasionally a startled horse whinny, the high-pitched shriek of breaking glass, the endless grunting and moaning from hundreds of workers. The city was like a gigantic wood and stone beast in the process of awakening.

Each building was more beautiful and stately than the last, adorned with the most incredible woodwork, wide bay windows, slate and tile and brick facades, with various peculiar ornaments and carvings. Houses were built so close together there was scarcely enough space to walk between them. With the land on Perry Farm, I could have built four neighborhood streets and housed dozens of families.

The mass commotion grew ever louder and more chaotic as we turned off the main road and down a wide thoroughfare. We'd gone barely twenty feet before the carriage stopped. The street was packed with dozens of other carriages, carts, open-air farm wagons, omnibuses, and the most varied array of pedestrians I'd ever seen. Sailors with jaunty caps and wind-burned cheeks, gentlemen in frock coats and striped trousers, merchants and shopkeepers in long white aprons cleaning windows or eying their displayed merchandise, factory workers in dull tattered clothing and coal-smoked faces hurrying down the road, boys and girls chasing both each other and the pigeons, women in wide walking dresses with lacy parasols chatting with one another, looking like colorful birds in white gloves and light shawls.

My exhaustion was vanishing, replaced by a growing feeling of anticipation. I was surprised to find myself enthralled by the movement and activity. Like the entire city was devoted to a new beginning. At last, we had made our way down the incredibly busy thoroughfare. The carriage turned left, and Aunt Curtis pointed to the street sign.

"This is Pearl Street, where the fire started."

Blackened ruins stood between the general bustle of foot traffic and the endless construction. Brick and wooden stumps rose haphazardly from the ground. Here and there a lone doorway, the remains of a smashed window. I smelled smoke mixed with the scent of freshly cut lumber. In one large vacant lot was a heap of charcoal-colored bricks beside a stack of half-burnt boards. The contrast between the destruction and the immense building projects was quite humbling. Thank goodness the Perry Farm never suffered any fire devastation.

"Two people lost their lives," Aunt Curtis was saying. "But thousands were left homeless. The United States Army had to provide tents and many lived on Munjoy Hill for months."

"My heavens," Lara said. "Then these buildings along here must be new."

Aunt Curtis nodded. "We're coming to Middle Street. This is the site of new Vallencourt buildings, completed last year."

We turned right onto Middle Street. My sister and I gaped at the beautiful new brick buildings lining the street. They towered above the cobblestones, with arched fronts on the first floor and verdigris sloped roofs. I'd never seen so many windows, each reflecting the brilliant October sunlight. One of the buildings sat at an angle of two intersecting streets, its bow front end curved like a huge brick ship. The first floors were occupied by merchants, druggists, grocers, restaurants, business offices, and stores.

"This is Spring Street," Aunt Curtis said after we had crossed a busy intersection. "The Curtis House is at the corner of Spring and High Streets."

The commerce buildings were left behind, and we drove down a tree-lined street with gaslight lanterns and large comfortable homes. We were on a high slope overlooking the busy and cheerful harbor of Portland. Sailing vessels mingled amidst steamships and pleasure boats. The size of the harbor was incredible. Bayview's entire environs could fit inside with room to spare. A bridge spanned the harbor, arcing over churning paddle wheels and bright white sails. Beyond the dazzling blue sea was another stretch of land with more homes and buildings. It was such a pretty view, made lovelier by the dappled fall foliage.

"This is where you live?" Lara asked.

"Yes," Aunt Curtis said. "At one time, my house belonged to a wealthy shipping merchant."

The carriage slowed. We were approaching the intersection of Spring and High Streets. At the corner stood an enormous brick home, its size rivaling that of the Perry Farm barn. Lara's wide-eyed gaze was enraptured. She turned and clasped my hand.

"Oh my goodness, Esther. It's amazing."

"It is," I admitted, unable to believe this was where Mother's sister had lived all our lives.

A low ornate cast iron fence encircled the home. Mr. Murton expertly wheeled the horses between two stone sentinels and into a bricked carriageway. Lara pressed next to me and we gazed up at the impressive three-story height, all the way to the white railing at the top. Each window was framed in white with thick black shutters set flat against the brick. It was such an elegant and stately home. Lara and I would be staying here all winter. It was better than I could have hoped for.

The carriage pulled up to the carriage house. Mr. Murton stepped out and opened the carriage door for us. On the side of the house was a door with a triangular pediment over it and a set of stone steps. Upon descending from the carriage, I walked over to it.

"Miss Perry," Aunt Curtis said. I paused. "If you wish to be treated as a servant, then by all means go through the kitchen door." She gestured to the front of the house. "I go only through the front door."

I fell in behind her and Lara as we walked up to the front of the house. The front door was situated in the center of the front of the house. A half-circle crowned the door, jutting out from the brick and supported by thick columns. We had just stepped under this interesting portico when the door promptly opened and a well-dressed gentleman of impeccable attire appeared. No one in Bayview could afford a servant of his stature, for he was clearly the butler. His face was round, his eyes a pale color and sharply alert. His gray hair was oiled and slick in the sunlight.

"Ah, Jakes," Aunt Curtis said with a sense of relief. "The luggage is for the southeast bedroom. Prepare two extra places for supper."

He bowed to her. "Indeed, ma'am. The young miss and master are in the parlor. Supper on the table in a quarter hour."

"Hello to you, Mr. James," Lara said brightly. "I've never met a butler before."

The servant stepped aside to allow us entry. Aunt Curtis, of course, was the first to walk into her home, untying her bonnet as she did so. Lara and I eagerly followed her.

"It is Mr. Jakes," the servant corrected. "I proudly serve the Curtis family."

After taking our outer garments and placing them on a tall ornate hall tree, he turned and strode down the hall. I was about to say something to Lara, but both of us stopped in mid-gesture, for we were standing at the entrance to a splendid home.

The front hall was enormous, as large as the parlor in Bayview. Before us was a grand wide staircase vaulting up to the open second floor, its wrap-around bannister curving above our heads. A huge palladian window stood prominently at the top of the staircase, lighting up the hall. Ornately flourished gold wallpaper decorated the walls, curving like the waves of the sea. At our feet was a richly ornamented carpet with large patterned squares, like we stood on a marble floor. Everywhere I looked was another decoration, whether it was the curled scrolls on the newel posts, the carving above a side door, or the Chinese vases on the hall tables. It made our home in Bayview seem shabbier than I'd ever thought before.

"Hello, Mother."

A side door opened and a lady of my own age stepped into the hall. She was wearing the finest dress I had ever seen, in a wine colored silk, the cut the height of fashion. Jewels flashed from her neck, her ears, and her fingers. Her hair was as dark as mine and framed her face in pleasing curls. Her eyes were a rich deep brown, her skin a creamy pale, her lips full and sporting the same half-smirk as her mother. At once, I recognized facial similarities in mother and daughter, though their natural colorings were as different as diamond and obsidian. It must be my cousin, Jane.

Behind her was a boyish faced young man with a full head of thick blond hair flopping over friendly blue eyes. He wore a dark evening jacket, richly patterned waistcoat and light trousers. He tossed back the rest of a glass of wine and extended a hand, grinning like a schoolboy.

"Pleased to meet you!" The way he said it, so welcoming and kindly, made me instantly warm to him. Such a difference from his mother and stand-offish sister. "I'm Elliot Curtis. And you are, pretty lady?"

He took my sister's hand and kissed it with a gentlemanly flourish. Lara was charmed and broke into a wide smile that matched his.

"Lara Perry, sir. How kind of you to welcome us. This is my sister, Esther."

I stepped out from behind Aunt Curtis and also received a kiss on my hand. His sister was not smiling.

"You must be Miss Jane Curtis," I said politely.

"I must be," she said flatly. We nodded to one another.

"Good to meet you, Miss Curtis," Lara said, her tone slightly less exuberant than with Elliot. "Your home here is lovely. It's much bigger than ours in Bayview. I hear you have horses, too."

"We do," Elliot said, and the two blond cousins began chatting amiably about the horses in the stables.

Aunt Curtis, Jane and I walked into the parlor. The hall's grandness was little compared to the formal elegance of the front parlor. It was decorated in rich blues and emeralds, with a huge marble fireplace and a lovely assortment of gilded paintings and burnished tables.

But every beautiful object faded as soon as I saw the piano.

Oh, how I wanted to run right over and touch the keys! To sit on the lovely wooden bench and try a song. It was such an instrument of skilled craftsmanship, finely built and sturdy, a square grand stretching the entire length of the parlor wall. Lovely oil candelabras glazed yellow light over the ivory keys, and an open book of sheet music sat invitingly on the stand.

Jane seated herself in a plush lady's chair. "Father will not be joining us for dinner."

My aunt sat down, and I perched on the emerald green sofa, careful not to convey the slightest hint of country manners. Though I felt like a drab gray bird in a flock of peacocks.

"Dr. Curtis is quite busy," Aunt Curtis said to me. "There are plenty of construction mishaps."

I could see why, with the vast numbers of workers we'd seen in the city. When Elliot and Lara came into the parlor, I smiled, since Lara was simultaneously chatting and staring around the lovely room. Then she noticed the piano and gasped.

"Oh! I told you it would be a fine instrument, Esther. You must be excited to play for us."

I wished she'd kept her exuberance concealed, for Jane's reaction was enough to let me know it was ill-received. With an arched brow eerily similar to her mother's, she rose from the sofa and swept over to the piano.

"Miss Perry plays?"

"I do," I said.

"She will perform for us when the Vallencourts dine on Saturday evening," Aunt Curtis said. "Though she has been disadvantaged without Mr. Lambson's formal training."

Jane reached over and closed the sheet music book. "His masterful techniques require a pupil of considerable talent. And you have music?"

"I do," I repeated, in the same tone.

"Then we shall hear your performance," Jane said.

There was a knock on the door, and upon Aunt Curtis's grant for an entrance, an older woman entered. She was of Sarah's age and height, though that was where the similarities ended. Her keen eyes could not have been less kindly, her stiff posture less warm. Furrows on either side of her mouth deepened as she peered first at Lara and then at me.

"Dinner is ready, ma'am."

"Thank you, Mrs. Keswick."

Aunt Curtis rose from the sofa and, together with Jane, walked from the parlor.

Elliot held out an arm. "I'll escort you, Miss Perry."

I grasped it as I would have taken the arm of a rescuer, feeling a little more at ease. My cousin was a gentleman, and that was a blessing.

"Thank you, sir," I said. "I appreciate it."

"My pleasure, though I am merely Elliot. If I may call you Esther, so that we should not be strangers."

I smiled. "Yes, you may."

"He already calls me Lara," my sister enthused. "I can't get over how gorgeous the piano is. I'm looking forward to hearing you play on Saturday, Esther."

"I am too, Lara."

I hoped my smile conveyed more good feelings than I felt. I was grateful for Elliot's good hospitality and easy kindness, for it was rare in his family. And as for my uncle, who was to say?

I could not. But I hoped his character was less disagreeable than his wife's or his daughter's. For if I was to spend six months in this family, any reprieve from new enemies was gladly welcomed.

10

"Neither Aunt Curtis nor Jane were very civil towards you at dinner," Lara said.

We were journeying upstairs to our new chambers. Mrs. Keswick, the pinch-faced and rather brusque housekeeper, turned about as we approached the stair landing.

"You'd best not speak ill of the mistresses," she quipped. "I'd not myself be quick to take in country orphans."

"We are still family, Mrs. Keswick," Lara said. "I'd want to offer assistance to those who needed it."

The housekeeper said nothing, but rather lifted her skirts and continued up the steps. Though it could not have been later than eight o'clock, the view beyond the palladian window showed darkest night. Glowing lamps illuminated the second floor landing. Mrs. Keswick carried a small chamber stick.

Moments before, we had said good-night to our aunt and cousins in the parlor. Elliot was kind with his good-night parting, but in what was fast becoming typical fashion, his mother and sister did not follow suit. Dinner topics never strayed too far from Lara and myself. There was an animated discussion of our upbringing, how we had been schooled, and daily chores at Perry Farm. I was tired from the questioning and the lengthy journey. Lara was right about the incivility, but I merely wanted to go to bed.

Mrs. Keswick turned right at the stair landing and we walked up the final steps to the second floor. There were two doors on the left-hand side of the landing and two doors opposite on the right-hand side. Both halves of the landing were connected by a smoothly curved railing on the opposite end of the house. A second palladian window looked out onto the top of the portico over the front door. As exhausted as I was, I couldn't help admiring the pleasing construction and how grand the interior architecture appeared. I leaned against the banister, looking down into the front hallway below. Mrs. Keswick paused by the first door on the left.

"You will have no need of going through this door. It leads to the servant's staircase and the northeast bedroom."

"Does Elliot stay here?" Lara said.

"It is not used."

She continued down the landing and we passed by the unused bedroom door. Its handsome appearance, complete with a large brass doorknob and crowning triangular pediment, added elegance to its secretive contents. We came to the second door on the left-hand side of the landing, which I guessed was the southeast bedroom.

Mrs. Keswick removed a set of keys from her apron pocket and unlocked the door. My immediate reaction to seeing our new quarters was astonishment. The room was enormous. A massively wide fireplace dominated the opposite wall, stretching up to the ceiling and decorated with paneling and crown molding. Each of the three tall multi-paned windows featured a deep window seat. The large four-poster bed had been made ready, with white bedspread and counterpanes. The remainder of the furniture was of handsome craftsmanship, including a pair of bureaus, a chifforobe, a dressing table, a wash stand, two small side tables and various chairs.

Lara went right over to one of the front windows, pushed back its inner shutters and looked down to Spring Street below.

"Oh, Esther, you can almost see the ocean from here. This is such a lovely room!"

I joined her, amazed by the view and how grandly the house was situated. Beyond the manicured front lawn, Spring Street was lit with lovely gaslights on this autumn evening. We could see down the slope of High Street towards the wharves. Several homes and buildings blocked the house from complete harbor scenery, but it was splendid nonetheless.

"Thank you, Mrs. Keswick," I said to the housekeeper.

Half a smile graced her thin lips, but then she became serious again. She pointed to a door in the back of the room, nearly hidden by the bed's massive size.

"That door is always locked. Do not ask for the key."

I exchanged glances with Lara. For some pressing reason, we were seemingly not allowed to access it. Not that I would want to, for it presumably led to the servants' staircase.

"Across the hall is Mr. and Mrs. Curtis's bedchamber and Miss Curtis's is adjacent to theirs."

"Where does Elliot sleep?" Lara asked.

"He has taken quarters upstairs while you are here."

"With the servants?" I said. "I hope we are not inconveniencing him."

"It was the young master's wish."

Mrs. Keswick bid us a good-night and left us to get settled. My dilapidated carpet-bag sat on the bed, a forlorn contrast between its worn tapestry and the snowy bedspread. Lara peered inside the bureau drawers and made funny faces at herself in the dressing table mirror. I chuckled as I opened my carpet-bag and took out my things.

"I wonder why our cousin did not choose to stay in the northeast bedroom, rather than move upstairs."

"You heard Mrs. Keswick." She pinched her lips and said in a near-perfect impression: "It is not used."

"Lara," I laughed. "You had better not do that in front of her."

"I won't. Though I agree about Elliot's decision, Esther. Why anyone would want to go up there is beyond me. I wonder ..."

I knew what she was thinking, for I admitted I was almost as curious. She ventured over to the northeast bedroom door and tried to open it. The doorknob barely moved beneath her hand.

"No luck. But why wouldn't it be used?"

I shrugged. "It is not for us to question. I know that you want to, but we are guests of the Curtis family and must respect their privacy. I hope you do not let your curiosity prevent you from being polite."

She scoffed and went over to her trunk, placed at the foot of the bed. "I will try to behave better, Esther. I just wish we could talk about Mother. Don't you feel curious about all of this?"

I opened a bureau drawer and placed my clothes inside. "And we have not yet met our uncle or the royal Vallencourts, either."

"Royal!" She laughed. "They do sound like an uppity bunch, don't they? Well, if they examine us like Aunt Curtis and Jane did about our country bumpkin life, then I may have to swear off all dinners."

Lara's humor made me smile, but there was a biting truth to it. "You know we can't do that. No, we shall attend dinners, no matter what Jane says about me being married to the farm and having no time for suitors."

It pained me to recall her observation, for I thought of Caleb. Oh, he'd be harvesting apples on the Hodges farm by now. It was not hard to imagine him sharing a laugh with Mr. Hodges. At my expense, of course.

"Jane seems quite eager to see Mr. Henry Vallencourt." Lara untied her hair ribbons and began unbraiding the golden strands. "She said he was the most eligible bachelor in Portland. And if he is, then I'd want to marry him, too."

"Marry him?" I sputtered. "Without setting eyes on him or considering the proportion of his faults to his virtues?"

"He has money, Esther. He could afford to let me buy all the horses I want." She combed her fingers through her hair. "We'll see if he and Jane are a good match. She is well-bred, but she does not know anything about horses nor does she care to. I am beginning to believe Aunt Curtis that she is not let near the stables."

"Well, her interests lie elsewhere. I'm sure Elliot would let you near the stables, if you asked him."

"He's quite the gentleman, I think."

"Yes. He is."

I pulled my sheet music folio out from the carpet-bag. It smelled like home, a comforting musky scent of leather, hay and dried flowers. I ran my fingers over Sarah's stitched cover. The lovely white house with a gray barn, Camden hills rising behind, the sun and clouds, the green pastures, the horses and cows in the meadows.

Lara came over and sat on the bed beside me, her head resting against my shoulder. "Oh, Esther. I miss Sarge and Jacob. I feel I can like it here, but it's not the same."

It wasn't the same. The farm was my home. The Curtis House, as grand and comfortable as it was, was a temporary shelter. It could never be my home.

Not for all the money in the world.

11

Our first few days at the Curtis House passed uneventfully. Lara and I shared breakfast trays in our room in the morning, visited with our cousins during the day, and dined with them in the evening. Lara did most of the talking, while I read or sewed quietly.

However, I hadn't set eyes on my elusive uncle. The explanation I received was that he was busy, so I accepted it. No one had refuted the opinion that he resembled the women in his family more than his kindly son, so his absence remained a perfect excuse to continue to think of him that way.

Despite her opinion of Jane's formality, Lara got along well with her cousin. It was not due to Jane's personality softening upon being better acquainted, but rather Lara's cheery nature that endeared her to most anybody. Her natural charm stemmed from an innocent desire to learn more about others. Lara was a happy girl, and even one as cold and reserved as Jane Curtis couldn't help but smile in amusement.

But amusement couldn't make up for the lack of proper society. Being corrected by Aunt Curtis had become their most common excuse for conversation. The evening before the Vallencourts were to dine, Lara was unusually high-spirited. Elliot gripped his chest in the throes of uproarious laughter.

"My goodness, Lara," he said, daubing his tear-stained face. "I can only imagine a silly young thing like yourself chasing those ducklings about the yard!"

I smiled and sipped my wine. The duckling story was from happier times before Father left, and it never failed to bring light-heartedness to its listeners.

"And with my bloomers in full view. A wonder that I hadn't known half my dress was torn off." Lara shook her head. "Um, I'm sorry Aunt Curtis. I suppose this isn't appropriate supper conversation."

Jane, trying to hide her giggles behind her fan, answered before her mother could. "I vote that Miss Lara may be forgiven her indecent choice of topics. It has brought great humor to our table. What say you, Mother?"

"Thank you, cousin Jane!" Lara beamed. "Oh, you are being kinder to me than at my first dinner. If you are half as decent towards Esther, then you'll be laughing every night that we are here."

Color flamed my cheeks, and I narrowed my eyes at my sister. Give her even the slightest encouragement and she ran over it like a toddler with muddy feet.

"Aunt Curtis, I do apologize for -"

My guardian's raised hand silenced me. She glared harshly at Lara, who seemed to shrivel in her chair. Elliot suddenly became interested in his soup.

"Miss Perry, you are not to speak on your sister's behalf again. As for Miss Lara, we begin the instruction for your employment after church on Sunday. Strict study and application will curtail these exuberant outbursts."

"Yes, ma'am," Lara mumbled.

I could tell she wished to ask questions about her new employment, but she didn't. After a few moments of silence, she set her fork down and said in as mature a voice as she could:

"You are right, Aunt Curtis. An occupation would help me perfect my decorum."

"That was a ladylike response. I am pleased." She smiled at Lara, but her cold eyes were upon me. "Very pleased."

I felt like a moth trapped beneath her magnifying glass. I squirmed in my seat and did not feel comfortable again until the meal was finished. After an hour in the parlor spent listening to Lara learn about other ladylike habits, I pardoned myself with a headache and retired to my room.

I closed the bedroom door behind me and let out a great sigh. Not even my sister's cheerful presence lessened the strain of living under my aunt's constant scrutiny and Jane's mocking questions.

I slipped off my house shoes and began unpinning my hair as I crossed to one of the front windows. Below me was the calm activity of a fall evening on Spring Street. The street was empty save for a few carriages. A couple strolled by, hands intertwined. They paused beneath a gas lamp to share a loving embrace. When he began to paw at her, she laughed and pulled him down the street. For some reason, I thought of Caleb and I together.

"Nonsense," I muttered out loud.

But I couldn't help admitting I thought of him. Too often. He didn't want to marry me, and I had to live within that heartbreaking truth. No matter how many times I remembered his eyes.

As I stood at the window, absentmindedly twirling my hair around my finger, a man in the street caught my attention. Dressed in a frock coat and dark trousers, he was moving very quickly. He dodged a slow carriage, crossed the street and hastened down the brick sidewalk. With a start, I realized his destination was the house.

Was he my uncle?

He strode along the fence, entered the gates and went right to the front door. I left my spot by the window and pressed an ear to the bedroom door. Sure enough, within a moment I heard Mrs. Keswick's clipped voice in the hall. He was either Ambrose Curtis or a stranger showing up at a late hour. But the latter explanation wasn't plausible, since his heavy footsteps ascended the stairwell. He sighed so loudly I could hear it through the wall.

I put my hand to the doorknob, curiosity heightened. My timing was perfect, for as he crossed the landing he noticed the open door. His eyes flashed black beneath his mussed hair, a look so intense and electric it was as if I'd been witness to something I should not have seen.

Confused, I started to close the door. But he stopped on the landing, breathing heavily from the exertion of his walk and his swift climb up the stairs. His appearance was so unkempt he didn't seem to belong in the Curtis House. His sleeves were stained with large dark red blotches and his waistcoat ripped at the collar. His cravat was askew and his face was haggard.

"Excuse me, sir," I said when my voice found me. "Good night."

"No," he said in a commanding tone. "Come out, girl. Don't stand there."

I gulped, pressing my lips together. His manner was as coarse as his appearance. Well, I was no meek violet and had dealt with men of far less delicacy. After opening the door, I squared my shoulders and walked out to greet him. His intense stare followed me, but I showed no fear or trepidation.

"My name is Esther Perry, sir." I gave a quick curtsey. "We have not met."

He looked at me. His shoulders slackened and his frown vanished. His eyes were not welcoming, but neither were they unkind. He regarded me with the strangest affected look, half scrutiny and half deep distress.

"You're right. I am Ambrose Curtis."

Of his character, I could deduce nothing. But it took little imagination to wonder why his shirt was stained and where he had been since my arrival.

"You work hard, sir."

He looked at my hands, still calloused from weeks of harvesting. "So do you."

We stood on the landing a moment longer, and I found myself unexpectedly relaxing in his presence. He was a man of authority in the city and held himself with it. I had no more authority than the scullery maid in the kitchen, but I sensed he would not patronize me. As opposed to his wife.

"Thank you for offering a home to my sister and myself."

Rather than warmth, he surprised me by furrowing his brow. When he spoke, his jaw was clenched.

"A home you have sorely needed."

For a moment I thought I had angered him. But he was not looking at me. He was looking at his own bedchamber door.

"We have come to stay," I said, partly to soothe his agitation and partly to inform him. "It's late. You should rest, sir."

He reached down, took my hand and kissed it with a ferocious yet tender passion. My breath let out sharply and I wanted to tear my hand away.

"There is no rest for me. Not while there is still much to do."

The look on his face was similar to one I'd had on my own countenance scarcely a fortnight ago. Ambrose was a man of intense burdens, and I would do well to not cause him any further trouble.

"You are happy here, Esther?" he suddenly asked.

"Yes, sir."

"That is a comfort." He was still holding my hand and brought it to his lips once more. But this time he barely kissed my fingers. "Stay as you are. Never change."

This instruction confused me, but it was delivered with such force that I nodded in agreement. He dropped my hand and swiftly strode down the landing. As I turned to go into my own chamber, he stopped before the locked bedroom door. I'd never seen a single person of the household emerge from that mysterious room. He produced a key from his stained waistcoat and inserted it into the lock.

Then he abruptly turned and stared at me. His eyes were so pained he looked like a wounded animal. I'd never seen anyone look like that before. With another great sigh, he tore his gaze away and went into the room. The door clicked shut.

I slowly closed my own chamber door and went to the bed. I sat on the white bedspread for a long time, tracing the embroidery with my finger. My meeting with Ambrose Curtis puzzled me more than it answered my questions. As I heard Lara come up the stairs, I decided not to tell her that my uncle and I had become acquainted.

He was a complete mystery.

12

My meeting with Ambrose Curtis dominated my thoughts the following day, but the rest of the household prepared to receive the Vallencourts. If their status in the city was not evident by the illustrious name and fortune, then the hubbub accompanying their arrival sealed it. Several Vallencourt servants were sent over to help, including an extra cook to prepare their meals the way they were preferred.

Lara and I kept mostly to the parlor, staying out of the way. Mr. Jakes and Mrs. Keswick directed the house traffic like policemen. Maids and footmen bustled about with freshly laundered table linens, polishing cloths, great quantities of vegetables and butcher cuts, and hothouse flower bouquets.

Neither of us had ever seen anyone with a social status as elevated as the Vallencourts, let alone been able to dine with them. Jane was given the task of supplying both of us with dinner dresses. Our mourning frocks were not deemed suitable. I balked, since it was disrespectful to not wear black while still grieving my mother.

"Then you will not be allowed to come down," Jane said. "And you are not to mention your mother's name, especially amongst the Vallencourts."

I stood in the doorway of her bedchamber, my arms crossed over my chest.

"She was your aunt as well as my mother. If that is the way of it, then I will not dine."

"Oh, Esther," Lara pleaded. "It is only for one evening."

I would not do it for a single person in Portland, but I would for Lara. Still grumbling, I reluctantly accepted the plainest of Jane's dresses, a navy silk. With a laugh, she said I could have the old thing, for it suited a country girl.

After being dressed by one of the maids, I re-entered her bedroom to find both my sister and cousin quite done up in incredible finery. Jane pinched a section of my navy skirt and twisted the fabric between her fingers.

"Henry Vallencourt will have trouble distinguishing you from a maid."

"I am not interested in impressing my appearance upon him," I said.

Lara was clothed in the prettiest of blue satins that perfectly matched her eyes. Jane was pleased and petted her like a doll. The two of them fawned before the cheval mirror, and Lara twirled the layers and layers of fabric about.

"Oh, if Jacob Hodges could only see me!"

Jane huffed. "No country boy could possibly hope to be in your presence, Miss Lara. Let us go to the parlor and await our guests."

The two traipsed from the room, Lara cheerfully complaining that her borrowed shoes were too large. I retrieved the sheet music folio before following them downstairs. I was looking forward to at last being able to play. The parlor had been buffed, polished and dusted to perfection. From across the hall, I could hear the maids and manservants setting up the dinner table.

I crossed over to the piano and set the sheet music folio upon the stand. Jane rose from the sofa and approached the piano.

"What, Miss Perry, is this? Your music collection?" She picked up the folio and stared at the cover. "My, what fine and even stitching. Oh, and it looks like a farm."

"It was a gift from my housekeeper," I said evenly. "Yes, the embroidery accurately depicts Perry Farm."

"Isn't it lovely?" Lara asked from her seat by the fire.

But Jane didn't answer her. She opened the folio and inspected each of the music pieces.

"Hmm," she kept saying. "I see."

Her reaction was as expected. I would have been hard-pressed to keep curt remarks to myself should she be insulting.

"It's chilly tonight." Lara rubbed her hands before the fire. "Play a waltz or a polka, Esther. I'm sure cousin Jane is dying for a dance as much as I am."

Jane slapped the folio covers shut and put it back on the stand. "And what makes you think I desire a dance, Miss Lara?"

My sister giggled. "Why, to be partner to Mr. Henry Vallencourt, of course."

"An idle gossiper you are. Wicked young thing."

"It's true!" Lara cried. She smiled at me. "Esther, play any piece you want. But I still request something lively."

"Then I shall oblige," I said and did not have the opportunity to add anything else, for carriage wheels crunched over the bricked carriageway. Jane and Lara hurried to the front parlor windows to catch a glimpse of the Vallencourts' arrival. From the hall, I could hear Aunt Curtis and her husband descending the staircase, apparently engaged in a heated discussion.

"It is not to be borne again, Ambrose."

"I have a duty to my patients, Lucia. You assured me that it was not so great an inconvenience."

I caught no more of their conversation, for a great commotion was heard in the hall. Lara and Jane hastened to greet our visitors, and the house was suddenly filled with a chorus of voices. There was Lara's bubbly laughter, a sly remark from Jane, Elliot's boisterous greetings, and others that were not recognizable. I didn't want to leave the quiet parlor nor the piano. But I would receive a reprimand for not appearing with the Curtis family, so I sighed and went to the door.

A laughing young lady, whom I guessed was Alexandra Vallencourt and Henry's younger sister, removed her cloak and bonnet. She was sweet-faced, young and quite beautiful. Her eyes were blue, her hair a light auburn brown. She wore a soft lavender dinner dress of refined fit and decoration. Pearl drops dangled from her ears and she wore a matching pearl necklace.

Behind her stood a handsome older woman, attired in a deeper purple gown. Mrs. Vallencourt was definitely Alexandra's mother, for she shared her general coloring. Her husband, the Vallencourt patriarch, handed his top hat and cane to Mr. Jakes, revealing salt-and-pepper hair and a high brow. He greeted Ambrose with a frank and open manner, exhibiting a friendliness that reminded me of Elliot.

"This is Lara Perry," Aunt Curtis was saying as I quietly slipped into the hall. Lara smiled at Alexandra.

"Pleased to meet you, Mr. and Mrs. Vallencourt." She bowed expertly, and I hoped neither of her new acquaintances thought much of her rural upbringing. "And you as well, Miss Alexandra."

"My goodness, you are a sweet young thing," Alexandra gushed and grasped her new little friend's shoulders. "So well-mannered, Mrs. Curtis."

"Indeed, Lucia," Mrs. Vallencourt added. "You have done well to take out the country and put in the city."

Amidst the bustle it was easy to be disregarded. I soon noticed someone else was not too keen on making introductions. Behind Mr. Vallencourt, standing off to the side and removing his coat and hat, was a handsome young man. Jane's eyes were fixed upon him as if he were the only person in the room worth her precious attention. Yet he wasn't paying her the slightest notice. Nor anyone else, I realized.

He was quite tall, taller than Elliot, and about my age. But his impeccable dress and formality gave him a sense of gravitas, as if he was a man of more mature years. He stood as rooted as a pine, feet planted apart and hands tucked behind his back. Brown hair swept about his temples. Steady brown eyes surveyed the chaotic excitement with a calm importance, as if he was captain on the deck of a ship.

"Henry!"

So this was the Henry Vallencourt my sister said would buy her horses. Mrs. Vallencourt clasped his shoulder with her jewel-encrusted hand. He looked bored and a bit peeved at being singled out. Jane darted through the crowd and went right up to him.

"Thank you for coming to dine with us tonight, Mr. Vallencourt."

Her breathless welcome was humorous, her curtsey over the top. Lara caught my eye and we shared a silent giggle over her conduct. Yes, with Lara by my side, this dinner could be somewhat bearable.

Ambrose next addressed our silent guest. "Henry, may I present Miss Lara Perry and Miss Esther Perry."

Henry Vallencourt grasped my hand and kissed it with perfunctory politeness.

"Good evening, Miss Perry," he said quietly.

I spared him a silly introduction or inauthentic airs. Instead, I met his gaze and received his nod in return. He kissed my sister's hand and greeted her in exactly the same way.

"Why, it is nice to meet you, sir," Lara said. "Your sister was telling me about your fine horses."

She did not notice, thankfully, that his eyes dulled. He was either not interested in her or horses. As the others made their way across the hall to the dining room, I realized his nod to me had been more than acknowledgment. He'd given me a gesture of respect. Jane led him into the dining room the way I'd drag a stubborn dog. He endured the feminine chatter over his arrival with few remarks.

When at last I entered the dining room, for I brought up the rear of the party, a friendly disagreement had sprung up as to who would sit next to the most eligible bachelor in Portland. Jane insisted upon her way and won out, so Henry was placed between her and his mother. Aunt Curtis sat next to Mrs. Vallencourt, with Lara to her side, then Elliot, Alexandra, Mr. Vallencourt, myself and Dr. Curtis between me and Jane. It was quite an ordeal, and my aunt muttered to Mrs. Vallencourt that the seating arrangements should have been worked out beforehand.

Finding myself seated beside Mr. Vallencourt proved to be an unexpected bonus, for in the first course I asked him about his business. In between sips of oyster soup, he regaled me with stories about heading the grandiose architectural firm busily rebuilding Portland.

"Yes, we passed some of your buildings on our way into town," I said. "I was amazed by the sheer immensity of the construction projects."

"Day and night, Miss Perry. Day and night." He wiped his mouth with his napkin. "Dr. Curtis can tell you more about the workers."

"There are thousands." Ambrose had barely touched his wine or his first course. "It would be helpful if they were offered some sort of compensation when they miss work due to injuries."

"Ah," Mr. Vallencourt said, wagging his finger at my uncle. "Then they'll come begging me for money for this and money for that. You are a poor businessman, Ambrose."

"I have no passion for architecture," Dr. Curtis admitted. He looked over at Henry, who was enjoying his dinner and also partaking in conversation with Jane. "Your son was extremely dedicated at one time, Leonard."

"He was." Mr. Vallencourt looked over at Henry, a fleeting sense of regret passing over his face. "He loved the profession more than I did. Not too long ago, he cared about vestibules, chamber placements, and how wide a hallway ought to be."

"These details are of great importance," I said. "I helped my father with building repair and restoration. Without proper knowledge of architecture, the buildings would have been in danger of rot or even collapse."

Mr. Vallencourt took a bite of his duck course. "Were there any professionally designed buildings in this town?"

"None like here, sir," I said. "Yet I don't feel one needs to be a professional architect to appreciate its benefits."

"Indeed." Ambrose brought his wineglass to his lips. "As one does not have to be a painter to appreciate art or a musician to appreciate music."

"Yes." I smiled and felt relaxed. My uncle's behavior from last night was no less astonishing, but he was being kind in his own way. He made me feel included and acknowledged, regardless of my lack of situation or finances.

So, it was with disappointment that he had to leave halfway through the dinner. A message arrived from his medical office. It seemed to be a matter of great urgency, for he rose from the dinner table, bade us a quick good-night, and hurried from the house.

"He is not a good businessman," Mr. Vallencourt said to me, "but he is an excellent doctor. We each have our virtues."

I set my wineglass down, fingering the stem. Candlelight flickered through the glass, and it looked as if the contents were ablaze. Henry Vallencourt had also lapsed into silence. I took the opportunity to extend politeness, less he should think I was a mute rustic.

"Henry Vallencourt, sir."

"Yes?" He was not looking at me.

"You know where my sister and I reside," I began, but at a glance from Aunt Curtis hastened to add: "At least temporarily. Where might your home be?"

He chewed thoughtfully for a moment and then met my gaze. I was surprised by the sudden mischievousness in his eyes. The table guests fell to silence until all noise had stopped. Henry's mother was less inclined to let my query go unanswered.

"My dear Henry, the Perry girls are new to Portland. This is your first time in the city, correct?"

"Yes," I said. "I had obligations other than traveling."

"Our home," she began, but her son presumably decided he could speak to a farm-girl. After lowering his napkin, he held up his hand.

"I'll tell her, Mother. We live on Danforth Street. It is a ten-minute carriage ride from here."

"I see." Not knowing how far a carriage could travel in ten minutes, I said, "Then it would not be far to walk."

"Walk?" Mrs. Vallencourt uttered in a tone that suggested any visitors on foot would be suspect of ulterior motives.

"Mabel, you must excuse Miss Perry," Aunt Curtis said icily.

"Yes, Mrs. Vallencourt," Jane chimed in. "She has not had access to modern transportation."

Henry clasped Jane's hand and looked directly at me. "You are right, Miss Perry. It would be a walk of short distance. High Street and Danforth Street connect after the next block. Do keep in mind that Portland is rather hilly."

"Sir, if you think I'll overexert myself walking two blocks, you are mistaken," I said as politely as I could. Inside, I was fuming. "Along with my country manners, I have a healthy constitution."

Henry's mocking gaze disappeared, replaced by a serious frown. Both Jane and Aunt Curtis narrowed their eyes in unison annoyance. I was saved from any future interrogation by the announcement of dessert. Mrs. Keswick and the servants removed our dinner plates and replaced them with a spiced apple tart.

As I smelled the apples and looked down at the dessert, my heart gave an unexpected pang. Those apple trees in our orchard hung ripe with fruit. Fruit I couldn't pick, nor could I have afforded to hire anyone to pick them. Mr. Hodges owned them.

Lara was not sharing my melancholy, but rather chatting with Alexandra. Henry resumed his conversation with Jane, and Aunt Curtis was engrossed in a fierce whisper with Mrs. Vallencourt.

"Don't let them get to you, Esther," Elliot said. "I don't think the Vallencourts have even been to a farm."

I gave him a smile for his kindness. "Thank you, Elliot. You should have seen our orchards."

"You could visit the Public Market. There are merchants with goods from all over Cumberland County. It is a fine place, especially when the weather is agreeable."

"I would like to go." I felt somewhat cheered, to think of a market stall piled high with fresh farm produce. "And I shall walk there."

"What's this about more walking?" Aunt Curtis had sharp ears. "Miss Perry, you are welcome to take the carriage whenever you travel in Portland."

Elliot laughed. I was glad he didn't take his mother too seriously.

"Mother, the Public Market is only three blocks up Congress Street. I frequently walked there as a child."

Alexandra smiled sweetly at Elliot. "Yes, I accompanied you."

That look passed between Lara and Jacob many a time. Elliot flushed and chuckled, presumably at the memory of them walking together.

"Thank you, ma'am," I said to Aunt Curtis. "I appreciate the offer to use the carriage."

She stopped paying attention to my personal traveling habits and returned to her private conversation with Mrs. Vallencourt. Mr. Vallencourt made full use of a toothpick to scratch his teeth. The gnawing sound reminded me so much of a mouse that used to nibble on our chicken coop feed boxes I suppressed a laugh behind my napkin.

"Good to see you've regained your spirits," Elliot said.

"Thanks to the good company."

Henry Vallencourt swallowed the rest of his wine and motioned for a servant to refill his glass. "Mother, what are you and Mrs. Curtis discussing?"

"Your future, of course."

Mrs. Vallencourt looked at Jane Curtis, who blushed under the candlelight. It was more like the glow of satisfaction, such as when I had corralled one of the stray piglets who got loose. Jane was pleased with the catch she had landed.

Too pleased.

Whatever she thought of her means to become better acquainted with Henry Vallencourt, Lara had picked up on it. The remainder of the dinner was only a few more minutes before plates were cleared and the entire party rose and made their way to the parlor.

Elliot paused before Miss Alexandra to offer his arm, and I smiled at their mutual affection towards one another. Aunt Curtis and Mrs. Vallencourt walked as a pair behind their eldest children, thus ensuring their match for the short distance between the dining room and the parlor. Mr. Vallencourt demonstrated an affable and big-hearted nature by asking for Lara upon one arm and myself upon the other. He declared us both remarkably well-bred, considering where we had come from.

Lara laughed. "There are schools in Bayview, Mr. Vallencourt. We weren't raised by wolves like Romulus and Remus, sir."

"And literate as well." Our guest laughed alongside her, utterly charmed. "You have a talent for setting others at ease."

"You do as well, sir," I said with a smile.

He may have been quick to judge my uncle and seemed not to know anything about farm life, but he was as fine a person as I'd ever met in Bayview. He paused in the hallway, gesturing for us to enter the parlor before him.

"Quite the flatterer, Miss Perry. It is a shame you are a woman, for you would be suited for a public position."

"Such praise, sir, when you know me so little."

"Ah, but I am an excellent judge of true character." He winked. "You quite remind me of your uncle, I daresay. A steady head on strong shoulders."

We walked into the parlor and took our seats upon the sofa and chairs.

"Yes," Lara mused. "I suppose Esther is alike to him, at least in appearance. And they both hardly utter a word, but when they do it is spot-on accurate, I'll say."

I laughed. "Thank you, Lara. You manage to both compliment and denounce at the same time."

She blushed. "Oh, Esther, I mean silly nothings by what I say. Aunt Curtis has quite a task on her hands, I'm afraid."

Mrs. Vallencourt accepted a cup of tea from the tray Mrs. Keswick had brought into the parlor, then set it upon the table and addressed my cousin.

"Dear Jane, I heard from your mother that you are to play for us this evening."

From her place on the sofa beside Henry, Jane was disinclined to vacate his side, even to show off her considerable talents over her poor relation. I rose to my feet, a gesture that received a smirk from my cousin and a considerable frown from my aunt.

"Pardon me, Mrs. Vallencourt. If you shall excuse my abruptness, I wish to entertain you at the piano. You see that I have brought my own music."

"Why, yes," Jane said. "Miss Perry has boasted long enough about her ability. Let us hear it at last."

With this encouragement, I walked over to the piano. The keys shone with a creamy luster beneath the gaslight chandelier. I ran my hand along its shiny top, the wood warm and smooth beneath my fingertip.

Mr. Jakes pulled out the bench. I smiled, a deep glow alighting within me. As I took my seat, for the first time since arriving at the Curtis House I felt truly comfortable. My feet found the pedals, pressing first the left foot and then the right foot. It was like a little dance with the piano before the music began.

I opened the sheet music folio, past the *Pathetique* I had last played at the farm and to a Johann Sebastian Bach sonata, the *French Suite Number Five*. The steady tempo and evenness of the Baroque period was suitably light for my intended audience. The Romantic pieces were for myself when I was alone.

I began the first movement, the *Allemande*, its dance-like gracefulness and elegance complementing the gentility of the Vallencourt guests. I played it slower than the suggested tempo, but as I had never heard it played by any other than myself, it more than sufficed. It was a rather short piece and I soon came to the final chord. A polite applause accompanied my completion.

"Your technique is sound," Mrs. Vallencourt said. "You would only need a few lessons from Mr. Lambson and then the overall impression would be complete. Polished, I daresay."

Mr. Vallencourt patted his wife's knee. "My dear, you cannot hope to have an ear for music you have never attempted."

"Thank you, Mr. and Mrs. Vallencourt," I said. "I appreciate all listeners."

Henry Vallencourt rose from his seat beside Jane and approached the piano. From over my shoulder, he scrutinized the Bach piece with great interest. It took me a bit by surprise, for I didn't think he had paid attention to me.

"A good start. Played rather well. Yet, I believe you mistake the composer." He came around to my side, pointing to the notation above the first measure. "You think it should have been played legato rather than adagio?"

"I mistake no one sir," I said quietly, "least of all the composer. Have you been schooled in music?"

He laughed and I felt prickled with annoyance. Why could he not entertain my cousin, rather than nitpick my piano playing?

"Mother started me in voice lessons when I was three." A mocking grin still played at his lips. "So, yes Miss Perry, I have been schooled in music."

"I see. But as you are not going to demonstrate your instrument, let me kindly play mine."

His grin turned from scorn to genuine amusement. I would have none of his opinions anymore. Wasn't Jane going to play for us this evening?

"I say, Esther," Elliot said as he came over to the piano. He tossed back the rest of his drink. "Lara says she requested a song for us to dance to!"

Henry suddenly reached out and plucked the sheet music folio. He flipped through the pages with a polite but intrigued quickness, until he at last came to a piece he preferred and set it back upon the stand. It was a Strauss waltz.

"It seems you have a piano version of the *Morning Papers Waltz*." Henry gave me a pat on the shoulder as patronizing as if I was five years old. "Please begin as soon as the dancers have assembled with their partners."

I positioned my feet above the pedals and my hands above the keys. "Miss Curtis is in want of a partner, sir. Not I."

He looked at me strangely, then over at Jane, who was laughing along with Alexandra and Lara. Thankfully, he said not another word to me and instead walked over to Jane and asked for her hand in dance. She rose to her feet, accepting his hand in her own gloved fingers. Elliot gave me a smile, and I smiled back. When he reached up to loosen his cravat, I leaned over.

"Ask her, Elliot," I whispered. "She will not decline."

"I do not know what you mean," he said with a grin, but as he spoke he was setting his glass on top of the piano. He walked over, gave a bow to Alexandra and held out his hand for her.

"Please accept this dance with me," he said with such earnestness and hope I smiled widely and began the song.

Mr. and Mrs. Vallencourt rose from the sofa and joined their children. The parlor soon came to life with the playful tune. Henry and Jane danced expertly about the room, their light steps causing the candlelight to flicker. Lara clamped her hand on her mouth, trying not to burst out laughing. I shared her enjoyment, for Elliot and Alexandra danced with such dedication to remembering the steps. It was quite funny. Aunt Curtis opened her fan, and I glimpsed her satisfied smile behind it.

When the final chord came to an end, I received an enthusiastic ovation. Miss Alexandra was both polite and sincere in her praise. Mrs. Vallencourt complimented me on my technique, on which she couldn't claim authority, and Mr. Vallencourt said how charming it was to hear an orchestral waltz played on the piano. Jane was silent and so was her mother, but Lara's clapping was heard above all others. Elliot couldn't speak, since he was overcome with both the physical and emotional exertion of dancing with Alexandra.

The last notes not only signaled the end of the waltz but also the evening. No sooner had I risen from the piano than Mr. Jakes and Mrs. Keswick were fetching the guests' cloaks and hats. Everyone was making their way towards the front door.

The clamor accompanying the Vallencourts' departure matched their arrival, with the exception of Henry contributing his share of farewells. As I watched Mr. Jakes help him into his wool coat, I thought to myself that Jane could have him. What a pair they'd make, snickering from behind their wine glasses at those less fortunate. They'd have the grandest home in town, but it would be lacking warmth, true comfort, and the ease of shared casual companionship. Jane might invite Lara to entertain her, but my name would be irrevocably off the guest list.

"Good-night to you, Miss Lara."

My sister wished Henry a hearty evening farewell and implored him to come back any time. Whether she was in a position to offer such hospitality was irrelevant and, for the first time that evening, he broke into a genuine smile.

"And you, Miss Perry," he said as I received the customary kiss to my hand. "Thank you for providing both myself and Bach your musical interpretations."

"Good-night, sir," I said. "I wish you luck in your endeavors. I don't recall who said architecture is frozen music, but I believe it is true."

Henry's father chuckled. "Well said, Miss Perry. It was Goethe. Fine words. We shall look forward to your company once more. A good night!"

He and his wife, along with a flushed and happy Alexandra, stepped out. Yet Henry lingered in the front hall a little longer, and for a moment I thought it was to spend an extra minute with Jane.

But after he had stepped from her side and gone to the door, he turned back ... to look at me. His features were flat, his face handsome, yet reserved. I thought I caught a tiny flicker in his eyes, but then he opened the door and left.

Aunt Curtis and Jane picked up their skirts and walked upstairs, laughing gaily about how fortunate it was to have such illustrious acquaintances.

My skin felt both cool and warm. I stood alone in the grand front hall, listening to Lara chatter with Elliot, the songs on the piano still ringing in my ears.

13

"Thank you for joining us in congregation this morning. All rise for the Lord's prayer."

The minister paused and adjusted his eyeglasses. I hugged my shawl tighter about my shoulders as I got to my feet. The church was unheated and the hard pew chilled my body.

"Our Father, who art in heaven, hallowed be thy name. Thy kingdom come, thy will be done, on earth as it is in heaven. Give us this day our daily bread. And forgive us our trespasses, as we forgive those that trespass against us. And lead us not into temptation; but deliver us from evil. For thine is the kingdom, the power, and the glory, for ever and ever. Amen."

The prayer was my mother's favorite. After receiving the War Department telegram announcing my father's death, she gathered my sister and I into the parlor. We sat together on the sofa, quietly reciting the Lord's Prayer. The memory felt both aching and comforting, as I felt my mother's presence. The minister motioned for us to be seated.

I blew on my fingers and rubbed my palms together. Elliot sat beside me, drumming his fingers on the charcoal lining of his hat. Ambrose Curtis was seated on my other side, silent and imposing. He hadn't said a word all morning about his whereabouts last night.

The Vallencourt family occupied the more comfortable and expensive seats up front. Henry had turned about once or twice during the sermon to glance at Jane, who of course was enjoying his extra attention. I still wondered at his words from last night and tried not to dwell too much on them. That my thoughts had even strayed to what he said was strange, as was the nervousness I felt whenever he turned around. Stop being girlish, I admonished myself, surprised I even needed to keep my feelings in check.

"The Lord's Prayer ends in Verse Thirteen of Matthew, Chapter Six. But it is Verses Fourteen and Fifteen I wish to speak of today. Let me read them to you."

'For if you forgive other people when they sin against you, your heavenly Father will also forgive you. But if you do not forgive others their sins, your Father will not forgive your sins.' These powerful words of forgiveness must not be set aside."

He looked up from the pulpit. An old lady snored softly in the pew behind me, and Lara was trying not to giggle.

"If your Father, your Lord and master, does not forgive your sins, then there is no eternal glory for you in the kingdom of heaven. It matters not what good deeds you do on this earth. It matters not what good deeds your parents or your acquaintances have done. But, as is stated here in Verse Fourteen, if you do forgive other people, then you are forgiven by the divine. Forgiveness is asked for and required by the Lord. If you do not forgive, you will have upheld the greatest sin. The sin of condemning yourself."

My uncle shifted in his seat. He clutched his gloves as if holding on to them for sustenance. Once the final words of the sermon had been spoken, he turned to me with a kindly smile. I'd never seen anyone look so open and so tense at the same time. It was not the first time I'd thought of him as a man of burdens.

Elliot was a man of no burdens, save for the impending affection he held for Miss Alexandra Vallencourt. Each time Henry had turned around, Elliot had moved sideways to see if his sister would follow suit. It was quite charming. He was young, barely older than twenty, but as eager as Jane to secure a match with the most illustrious family in Portland.

"Amen," the minister concluded, and the congregation echoed his solemn finish.

My uncle and I got to our feet, and Elliot helped his mother arise. Lara rolled her eyes in tired protest of both the early hour for church and also the minister's sermon. I frowned, trying silently to remind her of social propriety, and she looked abashed.

We made our way out of the church and into the small cobblestone yard where the carriages were parked. The First Parish Church was on Congress Street, the main thoroughfare that had enthralled me upon first entering the city. Aunt Curtis put a hand on my sister's arm.

"Miss Lara, if I could have a word with you?"

Lara looked at me, her expression somber. My aunt was again not pleased with her behavior. Well, I'd done what I could. She had to learn.

All of a sudden Henry Vallencourt appeared from the crowd. He approached our party and made a polite bow to both my aunt and uncle. Jane lifted her nose, nodding to him. He addressed my guardians in a formal but rather hurried voice.

"Mr. and Mrs. Curtis, may I request a drive with Miss Curtis in my carriage?"

"You wish to be unescorted?" Ambrose said, as if it were the most ordinary thing in the world for a young man to request time alone with his daughter. "I see no problem with it, Henry."

"Nor I," my aunt added in the kindest, most affable tone I'd ever heard. "Jane, do have a wonderful afternoon. We will expect you for supper this evening."

Lara chuckled, and Elliot couldn't prevent his wide smile. Jane accepted Henry's arm and her look of satisfaction could not have been more pronounced. Her parents, brother, Lara and I watched her ascend the

Vallencourt carriage steps as if she boarded a train to an exotic destination.

After they had pulled from the churchyard, Aunt Curtis beckoned to my sister for a private conversation. Ambrose took out his pocketwatch, checking the time against the large clock tower.

"So, here we must part." He tipped his hat. "I am not allowed many hours from work."

"Your office is nearby?" I said.

"Yes." He pointed up Congress Street, in the opposite direction we had driven from the house. "It is across from Lincoln Park on Federal Street, two blocks from here. Portland is an easy city for walking."

"It is," Elliot said with a laugh. "If only you had attended our first dinner, Father. It seems Esther shares your passion for walking."

My uncle looked at me oddly. I blushed, for his look was curiously unguarded, as if he expected to confide in me. But Aunt Curtis and Lara approached, so his face assumed its professional mask once more. He gave us a quick bow, and without another word took up his cane and started up the street.

"Father will go on foot to the office," Elliot explained to his mother, as if it wasn't obvious.

"I see," she said. "Well, it is fortunate he has decided, for I was going to beg the carriage from him. Miss Lara and I are bound on a special errand."

"She's taking me to Grombey and Sons druggists!" Lara blurted. I clasped her hand and shared her exuberant smile. "I imagine it's well stocked with fixings and items for my use."

"That is kind of you, Aunt Curtis," I said. "Lara has talked of nothing else since our arrival."

"But first we'll take you home, Esther," Lara said.

"There is no need for us to be escorted," Elliot said. "What is a sunny October day for, if not to be enjoyed. We shall walk home."

Aunt Curtis was not at first in full agreement with this decision, but since it was already one o'clock and the time to drop us off would have severely cut into her plans, she acquiesced. Lara gave me a quick kiss on the cheek and climbed into the carriage with her aunt. I tied my cloak strings tighter about my neck and waved goodbye to her as the carriage pulled from the churchyard.

Elliot offered his arm to me. "Shall we, my cousin?"

My gloved hands wrapped about his woolen elbow. "Thank you, Elliot. When I first arrived at your home, I did not think my desire to walk would be called into question."

He smiled. "Mother is proud of her carriage assortment, so it is less a matter of exercise and more of appearance."

"I see."

We started our leisurely stroll down Congress Street. It was the first time I had seen the city from its ground level, and it was even more bewildering than from behind carriage windows. Elliot tipped his hat to a number of acquaintances making their way about on this lovely fall afternoon. He pointed out a favorite restaurant, introduced me to several old schoolfellows, and shared stories about going to school and playing in the Deering's Woods park.

I, however, could not stop thinking about Jane and her object of attention riding about in a rare seclusion. He had no other motive for suggesting their intimacy than to ask for her hand. Yet I had not seen any undue display of affection, even at dinner last night. Was their dance proof of his attachment? Granted, she was the most beautiful young lady I'd ever seen and as fine and well-bred as the Vallencourts could wish her. Her entire life was consumed in those feminine pursuits that gentlemen admired. But I found her idle, selfish, and unconcerned with the welfare of those less fortunate.

"It seems I am to gain a brother," Elliot said, as if to mirror my thoughts. "Henry has pursued Jane for months, so it is almost certain."

"I confess I have been wondering the same. They danced together well last night, I thought."

"They did," he admitted. "Thank you for encouraging me as well. I have known Miss Alexandra all my life, and she has become the finest of young ladies."

"You have been long acquainted with the Vallencourts?"

"Goodness, yes." He laughed. "Also Henry, of course. I sympathize with his father's disappointment, for he used to be different."

"Now that you mention it, last night Mr. Vallencourt confessed Henry was at one time interested in architecture. Is he pursuing another profession?"

Elliot shrugged. "No, not that I know. He just brags about hiring more manservants and his new dinner suits. He was at one time ambitious and steadfast about his future career. Everyone knew he would join the architectural firm alongside his father."

A young man claiming to be ambitious and steadfast could not hope to find lasting companionship with a woman who denounced such things. If Henry had kept to his original character, he would not be riding around with Jane today.

"It seems his attentions have become diverted," I said.

"It is odd," Elliot said. "A few years ago, Henry little cared for my sister. Then his acquaintance with my family changed, and he has pursued her ever since."

"She is a great beauty," I said. "I confess I am no expert on relations. So as her cousin, I wish her happiness in her choice."

I was no expert, indeed. Every time I thought of Henry and Jane, my heart recalled my own affections towards Caleb. I had no right to question and judge. What did I know of their obligations and feelings? Their parents were so approving of the match that there must be some deeper connection I had not seen. Henry and I were acquainted less than twenty-four hours, so my first impression could be seriously wrong. I knew enough to see the ill merits in a hasty opinion.

I missed the farm. Life was far simpler when my future was clear. After marrying, I'd take care of Perry Farm the remainder of my days. Portland was an amazing place, but its great population required close society with different types of people. The more relationships entered my life, the more complex it became. I resolved to try and keep my personal business to myself, less it should invite further scrutiny or unnecessarily entangle me in others' emotional agitations.

For the fourth time since my arrival, Elliot declared how pleased he was that Lara and I had come to stay. With his father largely absent and his mother and sister a united pair, he could not help but be glad for amiable company.

I smiled and squeezed his arm. "Thank you, Elliot. Lara and I are pleased ourselves, to find such kindness."

"You have settled into your room, I hope? I love the view from those front windows. I've spent happy hours watching the boats in the harbor."

"Yes, we are quite comfortable. But, Elliot," I added, "I am not content about forcing you upstairs. You should not be in discomfort while we are here."

"I am not at all." He shook his head. "An old billiards room was specially converted for my purpose. I am well-acquainted with our servants and find no qualms in sharing their quarters."

None other in his family would have been so accommodating, and his consideration was all the more special for its rarity. By now, we had reached High Street, so we turned left down the sloping road. I glimpsed the Curtis House at the corner of High and Spring Streets. But I could not forget the strange boarding situation and again addressed the subject.

"Could you not have moved into the northeast bedchamber? It must be more convenient than the third floor. And you could have been directly adjacent our room."

He did not answer me at first. Uneasily, I felt I had pried into a personal matter, but of course I knew not what. Both Lara and I would enjoy rooming beside Elliot, with nothing but a door separating us.

"That bedroom is not used," he said at last.

It was the same way Mrs. Keswick had described it, in the same tone of voice. He stopped abruptly and turned to me, leaning close and speaking in a low tone.

"Esther, we are not to speak of it. I am sorry if it feels like a breach of trust, but do not inquire again. I hope you understand."

I nodded. "My own mother's name is not to be mentioned, either. There is much I do not know, but I won't put your confidence at risk."

He looked relieved and the uneasiness about his manner vanished. Once more, he tucked my arm in his and we continued down the street. As we approached the house, Elliot put a hand to his eyes.

"It seems we are not the first ones to arrive."

He was right, for the Vallencourt carriage was parked in the carriageway. We entered the gates and walked up to the front door. No sooner had we reached the portico than the door opened and Henry Vallencourt emerged from the house. I was surprised by the sudden rush of feeling, the quickened heartbeat and strange flush in my cheeks. Henry halted on the steps and nodded to us.

"Good afternoon, Mr. Curtis. Miss Perry."

"We hope it was a good afternoon for yourself as well, Henry." Elliot cocked his head, a mischievous grin playing at his mouth. "And for Jane."

"Thank you for inquiring."

"Hopefully your own inquiry was made with equal intimacy."

His playfulness was making Henry uncomfortable. My cousin had the same ability as Lara to take joking too far.

"I am chilled from our walk," I said to Elliot. "Please have your cook brew a cup of tea for me. I shall take it in my room."

"Of course, Esther."

He tipped his hat to Henry, gave me a smile and then promptly stepped into the house, whistling the waltz tune I'd played last night. I made as if to follow him and was passing by Mr. Vallencourt when he caught my eye.

"Your cousin mentioned that you wanted to be mistress of your family farm."

"Yes," I said. "Its occupations would have suited me perfectly."

"You desired nothing more for yourself, then."

"I was not looking for another position." In the light, his eyes were a warm brown. "It would have required great responsibility and conduct. I was honored to assume it."

"I see. Good day to you, Miss Perry."

He continued down the front walk towards the carriageway. I wondered why he brought up the subject, but no doubt Jane had spoken of it degradingly. Had he asked her to marry him this afternoon?

When I at last entered the house and heard both of my cousins speaking excitedly to one another in the parlor, it appeared I would hear of Jane's impending engagement before the evening had come to a close.

But before then, I wanted to rest and so I ascended the stairs to my bedchamber. Passing by the locked bedroom that was plainly not used, I thought how fortunate it was that Elliot was kind. I didn't know what role I was to play in this new life in Portland, but I hoped it would showcase my better talents.

No matter what level the position.

14

"I thought he'd never ask!" Aunt Curtis gushed. "My dear Jane, I am pleased with how you have conducted yourself throughout such a lengthy courtship. I never saw a girl so patient and determined to obtain her intended's proposal."

"It is a good thing he did ask, Mother," Jane said as we settled ourselves in the carriage the following morning. "You see patience in it, but I was severely tested upon this for months. What reason had he to be so guarded in his affections? I should have preferred Charles Stevens' more direct way."

"Ah, but he wanted Anna Brooking, dear, and you could have done nothing about that." Aunt Curtis was waving her fan so rapidly it looked like a hummingbird's wing. "And you, Miss Lara, what do you think of the match?"

Lara, lost in her own reverie about making lady's toilette articles with the items purchased at the druggist's yesterday, could at first make no reply. I gave a half-smile and nudged her elbow. She'd come into the bedroom last night clutching two brown paper sacks filled with herbal concoctions, glass bottles and oils. I'd never seen her more eager to begin a new project.

"Well, Aunt Curtis," she began with a blush. "I knew Henry would ask her the moment I met him. I even told Esther that night I'd marry him, too, if he asked me."

"Lara!" I admonished. "Please do not speak your opinion so freely."

"On the contrary, Miss Perry," Aunt Curtis interrupted. "I appreciate the innocence and girlishness of your sister."

I was instantly puzzled, since before Lara was deemed uncouth and unladylike. Could my sister's nature have won over Aunt Curtis so as to elicit a reverse of opinion? Not likely. As happy as she was for her daughter's fortunate match, my aunt could not change her personality any more than a tiger its stripes. Neither could Jane, for she languished again and again in her mother's praise. Praise that would not have been so frequent had the suitor not been so rich.

"I have longed for a Curtis and Vallencourt alignment ever since the two of you were infants." Aunt Curtis took a handkerchief from her reticule and daubed her dry eyes. "How happy Mabel and I will be, secure and comforted."

"Does Dr. Curtis know of the proposal?" I asked. "He is required to give his consent, is he not?"

My directness was improper, but he had not come home last night nor this morning. As I suspected, my question brought indignation. Jane reached over and pinched a piece of my gray wool dress.

"Those who wear such drab things cannot help but think drab thoughts. Perhaps, Miss Perry, you fancy yourself a match to Henry Vallencourt instead?"

The bride and her mother shared a mocking laugh that was far too loud and lasted far too long.

"You can't spoil this shopping trip with your negativity," Aunt Curtis said. "My husband has no intention of denying the inevitable. Jane and Henry will marry. Dr. Curtis and I have been in complete agreement. You should count yourself fortunate to participate as a bridesmaid."

"Only if you refuse to wear gray, black or any other dark color," Jane said. "My bridesmaids will be wearing the prettiest of coral pinks."

A costly color for a dressmaker, I thought. Even if I was included in the bridal party, my dress's expense would be deducted from the room and board expenses I was already accruing. But I shared none of these thoughts and forced myself to speak of more benign topics like the weather and what flowers Jane would like at the church.

Aunt Curtis had planned a shopping trip to celebrate her daughter's engagement, so our day was quite busy. We stopped at merchants and dress warehouses, purchasing fabrics, ribbons, trims and even a brand-new set of traveling luggage for Jane's trousseau. Dressmakers, tailors, leather workers, lace-makers, corset-builders and seamstresses prepared to contribute their laborious talents to creating the finest wedding Portland had ever seen. Jane wasn't going to allow them the full amount of time until the wedding date for their labor. The garments and items were needed and no amount of protest over the extreme skill required to bead or stitch would be heard.

I had no choice but to tag along, like a stubborn puppy, after my insistent cousin and her fawning mother, in this bridal preparation of the most outlandish proportions. I'd once thought of myself getting married in Bayview's white wooden church, in my prettiest cotton dress with a bouquet of wildflowers. After an afternoon of dancing on our lawn at Perry Farm, my husband and I would then sign our names at Mr. Greene's office as the joint owners and continue the life I'd wanted to live.

That life was gone. As we passed by the harvest market in Market Square on Congress Street, I saw sunflowers and tears came to my eyes. Our luncheon at a fine hotel restaurant included Apple Brown Betty for dessert, one of my favorite dishes to make in October. Lara shared my melancholy, for we walked by a carriage horse that could have been Sarge's twin. She ran up to him and stroked his velvety muzzle. Like all equines, he submitted to her loving treatment. But then we had to move on, and I held her hand to comfort her.

When at last Mr. Murton brought the carriage for us, the afternoon's sunlight had faded and long shadows stretched across the sidewalk. We settled ourselves in and began the journey up High Street to the house. Jane was persnickety about a dressmaker's response, and Aunt Curtis planned the elaborate reception menu. Then my aunt abruptly paused in mid-sentence and turned to Lara.

"You seemed quite compatible with Alexandra Vallencourt at dinner this past Saturday."

"Yes, ma'am. She told me of a pony she'd once owned. She called it Cookie, which I thought was the sweetest name."

"I do remember that little creature," Aunt Curtis said. "Did you know Miss Alexandra was educated by the best tutors and governesses in Portland? She has become an excellent example to influence any young lady."

"Mother and Father taught me reading and writing. There was a school in Bayview, but I missed months due to harvesting and farm-work."

It was the response I feared she would give. Exposing our lack of education in such an explicit way could not help our reputation. Aunt Curtis cocked her head, tapping her closed fan against her chin.

"Well, then you have been sorely disadvantaged. Don't worry, Miss Lara, it was through no fault of your own." She paused. "But I do have an idea as to how we can remedy it."

"Will I get a private tutor?" Lara asked eagerly.

Aunt Curtis leaned forward, pointing her fan at my sister. "How would you like to become a companion to Miss Alexandra Vallencourt? She will be your tutor, and educate you in all feminine pursuits."

"Have her teach me how to be a lady?" Lara looked surprised. "Gosh, that sounds wonderful. I'm sure she knows beauty recipes."

My stomach churned in my belly. Lara saw opportunity, whereas I could not help but feel a strange sense of unease. Jane smiled.

"She'd be only too happy to share her knowledge with you. I'd consider myself flattered to be asked."

"Think how great a teacher she will be for you, Miss Lara," my aunt added. "And you will get to see the Vallencourt mansion. They have the finest greenhouse in town and you will dine with them as well. How exciting."

Jane smirked. "Mother, you forget they have such pretty dapple gray horses. I'm sure Miss Lara would like to see them."

My cousin knew Lara well, for her face lit up like a lantern. "Oh, really?"

"Yes, how silly of me to forget." Aunt Curtis laughed. "And fine polished saddles, too."

I had a hard time understanding what exactly was being planned, but my sister lapped it up like a kitten. She grasped my hand and squeezed it with excited glee.

"They must have a piano, too."

"Yes. A grand Steinway," Jane said curtly. "Alexandra being such an accomplished lady, she is proficient in music. However, I believe you are mistaken about your sister, Miss Lara."

"Jane is quite right," Aunt Curtis said. "Miss Alexandra cannot possibly take two companions, nor I will be deprived of both of my guests. You will be going by yourself."

"Without Esther?" The thought had never occurred to Lara that she could do things without me. Her blue eyes grew fearful. "But if they live in a home as grand as yours, there must be room for us both."

"Thank you, Lara," I said quietly. "However, you will be Miss Alexandra's exclusive companion."

"Your sister is not only a fine pianist, but an intelligent young lady," Aunt Curtis said. "Do not fret, Lara dear. You will be far too happy to miss your sister."

"It's only a short walk, anyway," I said, remembering our dinner conversation.

Aunt Curtis and Jane both grimaced at me. My walking preference would never endear itself. But it was a means of independence, and, if what Henry had said at dinner Saturday night was true, then I could walk to the Vallencourt mansion in ten minutes.

"Well, then I shall have to tell you all about it won't I, Esther?" Lara said, wonder restored in her eyes. "How long shall I be staying?"

Her query was asked at the moment we pulled into the Curtis House carriageway. But before Aunt Curtis could answer, we all sensed something was amiss. The front door was wide open and servants were dashing about between the home and the carriage-house.

Suddenly, Elliot came running out of the house as if his jacket had caught fire. He ran down the walkway and right up to the moving carriage. Mr. Murton yanked on the reins.

"Whoa!" he shouted.

The horses skidded to a halt and the wheels ground into the cobblestones. I jerked forward across the seat, grasping Lara to prevent her from pitching into the glass window. My knees ached with the buckled weight. With the carriage still rocking from its abrupt stop, Aunt Curtis opened the door in a huff.

"Elliot, what is the meaning of this?"

"Father needs the carriage immediately! He has been waiting all day. He must leave!"

"Whatever for?" Jane demanded. "Elliot!"

Her brother ignored her. He grabbed the carriage steps to bring them down.

"Mother, come! Let me escort you."

While Elliot implored his mother to move quicker, I suddenly noticed Ambrose. He rushed out of the front door and hurried over to the carriage. He wore a simple traveling jacket and a plain suit, carrying a leather doctor's bag and a crumpled piece of paper the yellow color of a telegram. He nearly ran into his wife, who had just descended and stood adamantly in the carriageway, hands on her hips.

"Ambrose, why are you running about so hurriedly? Where are you going?"

He waved the telegram before her eyes. "There is no time to explain, Lucia. I have to leave at once without delay. Ladies, please. If you will."

Jane crossed her arms and stuck her nose up. I, however, took Lara's hand and got out of the carriage.

"Jane, now!"

Ambrose spoke so loudly the hairs on the back of my neck stood up. But his order snapped Jane to attention. She gathered her skirts and swiftly stepped down from the carriage.

"You have no right to be rude, Father," she scolded. "For you have not yet told us the reason for your departure."

"You want to know, then?" He tossed the doctor's bag and telegram into the carriage. "The reason is that your brother is alive."

Color drained from both Aunt Curtis's and Jane's faces. They looked quite ill. Lara and I were similarly shocked. Who was this brother? Where was he and why did he require my uncle? Jane appeared pale enough to faint, and Aunt Curtis had a hand to her mouth. She shared an odd look with her daughter.

"Ambrose, you have heard from him?"

"To the train depot!" my uncle shouted.

He boarded the carriage and slammed the door shut. Mr. Murton quickly turned the carriage about and sped out into Spring Street.

In a rush of dust and swirling autumn leaves, he was gone.

15

"Another brother?" Lara blurted. "Who is he? What's his name?"

Courtesy evaporated from Aunt Curtis's face as if she'd been turned to stone. Jane's lips were trembling, and she didn't answer Lara, though she plainly could have. Instead, she hurried past us into the house, slamming the front door behind her. I didn't know what to say. Finding out a brother was alive seemed a cause for celebration, not upset. As for my aunt, she soon was able to compose herself and promptly ordered us to remain in our bedchamber until supper was announced.

"I'll escort them inside Mother," Elliot said.

"Where did your father say he was going?"

Elliot looked as if he might conceal the answer or even lie. But his mother's eyes bore into him with tenacity.

"I believe he said Virginia."

"It is expected," Aunt Curtis said, as if her husband going to Virginia was commonplace. "You are needed at the doctor's office. Let us hope the training you have received will serve you. Go! I'll send a servant to deliver your things."

With Ambrose gone, the city's inhabitants would be in dire need of medical attention. I was surprised my aunt had the presence of mind to take care of his position. Elliot could not afford to linger, so he bid Lara and I a hasty good-night and started up Spring Street.

"I thought I told you ladies to retire."

"Forgive me, Aunt Curtis," Lara said, "but who is this brother? Can you not tell us? When will our uncle return?"

"So, Phoebe never taught you not to pry into others' affairs."

Her mention of Mother's name, up until now a forbidden utterance, stunned both Lara and me. We were instantly silent.

"No further inquiry will be tolerated. Dr. Curtis is away on private business and that is final. I will not have this incident damage my family's reputation, standing, or solidity either within my household or the city. Is that understood?"

I wasn't sure Lara understood, but I did and perfectly well. This mysterious brother was another unmentionable topic. In addition, I wasn't to find out why Ambrose had gone to Virginia.

Without another word, I took Lara's hand and led her inside the house and upstairs. Once inside our bedchamber, I began taking off my cloak and bonnet. But Lara went straight to the front window and peered out, as if trying to locate her lost uncle. She continued to pace about the room, wondering aloud what had happened in the carriageway, until I snapped at her and told her to sit.

"Why should I?" She folded her arms and pouted. "We can't speak of Mother or ask about Uncle's whereabouts. Nobody says anything in this house and look at us - right next to a locked bedroom!"

I sat down on the bedspread, feeling the keenness of her frustration but not being free to display it as openly.

"A locked bedroom ..." Lara swept past me and over to it. "Esther, do you think it could have belonged to this brother? He's never been mentioned before."

I shrugged. "Lara, it may have belonged to him, but we cannot ask. There must be some reason, as there is a reason for everything else we can't talk about. We are not supposed to know."

She shook her head. "I do not understand you, Esther. You never question! I feel like these people are half-strangers, for all the truth they reveal."

"I do question the need for secrecy about these topics, but I cannot go searching for the answers. I am responsible for our welfare here, Lara. I promised Mother I would look after you, and I feel that to betray Aunt Curtis's trust would cause severe harm."

Lara sighed, still gazing wistfully at the locked door. Then she went over to the dressing-table, strewn with the items for toilette articles, and sat down dejectedly. She pushed aside the dried rosebuds and bottles, resting her chin in her hands and staring into the looking-glass.

I sat on the bed for a long time, staring down at the striped pattern of my gray wool dress and trying to calm my agitations. I felt so much, like a vessel of water about to tip over. My eyes blurred and I wiped the tears away. I couldn't help Lara, and oh, how I wanted to. I wanted to talk about Mother. I wanted to converse freely with my aunt and to have my uncle's presence in the house once more. With him gone, I felt strangely vulnerable. And the conversation about Lara becoming Alexandra's companion disquieted me as well, though I didn't know why.

I finally stood and went over to Lara. Grasping her shoulders, I leaned down and gave her a kiss on the cheek.

"I'm sorry, Lara, for these troubles. I should have found us a better living situation."

She looked up at me. "Do not blame yourself, Esther. I will try not to ask about all these secretive things. It is hard, you know."

It was, but we had to be strong.

A few minutes later, a beef stew supper was served to our room on trays. We ate quietly and talked about the amazing places we'd visited in Portland that day. The busy shopping trip and the commotion surrounding Ambrose's departure made us quite sleepy. Long after Lara had fallen asleep, I lay awake in bed and stared up at the ceiling, my agitated thoughts whirling and whirling.

In the morning, our spirits had improved despite the fact the sunlight had vanished and gray clouds hung over the harbor. Lara regained her enthusiasm about making beauty items, and she was showing me a recipe book when there was a knock at the door.

I finished pinning up my hair and went to answer it. Mrs. Keswick stood on the landing, jingling her keys. She wore an especially pinched expression, even more pinched than usual.

"You're wanted in the parlor, Miss Perry. Alone."

I glanced back at my sister. "Save our place, Lara. I shouldn't be long."

"Of course." She went back to reading.

I made my way downstairs. Autumn leaves swirled outside the windows, their colors dulled by the ashen light. Candles had been lit in the front hall sconces. I wondered if Elliot had come home last night. He'd probably be as consumed with work as his father was.

I was so lost in thought, thinking of Elliot's absence, that when I at last reached the parlor door and knocked, the curt reply startled me.

"Come in."

It was my aunt.

Why did she want to see me so early? I opened the door and entered. The parlor looked empty and cold, though a fire had been built up and there were several lamps lit. A persistent wind whooshed against the large front windows.

Aunt Curtis was seated on the parlor sofa, clothed in a rich green dress and cream lace cap, looking quite regal and smug. I felt instantly on edge, as if I was about to be tested.

"Sit down."

I seated myself in the large wingback chair opposite her. As my aunt regarded me, I began to feel increasingly under scrutiny, an insect under her penetrating microscope.

"Elliot did not return from the office last night. I expect the medical position's demands will keep him absent from home."

I nodded. Ambrose Curtis's position could not be an easy one to fill. I hoped I'd be able to visit him and perhaps bring items to ease his burden.

"Alexandra and Henry Vallencourt are arriving early this afternoon. They will stay for a brief luncheon, and then Lara will go with them to the Vallencourt residence."

This was not unusual, given the conversation in the carriage yesterday. It still was a separation from my dear sister that I did not care for.

"You will not be joining them, as I said yesterday."

"Yes, ma'am." Aunt Curtis and Jane were not the best of company, but Lara would want me to call and write. "Is Dr. Curtis expected away for a long time?"

"How am I to know?" Her smile reminded me of a fox who had cornered a hen. "If the telegram's contents are true, then it will be months. Travel is difficult in the winter."

Too difficult for Ambrose to come home. All the questions puzzling me began to slip from my mind, leaving a fearful numbness. Aunt Curtis yawned and picked up a fan. She fanned herself slowly, though the room was not warm.

"When I arrived at your farm in Bayview, I was appalled at how deplorable your situation was. It was obvious that Phoebe made a poor choice in marriage. After I left your farm that afternoon, I journeyed to see Mr. Silas Greene."

"The lawyer?" I said, startled. "What was your business with him?"

"I saw the will." She stopped fanning and peered at me. "George Perry squandered a meager fortune and left his daughters with nothing."

Pain I had been trying to heal came rushing to the surface. My heart felt as full and heavy as a wet stone. Bitter tears burned the corners of my eyelids, and the lump in my throat was almost too large to swallow. Shame, such shame my father had brought upon our family.

"I told you that I do not extend charity. Seeing to your welfare was a request from my husband I was obliged to fulfill. Now, I can exercise the discipline and restraint as is my want."

I remembered Ambrose's face as he stood in my bedchamber doorway that night, his shirt stained with his patients' blood. *A home you have sorely needed.* He was the one who offered that home to me. Not my aunt.

"This afternoon, once your sister leaves, you will pack your things. I am moving you to the third floor. I let a housemaid go last week and your service is required."

Service? For a moment, I was confused and cocked my head, struggling to comprehend.

"I'm afraid I don't understand -"

"This is not a boarding-house, Esther."

I was to work. As one of the help. The realization made me feel stripped and bare before her. But I kept my mouth shut. I could do nothing but keep a steady gaze upon her eyes.

"Report to the kitchen at five o'clock tomorrow morning. You will be under Adelaide's supervision." She paused, looking me up and down. "You have another dress, I presume?"

I looked down at my dark skirts. "I am still in mourning for my mother."

"It is not acceptable." She reached for a goblet of water and sipped. "Your new position will not be made known to your sister or to the Vallencourt family. You are not to speak of it to anyone."

"Then I won't see Lara."

"Don't think I won't keep you busy. This house is filthy, and you won't have time to think of your sister's absence. I daresay you won't notice she's gone."

You daresay? I'd never spent a night away from Lara. How could I forget her? It took every last ounce of composure to keep from dropping to my knees, face in hands. I accepted Father leaving for war. I endured Mother's passing. But to lose Lara ... I could barely think of it without breaking inside.

"You'll work here until Dr. Curtis returns. Your room and meals will be enough to cover your expenses, so there are no wages. If my instructions are unclear, speak now."

I clasped my hands. Despair churned inside me until I felt it stiffen and flare into anger. How dare she keep me from seeing Lara! How dare she twist my need for a secure home into an imprisoned confinement of drudgery! I inhaled so deeply my corset laces dug into my back, but when I at last spoke, my voice was composed. I would bear this. I must.

"I understand, Aunt Curtis."

Ten days. It had been ten days since arriving in Portland, twelve days since leaving Perry Farm, and one month ago was the day my mother died. In one month I had lost everything I knew. I had never fallen so far so fast.

"Send Lara down here. And not a word to her. You are dismissed."

I was numb as I walked back upstairs. Feeling had drained from my limbs. I was losing Lara. My family. Never before had this year's losses felt so pressing upon me. They squeezed every last drop from me, until I felt both too empty and too full, starving to keep everything close to me.

"Esther, this recipe looks easy. You can help me, if you want."

I swallowed hard. "Perhaps, if there's time. Aunt Curtis wants to see you."

"All right!" She snapped the book shut and jumped up from the dressing-table. "What is the matter? You look pale."

"Nothing. I'm a bit tired."

"Oh, well you'll have plenty of time to rest. I don't suspect we'll be out shopping again today."

I slowly walked to the bed and sat down. "No, I should think not."

Lara shrugged and happily skipped from the room. Even the sound of her light footsteps on the stairwell made my heart ache.

I wept and didn't know I was weeping until a tear dropped onto the embroidery. The weight of my new situation pulling me downwards, ever downwards.

I leaned over and sobbed. Oh, to lose her. And I had lost my home ... I could still hear Lara laughing as she rode Sarge around the paddock. The piano notes echoing painfully in my mind. Mother's frail whisper. Take care of her, Esther. You're strong! You know you're strong.

I didn't want to be strong. Not if it meant I must be tested like this. I didn't want to lose everything. I wanted to keep it safe, locked in my arms. Never let go. Never leave me. Mother, why was I never told I'd have to do this? I couldn't say goodbye to everything. If that was strength, then let me be weak. I didn't care anymore. I wanted Lara. I wanted us together. She was all I had left.

For if I lost her, then I may as well lose myself. And who would ever find me again?

16

Lara flitted about our bedchamber, gathering her dresses and packing them. Aunt Curtis gave her a gigantic new trunk, since "it was shocking for a lady to appear at the Vallencourts with unattractive things." My forlorn carpet-bag sat quietly in the corner, exuding a comfortably shabby glory. I smiled ruefully. All I contained in the world fit in its stretched tapestry.

"You are not going to wear the mourning dress, then?" I asked. Lara had left it hanging in the wardrobe.

"Esther, I'm not going to show up at the Vallencourts wearing black. Aunt Curtis wouldn't let me leave the house if I looked like such a drab old maid."

Her cheery tone stung. I couldn't tell her that in the morning, I would be less than a maid. A maid without wages was a slave, no better than the poor Negroes my father died for.

I absentmindedly played with one of her gloves. Aunt Curtis, of course, had seen to it that Lara's appearance would suit the uppity Vallencourt taste. From Jane's wardrobe came an extraordinary array of pretty new clothes. Two pairs of gloves, three day dresses, two visiting dresses, a ball dress, three bonnets, two pairs of stockings, several petticoats, and even an unworn chemise. I half-wondered whether it would all fit in the traveling trunk.

"Lara, would you say we are of similar size?"

She giggled. "You can't have my new dresses!"

"No, silly," I said, smiling. "I wanted to ask for your old dress, the brown calico."

"Whatever for?" she sniffed. "It's the ugliest one I have."

And would be perfect for chores. "You'd have no use for it. What would Mrs. Vallencourt think if you appeared at dinner wearing a faded calico?"

That sealed her decision. I knew my sister couldn't fathom wearing the shapeless thing again. I thanked her when she fished the dress from the wardrobe and handed it to me.

"You worry me, Esther, the things you insist on wearing." She shook her head. "Well, it matches your hair. I'm sure you could make yourself look becoming."

I laughed. "I hope you enjoy your time with Miss Alexandra. It would please me if you would write often."

"In between French lessons, dinner parties, and balls I don't see as how I'll have the time," she said with a sweet joking air.

How could I be melancholy when she brought me such joy? She placed the last of her things in the trunk, closed the lid, and sat beside me. She reached over and played with my long dark brown braid. I longed to clasp her and never let her out of my sight again. Oh, Lara, if you only knew.

"Of course I'll write." She patted my hand. "Do me a favor and don't frown. Mother would not want you so dreary."

I must bear this parting. I could, for I was stronger than Lara. I had learned to be.

"Are you being dreary again?" she chided me. "Come here, Esther."

I leaned forward and we embraced. Sorrow drained from my throat and disappeared. Was it so difficult to be cheerful? I had a place to live, a comfortable bed, hot meals. I had something greater than French lessons or dinner parties.

I had hope.

Lara gave me a sweet kiss on the cheek, then sat back. I wasn't allowed to tell her of my situation, but in that moment I was willing to break any rule Aunt Curtis devised to imprison me. But before I could, I heard the clip-clopping of horses' hooves and crunch of carriage wheels on the carriageway. Lara sprang up and went to investigate, leaning expectantly on the window seat.

"The Vallencourts are here in their grand carriage - and to think I shall ride in it!"

"Perhaps I can join you someday," I said, forcing myself to share her enthusiasm.

She crossed over to the cheval mirror, pinching her cheeks. "I wish you could come, too. But I will tell you all about it!"

"You look beautiful."

She truly did. Her traveling dress, another hand-me-down from Jane, was a lovely goldenrod yellow that made her curls glow. She looked as fresh and happy as a marigold, on her way to a new place. For the tiniest of moments, I shared her joy.

But then she hurried from the room and I felt cold. It was just as well it was drizzling outside, for no sunny thoughts came to mind. I slipped into my wool house shoes, straightened my lace collar, and quietly closed the door behind me.

Henry and Alexandra were handing their wet outerwear to Mr. Jakes while my sister greeted them with a stream of friendly chatter. Jane perched in the dining room doorway, her arms crossed and her face frozen with a strange stiffness. When I began walking down the staircase, she didn't look up, but her future sister-in-law did.

"Good afternoon, Miss Perry," Alexandra said. "I must thank you for letting your sister spend the winter in my company. I'll take good care of her, I promise."

Eased by Alexandra's kindness, I returned her smile. "She has been delighted by the prospect since it was first suggested."

"Will Mr. Elliot Curtis be joining us for luncheon?" Her question was innocently delivered, but a high shade of pink flushed her cheeks.

"I'm afraid he will not," I said. "He has assumed his father's position at the medical office until further notice."

Alexandra nodded, then she and Lara entered the dining room. Jane stepped aside to allow them entry, but she didn't leave the hall.

"That is honorable of him, to have taken on such responsibility," Henry said.

"My cousin's affability and kindness would make him well-suited to ease ill patients," I said.

"Elliot's manners are quite unguarded," Jane said before her fiancee could reply. "Shall we, Mr. Vallencourt?"

Henry held his arm out for my cousin and walked with her into the dining room. I followed behind them, wondering how long our conversation would have continued without the interruption. As we seated ourselves about the dining table, I wished my uncle were in his chair at the head of the table and Elliot in his former seat. The two allies I'd formed in the house were absent, and their vacancy made it more apparent how alone I was.

"So nice to have you join us," Aunt Curtis said to Henry. "We had a wonderful shopping excursion yesterday to choose wedding attire and decorations."

If there was any indication Henry doubted the match, it didn't show on his face. But he did look more grave than usual and it took him some time to reply.

"Miss Curtis has requested a wedding date of April the ninth. I should like to assist in drawing up the invitation list before it is sent to the stationer's."

"April ninth is a fine day. Jane did hope to get married in the spring."

"We will create the list as soon as possible," Jane said. "My finishing school friends in Boston and New York would love to attend. I shall also include the Portland mayor and his family."

"Of course," said Aunt Curtis. "A wedding is a perfect place to further societal acquaintances."

I quietly partook of my pumpkin soup, half-listening to Alexandra and Lara talk about the guest quarters at the Vallencourt mansion. But Henry's odd mannerisms drew my attention. He barely touched his first course, he wasn't engaged in conversation, and his brows were drawn together in a look of agitation. After a half-hearted attempt to sip his wine, he set the glass down, took a deep breath and addressed Aunt Curtis.

"I want Mr. Gabriel Curtis included on the guest list."

My aunt seemed to have expected this puzzling request, for her facial expression didn't change. Jane looked paler, but then her cheeks colored with anger. Alexandra looked uncomfortable, and my own confusion mirrored Lara's. Suddenly, I realized exactly who Gabriel Curtis might be.

"Very well, Mr. Vallencourt," Aunt Curtis said icily. "Yet, may I be so bold as to remind you not to depend on his appearance. My husband gave me no word on his condition. We were only informed that he was alive and in Virginia."

Lara laughed out loud. "Gabriel is your brother? Then he must be the owner of the northeast bedroom."

"Hush, Lara," I whispered.

But Henry didn't admonish my sister. "You are correct, Miss Lara. His place at the wedding is irrefutable. I appreciate his name added to the invitation list."

Jane smirked. "You see, Alexandra, how your mentorship is required to sculpt Miss Lara's behavior. She has been quite unschooled."

"It is my privilege," Alexandra said. "We shall enjoy having her."

And with that, the conversation about Gabriel was dropped and the new topic of Lara's stay was resumed. Lara forgot her questions, yet I couldn't. From the moment Aunt Curtis's carriage had appeared in the farmyard, there had been nothing but questions and more questions. I could spend three hours a day trying to figure out the mysteries of this family.

Henry appeared to lose his former agitation and again bestowed much attention on his fiancee. Lara even got him to laugh after telling a story about getting her boots stuck in the mud of our old horse paddock.

"Esther scolded me, of course, but I wasn't going to let muddy boots spoil my daily ride."

"My, Miss Perry," Henry said, looking at me. "It seems you were the first to sculpt your sister's behavior."

"In some ways, sir," I said, "as she attempts to sculpt mine."

The luncheon had come to a close. Servants pulled our chairs out and we rose from the table. A pang constricted my throat, as I realized with alarm my time with my sister was ending.

"Esther can be too dreary," Lara said. "But she is kind and capable. There would have been no better mistress of Perry Farm."

I cast my eyes down at my feet. Oh, Lara, I will miss you. After we entered the hall, Mr. Jakes approached the Vallencourts with their cloaks and hats. To my surprise, Henry waved him away.

"Let us not depart yet. I should like to hear both Miss Curtis and Miss Perry play a song on the piano."

Alexandra smiled. "Oh, Henry, what a wonderful idea."

Lara grinned. "It is, Mr. Vallencourt. I won't be hearing Esther play for a long time, so this means a lot to me."

"It will be a pleasure. Shall we?"

He escorted Jane into the parlor, then took his seat upon the sofa. Aunt Curtis, Lara and Alexandra sat down, while Jane and I approached the piano. My sheet music folio still sat on the stand, as it had on Saturday night. But this time felt like the afternoon I'd played the *Pathetique Sonata*, my heart aching over Perry Farm. I could think of no better piece to mirror both the sorrow of losing my sister and the hope we would be reunited soon. Jane brushed past me and handed me the folio.

"I do not need music." She turned to her expectant audience. "I shall play Mozart's piano sonata number sixteen in C major. This is the first movement."

I sat down in a nearby chair, in complete view of her flying fingers. Up and down the scales she trilled, like a seabird dipping and soaring above Portland harbor. Her technique was sound and her fingering flawless. I'd never heard a pianist exhibit such incredible skill, and I was awestruck by her talent. Mr. Lambson lived up to the praise his pupil had bestowed upon him. When she finished, I applauded Jane as an admiring peer. To compare myself to her was as useless as comparing Jenny Lind with a goose.

Jane stood and moved aside to occupy the chair I'd vacated. Whether her eyes would be on my fingers or on Henry was easy to guess. Since I could think of no other piece than the *Pathetique*, I set the open folio on the stand and sat down.

"This is Beethoven piano sonata number eight, also known as the *Pathetique*. I shall play the second movement."

That soft, sad beginning, on so fine an instrument, was as pleasurable as it was anguish. My left hand tilting, the response from the ivory keys like a delicate whisper. My right hand played the ascending notes. With the music unfolding, I was again in the parlor at Perry Farm. The smell of hay and crisp apples drifting through the windows. A nicker from Sarge in the pasture. Harvested vegetables in bushel baskets on the cart. The way the wind stirred in the barn. It was mine once again.

At last, I played the final chord and emerged from my reverie. I felt diffused and also deeply satisfied from performing a song as perfectly as could be. Then the sound of applause rang in the parlor. I rose from the piano bench and turned around. Henry, Alexandra and Lara were on their feet, clapping vigorously.

"Oh, Esther, that was gloriously beautiful," Lara said. "You play so well."

I blushed. "It was for you, dearest. Have a lovely time this winter. I will see you as soon as I can."

"Yes, Miss Perry," said Alexandra. "We would love to have you visit and play our piano."

"I thank you for the offer."

"Well, we have had a fine afternoon of musical talent," Aunt Curtis said as she rose to her feet. "I dearly thank both Henry and Alexandra for their visit today. Say good-bye to your sister, Miss Perry."

We all walked into the front hall. Mr. Jakes waited with cloaks and hats.

"It is only a farewell," I said. "Until we meet again."

Lara nodded, but I heard her give a sniff. She turned towards me and gave me a huge embrace. I could not speak and held her as long as I could.

But then she broke from me and was gone from the house with Alexandra, ascending the Vallencourt carriage steps and as excited as could be about her new situation.

Henry bowed to Jane. "A good day to you, Miss Curtis. Thank you for the exceptional concert."

"It was a pleasure, Mr. Vallencourt," Jane said. "I will be taking your suggestion into account as I draw up the invitation list."

"My request is firm." Mr. Jakes handed him his hat and walking stick, and then Henry looked at me. "It was quite the rendition of the *Pathetique Sonata*, Miss Perry. If architecture is frozen music, then you played a temple."

Jane glared at me, but I ignored her and nodded politely to her fiancee. Judging by his first reaction to my playing, Henry preferred constructive criticism over pure flattery. To have softened his viewpoint on my unlearned technique was high praise indeed.

He gave Jane one final kiss on the hand and headed out to the carriage. I couldn't help but feel pleasure at his respectful admiration. I had no beauty, no money, and no family. There was nothing to recommend me to Henry Vallencourt, nor was he available for eligibility. My station was like the low notes on a piano, and he was several octaves above. I knew how far apart we were.

The Vallencourt carriage pulled from the house and turned onto High Street. A ten minute carriage ride could have been a hundred mile walk for all I knew. Jane turned and headed back into the parlor without a word to me. The door to the dining room opened, and Mrs. Keswick appeared in the hall.

"You're to be moved upstairs."

"I shall do so after supper, Mrs. Keswick."

She scowled. "You're no longer a guest. I command the servants in this house. Follow me."

I reluctantly picked up my skirts and started up the staircase behind her. My strength and hope began to sink as the enormity of my new position gaped before me. Like Gabriel Curtis, I would not spoken of by anyone. I wouldn't see Lara. I wouldn't see Elliot. I wouldn't see Henry.

But even if Henry could see me, I'd be nothing more than a farmer's daughter who couldn't afford a sheet of music.

17

I rose from the cot, took up my shawl, and went to the window. My feet were cold on the bare floor. The walls were old plaster with great stained patches of soot. A torn lithograph in a shabby wooden frame hung from a rusty nail. It was a servant's room, no more luxurious than a shed. I pressed my forehead against the cool glass, comforted by its solid form. If there had been no glass, I would step through the window and plunge into the courtyard below.

Lara was gone.

The silence of her absence closed around me. Forty-eight hours earlier, I'd been settling into these cozy fall days. Henry's laughter rang in my head, and I could feel Lara's parting kiss on my cheek. Elliot's kindness was a welcome comfort after being wrenched from my home.

How could these memories be more real than the life I lived now? It was like the day in Silas Greene's office, staring at the massive debts and feeling the tide pull me under.

Would I ever stop losing everything?

Ting ting. Ting ting.

The servant's bell. I turned down the bedclothes and dressed in

Lara's calico. I pinned up my hair, checking my reflection in the wall looking-glass. The simple house dress was shapeless and unflattering, but sturdy enough for a working life. The only ornament was the rather austere lace collar. I actually looked like I had the day Caleb declared his love for me, and I felt like my old self again.

I tucked my handkerchief in my pocket, gave my cheeks a final pinch, and cautiously opened the door. In the third floor hall, servants fiddled with last-minute preparations - tying cravats, adjusting aprons - and then hurried down the back staircase. Nobody noticed me, nor did I expect them to. Aunt Curtis relayed my situation to Mrs. Keswick, who then told the staff to leave me alone.

I took my place in the busy surge of servants, and descended the narrow back stairs with as much confidence as I could muster. Soon, I emerged into the dark hot back kitchen. The layout was similar to the kitchen at Perry Farm, but much larger. Several girls bustled about, a blur of activity before my eyes. My stomach rumbled. Roasting coffee beans, brewing tea, toasting bread, hot biscuits in the oven, creamy butter.

"Yes, that's what I did! Though do you think she paid it any mind?"

A maid stood beside the butcher block table in the center of the kitchen. She wiped her beading forehead with her forearm, then furiously rolled out a lump of sticky dough. She reached in a bowl of small black fruits that looked like currants, and sprinkled them in the dough.

"I haven't a notion as to what goes through that woman's head, Addy!"

A stout red-faced woman stirred a large cast iron kettle on the range. She pulled her wooden spoon from the murky mess and tasted it, so I assumed she was the cook.

Two trays with complete silver tea services sat on the sideboard by the door. One for Jane and one for Aunt Curtis. It dawned on me that I was watching the incredible ordeal of preparing breakfast. The maid, whom I took to be Adelaide, turned to a thin young girl scrubbing pans in the metal sink.

"You ready with that baking sheet, Peg?"

The girl, a lowly scullery maid, scrubbed harder. The cook stuck the spoon back in the kettle, grabbed a thick hot pad, and after a struggle with the clanging range door, brought up a fresh batch of breakfast biscuits. She scooted them on the sideboard and turned around in time to see me. She was bulky and frowning, and her nose was so large and pointed she reminded me at once of a rhinoceros.

"And what straggler visits us this morning?" she announced.

Adelaide and Peg stared at me. I hastened across the room, grabbed the hot pad the cook had used for the biscuits, and swooped the whistling teakettle from the range. It was heavier than I thought, and my arm and shoulder muscles groaned in pain. I set the teakettle down on the butcher block table.

Thankfully, none of the servants said a word. As I inspected each of the teapots for tea leaves, the scullery maid went back to work, and the cook returned to the range. Adelaide's biscuit dough was ready for a new batch, so she started looking around for the biscuit cutter. She wiped her forehead again, a gesture that reminded me of Lara when she'd come in after an arduous ride.

Despite her blond hair and blue eyes, Adelaide didn't resemble my sister at all. Her hair was dull and flat, streaked with a mousy brown, and haphazardly pinned back beneath her cap. Her eyes were grayed like the sea on a winter's day and ringed with purplish skin.

"Good morning, Adelaide," I said quietly. "I'm Esther Perry. I'm working here under your guidance."

"Mrs. Curtis let a maid go last week," Adelaide said. "She was from Montreal, named Sophie."

"I am sorry to hear of it," I said, for Adelaide's tone of voice sounded of bitterness and regret. I picked up the biscuit cutter. "Here."

The scullery maid passed me the washed and dried baking sheet. Adelaide snatched the biscuit cutter and punched it through the dough. I managed to find a spatula on the cluttered table and scooped the dough circles onto the baking sheet. Adelaide spaced them out slightly so they would have room to rise.

The cook wiped her hands on the rotating dishtowel. "Well, you've got yourself a right helper, Addy. Good on you."

My new instructor didn't look pleased. She grabbed the hot pad, slid the raw biscuits into the oven and slammed the oven door with a loud clang. I put myself to use scooping gooseberry jelly into small cups for each tray. The cook poured the teakettle water into the two teapots, rapidly stirring the tea leaves.

As soon as the scullery maid had scrubbed another dish, it was needed. I promptly became part of the incessant rhythm of working. Within a short time the two trays heaped high with hot biscuits, jelly, toast, cream, sugar, tea, coffee, and butter. I had pressed this last precious ingredient into the butter mold and popped out tiny flowers onto a plate. The machine-like movements of the kitchen staff was a marvel. I'd never realized how much work went into one simplistic meal.

Adelaide reached up into a corner and pulled a tassel. Another maid appeared at the kitchen doorway, summoned by the bell. After Adelaide handed her a tray, she turned and addressed me.

"Stay in the kitchen, girl. I wait on the missus personally."

And proud of it, I thought, as she sniffed at me. I wasn't serving either my aunt or my cousin, nor was I going to to be called by my name. Adelaide followed the other maid out of the kitchen.

"It's the only time she's allowed to use the front stairs," Peg explained quietly, then picked up a scrubber and went back to work.

So I had a new staircase to go along with my new servants' position. Well, at least the back stairs had a handrail. I'd do my best not to drop or spill anything.

The cook gathered the teakettle, baking pans, butter mold, toast rack, mixing bowls and an armful of utensils, dumping them in the sink. Poor Peg was swamped. I rolled up my sleeves, dipped a scrubber in the soap bucket and started tackling the dirty dishes. The cook banged away behind us like an industrial steamship, readying the noonday meal.

By the time Adelaide returned, Peg and I had emptied the sink together. The senior maid said nothing, but the scullery girl smiled at me.

A scullery maid position was the lowest in the household, but I felt even lower if it could be possible. The other maid who had carried the second tray brushed past us with an armful of Jane's clothing and disappeared out the back door.

"That's Josie," Peg said. "She's my cousin."

"Enough, Peg," Adelaide snapped. "Just because the dishes are done doesn't give you time for idleness. Go help her."

Peg wiped her hands, gave a curtsey of submission and hurried after Josie. I bit my lip, doing my best to remind myself I was also under Adelaide's supervision and not to question her.

"Fix your hair," she said to me. "Roll your sleeves down. You'd better be a fast learner, because I don't repeat myself."

While I readied my attire, she fetched two wooden buckets filled with cleaning supplies. I took a bucket and followed her out of the kitchen and into the hall.

"When are we to eat breakfast?" I asked.

"An impatient thing you are. Missus requested your presence in one hour. She will go over the schedule with you."

As brusque as Adelaide was, the thought of seeing Aunt Curtis this morning made my new situation more deplorable. Well, once I received the schedule and became accustomed to it, my feelings would be more at ease. I never shied away from work. To be ordered around grated on my nerves, but I had little doubt I'd prove to be Adelaide's competent pupil.

Once inside the front parlor, Adelaide set me to work cleaning the fireplace. My first task was also the dirtiest, for the fireplace was in constant use due to the chilly weather. I swept ashes with the fireplace brush and dustpan, dumping them into the little cinder-pail next to the hearth. Then I took black-lead and polishing brushes from the cleaning bucket and blacked the grate as well as I could.

The parlor was quite an immense room, but I had to admire my mentor for how efficiently she worked. She dusted, polished the furniture, and scrubbed the window panes. I wiped down the andirons with a sooty cloth.

"You would like me to light the fire as well?" I asked.

Adelaide was on her hands and knees, brushing the rug so furiously her cheeks were two bright pink circles. She gave me a look as if I'd asked the dumbest question imaginable. Of course, Esther, I grumbled silently. It is October and the parlor requires a fire everyday. It was not a decision I'd ever had to make, but gained a new respect for the ones who did.

I found fresh coals in the coal-hod and set about laying them in the grate with fireplace tongs. Matches and pieces of torn paper were in a muslin bag in the wooden bucket. I sprinkled the paper throughout the coals and struck a match. The lovely satisfaction upon seeing the cheerful blaze warmed me and the room. I blew on the little fire and rejoiced in my small victory.

But my appearance was nothing to celebrate. My hands were black and my sleeve-cuffs grayed by ash. Adelaide had succeeded in tidying the parlor, but I couldn't even touch a doorknob without sullying it. She came over to inspect my work.

"Wash up. After you speak with the missus, meet me in the dining room."

I didn't know whether I'd done well with my first task. No criticism could be good praise. I put the cleaning supplies back in the bucket with cleaning supplies and returned it to the kitchen. After as thorough a scrub as I could muster, I smoothed my hair and crept up the back staircase to the second floor.

There was a door at the second floor, so I slowly opened it and stepped into a narrow enclosed hallway I'd never seen before. With a start, I realized I was in the space between my old bedchamber and that of my absent cousin, Gabriel. The northeast bedchamber wasn't adjacent to my old room as I'd always thought. A hallway separated them. Furthermore, his room wasn't directly accessible by the second floor landing, either. He had been quite removed from the rest of his family, even when he was living here.

It wasn't my place to guess the reason for his absence. Henry was firmly adamant about him being on the guest list. Perhaps they'd been friends, enough for Henry to want to see him again. But I didn't have the time or the evidence to speculate further.

I emerged from the little hallway out onto the landing and crossed over to my aunt's bedchamber. It was the first time I'd been inside her room, which added more dread to my cautious knock. I took a deep breath and waited for the command to enter.

The master bedchamber was exquisitely decorated in a rich palette of burgundy and cream. Huge silk drapes framed the large windows, and the fireplace was as massive as the one downstairs in the parlor. The bed looked fit for a queen with an impressive arched canopy and elegant carving. Dressed in her casual morningwear, my aunt sat at her dressing-table.

"Good morning, ma'am," I said quietly.

"The first rule of a maid," Aunt Curtis interrupted, "is to speak as little as possible."

I tucked my hands behind my back and said not another word. The mantel clock ticked. It was eight o'clock in the morning on my first day as her servant. She took a sheet of paper from the table and handed it to me.

"The list of duties. Adelaide is your immediate superior. You also assist the other maids as needed."

I nodded, keeping as calm and respectful as I could. Rather than pleasing my aunt, this made her more cross.

"Do not address Mrs. Keswick, Mr. Jakes, Jane or myself. You are to conduct yourself with a polite sense of invisibility."

Not that my opinions had ever been sought, so becoming invisible wasn't a drastic change. After a moment's pause to allow her orders to sink in, my aunt continued.

"Elliot has his medical duties, so you can expect a high degree of absence from him. No music, errands, letters or any other activity that prevents you from performing a high degree of service."

All I had were my memories. Memories of my hands upon the keys, memories of songs, memories of a walk in the fresh air, memories of my cousin's friendship. Aunt Curtis didn't trust me enough to allow the slightest luxury. She sat back, looking me up and down as if I was a hog at a market.

"You are suitably dressed. It won't be a problem to retain such low standards, for that is how you were raised."

I took quiet deep breaths, forcing my expression to assume a flat mask. The wound from losing my mother had reopened and rent a rip inside me I struggled to heal. But my conduct would speak as highly of her life as any lesson she ever taught me.

"Work inspections are held on a regular basis. Mrs. Keswick pays particular attention to detail in her reports."

She rose from her dressing-table and walked over to a large low bureau, upon which sat an oil lamp and a small wooden box. She opened the box and took out a jewelry set, holding each piece up to the light. The gems glittered in the morning sunlight.

"Did you know that maids are the number one suspect in stolen property?"

I shook my head. The long snaky necklace dangled from her fist, the earrings pinched between her fingers. She stood before me, her face inches from mine, the jewelry held right at my eye-level.

"I will be watching every move you make, girl."

I had no doubt she would. Her eyes bore into mine for what felt like an hour, then she returned to her dressing-table.

"Take the chamber-pot on your way out."

I tucked the schedule sheet under my arm and went over to the bed to retrieve the item. Holding it out before me and trying to ignore the sound and smell of its contents, I swiftly left the room.

No sooner had I closed her door than Mrs. Keswick appeared at the top of the stairs. I pressed my back to the wall and bowed my head. She walked right by me, sniffing as she did so, and paused at my aunt's bedchamber door before entering.

I thought she might say something, but she did not and entered the room without a word. I continued down the landing and had almost set foot on the staircase before I remembered I was not supposed to use it.

So, I backtracked and returned to the little hallway between my old bedchamber and Gabriel's.

A lovely rush of memories about Henry warmed me from inside, surprising and comforting at the same time. His respectful nod in the hall, the way he had first criticized my music and then praised it, our conversation under the portico. But then I opened the door to the back staircase, looked down into the dark and the memories vanished.

He was as lost to me as my old life at Perry Farm.

18

Thus equipped with my schedule sheet and under the ever-vigilant eyes of Mrs. Keswick, my days passed. My peace of mind had become severely interrupted and a strange fearfulness accompanied my every endeavor. I felt I was constantly being watched, and to some extent, I was. Not one second could I let down my guard and just be. To make my discomfort more unbearable, nervous tension cramped my belly. I declined so many meals Adelaide confronted me and said that if I did not eat, she would report me. So I forced down the leftovers from the dining table with the rest of the servants.

On the morning of my eighth day, I was released from Adelaide's mentorship and sent alone to clean my former bedchamber. I stood by the freshly made bed, allowing the tears to flow and my sobs to echo.

Lara. Standing by the front windows, eagerly watching the Vallencourt carriage. Sitting at the dressing-table arranging her lady's toilette articles. Do not be so dreary, Esther. Her laughter so loud I half-expected to turn and for her to be there.

But she was not. Across the landing, Adelaide grunted as she cleaned the master bedchamber. It was time to get back to work.

Hours stretched, slowly bled into days, then weeks. Exhaustion became my silent and ever-present enemy, stealing time and energy at whim. Sometimes I'd find myself kneeling by a fireplace or rubbing soap on my hands at the kitchen sink without knowing how I'd gotten there. I was not allowed to sit or rest, and felt a bitter jealousy when Mrs. Keswick took afternoon tea and Rosie the cook had Sundays off.

As November wore on, the days varied from blustery and cold to dry and sunny. I'd awake each morning in my unheated servant's room with numb fingers and chilled feet. My favorite chore of the day was to light the fires in the morning, for the cheerful blaze never failed to warm me.

Neither my aunt nor Jane ever acknowledged me. Adelaide uttered either criticisms or orders. Peg smiled and occasionally spoke when we'd wash dishes together, but Josie was too busy and the cook too brusque. It was not enough to just lose my family and my home. Now I was cut off from congenial society with almost no cordiality.

One morning, however, a bit of news was startling enough to shake me from my weariness like cold water to the face. I was preparing tea for the breakfast trays when Mrs. Keswick poked her head into the kitchen and summoned Rosie. The cook looked quite surprised, wiped her red hands and met the housekeeper out in the hall.

"Must be about Thanksgivin'," Peg whispered.

I leaned as far towards the kitchen door as I could, for any plans about Thanksgiving could include guests ... and maybe Lara. Sure enough, just as my leg began to cramp from supporting my weight, I heard what sounded like the most beautiful piano sonata to my ears.

"Yes, Mrs. Keswick, so the Vallencourt family will dine."

For the first time in three weeks, hope seared through my breast. I was shocked at how electrifying it felt, to awaken from a prolonged darkness and dare to think I could see my sister - and Henry - again. For a moment, I stood frozen at the chopping table. Then Adelaide's frown alerted me and I got back to work. But I could not quiet or forget my feelings. When Rosie came back into the kitchen, she was silent about her meeting with the housekeeper.

About twenty minutes later, however, this news received a disheartening postscript. There was another knock at the kitchen door that we all thought was Mrs. Keswick again, but when Adelaide answered it, Jane swept into the room.

All activity stopped. Peg and I both turned around from our position at the sink, tucked our hands behind our backs and bowed our heads. Adelaide pressed herself up against the wall to allow her mistress to pass, and Rosie clumsily curtsied with a slotted spoon in her hand. Jane paused in the middle of the kitchen, like a queen surveying her subjects. She handed a sheet of paper to Rosie, careful not to bump her lovely daydress against any sullied surface.

"Mother and I have drawn up the menu for Thanksgiving on Thursday. Please take note of the courses and their respective wines. Service for two only this year. There will be none other."

"Yes, miss."

So Elliot was not to dine with us and neither were the Vallencourts. Or Lara. I should have expected such a disappointment, but I still felt extremely saddened.

Jane gave further instructions as to when each course would be served and the proper temperatures for cooking the turkey and oyster soup. Rosie crossed her arms over her ample bosom and suffered through the trite advice. Once finished, Jane turned to leave the kitchen. She apparently changed her mind, for she then approached Peg and I at the sink. The poor scullery maid trembled with anxious fear.

Jane stopped before me. "You will serve us on Thursday. Mother explicitly requested."

I didn't move. Except for cleaning the fireplace, I'd not set foot in the dining room since the last luncheon spent with Lara. Jane stared down the length of her nose at me for a long time, and though I could not see her face, I could well picture it. Her arched eyebrow, her dark glittering eyes set against her alabaster skin, her black hair curled about her face. She was a creature to behold, but I did not fear her.

Satisfied with her control over me, she picked up her skirts and marched out of the kitchen. When I lifted my head, everyone in the room was staring at me. I turned back around and went back to washing the breakfast dishes. But I wasn't to be let alone yet.

"We start the training tonight, girl."

I nodded to Adelaide. I'd been on my own as far as cleaning, but setting up and serving so fine a dinner as Thanksgiving was another matter. Well, I had three days to learn.

But Adelaide thought three months too little a time to learn how to serve courses, let alone three days. She drilled me like a sergeant, snappy and uncivil towards my every mistake. If the soup spoon was less than one quarter of an inch out of place or if the wineglass was not filled to the exact line or if I hadn't approached the diner from the correct angle, I was made to feel like a fool. If I'd had a penny for every time I restarted the motions, I'd have walked from that dining room a wealthy woman.

On Wednesday evening, I did a final inspection with both Mrs. Keswick and Adelaide. I concentrated as hard as I would helping a mare to foal and passed their scrutiny with minor nitpicks. I was deemed ready, though still not an example of perfect service. I was lucky to escape with my dignity intact.

Rosie began her meal preparations for Thanksgiving that same night, and Adelaide woke me at three o'clock the next morning to assist. I sleepily donned the brown calico, smudged and faded from a month of work, and trudged down the back stairs. Rosie produced a menu card and had us all gather round to view it.

It was a complicated meal with an incredible amount of different dishes. The turkey, of course, with green onion and sage dressing. Then mashed potatoes, turnips, squash, onions, carrots, biscuits, gravy, pumpkin pie, apple pie, blackberry pie. It made my head ache just thinking about all the work we had to do.

"The missus will be served at two o'clock. I'll be takin' the turkey, and you two -" indicating Josie and me - "are preppin' the vegetables. Adelaide start on the pies and Peg can fill in as needed. Get to work!"

I'd never worked with Josie before. While the cook gave orders, Josie stood next to me tapping her fingernails against her teeth. Her hands were scraped raw and red from spending week after week in the hot washtub. Without saying a word, the laundry maid grabbed my hand, led me to the back of the kitchen, and pushed open the door.

We were in a pleasantly scented but unheated dry goods storage room. Bunches of dried herbs and flowers hung by twine from pegs, large barrels of flour and oats and apples and potatoes sat neatly labeled along a wall, and every available inch was occupied by lined baskets and crates. Josie took an empty basket down from a nail and handed it to me.

"I guess Elliot won't be eating with his mother and sister," I said, as an attempt to start conversation.

Josie looked at me oddly. "What of it?"

"Well," I began, but she was already moving towards the potato barrel and obviously not listening. "Never mind."

It made me miss Lara's company all the more. I followed Josie with my empty basket as we went from barrel to barrel. Josie scooped out the vegetables and dumped them into the basket. When the basket was full, I returned to the kitchen and emptied the contents into huge pottery bowls. Back and forth, back and forth. First the potatoes, then turnips, squash, onions, and carrots. I don't know how my feet kept moving and my back kept bending, for exhaustion hounded me.

Then Josie and I set to work peeling, scraping, and chopping. My back hurt from standing in one position, my knuckles were scraped and raw by the peeler, and my feet ached. Adelaide and Peg helped make biscuits, and the cook dressed the turkey before shoving it into the bake oven.

I was bone-tired and could barely keep my eyes open after four hours of sleep. When the clock chimed eight, I'd already been on my feet for five hours, and it was just now time to prepare the breakfast trays. Three weeks of practice took over my tired limbs, and the trays were soon ready. Adelaide was to deliver the one for Aunt Curtis, as usual, but then she motioned for me and pointed at Jane's tray. I shook my head. I'd seen enough of Jane this week.

Adelaide glared at me. "Girl, pick up the tray."

I crossed my arms. "I will only take it, Adelaide, if you accompany me into Jane's room."

To utter such a statement was almost beyond the maid's belief. But there was too much to do that day to argue. She gathered up the tray in a huff.

"Have it your way!"

I will, I thought. To strip me of wordly possessions, my family, and the things that brought me joy would mean nothing without retaining my dignity. I still had a right to ask for common decency, and Aunt Curtis couldn't take it from me.

The tray was heavy and unwieldy, rattling like a tin toy. Saucers, cups, plates, and silverware bumped against one another. Forcing my aching shoulders to steady, I followed Adelaide out of the kitchen and slowly up the main staircase. The novelty of using the front stairs was consumed by nervousness as I waited outside Aunt Curtis's bedchamber. Seconds ticked by, and Adelaide did not appear. Arms weak, fingers cramped, I could hold on no longer. I staggered down the landing and managed to prop the tray against the wall long enough to knock on Jane's door.

"Enter."

I turned the knob with white-knuckled fingers, straightened my aching back, and crept into my cousin's bedchamber. The last time I'd been here Lara was twirling about in a new dress and I was uninterested in Henry Vallencourt's opinion of my plain attire.

I approached the breakfast table, set the tray down, and bowed my head. Silently, I was trying to forge my feelings to a hardened iron. No matter what she said, I was ready.

Jane was half-propped on her pillow, her hair tied in rag-curls, the bedclothes pulled right up to her chin. She turned over on her side, presumably to go back to sleep. I didn't know what to do and stood mute.

"I do not require anything else, girl," she grumbled.

My heart leapt into my throat and prevented me from speaking. She didn't recognize me. Thank God! I turned and exited the room without drawing any more notice. I'd never been so grateful for Jane's idleness in my life.

Adelaide still hadn't emerged from my aunt's room, so I walked down the back stairs and returned to the kitchen. The rest of the work preparing Thanksgiving consumed my hands and my mind dulled, but I scolded myself for being so fearful. What did Jane have over me, that she could ignite such feelings? She had Henry's hand, to be sure, but they were not married yet. Absence could make the heart grow fonder, or it could remind both parties of their mutual disaffection.

For that matter, what did Aunt Curtis have over me? While Jane could claim snobbery or greed as a motive for cruelty, I still couldn't answer that question about my aunt. Why she wanted me in so low a station. Why she treated me with either indifference or obvious insensitivity. She hadn't been compassionate about my mother's death, concerned with my well-being, or open about her past.

Why?

I had to find out, no matter what the consequences. She could not keep me like this forever. My uncle would return eventually. My sister and I would be reunited. I must rally, or I'd go mad with relentless querying.

At half-past one, the meal was finally ready, though I was too exhausted to feel victorious. Rosie and Adelaide removed the gigantic turkey from the oven, its skin as golden as sunshine. Potatoes were mashed, oyster soup bubbled on the range, turnips and squash were spooned into china serving dishes. An exquisite dessert platter boasted baked pears in a cinnamon glaze, apple pie, pumpkin pie, and blackberry pie.

Mrs. Keswick entered the kitchen, her lips in a thin line, her hands clasped.

"The ladies are seated and ready for service."

Was she staring at me or was it my imagination? I was too weary to tell, and the thought of performing an entire dinner service in my condition was overwhelming. Mr. Jakes stepped into the kitchen and lifted the huge turkey platter, hoisting it to his shoulder and carrying it to the dining room. Adelaide followed with the tureen of oyster soup, then Josie with the mashed potatoes, me with the turnips and squash, and Peg with the gravy.

The dining room was delightfully decorated. A centerpiece of pomander balls and fall leaves in a silver footed bowl scented the room with spicy clove. Bittersweet branches poked from the vases, and a huge pumpkin and gourd display was strewn across the fireplace mantel.

My aunt and cousin were already seated, dressed in lovely autumn colors of burgundy and gold, complementing the decorating. One by one, the servants and I set our food on the sideboard. Mr. Jakes poured wine, then placed the turkey platter on the table and began carving.

"Why, Mr. Jakes, you are ever so talented," Aunt Curtis praised.

Jane sipped her wine. "So well-trained, too."

The butler's ears turned pink, and he coughed a bit. Oyster soup was the first course, so Adelaide expertly filled the two soup bowls. Josie placed two buttery heaps of mashed potatoes on the dinner plates. I watched her, agitation making my knees weak and throat dry. At last, it was time for me to serve the turnip and squash.

I swallowed and stepped forward. I carefully set the two china dishes on the table, then reached for Jane's plate. My sleeve was dangerously close to a lit candle, but I managed to avoid it. Then I deftly spooned equal amounts of turnip and squash on her plate and handed it back. It clattered too loudly when I set it down, but at least nothing spilled or slid off onto the ivory tablecloth. I took a deep breath and reached for my aunt's plate.

Aunt Curtis turned to Jane. "Mrs. Vallencourt should be sending along the invitation within the week. I know this year's Christmas party will be one to remember."

A Christmas party! Oh my goodness, I'd see Lara! I was so excited I smacked the spoon handle against my aunt's plate. Jane glared at me.

"Clumsy fool you are, girl."

I said nothing, for I couldn't. I humbly set the plate before my aunt, then went to stand by the sideboard. Bowing my head, I stared down at my hands, secretly delighted when conversation returned to the party.

"We'll go to the dressmaker's on Monday," Aunt Curtis continued. "I must have you looking your best for Henry."

"Of course, Mother. Oh, wasn't he so handsome last year? I should think a velvet of a deeper color would show off my complexion to its best. Alexandra will wear yellow. She always does."

"My muff is in such shabby condition. I must have a new one. And the carriage interior is deplorable."

This type of half-gossip half-critical conversing continued for some time. My mind slowly quieted, but with the dissipation of my agitation extreme fatigue weighted my limbs.

My aunt and cousin eventually finished their courses. Mr. Jakes presented them with the brimming dessert tray. I shared in the 'oohs' and 'aahs,' since it looked delightful. My stomach rumbled in hunger, my meager luncheon of bread and cheese long ago.

Mrs. Keswick brought out the coffee, then dismissed Adelaide, Josie, Peg and myself. We trudged back to the kitchen, quite jealous of the housekeeper's ability to join her mistresses at the table for sweets. My destination was the sink, so I began rolling up my sleeves. But Adelaide stopped me.

"Return to the dining room and wait to clear the table."

"It could be another hour," I said. "Peg needs help with the dishes."

"You don't give orders," she snapped. "Do it."

Anger flared up the back of my neck, making my head ache. Grumbling, I rolled my sleeves back down and left the kitchen. As I stomped up the hall, I was so peeved I could barely see straight. Oh, I don't give orders, do I? I just have to do what you say? I'm not a servant. I'm a member of this family! I thrust my hand towards the dining room door and was about to fling it open when my aunt's voice stopped me cold.

"You'd better pray he doesn't bring him home."

Who? I froze, straining to hear more. Were they talking about my uncle?

"Don't worry, Mother." It was Jane. "The money will still be mine. Your priority is to ensure this wedding occurs."

The money. I was right. Jane did not seek Henry's affections for their own sake. She wanted the Vallencourt fortune like a prospector sought gold.

"Of course I will, dear. You've done well, Jane. He won't go back to the way he was."

Mr. Vallencourt bemoaned his son's lack of ambition. *He loved the profession more than I did.* It was as I feared. My cousin not only preyed upon Henry's fortune, but relentlessly sought to make him forget his own career passions. Oh, God. I didn't want to hear anymore.

I forced myself to turn the doorknob and enter the dining room. My head was bowed, so I could not see either my aunt's or cousin's faces. But they gave no indication they had been overheard, except to change the conversation back to the Vallencourt Christmas party.

After a few minutes of pointless prattle, the two ladies at last stood from the dining table and left the room. Mrs. Keswick also rose and approached me.

"Clear the table."

"Yes, ma'am."

She followed her mistresses out of the room. I slowly walked over to the table, staring at the plates of crumbs and empty coffee cups. Jane didn't love Henry. She couldn't love him at the same time she discouraged him from following his ambitions. She wanted his money, and she hoped her father would not come home and discover her true motive for securing the Vallencourt name.

Jane didn't love Henry. The only question remained - did he love her?

19

Thanksgiving left me so beaten with exhaustion I barely thought of what I'd heard between my aunt and cousin. I stood at the sink beside Peg and washed dishes for two days, mind and body both numb. Sometimes Henry's face would float into my vision like a phantom dream, but then it disappeared again. I didn't know what to do with my discovery about Jane's feelings.

One early morning several days after the dinner, an unexpected development occurred in my situation. I'd just completed lighting the parlor fire when Adelaide interrupted me.

"You're needed upstairs. The missus wants you for dressing."

"Aunt Curtis?" I blurted. "Mrs. Keswick dresses her."

"Not today, girl," she grumbled. "And take the letter up."

"What letter?"

She didn't answer me and stomped off to brush down the curtains. I wiped fireplace ash on my soiled apron, returned the cleaning bucket to the kitchen, and walked up the hall to the front entry. Upon the side table was a small silver tray with an embossed envelope. I picked it up, peering at the envelope. It appeared blank, so I carefully turned it over.

A large "V" scrolled across the surface. My heart suddenly flipped in my chest. It was a letter from the Vallencourts! Oh, good God. Would it be Henry Vallencourt's words within the envelope? Or a remark from his mother about Lara's conduct? What if it was from Lara herself?

Joy fired through me, and I broke into a wide smile. I knew what this was. It was the invitation to the Vallencourt Christmas party. It had to be. And, knowing my sister, I would be invited as well. I only had to bear a few more weeks of my situation, and then I'd see her again.

Not even the trepidation of dressing my aunt deterred my steps from lightly ascending the main staircase. I traced a hand along the slick wood banister, making my way down the upstairs landing. A table clock ticked the early hour. When I came to the master bedchamber door, I paused before knocking.

"I can you hear you there, girl."

I pushed open the door and entered quietly, remembering Aunt Curtis's earlier admonishment to be as silent as I could. A fire had been lit, and the room was cozily warm. The breakfast tray sat on a side table, and my aunt sipped her morning tea. She sat perched at her dressing table, the same as I'd last been here, but this time wore nothing but a chemise and petticoat. Her hoop skirt and corset were laid across the bed, and a blue wool dress hung on a wall hook next to the bureau.

"Leave the envelope on the table and come here."

I slid the tray next to the breakfast items and approached my aunt, not quite knowing what I was expected to do.

"The Vallencourts have written."

I tucked my hands at my waist to keep from fidgeting and nodded. Aunt Curtis quietly sipped her tea, watching me. I gently breathed to keep myself calm, but I felt such an ache in my stomach I wanted to lie down. She finally set her teacup down.

"Mrs. Keswick reports you have been consistent in performing your duties. I am assigning a new task this morning. You will dress me."

I nodded again, still feeling unsure. She crossed her arms.

"Well, girl?"

I guessed it was time to begin. Of course I could dress myself, but Aunt Curtis's exacting standards would not accept sloppy service. I went over to the bed and fetched her hoop skirt, then placed it on the rug at her feet. She stood from her dressing table, stepped within the center of the hoop, and I gathered it up to her waist. She turned about, and I tied the hoop strings firmly.

"I like my corset tight," she said. "You should wear yours tighter."

A corset did little to shape my slim size, but my aunt's curvier figure demanded rigidity. I tucked the corset around her middle and started lacing the back. Aunt Curtis was several inches taller than I, and my knees buckled as I bent lower and lower. Bracing my foot against the floor, I pulled tighter.

"I received a letter from Dr. Curtis. He will be away the remainder of the winter."

I was glad I was behind her so she couldn't see my disappointment. But I bore his absence better than I did Lara's.

After several more minutes of tugging to such a great extent I feared a rib would crack, she was satisfied. I'd never have a corset that tight, no matter if she checked my laces every day. I placed on her corset cover and buttoned it up in the back. Then her two petticoats, tied at her waist to cover the hoop skirt.

Finally, it was time for the dress. It was a beautiful sky blue wool, a pretty color for her eyes and her frosted hair. I carefully took it down off the hook, marveling at the lovely cream embroidery and matching buttons, the soft fineness of the material, and how masterful the tailoring was. I'd seen my aunt in finer gowns, but this blue dress was my favorite. I could see myself wearing something like it, for it was simple and also meticulously constructed.

I brought the dress over my aunt's head, smoothed it over her shoulders and curvy torso, then billowed it above her petticoats. She shook her hips and gave two little jumps to straighten the dress. I buttoned up the back and inspected the voluminous skirt, straightening tiny wrinkles and creases.

"Now the dusting. And my shoes."

I fetched a small hand-held broom from the fireplace mantel and brushed minute specks of dust from her skirts. Aunt Curtis sat at the dressing-table while I fitted her feet into each black leather boot and laced them.

"That will do, girl."

She looked at herself in the mirror, dressed and ready for the day. It took me five minutes to slip on my corset, petticoat, and the old brown calico. I sighed at the differences between us. Why would Henry Vallencourt look twice at a girl in plain calico?

He wouldn't.

"I'll be the one to put my jewelry on. Servants steal, as you recall."

How could I forget. Aunt Curtis went to her jewelry box and retrieved her necklace, earrings, and rings. As she deftly slipped them on, I thought of the morning she'd held them up in front of my eyes. She kept me in my place, as was her want.

"You will dress me for supper tonight, and undress me this evening."

I'd performed my duties well enough. She dabbed a spot of powder on her cheeks, took up a pair of gloves, and went to the little table to look at the invitation. The chamber-pot was by the bedside, like the last time I was here. But today I knew it was my duty to take care of it, so without a request I picked it up. I swallowed my disgust, trying to ignore its liquid weight and the sloshing sound inside. At least it had a cover. My aunt had the courtesy to give me a smirk of satisfaction.

"It is the Christmas party invitation. You, of course, are not attending."

I could have crumpled to a heap on the floor, chamber-pot and all. To not see Lara at Thanksgiving was justifiable, and I bore it rather well, for being so utterly exhausted. Yet this party was the one thing I could not bear exclusion from. It was the closest I'd come to tears in front of anyone since the day my sister left and my eyes stung. Then I thought of my mother.

These are dark days, Esther. But lighter ones do come. The day we'd received the war telegram, she'd comforted me with these words. I believed her, even though I'd seen more dark days than I could count. Let a hope in better days help me.

"Mother, are you ready?"

Jane was calling from the front hall. Aunt Curtis set the invitation down, picked up her gloves, and brushed past me out onto the landing.

"Good morning, Jane! Is Mr. Jakes readying the carriage?"

I didn't hear her daughter's reply, for I was closing the master bedchamber door. Jane and Aunt Curtis were helped into their cloaks and bonnets for a journey out.

I slipped into the little side hallway and followed the back staircase down to the kitchen, then brought the chamber-pot over to the sink. Rosie paid me no heed, clanging lids and pots about as she prepared the luncheon. After emptying and scrubbing the pot, I was about to go back up the servant's staircase, when a sudden idea came to me.

The piano.

I'd been in the parlor since my sister's departure, but always under Adelaide's watchful eye, and I hadn't gone near the instrument. I wasn't even allowed to polish it. But in that moment, standing in the kitchen with the clean chamber-pot, I had to see it again. I was alone and there wouldn't be any harm. The ladies were out. My heart beat faster with delicious excitement.

I tip-toed past Rosie, who didn't even turn around, and stepped out into the center hall. Taking care that neither Mrs. Keswick or Mr. Jakes should see me, I crept up the hall to the parlor. Peeking past the door, I was relieved to find the room empty. I slipped inside, quietly closing the door behind me.

I was alone with the piano. I set down the chamber-pot and walked towards it, reaching out and touching its dark mahogany carvings. Oh, it was so beautiful. Sometimes I could hear Jane practicing. It made my heart ache so greatly I felt it would drop out of me.

"I wish I could play," I murmured. "The *Pathetique*."

My music folio was tucked away in the carpet-bag upstairs in my servants' room. The last time I'd played was the afternoon Lara left. I longed for her return, if only to be able to sit and touch these ivory keys once more. I gazed upon the piano, conjuring up its beautiful music in my mind, trying desperately to feel as content and full as I did when I played. I lingered in the parlor for as long as I dared. But footsteps sounded in the dining room across the hall. It was time to go.

After quietly closing the door, I returned to the kitchen and climbed the back stairs. I hummed the opening measures of the *Pathetique Sonata*, and felt a little better. I was glad I was not caught! Once I was back inside the master bedchamber, I placed the clean chamber-pot beside my aunt's bed. Even one tiny moment to cheer myself made all the difference. I was on my way out when I spotted the silver tray.

The Vallencourt invitation.

My heart nearly stopped. No, Esther. You just broke orders by touching the piano. You mustn't. Don't torture yourself. You can't even go …

I glanced towards the open bedroom door. Adelaide grunted as she scrubbed the front windows of my old bedchamber across the landing. She wouldn't hear me.

One look, then. I had to know.

27th November, 1868

Dear Mrs. Ambrose Curtis,

It is with great privilege that we request the honor of your presence at our annual Christmas party, to be held upon Thursday, December the 24th at half past seven o'clock. This invitation extends to Miss Jane Curtis and Mr. Elliot Curtis.

Please RSVP by Friday, December 5th. We hope to receive the pleasure of your company.

Sincerely,

Mr. & Mrs.

Leonard Vallencourt

Postscript:
Miss Lara Perry has made a special request that Miss Esther Perry should attend, if her health prevails.

I pulled the invitation from my eyes. I was invited to the Christmas party! I would see Lara! I let out a gasp that felt like the unlocking of a forbidden door. A fire was growing inside me, awakening a heat I'd tried to douse.

With this request, my aunt had to let me go. My health was fine, and Aunt Curtis would never turn down Mrs. Vallencourt. Nobody in Portland did. I was invited.

The fire in my belly sent a blaze of heat through my limbs and my heart felt as light as a petal. I wanted to run outside and down Spring Street shouting with joy. To have one tiny glimmer of a better life, to have all my troubles worth what I had borne. I would see Lara. And Henry...

"What are you doing?"

Adelaide glared at me from the doorway. My joy snapped into fear and I dropped the invitation onto the tray.

"I can go to the Vallencourt Christmas party," I blurted. "I am invited."

She stared at me. For a moment, a look of compassion flitted across her plain face. But then she dropped her arms and abruptly left the doorway. I rushed after her, in time to see her reach the main staircase and fly down its steps with the utmost haste. My God, what was she doing? We weren't allowed to use the main staircase, but I didn't let my rule-breaking prevent me from following her.

I was too late. She had gone straight into the parlor, where Mrs. Keswick was enjoying a cup of tea before the fire. I froze in the doorway, my hope struggling not to drown. My moment of beauty with the piano, my utter delight to see Lara. All dissolving, as Adelaide relayed my faults.

"She read it, Mrs. Keswick."

The housekeeper set her teacup down and rose from the chair. It was ridiculous to hide like a mouse, so I slowly walked over to her, my head bowed and hands tucked behind my back. She would tell my aunt and the consequences would be severe.

"Well, girl. I shouldn't have expected more."

Her standards for both cleanliness and conduct were so high Queen Victoria couldn't meet them.

"I perform my duties to the best of my ability, ma'am," I said.

Adelaide's mouth dropped open at my boldness. The housekeeper was also speechless and it took her a moment to compose herself. When she at last spoke again, her voice was as piercing as a blade.

"A vicious pride you have, girl. It was the same in Phoebe Sullivan, and it brought about her downfall."

Her words seeped into me, burning like a poison. I wanted to make my mother proud. I hoped she was.

"The sins of the parents pass down to their children." She paused after such a damning declaration. "I will inform my mistress of your conduct. I am also giving both Adelaide and Josie the week off with double pay. You are dismissed, Adelaide, until next Monday morning."

The housemaid couldn't have been happier than if Mrs. Keswick had given her a sack of gold. She gave a quick curtsey and hurried off to tell Josie of their amazing success.

"You assume the duties of both maids by yourself."

My workload was tripled. It was not only the extra cleaning, but the laundry that became daunting. Josie ensured the linens, textiles and clothing items were washed, dried and ironed, and it took her all week. I couldn't possibly hope to complete all of these duties alone. And Mrs. Keswick knew it.

"This situation sets me up for failure, ma'am."

She smiled cruelly. "You have only to look to your parentage for that. Good day."

Somehow, I didn't feel anything. All emotion had drained from me, leaving a strange numbness. I returned to the kitchen and walked up the back staircase.

When I thought of my mother, I remembered her kindness. She willingly accepted the task of raising two daughters, though she was horribly strained by thousands of dollars of debt. She faced hardship with grace and maturity. She didn't want to burden me. I, too, was faced with a great task. And I didn't want to burden Lara.

I finally understood why my mother had kept me from her troubles. She loved me, as I loved my sister.

There was no sin in our silence.

20

Renewed by my forgiveness and understanding of my mother, I concentrated exclusively on my duties. Every time I picked up an armful of clothing, polished a table, swept the hallway, or scrubbed a chamber-pot, I focused on what I was doing and not how much I had yet to do. Peg kindly stepped in to help with the laundry, so an extra pair of hands scrubbed, wrung and hung sheets, chemises, stockings, petticoats, bodices, and skirts.

Even so, the work took its toll on me. My lower back ached like I'd been beaten with a hammer, my calves were tight and sore, and my knees throbbed like rotten teeth.

I was taking a fifteen minute break to eat supper in the kitchen, when I was summoned to the parlor. Aunt Curtis and Jane had arrived home, so I wasn't surprised they wanted to discuss my encounter with the housekeeper.

"An interesting week you have ahead of you, girl. Mrs. Keswick made an excellent decision."

Like I had that morning, I stood quietly before my aunt, hands tucked behind my back. Submissive to her every whim.

"There will be a new development in your situation."

The knot that had been growing in my stomach turned into a tight rubber ball. Whatever kind of new development, it wouldn't benefit me.

"Jane and I met Elliot today in Market Square. He has requested your assistance with work at the doctor's office."

The knot disappeared and I felt an enormous lifting of my shoulders, as if I was a marionette on strings. Even in such a trying capacity as helping at the doctor's office, Elliot's amiable companionship would be more than worth our troubles.

"Beginning next week, you shall assist him on Tuesdays and Thursdays. Mondays, Wednesdays, Fridays, Saturdays and Sundays are for household duties. Elliot will pay you two dollars a day. However, since I am losing your help here, all pay he gives to you is turned over to me."

I wouldn't see a dime from my efforts, and my workload would consume eighty hours of each week. Yet, somehow, I was looking forward to a new schedule.

"At six o'clock on Tuesday morning you are required at the doctor's office. No word of your position to Elliot. You wouldn't want to make your situation worse, would you?"

"No, ma'am."

"You are dismissed."

I ignored my pained back and throbbing knees and got back to work. Each night for the next seven days, I limped upstairs to the third floor and sat on my cot. Thinking about the doctor's office and how delighted I'd be to see Elliot. When Adelaide and Josie returned on Monday, it actually felt odd to have the extra help. But I gladly welcomed it!

At five o'clock on Tuesday morning, I awoke in utter darkness with a strange excitement stirring my breast. I pinned up my hair by the light of a candle and pinched my cheeks. An ironic smile tugged at my lips as I set off from the house and walked down the carriageway. After all of the fuss over my preference to walking, that was exactly what I was doing. Bracing December air hit my nose and lungs with a blast of renewed energy. At some point during my horrific week, autumn had vanished and winter had come. I could smell snow in the air as I rustled through the dead leaves on the sidewalk.

I was free from the confining walls of the Curtis House, free from Aunt Lucia, free from Mrs. Keswick and Adelaide. I was free.

A seagull cawed, waking its neighbors. The birds floated on ocean breezes, jabbering amongst themselves. Between the houses on Spring Street, I glimpsed tall smokestacks and chugging steamship wheels in the harbor. Portland was surprisingly hilly, buckles of land squished into the peninsula like a sock bunched in a shoe. The city had been closed off to me for a month.

I couldn't believe how revived I felt smelling the sea air, nodding to passersby, listening to workers pound hammers and carriage wheels slosh through dried mud. As I turned left onto Temple Street, the activity increased until my senses were saturated with its vibrancy.

Portland's liveliness had captivated me from the start, and I was surprised to realize I was falling in love with the city. It was like I'd closed a trunk full of memories of my old life and cracked open the lid on a new life. The farm taught me how to assume my duties with diligence and responsibility. Portland awakened me to all of the possibilities inherent in myself and other people.

Passing Middle Street, I came to Federal Street and turned right. After a few short blocks, the leafless trees of Lincoln Park came into view. At last, I came to the corner of Federal and Pearl Streets, with the park opposite on the other side of the street.

A large wooden structure sat right on the corner, and at first it looked like a white clapboard house. But the double front doors were too wide and the roof too flattened. A sign dangled from chains hung outside the doors, which I read aloud.

"Ambrose Curtis. Medical Doctor and Purveyor of Health Remedies for Gentlemen, Ladies and Children."

Doc Wilson in Bayview conducted his business from his front parlor, so to have an entire office was impressive. I walked up the wide porch steps. A gentleman patient exiting the building was kind enough to open the door for me. I thanked him and entered a waiting room with wooden benches, footstools, a tall grandfather clock and a cozy potbelly stove. Three narrow shelves supported an assortment of books and boxes filled with clean bandages. An "Occupied" sign dangled from a hook on the back of a door in the rear of the room.

It seemed Elliot was seeing a patient. I took a seat on one of the benches beside a wheezing elderly lady who spent the next quarter-hour struggling for breath. Finally, the door opened and an older gentleman emerged. The elderly woman stood up and accompanied him out the door, her arm tucked sweetly in his.

"Esther?"

Elliot stood in the doorway, wiping his hands on a towel. I sprang from the wooden bench and over to my cousin. My joy turned to concern, for he was much changed since our last meeting. He looked older, his skin was quite pale, and all formality in dressing had been exchanged for a simple brown suit and long apron. But a smile enlivened his thinned face, and he clasped my hands in excitement.

"Elliot, are you ill?"

"Gracious, no. Nor could I afford to be. Oh, it's so good to see you! Come into the examination room."

He closed the door after I'd walked in behind him. Never before had I seen such a modern medical facility. A large curtain divided the room into two sections, an examination table on one side and sickbeds on the other side. Shelves lined the walls, crowded with glass bottles and containers of all shapes and sizes. On a side counter were different medical instruments, including some sinister looking knives. A little potbelly stove with a range-plate put out a modest amount of heat from the corner. But the most astonishing thing of all was a pump sink near the examination table.

"What fine quarters you have here," I said as I removed my outer things and hung the articles on hooks by the door. "What is the sink for?"

"Ah, this was my suggestion!" Despite Elliot's altered appearance, his giddiness was infectious. "I recommended to Father he wash his hands between patients and before surgeries. He was surprised at first, but it was quite the best decision, I daresay. Then, not two months later, I came to the office and the sink was installed. Capital, you think?"

"I do," I said, and had not the time to say anything else, for he interrupted me excitedly.

"Oh, Esther, it has been too long since last I enjoyed your company. You have come during a rare moment of quietness. My work here has utterly swamped me."

He showed me a ladder leaning against the back wall. A trap-door was built into the ceiling above it.

"It's my sleeping room. I have not even had the time to visit at home. I was in surgery on Thanksgiving day, but would have much rather dined with you."

I nodded, remembering how exhausted I had felt, too. "You were missed. Lara is at the Vallencourts, as you well know."

"I saw her the other day."

My heart leapt into my throat. "You did?"

"Miss Alexandra and Lara stopped by to wish me well and make sure I am attending their Christmas party."

"Yes, you have been expressly invited."

He leaned against the examination table. "You must be so happy to see your sister. I know I cannot wait to see Miss Alexandra. I will ask her for the first dance. It keeps me going here … when the -"

He stopped, and I realized he was trying to maintain a sense of normalcy for me. That he was all right. But no matter how much Elliot loved his profession, he was seriously over-burdened. God knows how little he'd slept or how poorly he'd eaten. He took out a handkerchief and wiped his brow.

"Well, in any case, we will see the Vallencourts at the party."

Not if Mrs. Keswick or Aunt Curtis had anything to say about my attendance. Well, perhaps Elliot could persuade his mother. He was not to know of my situation.

I smiled. "Yes, we will."

He crossed his arms casually over his chest, regarding me with a thoughtful look similar to one I'd seen on his father's face.

"You are different as well, Esther. Your figure is more thin. I hope my mother hasn't been too severe. Or Jane, for that matter."

I couldn't tell him the truth, and I feared if we stayed too long on the subject I might be tempted.

"Thank you, Elliot, but I am well. I am here to help you, but I confess I need some instruction. Though I attended my mother's sickbed, I am little educated in medical duties."

"There is no need for you to become a doctor overnight." He laughed at the thought, and I was pleased to see his cheeks regaining a healthy color. "I lack help in basic duties. Nothing glamorous, you know. You'll be bringing patients in from the waiting room to see me. You can fetch foodstuffs and prepare meals. Of course, there's the cleaning and preparing the examination table, then taking linens to the laundress. Oh, and you can administer medicines to those who occupy the sickbeds."

It was, in essence, little different than what I was obliged to do at the Curtis House. With the work of both places, I would also be quite over-burdened. He gave another little laugh.

"I'm sorry to sound like I need a servant more than a nurse, but it is true. All of these little things take time away from my patients."

I stepped forward and took his hand in mine. His fingers were chilled. "Thank you for recruiting my company."

"I had it in mind you might be lonely at home without your sister. Truth be told, neither my mother or Jane are good company. Well, the kind of good company a girl like yourself would prefer. So, you see I want your company and you want mine. Good things all around, eh?"

Tears came to my eyes. I couldn't help it. His open kindness and his thoughtfulness towards my situation. Nobody except Lara had treated me so well. I threw my arms about his neck in a wholehearted embrace.

"Oh, Elliot. I am so grateful."

"I am grateful too, Esther."

He patted my back, and I reluctantly stepped from him. He smiled for a moment, then his expression became contemplative.

"Has there been any word about Father or Gabriel?"

I shook my head. "All I know is that Dr. Curtis will be gone the remainder of the winter."

"I suspected as much. No doubt you have deduced that my brother is the owner of the locked northeast bedchamber."

I nodded. He dropped my hands and started walking about the room. I followed him, reading the labels on the glass canisters, staring in fascination at the specimen jars.

"Father was firm that Gabriel was not to be mentioned. Yet, now that he has been found, wherever he is, I feel I can at last speak of him to you. That day we walked home from church I was sworn to silence, so I apologize for not being open."

"I understand, Elliot."

He paused by the stove. "Gabriel is the eldest of the three of us. While I have always been attracted to this profession" - gesturing about the room as he spoke - "Gabriel was not. But Father had it in mind that he would be a doctor. So, from the age of ten my brother was apprenticed under rigorous training. He resented it so greatly that he would do anything not to come here."

Elliot led me through an opening in the curtain to the other side of the examination room. I looked at the row of neatly prepared cots. Elliot picked up a small glass medicine bottle, playing absentmindedly with it.

"Then the war started. I was twelve, and Gabriel was fifteen. At first, he didn't pay attention to it. But after the first battle, he changed. He started reading every newspaper account and attending recruiting rallies. He became obsessed. I guess it was no real surprise the following spring when one day we all awoke and he was gone."

"It was a hard time," I said quietly. "My own father also left us, in October of '61."

Elliot smiled sadly. "You can well imagine how Gabriel's decision affected my father. Oh, he was so angry and upset that he shut up that bedroom. We were not to speak my brother's name. He would be dead to us." He set the little bottle on a shelf. "Father was not the only one angry. There was a rumor Henry and Gabriel quarreled violently before my brother left, but I don't know if that's true."

"Henry Vallencourt?" I said. "Were they well-acquainted?"

"Of course. The best of friends, in fact. We all held out hope that Gabriel would return. But the war ended and he didn't. He was discharged from the army but never came home."

Neither did my father. "So, there has been no word of him until now."

Elliot nodded. "I hope Father can find him. He wasn't the same after Gabriel left. I've been working so hard I haven't stopped to think about having my brother home, but it would be ... wonderful indeed."

I reached for my cousin's arm and tucked it within mine. "This has rent your family in two. I dearly hope your father and brother come home safely, from wherever they are."

He bowed his head and sniffed. I felt his sorrow, for my life had also changed when a loved one departed. The war had done such damage to thousands of families. Neither Elliot nor I had set foot on a battlefield, but its sadness had stretched to nearly every family in the country. He patted my hand.

"You are so kind. I wish my mother and sister sympathized as you do." He left my side and went over to a large book opened on the side counter. "But between you and me, I think they're glad Gabriel never came home."

A memory stirred. The conversation I'd overheard at Thanksgiving. *You'd better pray he doesn't bring him home.* Why would Aunt Curtis not want her son home? I decided against telling Elliot what I had heard.

"No matter the circumstances, I'd want a brother to come home."

He took up a pen. "Well, in any case, it's time to get started on the real reason you're here, shall we?"

Elliot showed me the patient history book, which had a page for every Portland family his father treated. After each patient departed the office, I was to write down their reason for treatment, the date, and any patent remedies administered. Next, Elliot showed me where the mop and bucket were, how to operate the sink, the various herbal concoctions, pills, potions, elixirs and syrups on the shelves, how to clean the medical instruments, a list of grocers and butchers in the area for meals, and he also gave me the address for the laundress. It was a large amount of information to take in, but my mind had been so dulled from doing chores I welcomed the learning. Elliot praised his pupil's quick aptness, and I praised his good decision in choosing me.

Then there came a knock on the door and my first patient walked in. A wife with child close to the beginning of her confinement suffered from an upset stomach. I noted her name in the patient history book and stood by as an observer to my cousin's actions.

Elliot's general goodness extended to all he met. It was plain he had the gift for helping people, and gave her good counsel about eating less heavy meals in the evening. By the time she departed with a paper bag of ginger root, her calm had been restored.

As soon as the door closed behind her, I congratulated my cousin.

"What for?" he said. "Mrs. Stratton's condition was easily remedied."

"That is no small thing," I said. "You eased her nerves and soothed her mental troubles. You are a great doctor, Elliot."

He blushed, loosening his cravat. "I will not tolerate this flattery if you dish it out with hope to gain something."

I laughed. "I have gained so much by being here. This partnership benefits both of us."

A second patient walked in and time for chatting came to a close. We soon both became occupied with our respective duties. As I mopped floors, cleaned windows and dusted the specimen jars, I couldn't help but smile. I was doing the same thing I was at the Curtis House. But the company made all the difference.

I could do anything as long as the people I loved were by my side.

21

The morning of December the twenty-fourth dawned gray and frosty, snow swirling the streets of Portland. Not too many weeks ago, I had been forbidden from attending the Vallencourt Christmas party held on this wintery evening. But, as I'd hoped, my new partnership with Elliot convinced his mother I had as much right as anyone else in the Curtis family to attend. My conduct as a maid had also improved, thanks to a more cheerful mood, less snappishness towards Adelaide, and a higher degree of work ethic. The two days a week spent with Elliot were like blots of sunshine.

The day of the party fell on a Thursday, so I was supposed to be at the doctor's office. But the grand occasion made Elliot light-hearted enough to give me the day off. I received no such goodwill from his mother, and spent every waking hour until five o'clock cleaning the Curtis House. After a final polish of the dining room table and a few bites of stew from the kitchen, I hurried up to the third floor to get dressed.

I retrieved the same navy blue gown I'd worn the night I met Henry Vallencourt. After I had slipped it over my head and beheld myself in the tiny mirror, I felt quite nervous. He'd seen me in this old thing. What kind of impression could I hope to make dressed as plain as a wren? I sighed, adjusted the lace collar, and tried to push away jealous thoughts of those beautiful gowns at the dress warehouses.

After making my hair look as becoming as possible, I blew out the candle and descended the staircase to the second floor. As I emerged onto the second floor landing and closed Gabriel's door behind me, his brother came into the front hall blowing on his bare hands.

"Good gracious, it's cold!" Elliot looked up as I came down the stairs. "Why you look lovely, Esther."

"I see you've traded a doctor's apron for a dinner suit."

He stole a peep in the hall mirror and adjusted his bow tie. "Do you think Miss Alexandra will prefer it?"

I smiled as I reached the bottom of the stairs. He winked at me, picking imaginary specks off his shoulders. Then we were both interrupted by the entrance of Aunt Curtis and Jane from the parlor. Momentarily speechless, I stared at their exquisite gowns. Nothing either of them had worn before could compare to such luxurious dresses and jewels. My joy at seeing Elliot dimmed a bit, but I steadied and held my composure. I needed to be strong, for my aunt would not let anyone's presence deter her from exercising all power over me. It had been her course of action since the moment we met.

Mr. Jakes helped us into our outer things and neither my aunt or her daughter would look my way. We soon made our way out into the snow and into the carriage.

I hardly dared breathe on the short ride to the Vallencourts' home. I would see Lara! After two long months of working both for my aunt and for my cousin ... My mind whirled with the shock of it.

We had barely set off before we were turning onto Danforth Street. Elliot was as excited as I was, rubbing dew from the windows and grinning like a schoolboy. As we pulled up in front of the mansion, I became awestruck.

Its size was absolutely immense. The home was constructed of brown stone with a blocky central tower stretching high above the uppermost floors. The mansion's position on the slope of Danforth Street overlooking Portland harbor highlighted and enhanced its size. Thick columns supported a large porch, and a wide stone staircase led up to the massive front doors.

"My goodness," I said. "It's beautiful."

"Quite," Jane said.

I swallowed hard. She would be mistress of this grandeur soon. Though I'd met Henry Vallencourt and been witness to his formality, somehow I felt overwhelmed by his home. He was destined, as the eldest son, to inherit it someday. His wealth became painfully real in my mind, as if I'd been presented with stacks of gold coins. What a vast difference in our social stations! Not even two hours hence, I was emptying my aunt's chamber-pot.

Oh, and I'd wanted to be mistress of a farm. In his eyes, I might as well have been proud to empty chamber-pots the rest of my life. Biting my lip, I averted my gaze from the others.

We at last pulled to the end of the carriageway and the vehicle came to a stop. A pair of footmen immediately came up and pulled down the steps, then assisted each of us out into the snowy walkway. As if orchestrated by the heavens, it began to snow. Huge soft flakes spun and pinwheeled gently from the dark above. Landing on Elliot's blond hair, on my wool mittens, on Jane's feathered bonnet.

I walked slowly behind Aunt Curtis and my cousins as we followed the walkway around to the front of the mansion. Up the wide stone steps and to the front doors. Brushing the fresh snow from our clothes, blowing on fingers, stamping feet. The Vallencourt butler was waiting to usher us inside into the welcome of warmth. Suddenly all thoughts of snow and Henry vanished as if a veil had been lifted from my eyes.

Stunning.

Halting in the front foyer, it was the one word that came to mind and it repeated itself over and over as I gaped at my surroundings. This home was stunning. It was like each item of decoration had been elevated to a higher level than any other I'd seen before. A luxurious patterned

Oriental carpet was at my feet. The foyer chandelier swooped down from above, splaying globed arms and casting warm light upon me. In front of me, the central staircase swept up to the second floor, its intricate carvings and solid mahogany balustrade glowing like chocolate beneath the chandelier. The walls were painted with delicate frescoes, each a masterwork of form and color. Hall tables featured ornate golden candlesticks, huge porcelain vases, and enormous bowls filled with bountiful fruits.

"Excuse me, miss."

I was shook by my reverie by an amused-looking servant, whom I recognized at once as the housekeeper. She was quite large and pink-cheeked, winking at me as I handed over my cloak and bonnet. Her cheeriness was quite the opposite to Mrs. Keswick's sourness.

Aunt Curtis and my two cousins had already handed off their outer things and passed through a huge set of double-doors on the left wall. I swallowed and slowly stepped behind them into the parlor. If I thought the foyer was stunning, it did little to prepare me for the palatial grandeur of the parlor.

Oh, it was splendid! Decorated to the utmost in all the festivities of the season. Silver, gold, red, and green baubles, swags, festoons, drapes and garlands occupied every conceivable surface. An enormous Christmas tree was set up at the end of the room, bursting with ornaments and glittering with hundreds of tiny twinkling lights. Dancers in their floaty gowns and smart black dinner suits twirled past like a magical scene of years past. Warm candlelight bounced off the ornamented surfaces, luxurious fabrics, and burnished woods. It was like being in a princess's jewel box, and I was dazzled.

"Esther!"

Before I could register who had said my name, I caught a flash of blue eyes and gold curls. And then my sister was in my arms, her hair smelling sweetly of roses. It was both the most wondrous and most torturous moment, for I couldn't tell her of my troubles, nor escape into this fairyland with her.

When at last we parted, I stood back and beheld her. Our prolonged absence vanished as if it had never occurred. She looked more grown-up, her hair in a lovely curled style. Her shimmery silver dress made her skin glow, and she looked as radiant as an angel.

"Esther, I've missed you so much! It has been nearly two months!"

Her voice was like balm on my open wounds. I had no words. I couldn't speak. I had missed her more than I could ever express.

"I'm so glad I could come," I finally said.

I glimped my aunt standing next to Mrs. Vallencourt, surveying the scene with one eye on the dancers and the other on me. There wasn't much time before she separated me from Lara.

"Have you been cross with me?" Lara asked.

"Cross? Heavens, no. Why would you think that?"

"I've sent ever so many letters! Alexandra says she trusts the servant who delivers them, so why haven't you written?"

I laughed. I'd half-forgotten her sweet bluntness. Silk and jewels aside, there was a true farm girl before me. She'd rather be in a saddle than a lady's chair, even after all this time spent in such an exquisite place.

But I had no time to answer her, for my aunt approached us. Her voluminous skirts caused Lara to step aside. Again, I was parted from my dearest, but even the simplest contact with her had revived me like a bellows fans a fire. Being near her was warming, no matter how chilly the new company.

"Good evening, Miss Lara," Aunt Curtis said, with such a high degree of fake politeness I almost rolled my eyes. "Why, just look at you. The perfect picture of a fine lady."

"All thanks to Miss Alexandra, Aunt Curtis," Lara said.

Alexandra was at that moment heartily conversing by the Christmas tree with a pink-cheeked Elliot, but it wasn't the heat that caused his high color. And right beside them, in a formal dinner suit and plush embroidered waistcoat, was her brother. Henry, too, spoke with one of my cousins, though their conversation was contrasted by his stiffness and her hotly fanning herself. Even as I watched, he stifled a yawn behind his fist.

"Jane looks lovely tonight," Lara said politely.

"Thank you, my dear," my aunt returned with a smile. "Pray, let me steal your sister's company. Mr. Vallencourt has requested her opinion about an important matter, and she is needed."

The tiny heartbreak in my sister's eyes flooded me from the inside. We had just been reunited. Now to part again! I gave Lara a reluctant curtsey and a smile, then willed my feet to leave her side. I'd gone ten feet before I realized I was supposed to be searching for the master of the house.

I slipped between the onlookers standing about the room's perimeter. They drank champagne and enjoyed caviar toast points, chatting about how delightful the latest season had been, how soon the economy was recovering from the devastating city fire, and how strange it was that the latest fashion was a bustle and not a hoop. To think those ladies in Paris! How scandalous. I caught bits of their passing conversations, ignored their pitiful stares when they beheld my simple gown, the plainest in the room, and at last found Mr. Vallencourt enjoying social company in the rear of the parlor. A servant handed him a glass of punch in a crystal goblet and he knocked it back heartily, enjoying a laugh with his fellow businessmen. I approached the circle of suits with politeness and trepidation, but it wasn't long before one tapped Henry's father on the shoulder and he turned to acknowledge me with a grin.

"Ah, Miss Esther Perry! So good of you to come. You must be so pleased with your sister's progress with Alexandra."

"I am, sir," I said. "Thank you. Forgive me for interrupting, but you wished to speak with me?"

He looked dazed. I was obliged to mumble an apology and induce him to remember why he'd summoned me. But after an awkward pause, it was plain he'd never sought my opinion. Aunt Curtis wanted me away from Lara, and that was that. Foolish, I admonished myself. Esther, you're foolish.

I was about to excuse myself, when Mr. Vallencourt stepped from his acquaintances and came closer to me.

"No harm in asking, Miss Perry. News does travel fast in the city of

Portland. It seems you are the first of the Curtis family to know!"

"Know?" I said, confused. "Know what, sir?"

"About Henry and I, of course. I asked my son to be a partner in the Vallencourt Architectural Firm. This afternoon!"

"A partner!" I repeated. "That is a wonderful decision, sir. I congratulate you both."

"Yes, yes," he said off-handedly.

But the merriness in his eyes disappeared, and he glanced around the room before lowering his voice in a confidential tone.

"You seem like a steady girl with a good head on your shoulders, Miss Perry. I only wish I could say the same for Henry. Indeed, he has refused me. My wife says he will become more sensible in the spring once he has said his vows to Miss Curtis. With that level of obligation, he cannot hope but commit to his true path."

I couldn't say I was surprised to hear of this, but it was obvious it vexed his father greatly. "I am sorry to hear of his refusal. Is there another profession he prefers?"

"No, none at all." Mr. Vallencourt shook his head until his forehead glowed pink. "Once this wedding takes place, his mind will be changed. I'm sure of it."

I didn't know what to say. Henry shirking his duties? Shrugging off a profession? Not even the lowest man in Bayview would say no to heading a prestigious architectural firm. So much good Henry could do, and he refused it.

"Well," Mr. Vallencourt continued, "it is time for the toast. Henry must be present, so be a good girl and fetch him, Miss Perry."

"Yes, sir."

Still puzzled by this latest news, I struggled to maintain my composure. What had happened to elicit such a reaction, that I should suddenly feel nervous about speaking with Henry? The last I'd seen him, he was speaking with Jane by the tree, so I headed through the crowd in that direction. But I was surprised to find my elder cousin had replaced her fiancee's company with my aunt and sister. It ached to see Lara so close and not be able to speak to her privately. I hoped I'd get another chance this evening. Elliot and Alexandra were still chatting with equal vivacity. I'd never seen him look so happy.

I surveyed the room, but no sign of Henry Vallencourt. He wasn't partaking of sweets, speaking with friends, or dancing. He wasn't in the parlor at all, so I ducked out into the hallway. I peeked in the dining room, but no luck. Servants were clearing the table and brushing the rug. I'd be back to doing chores in the morning just like them. I quickly pushed the ugly thought out of my mind.

Walking down the hallway towards the back of the house, I passed by a wavy glass window. I paused to look in and realized it was a library. Along the walls were enclosed glass cases filled with books. I went to the door and quietly let myself in. The library was comfortable and cozy, decorated in a rich Gothic style with arched bookcase windows, a thick Persian rug, and carved trefoils.

But my attention suddenly went from the decoration to a familiar figure standing by the curtains. He was muttering to himself, and I overheard the final words of his private conversation.

"God damn it," was what it sounded like.

"Good evening, Mr. Vallencourt."

At the sound of my greeting, Henry turned and shoved his pocketwatch into his waistcoat. He appeared agitated, his hair disheveled and his face flushed. Upon seeing me, he looked even more ill at ease, as if I was a wind that had whipped up the air. A dozen thoughts crowded my mind. The handsomeness of his face, the conversation with Jane he'd had earlier, the way he'd looked at me as I played piano, my realization that Jane didn't love him, his refusal of his father's proposal.

"Sir," I began, my voice as strong as I could make it. "Your father is looking for you."

He froze, not greeting me and not saying a word. I decided not to wait for formalities or social niceties. I had to speak to him. I had to try, for my mind wouldn't let it rest.

"He confided in me about your meeting today. Please accept his proposal and become partner."

His jaw stiffened and he drew himself up to his full height, smoothing his waistcoat and brushing down his jacket lapels.

"Miss Perry," he said. "The girl who prefers to walk and thinks architecture is frozen music. The girl who plays Bach however she likes and Beethoven with incredible feeling."

I stood mutely, and without even thinking, tucked my hands behind my back. The way he mentioned these aspects of our acquaintance made me feel strangely at ease. He knew me and was not afraid to speak of it. I could do the same.

"Mr. Vallencourt," I replied. "The man who has the greatest of opportunities to make a real difference in his city. The man who says no to it."

He glowered at me, angered dark eyes beneath his gathered brow.

"Someone once called me a coward. But I am not afraid of the accusation. Good night."

He clenched his jacket lapels and stormed past me. In the half-second before he left the room, I tried one last time to convince myself he was like Caleb. I was again hanging my heart on someone unworthy, someone who shirked duties and played with hearts. But there was something different. Something Caleb never had.

"Don't lock it away any longer," I said. "Don't forget who you are, no matter what he said."

Henry had flung open the door and was about to leave when he stopped. He gave a wrenching sigh, then his shoulders slumped and he looked up at the ceiling. I knew then, and didn't know how I knew, that it was Gabriel. Gabriel had called him a coward. Gabriel had gone to war and Henry had stayed. Everything I'd heard from Elliot, Mr. Vallencourt and my uncle made sense.

When at last Henry spoke again, his voice was low and steady. But he did not turn around.

"You don't know of what you speak."

"He was different from you, sir," I said quietly. "His father forced him to be a doctor. He never had the passion for it. But you had a healthy ambition. I believe you'll feel that again."

Please turn around, I thought. Turn around and speak to me. Show me who you are, beneath the formalities.

"Good night."

He left the library, and I was alone. I had lost his good opinion by treading too far on his pride. Whatever had transpired between he and Gabriel before my cousin left for war had wounded him. It broke my heart to see such potential waste away in degrading pursuits, but there was nothing I could do.

I felt this helplessness as a girl, watching my father laze away at the farm and become indebted to creditors. I remembered the knocks on the door, the telegrams, the angry whispers from his enemies in Bayview. Once, I had been stopped in the street by the owner of Sloop Tavern demanding to be paid from George's latest gambling night. My father was so irresponsible I swore I would never be like that.

"Ah, there you are girl!"

Aunt Curtis emerged from the parlor into the hall. I was sitting in a hall chair, staring down at my feet.

"What is this? Have you paid your respects to Mr. Vallencourt yet?"

"Yes, ma'am," I said dully.

She fanned herself, spilling some of her champagne on me. "My goodness, it is warm! Fetch me some water, girl."

My cheeks felt hot, too, though it was not from the party. I didn't want to go back into the main parlor, but it was inadvisable to disobey Aunt Curtis. So, I reluctantly walked back inside.

Henry was standing by the Christmas tree, toasting champagne flutes with both Jane and my sister. My heart gave a sharp pang, and tears came to my eyes. I swallowed hard, made my way through the crowd, and stopped at the buffet table in the back of the room.

"Good evening, Esther."

Elliot, flushed and giddy from the excitement of spending all evening with his beloved, was also getting a drink. He poured water from the punch bowl into a goblet and handed it to me. I didn't feel like conversing, but then he began talking so fast I could barely keep up.

"Oh, Esther, you won't believe it. I had a right notion as we came to the party that it might happen! I am the happiest man alive!"

"Elliot," I said. "I do need another glass for your mother."

My request was lost upon him. He took out a handkerchief and daubed his glistening brow. Despite my horrible evening, Elliot's boyish cheerfulness made me smile. I reached for the punch bowl ladle. Suddenly, all the party attendees in the room began politely clapping. I filled the water glass and sipped it myself, turning around to face the front of the room. A bell rang.

"Attention! Attention all!"

Mr. Vallencourt stood directly in front of the brilliant tree with an arm around Henry, who looked more pleased than I thought he would being the center of attention. Alexandra stood on her father's other side, as flushed and giddy as Elliot. Mr. Vallencourt cleared his throat, then turned to Alexandra and warmly clasped her hands.

"Thank you so much for coming to our annual Christmas party. It has been a pleasure to see you all, especially you Mr. Mayor, Miss Pierce and you Senator, of course. Earlier this fall, my son Henry proposed to Miss Jane Curtis. His proposal was accepted, and a wedding date has been fixed for April ninth! Wedding plans are, of course, in place - but I leave these things to the ladies!"

He gave his wife a wink. Henry looked over at Jane, who was standing a few feet from him. She dipped her head in acquiescence and gave an expert little curtsey. He smiled, obviously enjoying himself, and tossed back the rest of his champagne while the crowd applauded. It was a complete reversal of his angry departure from me. Just as well, for I had tarnished his opinion of me. Mr. Vallencourt gave his son one final look of affected dissatisfaction before resuming his address.

"But I am pleased to inform you all that it is not the only good news you shall hear this evening!"

Alexandra squeezed her father's hand, her pretty face alight with excitement. Beside me, Elliot leaned over.

"I fear I am about to faint, Esther!"

"Miss Curtis's younger brother Elliot has made an offer of marriage to my daughter Alexandra Vallencourt!"

The room buzzed with whispers, and everyone turned around to see the would-be groom. Poor lovesick Elliot looked like he would topple over. I nudged him forward, and the crowd parted way for him to approach his love's side.

"I accept this happy union! Hear hear! So, look for the invitation to a double Vallencourt wedding!"

Now I was the one to nearly faint. A double wedding!

The whispers escalated to cheers for the two couples. Elliot haltingly approached Alexandra, trembling like a mouse, but she went right to him and kissed his cheek. Of course, the crowd roared louder. I smiled. She was a sweet young lady and he as kind a gentleman I'd ever met. But his sister and Henry ...

As the party attendees began congratulating the groom-to-be and his beautiful bride, I gazed at Henry from across the room. Dozens of people and servants divided us. He felt more lost to me than I ever thought he could be, and I didn't even know I'd wanted him to be by my side. I was no more than a farmer's daughter of no rank or family, with three dollars to my name. I gulped the rest of the water, filled a glass for my aunt, and left the parlor to the sound of a pretty waltz ringing in my ears.

Aunt Curtis was no longer in the hall, so she must have gone back into the parlor to celebrate the extraordinarily fortuitous matches her children had made. Elliot's future happiness was nearly written in stone, but Jane did not love her future husband.

"For heaven's sake," I muttered aloud. "If he is to be so blinded by her lack of character, then I was wrong. There is nothing under his irresponsibility to recommend him, either."

They were perfect for each other. Even if they had virtues, their more flawed traits did an equally excellent job of hiding them. What a pair!

I gave up searching for Aunt Curtis and set the glass on a hall table. The quiet foyer gave me a chance to breathe. I neither wanted to return to the parlor or wait for the Curtis ladies. The library seemed a good place to spend an hour or so, for amidst the hubbub I wouldn't be missed. So, I walked down the hall towards the glass windows I'd seen before.

Just past the staircase, I noticed another room that was rather dark. I would have kept walking, but then I spied the familiar glint of candlelight on ivory keys.

A piano!

My heart leaped. I slipped past the ajar door, into what appeared to be a small drawing room. After lighting several more candles and an oil lamp, the room glowed cozily.

Yes, everything I'd imagined about the Vallencourt piano was true. It was magically beautiful. Deep burnished mahogany the color of fine chocolate. Painted gold scrolls wound their way around the lid, and curvy carved legs ended in lion's paws. I touched the blue bench cushion, made of finest silk. I'd never seen such a luxurious instrument. It was like a throne for a queen.

Auld Lang Syne sat open on the piano music stand. I moved the bench out and seated myself upon the comfortable cushion. I slipped off my pinched evening shoes and placed stocking feet on the golden pedals.

"Should auld acquaintance be forgot," I sang as I ran my fingers up and down the smooth and wonderfully balanced keys.

Such a responsive touch, too. It was like being upgraded to the finest barouche after sitting in horse wagons my whole life. An exquisite pleasure.

My feet played with the pedals, first one and then the other. The little dance, like making a new acquaintance. When at last I felt calmed and settled, I started the song. Quietly at first, repeating the first few bars to luxuriate in the feel of the ivory keys. Then I began the opening verse and hummed along to the melody. Such a melancholy and nostalgic song.

Should auld acquaintance be forgot
And never brought to mind?
Should auld acquaintance be forgot
And the days of auld lang syne.

For auld lang syne, my dear.
For auld lang syne.
We'll drink a cup of kindness here
For the days of auld lang syne ...

After I ended the song, without even realizing it, I was in tears. My feet rested on the pedals. Leaning forward, I placed my elbows on the edge of the keys, my head in hands. Everything I'd felt, all the loss and sorrow, seemed so present. Like a song weeping inside me. I sniffed and finally sat back on the bench, wiping my eyes.

"You may borrow mine."

Startled, I looked up. And there was Henry Vallencourt. He held a handkerchief out to me. I was so shocked I stared at his hand for a moment before gratefully taking it and daubing my eyes. He could have used it himself, for he looked so sad.

"Thank you, sir."

I didn't know what else to say. Whether I should apologize for treading too far into his personal business or to congratulate him on his marriage, which I could hardly do so. I couldn't believe he had found me, that he had listened to my song.

But I was saved from continuing our conversation, for we were interrupted by quite the crowd. Jane, Aunt Curtis, Elliot and Alexandra all traipsed into the room. I immediately gave Henry the handkerchief and stood from the bench. Both Jane and her mother eyed me coldly. Jane swept to her intended's side and firmly placed his arm in hers, as if they were eternally locked together. Aunt Curtis reached over and closed the sheet music book with a slap.

"That is enough for one evening. The hour is late and we must be going."

Nobody moved. I stood next to the piano, one hand resting lightly on its lowest keys as if it needed a gentle caress. It was I who needed it, longing to stay in this room and never face the dull winter weeks ahead. Finally, Elliot stepped over to me and offered his arm. I lowered my eyes and reluctantly left the little drawing room, followed by the rest of our party.

The housekeeper was in the foyer, ready with our winter cloaks and bonnets. Lara was there, too, looking quite downcast at our imminent parting. How little time I'd had with her this evening. I should have tried to speak with her rather than play the piano. She came to me and wrapped her arms about me.

"Oh, Esther. I wish you could have stayed longer."

"Me, too," I said, and it was all I could say.

Her bright cheeriness shone like a loving beacon in my gray life. All too soon, Elliot was stepping out into the walkway and Aunt Curtis was tugging me from my sister's embrace. When I let go of her, it was like leaving warm shores for stormy waters.

It had stopped snowing and fresh powdery flakes dusted the mansion's front steps. Henry, his arm still tightly clasped in Jane's, followed us out to the carriage. After Aunt Curtis, Elliot, Jane and myself had taken our seats in the carriage, he paused at the door. Candleglow from the mansion's windows lit up his face, and I could see his eyes were still sad. I leaned against the carriage window, exhausted and wearied by my evening. He took Jane's gloved hand and kissed it.

"You were radiant this evening, Miss Curtis. I thoroughly enjoyed your company."

"Thank you, Mr. Vallencourt," she said. "It was a pleasure."

"Miss Perry."

I lifted my head. He was regarding me from the carriage window. Jane immediately glared at me. I bit my lip. He would admonish me again, like he had in the library. Only now, it would be in front of his fiancee and my aunt. More ammunition for their cruelty towards me. I nodded to him, bracing myself.

But the sadness was fading from his eyes, replaced by a warmth I'd not seen before.

"The girl who played the right song at the right time."

Then he stepped back from the carriage, tucking his hands behind his back. I didn't know what to say, but the tiniest glow began to warm me inside. He had complimented me. Elliot was grinning from across the carriage seat, and as expected Jane was furious.

"Well! You are not to speak to my fiancee!"

"I did not speak to him," I murmured. "He spoke first."

Indeed, he had. She could not argue with me and remained silent on our return drive to the Curtis House.

He had spoken first.

22

Startling, how quickly life returned to drudgery. It was like I was thrust from the jewel box of the Vallencourt mansion into a coal-hod. My memories of the jewel box were both beautiful and aching. The smell of Lara's hair as we embraced. The way Henry had looked whilst handing me the handkerchief.

Yet one memory kept reliving itself through my cousin. For several weeks after the party, Elliot could hardly focus at the office and whistled tune after tune. He'd loved Miss Alexandra for as long as he could remember, and between patients with winter head-colds and frostbite, he read me her letters about wedding preparations.

All anyone could talk about was the double wedding. I was once stopped in the street on my way back from the doctor's office by a stranger who could hardly believe the news. The wealthiest family uniting with one of the most respected families? It was like the royal marriages of olde when two countries became alliances.

But though Queen Victoria of England had adored her German Prince Albert, this match couldn't claim such deep affection. Jane didn't love Henry, and it made me feel more wretched than I admitted even to myself that he would be unhappy with her.

While word of the wedding was on everyone's lips, word of the intended Vallencourt partnership remained silent. Henry hadn't reneged on his decision despite my uncouth urging and remained idle without a profession.

For some reason, this didn't seem to interfere with Jane's opinion of him. A woman so obsessed with his fortune as to make a match of purely financial motives, and then not wish to see him obtain further success? It bothered me exceedingly.

My head hurt and my feet hurt, and some days it was enough simply to get through to the next hour. I stopped looking in mirrors, for my haggard appearance was like that of a beggar woman. My eyes watered from the brisk cold on my city walks, my knees ached with a dull pain, and lighting the Curtis House fires blasted my skin until my cheeks and fingers blistered and cracked. Elliot treated my ragged skin with comfrey poultices and sighed when I told him I was well-fed and cared for.

"You must be ill," he said quietly one afternoon.

I leaned the broom up against the wall and paused by the medical office window. Beyond the frosted glass children threw snowballs in Lincoln Park. It was a beautifully sunny January day.

"I'll speak to Mother," he went on. "She must put you to rest."

"No," I forced myself to say. "Elliot, you are very kind, but I am well at the house."

"Then let me give you the rest of the week off. I cannot bear to see you this way."

I crossed my arms over my chest, wrapping a shawl about my shoulders. "My dear cousin, you are so good to me and I have not asked for anything from you. Please respect my wishes on this matter and put thoughts of my health out of your head."

"I can't do that!" he cried. "You are dear to me."

"And you to me." I was glad he could not see my trembling lip. I took a deep breath. "Who next is scheduled to visit us?"

He looked over the visitor book. I returned to my broom and swept the floor, keeping my back to Elliot so he wouldn't see my tearful eyes. Of course I wanted to tell him. But I could not.

We both soon had reason to be more sorrowful, for a few moments later the door opened and a pitifully clad figure stumbled in. I abruptly stopped sweeping, feeling a rush of compassion for the poor man. Ratty hair concealed his dirty face, and he was bundled in a pile of wools and tweeds as if from a rag-bin. His feet were encased in newspapers wrapped with twine, his bare hands blue with cold.

Elliot immediately rushed to his side. "Sir! Sir, let me help you. Come and warm yourself by the fire. Esther!"

I was already filling a bowl of water to place on the stove. I raked the coals, inducing them to blaze. Elliot coaxed the man over to the examination table and started removing his outer blankets and shawls. I heard a gasp of surprise and looked up.

The man's hat had been removed - and he wasn't a man! A woman sat upon the table.

Elliot pushed back some of her hair to reveal what once had been a beautiful face. But now her skin was encrusted with sores, her blue eyes glassy and dull, her hair so twisted and dirty I could hardly tell what color it was.

"My God," I breathed. "She's a lady."

Elliot was at a loss for words. He stared at her with such pity and compassion it half-broke my heart. I knelt by her feet and began untying the twine and unwrapping the newspapers. Elliot kept murmuring "poor girl" and set to work preparing salves for her face. She didn't say a word, but gave a small sigh.

Once I'd removed all the newspapers, I fetched the bowl of hot water and set it beneath her feet so she could at last receive its warmth. Elliot and I attended upon her for the next hour, washing her feet, rubbing her hands, caring for her sores. Then I set to work trying to clean her hair. But it was so dirty there was no hope.

"Elliot," I said. "I'll have to cut her hair."

He paused, his hands covered in salves and creams. "It cannot be cleaned, then?"

I showed him the mats and snarls. It was in such poor condition that to brush it out would cause tremendous pain. Elliot sighed and indicated his medical tool-kit on the side counter.

"There's a pair of scissors in the kit. Do it quickly."

I patted the girl's hand. She didn't look at me, but I comforted her all the same. I straightened a length of hair, took the scissors and snipped the strands clear from her scalp. She didn't struggle, didn't utter a word. I took a deep breath and began cutting away her hair. It was greasy and horribly unclean, but I saw no ticks or mites. One by one the dark clumps of hair fell on the floor.

At last, we had finished what we could in the short-term. The girl looked a sight, her face swathed in cream, all of her hair cut away. Elliot and I helped her to gently rise from the examination table, and she half-stumbled half-walked beyond the curtain to a sick-bed. I pulled back the quilt and lowered her into bed. Elliot gave her firm instructions to stay and sleep. She quickly obliged and was soon resting quite peacefully.

Back on the other side of the curtain, I took the broom and began sweeping up her cut hair.

"What has happened to her?" I said.

Elliot shrugged. "We may never know. She might not be able to speak enough to tell us. She does exhibit symptoms of opium usage."

"Opium." I shook my head. "Poor thing."

"The best thing is to keep her clean and comfortable. I hate to go back on my offer, but even if I could, it is best you not take a day off."

I swept the hair into the dustpan. "I wouldn't, Elliot. You need me and so does she."

He looked saddened. "I will be glad when my father at last comes home. As much as I know of medicine, there is still so much to learn."

I gathered up the stranger's discarded blankets and clothes. "You are a good doctor, Elliot. I'll take these to the laundress."

"Thank you, Esther." He smiled. "I don't know what I did without you."

By the time I had returned, Elliot was busy with more patients. I peeked through the curtain every so often to check upon the girl's progress, but she was sleeping soundly. With our care, she had a good chance of recovery. I prepared our dinners and returned to my cleaning. Elliot asked for more salves, since I'd be back at the Curtis House tomorrow. So, I created a fresh batch for the strange sick girl.

At last, the hour grew near for my departure. It had started snowing, and a light wind whirled the fresh flakes outside the windows. Elliot helped me into my winter bonnet and mittens.

"Esther?"

"Yes, Elliot."

He wiped his surgical instruments with a cloth. "Would you like me to write to Lara? Tell her of how you have been helping me? Miss Alexandra confessed at the Christmas party she didn't know of your new situation."

"Oh, that would be delightful." I smiled. "I confess my sister scolded me about not writing to her, so letters would be much appreciated."

"Good. Well then, I shall do so. Have a good night, Nurse Esther."

"Good night, Doctor Curtis."

He smirked, waving me out into the wintry night. Yes, a letter to Lara, even though it was not of my own words, would be well-received. She would write back - and I could read her reply at the medical office without Aunt Curtis's knowing. A tiny gesture of goodwill to keep my spirits from swirling into the stagnant darkness.

I wrapped my hands in my wool cloak and walked back to the Curtis House. When I came to the end of Spring Street, I paused on the sidewalk. The stately brick home stood on the corner, lacy curtains in the windows, cheery lamplight from within. God, how I didn't want to go inside. I'd have rather stayed in the snow all night than return to my drab quarters.

Suddenly, an idea stole into my mind. Wait. I didn't have to return to the house yet. For at least a few minutes, my time was my own.

I turned left down High Street and descended the slope, Portland's dark harbor waters ahead of me. My footsteps felt lighter. Less than a ten-minute walk. Indeed, I'd have been surprised if it was five minutes, for I soon came upon the sign to Danforth Street. Scarcely had I started down the sidewalk when I was approaching the large trim front lawn, covered with snow. The stone fence and wide steps were a ghostly pale in the winter moonlight, the brownstone siding the color of dark gingerbread.

The Vallencourt mansion. It looked like a strange mythical palace. Candlelight glowed from second floor windows. Perhaps it was Lara's bedchamber. She'd so loved to look out the front windows of the Curtis House, and the view of the harbor was even better from here. I stood at the base of the mansion's wide stone steps, looking up at its huge grandeur, remembering the stunning interior.

Then suddenly, I was overcome by a strange feeling of relief. Relief that Lara was well provided for. Relief that she was warm and comfortable and happy in this place. It was hard being without her. It was hard working each week. It was hard.

"We'll be all right, Lara."

"Yes, as long as we have each other."

We still had each other. For too long, I'd pushed away my needs for comfort and enjoyment. Work was an honorable way to occupy my hands and give of my time. But it did not bring joy like my family did.

Had I wanted to be mistress of Perry Farm? Or was it thrust upon me by my father's ill-use of the position and then his absence?

It was time to go. I turned from the mansion and made my way back up High Street. I had to admit that I didn't know what I wanted. But it was enough to be satisfied I was doing the best I could. Once my uncle returned, maybe I could then settle into this new life. Here, without the farm.

Yes, I thought with a slow realization. I could be happy here.

23

No matter how bright the glow of Elliot's kindness warmed me, I only saw him two days a week. The rest of my hours spent at the Curtis House slowed down so greatly it was like time had stopped and I was wallowing in a stagnant sludge. I wanted my new life in Portland to be so much more than this. I felt demeaned, wasted, my talents unused like the piano keys I never touched in a song. The potential for beautiful music was hidden in the notes, but I could not find it.

My mind dulled with the endless monotony of tasks. Scrub the dishes, polish the silverware, fold the table linens, rearrange the centerpiece, dust the sideboard. At night before bed, I'd sit on my cot in the candlelight and look at my sheet music folio. But then I had to put it away, for it tortured me so.

As the winter weeks wore on, Henry Vallencourt's face became a memory, a watercolored image in my mind with his kind smile. When I thought of him, I felt a dull ache. I was struggling to learn what I wanted, and he didn't know what he wanted, either. Maybe he was right to refuse his father's proposition. Maybe I was wrong to judge him. Over and over, I had to remind myself he was marrying Jane. He was marrying Jane. On

April ninth, he was marrying Jane.

If I did not work to make Henry nothing but a memory, the longing for him would carve me as water carved rock. And I would wake to find a great crevice in my heart none could heal.

The girl at the doctor's office slowly recovered. Her sores cracked, split, and then began to fade. Her skin went from a pale and sickly green to a healthier pink. Her hair began to grow back, delighting both Elliot and I with its rich deep blond. The glassy sick look faded from her eyes. I sat by her side and told her stories, sang lullabies, and generally made her comfortable and cared for. But still she did not speak.

As soon as I came in to the office waiting room one February morning, Elliot met me at the door. He had such a frantic look I became alarmed.

"Elliot, what is wrong?"

"She spoke!" he burst out. "She asked for you. Come!"

I hurried to the sickbed area. She had asked for me? It had been weeks she'd been here, weeks of only outward healing and no response from within. But when Elliot pushed back the curtain, she was sitting up in bed. Her eyes were alight with life, her cheeks pink and devoid of any sores or markings, her pretty blond hair braided about her face. It was like June sunshine had come to visit our wintry world.

"Esther," she greeted.

I couldn't have been more astonished. I took off my bonnet, handing it to Elliot, then went to her side, and sat on the bed. To look in her face, bearing such a great resemblance to my own sister, made my heart so full I almost wept. She reached for my hand and I gladly took it.

"I am so glad to see you recovered," I said. "Elliot and I have been so curious to know where you are from and how you came to be so ill."

She smiled. "My name is Annie. I came to find my husband, and when I saw the name Curtis on the doctor's sign, I knew he'd be here."

Her speech had a pronounced accent. The girl was definitely not from Portland, nor even from Maine. But her mention of a husband puzzled me. I felt saddened that I was to tell her no such person was at the office. Perhaps she suffered mental confusion, which unfortunately we couldn't treat.

"Miss Annie," I said gently. "I'm afraid we cannot help you. Your husband isn't here. Only Elliot Curtis, as you can see, and he's intended for another lady. I'm sorry."

"No, ma'am," she said. "Not Mr. Elliot Curtis. His brother, Gabriel."

Elliot's mouth dropped open. "Gabriel! You are my brother's wife!"

She nodded. "We were married in Virginia six months ago."

Elliot and I stared at one another. Well, my first question about her accent had been answered. She was a Southern woman from Virginia. Her explanation also answered a second question as to why she had not decided to speak to us for so many weeks. A Southern woman to marry a Northern man, so soon after the wrenching war, was not a common complement for either of them. If Aunt Curtis and Jane treated a fellow Maine girl like myself with such contempt, think of a Virginian girl! I was immediately glad Miss Annie had chosen to come to the medical office instead of the Curtis House.

Elliot was amazed. "My God, he's been in Virginia this whole time. Miss Annie, we have had no word after Gabriel left for war. Can you please tell us where he is?"

"Yes, do tell us at once!" I said, nodding vigorously. "Dr. Curtis abruptly departed in October to find him. Have they been reunited?"

"One at a time! One at a time." Annie laughed. "My goodness, you all are like bees to honey!"

Elliot and I giggled. She took a deep breath, and looked at my cousin.

"I'll answer you first, doc. I do not know where my husband is, which is why I journeyed up to the North. And yes, Miss Esther" - turning to me - "his father did come down to Virginia in October, and they were reunited. I was the one who sent the telegram to Dr. Curtis. My poor Gabriel fell sick last summer. We tried everything, but he was getting worse and worse. Finally, he told me to send for the best doctor he knew. His father."

Her eyes darkened when she spoke of my uncle, and I felt uneasy.

What could be the reason for such a reaction? Surely Ambrose had not done either of them harm in any way. Elliot, however, swelled with pride upon hearing Ambrose's praise.

"I am a temporary substitute for my father's experience. He is, indeed, a greatly respected and admired physician. I do hope he was able to help my brother?"

"As for how good a doctor he is, I don't happen to know." Annie folded her arms, reminding me of Lara when she pouted. "We offered him hospitality and all the supplies he needed. Next thing I know, he's run off - and taken my husband with him!"

"What?" said Elliot and I in unison.

"It's true. I saw it myself. Took me two days to figure out where they were goin'. Finally, I learned from a neighbor that Doctor Curtis brought Gabriel to Boston."

A loud knock rapped on the door, and a man's voice bellowed for the physician. Elliot glanced at the clock, looking sheepish.

"Oh, I'm sorry Esther and Miss Annie. Excuse me."

"You have shown me such kindness, Doc Curtis. I can see why Gabriel spoke so well of you."

Blushing, Elliot left to see to the patient.

"Sounds like Mr. Abbott," I said. "I confess I'm unsure as to why my uncle would take Gabriel to Boston. Perhaps there was better medical care there."

She sniffed. "Well, maybe ... and you know him better than I. But I was madder than a shorn sheep. I packed all my things and spent my last dollars on the train ticket North. And what do you think happened when I got to Boston?"

I had a feeling, judging by her appearance when first we met, that her arrival was met with disappointment.

"Nothing. He wasn't there. I searched the whole city for weeks and didn't find him at all. Finally, I say that I've got to get to Portland. I know he had family up here, so here I came."

I sighed, resting my hand on hers in comfort. "I can't imagine the effort you have gone through to find Gabriel. You can stay here as long as you wish, for I do not believe - if I may be plain - that you would find hospitality at the Curtis House."

She nodded. She did understand, for no doubt Gabriel had never wanted to return home.

"Have you any family in Virginia that I can contact?"

She shook her head. "No. I live in Richmond. The war was ... well, my family is gone."

I nodded. "Except for my sister Lara, mine is, too."

She squeezed my fingers, and I began to feel a little better.

"Esther, you have treated me with such care. Even if you had known I was a Southern girl, it wouldn't have made a difference." She paused, then looked at me with a knowing smile. "That Doc Curtis is a handsome fellow, and quite the gentleman, too. It's a wonder he don't take more of a fancy to you."

I laughed out loud. "That would be a lovely idea, and I believe Elliot will make an excellent husband, but we are cousins. Our mothers were sisters."

She flushed. "Oh. Then I am glad to call you family, then."

"Both Elliot and I are glad you came to us."

On the other side of the curtain, Elliot wished a grumbling Mr. Abbott a good day. He reappeared on the sickbed side of the room, nodding to Miss Annie and me.

"Yes, Miss Annie," he said as he pulled up a chair and took a seat. "We are glad to have you."

Her eyes welled with happiness and relief. Elliot fished out a handkerchief and handed it to her. I knew what it felt like to be an outcast in a strange place and the joy of finding a sudden friendship. I'd found it in Elliot, and I in turn offered it to this girl. She, who looked so much like Lara, could claim the same family connection of love and strength in my heart.

"Help me find my husband," she said. "I do so worry for him."

"We will, Miss Annie." Elliot grabbed my shoulder. "Esther, you can return home and inform my mother. She can send telegrams to my father's acquaintances in Boston."

My heart gave a sudden leap of fearful apprehension. "Elliot, your idea is a sound one, but Aunt Curtis would not act upon it."

"She will, and she must," he insisted. "Esther, I beg you. It is imperative that we find my father and my brother."

I bit my lip, utterly torn between refusing him and returning to the Curtis House. There was no possible way my aunt would actively seek out her husband, when for months she had so clearly reveled in his absence. To inform her of this new development and hope to enlist her help was almost inconceivable.

"Esther, please!"

Reluctantly, I nodded. It was not my life alone involved. I couldn't let my cousin or Annie spend any more time than necessary separated from Gabriel. He must come home.

I rose from the bed and picked up my winter bonnet. With a promise to return in the morning with my errand completed, I put on my mittens and left the office. The February day was bright and sunny, but bitterly cold. My journey down Congress Street froze my cheeks and dried the inside of my nose, but my thoughts were quite occupied.

Why had my uncle separated Annie and Gabriel? Where had he taken his son? And what would Aunt Curtis say? As elated as I was that Annie had made a full recovery, the pit in my stomach would not be ignored. I felt nervous.

I turned onto Spring Street and hurried past the homes towards the Curtis House. It was the first time in months I'd felt relief upon seeing it at the corner of High Street. I entered the carriageway and had taken ten steps towards the back door, when I stopped and turned around to go in the front door.

I was not a servant today.

As expected, my use of the doorknocker brought Mr. Jakes. But to my surprise, his cravat was askew and his normally immaculate composure harried.

"Miss Perry!" he said, forgetting to call me the usual 'girl.'

"I am calling upon my aunt," I said. "Show me into the parlor."

"Mrs. Curtis is indisposed to see you," he replied with a sudden nasty look. "Good day."

And with that, the front door slammed in my face. For a second, I hardly believed he'd done so. But I was still under his command as part of the help. So, I shrugged and went around to the back door, where nobody would refuse me.

Everyone in the kitchen was frantic. Rosie banged away at the range as if her life depended on how much noise she could make with cast iron pots. Josie ran to and from the laundry room carrying mountainous loads, and Peg scurried from the sink to the range and back to the sink like a mouse. I caught the scullery maid's attention as she zipped past me again.

"Peg, what is going on?"

"Esther!" She looked both surprised and relieved. "Thank goodness you can help. The master has arrived!"

"What!"

"He's taken to his bed. And -" she lowered her voice, making it almost impossible to hear beneath Rosie's thundering - "he's brought Mr. Curtis. His son!"

She scurried off again. I was so shocked I stood in the middle of the kitchen, my mind blank and my limbs unable to move. All thought drained from my head like a hole in a water barrel.

But then the most incredible feeling spread throughout me. At first it was a trickle, a tiny stream. Then it grew and grew as it rushed into my arms and legs. I felt I was to burst, and I erupted into laughter. I stood in the kitchen with the servants running all about me, and laughed and laughed. I laughed so hard tears came to my eyes and my vision blurred. My stomach started hurting, but I kept laughing.

Rosie turned around and pointed her spoon at me like a lance. "Get off it, girl! You're not standing there all day!"

I felt so joyous I didn't care how she spoke to me. My uncle had returned. My cousin was home. My dark hours were over. The servants couldn't order me around, and Aunt Curtis wasn't my mistress any longer.

Still giggling like a school-girl, I turned on my heels and exited the house the way I'd entered. I skipped down Spring Street on my way to tell Elliot and Annie the good news.

Ambrose and Gabriel had returned.

24

My uncle and cousin may have returned, but my heady reaction to the news was quite short-lived. Annie slept most of the rest of the afternoon after complaining of a headache, and both Elliot and I were so busy with ailment-laden patients I hadn't time to think, let alone absorb the strange twist in my circumstances.

"There must be some way you can come home tonight," I said to Elliot at the end of the day.

He removed the stethoscope from his ears and straightened, his back cracking. "I'm afraid there isn't, Esther. Father hasn't come to relieve me, has he? Then here is where I'll stay."

There would be no persuading him, no matter how many years it had been since he'd seen his brother. I wished him a good-night and walked back to the house alone. On my way down Congress Street, I privately admitted that now that I'd had a chance to ponder my uncle's return, it was improbable my position would change. Nor was I likely to see Lara soon. As far as I knew Gabriel was still ill, so I'd be of more use quiet and duty-bound. The house was dark when I arrived, so I softly stole upstairs and went to bed.

In the morning, my feelings had calmed themselves. The time spent wearing my old calico and being a servant was coming to a close, but not yet. Standing before the little crooked mirror, I turned my head to one side and then the other. Would my uncle notice a change in me since autumn? It was like half a lifetime had passed.

The mood in the kitchen had also subdued. My breakfast duties were so rote, I made the biscuit dough and poured tea without a second thought. During a quiet moment, I sought Adelaide's attention.

"What is to become of my position?"

She slammed the butter mold onto the butter and dumped the pats on the butter plate.

"How should I know?" she said crossly. "You do as you're told."

Her brusque tone set my jaw and forced me to accept my reality. No more was spoken on the subject as we finished the breakfast trays. I was pleased to see a third tray for Ambrose, but my mysterious cousin received nothing but a pot of tea and the last crust of Sunday's bread. As I reached for a tray, Adelaide stopped me.

"Mrs. Keswick will help this morning, girl."

I stood by silently as the housekeeper entered the kitchen and stayed out of the servants' way until they had left. As Rosie began handing dirty dishes to Peg, I fell in to help. The little maid was unusually quiet and didn't offer a smile. When we were finished washing the breakfast dishes, I excused myself from the sink and stepped out the back door. Beyond the dry goods storage room was the laundry, where Josie was starching shirts. They were men's shirts, undoubtedly belonging to Ambrose. I felt a little better. He really was home.

"Have you received any word on my duties?" I asked.

Josie shook her head, and I started sorting soiled clothing. Josie was not curious about Dr. Curtis's return. She was, however, keenly interested in the double wedding and throughout the morning regaled me with a steady stream of gossip.

"Miss Curtis showed her new bridal dress in the parlor yesterday, so's I heard from Mrs. Keswick."

"Oh," was all I could think of to say.

The topic brought more than a few pangs to my heart. Henry lived three blocks away, but may as well have been on the moon. April ninth suddenly seemed a short time away.

After hanging the laundry with Josie, I wandered back to the kitchen. I felt constricted and strangely aimless. My aunt would be displeased to find me idle, while Ambrose would want me enjoying my quiet occupations at home. Since it was likely we would host a dinner party soon to announce my uncle's homecoming, I went into the dining room to polish the silver.

So intent was I in my small task that I passed an hour in the empty dining room, a box of flatware, coffee pitchers and urns on the table. There was something satisfying about keeping one's hands occupied when the mind and heart were fretful.

"Esther?"

I was so startled upon hearing my first name spoken in the house, I dropped my polishing cloth and the serving spoon. Fumbling for it in my lap, I hastily glanced up.

And there, leaning against the doorway in the shadowed hall, was Ambrose. He was so pale, thin and wan, I couldn't have recognized him on a sunny day. He looked as if someone had drawn out his life breath over a long period of time. Any joyous thought upon seeing his return was replaced by the nurse's instinct to see him comfortable. I set down the serving spoon and hurried to the doorway.

"Sir, let me assist you."

I tucked my shoulder beneath his arm and leaned a portion of his weight against my body, my arm encircling his back. His clothes were wrinkled and needed a washing, and his eyes were sunken and dark. But the thin-lipped smile he gave me was genuine pleasure.

"Esther, do not fuss. I cannot tell you how glad I am to see you."

"And I you, sir."

He clasped me about the waist. We slowly crossed the front hall and entered the parlor, where I helped him into the large wingback chair by the fire. I went to work building up the fire in such an expert fashion I barely got my hands dirty. I drew the curtains against the weak February sunlight and fetched a wool blanket from the back of the sofa to warm him. He sat as quietly and obediently as a child, watching me with a look of warm relief.

"If only I had been as well taken care of this long winter," he said.

"You were much missed, sir. It is a pleasure to have you home."

I finished placing his slippers upon his feet and offered to fetch any other item he needed, but he declined. He indicated he wanted me near him, so I drew over a chair and sat opposite him. A sense of quiet calm settled in me, and I realized it was the first time I had sat, truly sat and relaxed in the parlor since he left. He also looked serene, but then his thick black brows drew together in an expression of serious gravity.

"Gabriel is upstairs, resting. His condition is weak and the traveling was horrid. One inn ran out of coal."

Where had they traveled from? I shuddered to think of spending a freezing night at an unheated inn, especially in such an invalid condition. Where had he taken Gabriel after parting him from Annie? I found it difficult to think my uncle was capable of any deliberate cruelty. But he was also weak, so I did not wish to press him.

"Jane has gone out this morning. When she does return, I wish to speak with her urgently. Elliot, I presume, is at the doctor's office."

"Yes, sir. He has kept your position with great care and attentiveness."

"That is a blessing." He inhaled and let his breath out. "I apologize for not being able to converse more, but I wish to be alone. I am tired."

I rose from the chair. "I will prepare some tea. Would you like a book to read?"

"No, thank you." He sighed, still staring into the fire. "Rest this afternoon as well, Esther."

He had no idea how soothing those words were. To rest, to be at ease once more. It was a tiny luxury I had not known.

"I will, sir."

The firelight showed silvery strands streaking through his black hair. It had been a hard winter on both of us. I quietly left the room and, instead of going to the kitchen and up the back staircase, went to the front foyer. I paused at the base of the main staircase for a moment. Marveling at how simple a thing it was to be able to walk up the same stairs as the rest of the Curtis family.

Where Jane had gone this morning was anyone's guess, but Aunt Curtis must have accompanied her, for I met neither of them. I reached the second-floor landing, slipped past Gabriel's room and walked up the final stairs to my little shabby servant's room. My gray and black striped dress had hung on a wall hook ever since the night I'd moved to the room. I took it down and donned it with a tremendous relief. Lara's old calico had served me as well as I'd served the Curtis family.

When I looked at myself in the mirror, I looked like me. Perhaps a bit too thin, and my cheeks could use some color. But the face in the mirror was the Esther I knew, and not an unhappy maid struggling to work and aching for the life she'd known.

I adjusted the pretty lace collar at my throat, pinned up my hair, and went down the back staircase to the kitchen. Rosie was preparing a luncheon stew, so I set the kettle on the range to heat the water. Adelaide came back into the kitchen with the empty breakfast trays and placed them in the sink.

"You're not dressed properly," she said. "Dr. Curtis is in the parlor."

"Yes, he is," I said as I took a teacup and saucer from the china cupboard.

"Why didn't you tell me?"

I paused at the sideboard. A prickling of anger caused my teeth to clench. "With my uncle home, I am no longer under your authority."

Her eyes narrowed. "And who are you to be so ungrateful?"

"Who am I?" I dumped a teaspoon of sugar into the teacup. "I am a member of this family. And I am not a servant any longer."

Her eyes widened, and her lips moved as if to retort. But she snapped her mouth shut and stomped out of the kitchen. I poured hot water into

Ambrose's teacup and made a cup for myself. I set the two on a tray and stepped from the kitchen. As I made my way up the hall, Mr. Jakes approached the front door and opened it.

Aunt Curtis and Jane walked in, making plenty of noise with their incessant chatter and foot-stomping. Jane's cheeks were red from the cold, and my aunt dabbed her nose with a handkerchief as she removed her cloak and muff.

"Mother, they should come next Saturday. Tomorrow night is the opening of the play at the Jefferson Theatre. I do wish to go."

"Of course you do, dear."

Then, like a soldier locked on his target, Aunt Curtis spied me. Her expression changed from jovial and elated to serious, her eyes cold and her forehead lowered.

"What is it, girl?"

Emboldened by my recent exchange with Adelaide, I straightened my shoulders and announced: "Aunt Curtis, my name is Esther. Your husband is in the parlor and wishes to speak with Jane."

My aunt glowered. Jane, her eyebrows and nose as elevated as they could be, peered at me.

"Mother, do not twist your petticoats over her high opinion of herself. I shall go see what Father wants."

Aunt Curtis grimaced. "We shall go in together."

Arm in arm like a pair of paper dolls, the two ladies haughtily passed by me and swept into the parlor. I allowed myself a private chuckle over their ridiculousness before following them into the room. They had paused in front of Ambrose, neither of them bothering to greet him with pleasantries.

"What matter, pray tell, requires Jane's attention so urgently?" Aunt Curtis demanded.

"Yes, Father," Jane added.

I crossed over to the parlor table and set the tray down. Ambrose's gaze softened upon seeing me.

"Ah, thank you, Esther," he said pleasantly.

Jane cast her conceited glance at me, tapping her foot in impatience. "We will have this conversation in private."

Instead of leaving, I sat down in the chair I'd occupied earlier. Ambrose sipped his tea and then set the cup on the saucer.

"What I have to say is not a private matter, Jane," he said. "I have a task for you."

She stiffened, no doubt wondering if this task would interfere with her previous engagements. "What would you have me do?"

"Gabriel is ill. He requires more care than Mrs. Keswick can provide alone. You are to assist with his nursing until he recovers."

She stared at him. She couldn't have looked more surprised than if he'd asked her to empty his chamber-pot.

"You think me the ideal person for this? Whatever gave you the notion I have the time? I am soon to be married and wedding preparations are underway."

From the look on his face, my uncle anticipated her reaction. "This is not a request. Your brother needs your care."

Aunt Curtis, coldly silent up until now, slid a step closer to her husband. He did not appear ill at ease by her presence and continued to sip his tea.

"What you have requested of Jane is improper. I will not have my daughter acting so degradingly."

"Nursing her own brother is not degrading," my uncle said dryly. "But it appears both you and Jane lack the necessary compassion."

"Father, it is not a matter of compassion. I wish Gabriel a swift recovery." Jane took a step forward until both women were standing side by side before him. "But I have not been raised to perform such menial tasks."

"You know how sensitive ladies are to men and their indecencies," Aunt Curtis added. "We are not fit to be physicians like you."

Ambrose sat silently. He had heard more than enough and was struggling to keep his composure. His eyebrows were knitted, and his eyes crackled with such dark blackness, I feared he would overexert himself.

I rose from the chair and approached him.

"Sir, do not trouble yourself. I will nurse Gabriel."

He shook his head with curt decision. "No, Esther. You are a guest of my house, and I would not have you treated as an inferior."

I raised my eyes and looked straight at my aunt. "Do not worry, sir. I am not an inferior. Rest now. I will look after him."

"Ambrose," my aunt sneered, "you cannot possibly let Esther see to Gabriel. Let Adelaide or a hired nurse care for him."

She could argue with him all day as far as I was concerned. My uncle's position on this would not budge, and neither would mine. Unexpectedly, I was to meet my mysterious cousin, and I could not wait to tell him about his wife. And Henry. I smiled at my uncle and walked towards the parlor door.

"No, Lucia," Ambrose said. "Whether it is her duty or not, Esther is well-suited. She has her mother's kind heart."

As I opened the parlor door, I was overwhelmed by the rush of tears to my eyes. Buried feelings, hidden over the long snowy weeks as I'd struggled to keep to my duties. For months, my mother's name had never been mentioned. The one time it had, that morning with Mrs. Keswick, I was labeled a flawed copy of her sins.

My uncle's praise pained my heart, for it was the first time I'd heard words of compassion spoken about her. And that my kindness was a mirror of hers. I didn't know if Mother and Ambrose were well-acquainted, but she had shown him the best of herself.

Now he saw the same kindness in me.

25

While ascending the stairs to the second floor, I thought how funny it was that Elliot should be the one to help me become a better nurse, so then I could repay the favor by assisting his own brother. And only yesterday I had finally learned the true identity of my cousin's wife, so it would be a pleasure to tell him she was in town.

My aunt and uncle spoke in heated tones downstairs in the parlor. I didn't catch any words, though there was little doubt I was the subject of their contention. I turned right at the landing and crossed over to what I had privately nicknamed Gabriel's door. I opened the door and entered the little hallway partition separating the two bedchambers. For my entire duration in this house, the door on the left had been locked.

Not today.

Curiosity replaced any nervousness, but I still hesitated. The bedroom termed 'not used' was definitely now occupied, but by whom? Well, I couldn't discover the answer standing blankly on the landing. So, I quietly turned the brass knob. No stubbornness or struggling with the door. It simply opened, as if it had always been inclined to do so. I stepped into the room to meet my newest patient.

His room was the least spacious of the family bedchambers. It was not too much larger than a servant's room and just as plain. An old canopy bed of an antique style heavily draped with faded tapestries occupied a corner across from the sooty fireplace. There were hardly any other furnishings save a dented wash-stand and several dilapidated chairs. A pair of huge trunks took up much of the chamber's space, sprawled wide open and revealing an assortment of hastily packed items, including clothing, books, candle stubs, and tintypes. The only thing in the room that looked new were the large curtains, closed against the two windows and emitting scarcely a hint of the February daylight. I made my way through the dimness to one of the caned chairs, drew it up alongside the bed, and seated myself.

I had little view in the low light, but what I could see of my cousin's features as he slept greatly interested me. It was like I was a naturalist studying a new species of flower for the first time. His face was handsome, but not in a classic way like Henry, nor did he have Elliot's boyish look. He had a straight nose, full lips and thick black brows the same as his father's. His hair was also dark, richly deep, and lay in waves about his head. But his complexion was sallow, which I took to be the result of his illness.

I would have sat there for a while in silence without disturbing him. He soon stirred, pushing the tattered bedclothes down and turning onto his back. After a great long sigh, he at last opened his eyes and rubbed them.

"Sir?"

It was inevitable I'd startle him. He turned sharply towards me, his face still half in shadow.

"Sir, it's all right. You're home."

"I know where I am." His tone was flat, with the tiniest trace of a Virginia accent. "And you are?"

"Esther," I said, amused by his directness. "I'm to look after your care."

"What are your qualifications?"

I leaned back in the chair, folded my arms and regarded him for a long moment. Well, he'd inherited his brusqueness from his mother, no doubt about that.

"What qualifications would you like me to possess?" If he was to question me, I had questions for him!

"Competency with ill patients. The strong stomach required for the sick-room. A knowledge of medicines and remedies."

"That is quite the list of attributes, but I believe I have them." I leaned forward, enjoying his assessment of me. "I also have a witness, should you care to check."

"A credible witness, I hope." He stared up at the bed's canopy with a hand on his forehead. "I cannot have my health in the hands of a confident amateur."

"As credible as they come."

When I didn't say the name, Gabriel lay motionless. Finally, he looked at me, annoyed.

"Who, then?"

I chuckled. "Your wife."

A look of disbelief passed over his face, accompanied by a loud scoff. "Not only are you an amateur, you are deceitful. I would not speak of a wife if I had one, nor would I reveal personal details to a stranger."

I laughed. "You don't begin an acquaintance thinking the best of people."

Normally this kind of sparring would have set me ill at ease. But Gabriel's blunt manner struck me as funny. It would be even funnier when he realized I was telling the truth.

"You are mistaken on all three accusations, Gabriel," I continued, and he started at the sound of his name. "I am not an amateur, deceitful, or a stranger. I am your cousin, and I have been helping your brother Elliot as a nurse. Your wife, Annie, traveled up from Virginia, and she is currently at the doctor's office, eager to see you."

He clearly didn't know what to say in response, for he lay frozen and wide-eyed. All possible crossness had disappeared from his face, replaced by a set and determined brow. He suddenly pushed the bedclothes down and began rising with the strength of a healthy man. I immediately got to my feet and attempted to restrain him, but he thrashed his limbs.

"Calm yourself," I said sharply. "She is recovering and would not be able to see you anyway. You're no good a husband if you become more ill."

"Let me go, then," he shot back.

I acquiesced and released his arm. He begrudgingly lay back upon the pillow. But his eyes darted about and he looked wildly disturbed. After settling back upon the chair, I asked if he needed refreshments or hot water for his pitcher and ewer. He shook his head.

"You could have stricken me with the shock of this news. I wonder that you aren't here to do me more harm than good."

"That is unlikely. This illness has given you a large amount of distrust that isn't necessary. Or," I added after a moment's pause, "it has come not from illness but rather your family."

"My family doesn't understand me," he said in a low voice. "I may as well have been switched at birth."

I half-smiled. He was not happy to be back in his old room, at his childhood home. If it weren't for his poor state of health, he'd rush down to the doctor's office, grab his wife, and be on the next train south. But it would be at least a fortnight before he could rise from his bed, let alone manage such a journey.

"Tell me about Annie," I said, partly to take his mind from his agitation and partly to learn more. "How did you meet her?"

He didn't answer me for a long moment, and during that time I thought he had shut me out. I could have been Queen Victoria herself for all he cared. But he eventually turned his head sideways to look at me.

"No doubt Elliot has told you of my abrupt farewell. It's true. I left home to join the war. I was in many battles and campaigns as a private in the Fifth Maine Regiment. But at Petersburg I was wounded." He pointed down the bed. "In my lower leg. It was a clean shot. After I was discharged, I didn't want to come home. I didn't want to leave Virginia, either. So, I stole a Confederate uniform and pretended to be from Richmond."

His story was quite remarkable, not only for its adventure but in the way he was telling it. He'd created a new life for himself when his old one proved unsatisfactory. I'd also felt forced from my home, but under different circumstances.

"That's when I met Annie. Her father was dead, her mother was ill and they'd lost everything. I stayed with her when the Union soldiers captured and burned the city. I don't know how we survived, but we did. Her mother was killed. It was horrifying."

He stopped, breathing deeply.

"We sought quarters in an abandoned home and helped rebuild it after the war ended. I took a few odd jobs here and there for money, while Annie sewed clothes. It's not been easy, but we're happy together. We married in August. Then, on September fifteenth, I was stricken with a strange illness. I coughed for weeks and could barely work. It got worse and worse, so Annie said that I should contact Father. He was the best physician, and she had faith he could cure me. But she didn't know what he would do."

Gabriel then broke off his story and began to cough. The hairs on the back of my neck stood up. It was that wracking, fearful, awful cough. A rush of memories flooded my mind, so real I was struck dumb. Mother collapsing in the field, the doctor's damning prognosis. And September fifteenth was the day she died.

"Oh, God," I said. "I know what ails you, Gabriel. My mother ... she had the same cough. I cared for her last summer."

"Then," he wheezed, "you had better nurse me back to health. I must be with Annie again."

I nodded, trying to keep my composure. But I was in anguish. It was like the pain of that horrible night Mother died had resurfaced to torment me. I rose to my feet, then reached over and held my cousin's hand. His fingers were thin, his wrist a cold bone.

"You will recover. I lost my mother, but I won't lose you. I promise."

"Don't ... promise what you can't deliver, Esther," he said. "I've been let down by my family too many times."

"So have I," I said. "Rest now. I will return later."

He closed his eyes and turned onto his side, away from me. I pulled the bed curtains together and left him in relative peace. I had much to do to take care of my cousin. The gnawing fear in the back of my mind about Gabriel's illness would cause immense anxiety if I didn't calm myself and rest as well.

I walked up the back staircase and entered the servant's room. Then I gathered my carpet-bag with its sheet music folio and the rest of my meager belongings. I was packed and ready to leave this strange cold room, where I had cried so many tears and struggled against such pressing deep tides.

I stepped over to the window and gazed through the wavy glass. Months ago, I had stood here on an October morning in my shawl and bare feet, feeling as lost and alone as the last of a tree's leaves. I pressed my forehead against the glass. But instead of wishing I could plunge into the courtyard below, the glass cooled my heated brow. It was over.

After leaving the room, I walked down the stairs and entered my former bedchamber. I set the carpet-bag next to the bed and sat upon the white bedspread. The room was cold and quiet, and the shutters on the front windows were closed.

Yet, for the first time since coming to this house, it felt like I was home. Lara wasn't with me, but my uncle and Gabriel and Elliot were. I had rejoined my family as one of their own.

And I was a part of them.

26

I yawned and stirred, drawing my shawl across my shoulders. The room was chilly. I had fallen asleep in the chair across from Gabriel's bed. My neck ached, for I had lain curled against the wing of the armchair. I moved my head from side to side. At last I felt steady enough to rise, so I crossed over to the bed to check on my cousin.

He breathed evenly as he slept, his arm above his head, his thick lashes fluttering against his cheek. I was glad to see he hadn't grown weaker since yesterday. I had seen patients at the doctor's office who were far less ill and hadn't gone through such a harrowing ordeal as war and a perilous journey home.

Rubbing my shoulder, I reached beneath the bed and pulled out the chamber-pot. I couldn't help a half-smile as I thought of the weeks I'd performed such a degrading chore for my aunt, only to perform it for my cousin as well. But what a difference willingness made!

Gabriel did not awaken, and I crossed to the bedchamber door and closed it behind me. Sunlight shone through the hallway windows, one of those rare pleasant winter days with the sky as blue as a hyacinth. After I took care of Gabriel's chamber-pot, I'd draw a hot sponge bath and change into a fresh dress.

While descending the main staircase, I was surprised to hear the sound of horses' hooves in the carriageway. Somebody was arriving at an early hour. It must be Elliot or one of the other city doctors to call upon Ambrose.

Suddenly, the door blew open and there stood Henry Vallencourt. A mad rush sped through my belly and blasted my face with unexpected heat. At the same time, my stomach quivered and dropped to my knees. Embarrassed, I bowed my head.

"Miss Perry."

Any thought of vanishing without him noticing me was silenced. I had no choice but to look up into his eyes, holding the chamber-pot in front of me like a hideous offering.

"Good morning, Mr. Vallencourt. If you'll please excuse me, sir."

He chuckled. "You seem to be occupied. Very well, then."

Good heavens. I ducked and walked down the hallway out to the kitchen. After scrubbing the chamber-pot in the sink, I returned to the hallway. Voices were coming from the parlor, and it sounded like Henry and my uncle. Not wishing to interrupt, I made my way past the open parlor door. But my uncle called for me.

"Ah, Esther. Please come in."

I sucked in my breath and entered the room. Ambrose, looking in far better spirits than he had the previous afternoon, sat before a large cheery fire with a mug of coffee. Henry wiped his mouth with a napkin and stood as I entered. I nodded to both of them and walked over to stand in front of my uncle. He motioned for me to sit, and I thanked him as I did so.

"You look much improved, sir."

"Indeed, Esther, I am." He indicated his guest. "Henry has asked about Gabriel's condition. I told him you have become his nurse, so please inform him."

Henry looked at me earnestly with an openness I had not seen in him before. He did not resemble the frustrated young man at the Vallencourt mansion. I was taken aback by his change in manner, and it took me a moment to reply.

"He is resting, sir, and will recover. But I do not expect him to rise for at least twelve days."

"Traveling all that way in the winter?" Henry shook his head. "How deplorable."

"I had little choice," Ambrose said gravely. "I found him in such squalor and appalling conditions. I took him with me to Boston, to be seen by my finest colleagues. But when his illness worsened, we had to come home."

I was pleased to discover where Gabriel had been these past few months, though to not mention Annie was perhaps best at the moment. Her identity could be revealed once Gabriel recovered.

"So it seems." Henry sipped his coffee. "Well, Miss Perry, you have been put up to nursing duty. I should think your uncle would hire a servant for that."

"He could, sir," I said quietly. "But I wanted to help him."

He gave me a strange look, but Ambrose nodded. "Come now, Henry, you do not know Esther at all if you think she lacks the capability."

"That was not my assumption at all, I assure you Dr. Curtis."

But Henry was still looking at me strangely. So strangely that I had to look away.

Unfortunately, we were interrupted from further conversation by the entrance of his fiancee. Both Jane and her mother had at last made their appearance. They were still wearing wool cloaks and gloves, so they had returned home from being out. I expected the two harsh glances that I received, but not Henry's reaction. He did not rise from the sofa to greet her, a gesture unlike his formal breeding.

"Henry, dearest! What brings you to call upon us so early? I had it in mind you would not come until the afternoon."

"I wanted to see Gabriel," Henry said. "You have been out."

"Of course," Aunt Curtis said. "Jane has selected the flowers for the church bouquets. I tell you, Henry, it has been quite an ordeal for her to decide. She does want it to be perfect, you know."

"I see." He traced a finger around the rim of his coffee mug. "Your father tells me that Gabriel is being nursed back to health by Miss Perry."

Jane adjusted her hat, laughing in her off-handed way. "Can you believe I was asked to do such a thing?"

Henry looked up at her. "What do you mean?"

"Why, before Esther said she would. She dearly saved me from spending my days in the sick-room. I have not the stomach for such a duty."

Henry turned to my uncle. "Is this true, sir?"

Ambrose nodded. "I thought Jane more suited to the task, since Gabriel is her brother. However, she refused."

"And with good cause, Henry," Aunt Curtis said. "Your fiancee has not the time nor the proper training for it."

An uneasy silence settled upon Henry and he sat transfixed on the sofa, his brows knitted as if he was deep in thought.

"I am perplexed at your actions, Jane."

"Come, Henry," she said with a flip of her gloved hand. "What actions can you possibly have trouble with?"

"Refusing to take care of Gabriel. It shows a lack of compassion."

She folded her arms. "He called you such awful things and then ran off to war without telling a soul. What compassion should I show him?"

The room went deathly quiet. Aunt Curtis patted her daughter's hand, nodding in agreement. But my uncle's face was like an angry lion, his eyes burning beneath his dark brow. Henry also had such a grimness to his mouth he looked as if he was at a funeral. He set his mug on the saucer and clattered it on the table. Then for the first time since Jane and Aunt Curtis had entered the room, he rose to his feet. He gave a nod to Ambrose.

"Thank you for the coffee, sir. I believe I must be going."

"Why, you told me you had no other engagements today," Jane said.

"You were misinformed."

He strode towards the door with the utmost purpose. My aunt

sensed that something was quite amiss and hurried to block him from leaving.

"Can you not spare another hour? You see how Jane has desired your company."

He stopped and glared at her. Indeed, I was astonished at his behavior. It reminded me of the luncheon conversation the day he and Alexandra had arrived for Lara. He'd been so firm insisting on inviting Gabriel to the wedding. There was no way my aunt could change his mind.

"I will not stay another hour, Mrs. Curtis. That is my final decision."

His eyes were so resolved and his jaw so set, she had no choice but to step aside. He nodded to both her and her daughter and left the room. I could hear him fetching his things in the foyer. Then there was a slam as the door closed behind him.

Aunt Curtis stood motionless by the parlor doorway. Then her hands went right to her hips and she skewered Jane with her piercing gaze.

"Well, I'll be! What have you done, Jane?"

She crossed her arms. "I have done nothing amiss, Mother."

"Of course you have. You paraded yourself to be a frivolous fool who cares for nothing except flowers!"

"Ladies!" Ambrose barked. "Neither one of you had the decency to rise to the occasion and show a better side of yourself to Mr. Vallencourt. It is no wonder his opinion was soured this morning."

Without any other to blame, of course I was next to be targeted.

"Young lady," my aunt seethed, "I am severely disappointed. You goaded Mr. Vallencourt into expressing his opinion and it has soured against us."

Ambrose slammed his coffee mug. "Lucia, you are not to turn your bitterness upon Esther."

I could have withstood another hour of her raining anger. It made no difference to me since my uncle was home. Ambrose sighed.

"Esther, please go upstairs and look after Gabriel. Mr. Vallencourt will want to see him soon."

"Yes, sir."

I quietly retreated to the parlor doorway. With the tumult over Henry and Jane, I had not had the opportunity to ask when I could see Lara again. Even with Ambrose home, Aunt Curtis would do everything she could to keep me separated from my sister.

I stepped into the empty foyer and was on my way to the kitchen for the chamber-pot when the front door blew open. A man entered, rubbing his fingers together against the chilly blast of winter air. At first I thought it was Elliot. But then he lifted his head and I looked into the kindly eyes of Henry Vallencourt.

"Sir!" I exclaimed. "I'm sorry, I thought you had gone."

He blew on his hands, looking at me again in that rather friendly way. My heart suddenly began beating right in my throat. His gaze softened, and a broad smile played at his lips.

"You are right, Miss Perry. I had gone. But the carriage was about to pull away, and I realized I had not done something."

My curiosity heightened and my heart beat faster. "What is that, sir?"

He took off his glove and extended a hand. "I have not thanked you."

The rush in my stomach poured into my knees. My mind shut down and I stared blankly at his hand.

"For what, sir?"

"For helping Gabriel."

I cautiously stepped towards him. Then I reached forward and took his hand. All the room vanished and it was he and I alone, the grandfather clock ticking behind me and the warmth of his hand both comforting and strong.

"I also wish to relay a message," he said. "Miss Lara is eager to see you and has invited you to come to the house as soon as you are able."

Even despite his handsome presence, I couldn't help a chuckle. "My sister is quite forward to invite me herself without the master's permission."

"It is my wish as well," he said. "The rest of my family welcomes you gladly. But, I want Gabriel's good health assured before you arrive. I trust you will carry out your duty with your usual grace."

I nodded. "Yes, sir. I ... I know how much you value his friendship."

He clasped my hand, then gave me a tender smile. It was like I had been out on a fragile limb for so long, only to be caught and carried safely. I'd see Lara. And I would help my cousin, too.

Henry nodded one last time and then quietly shut the door behind him. I stood in the empty foyer, and though a wisp of icy wind chilled my ankles, my hand still felt his warmth.

"Did I hear Henry Vallencourt's voice?"

Jane peered at me from the parlor doorway. It wouldn't matter how I answered her and I didn't want to anyway, so I turned and began walking up the hall towards the kitchen.

"Miss Perry! You will answer me."

I stopped and faced her. "He was here, but he did not ask for you. Good day."

Her haughty sniff made me smile, and I returned to the kitchen with light steps. It was the little victories that made life so sweet.

27

"Do we have cayenne pepper!" I shouted above the din.

Shouting was a must this morning. Between Rosie's incessant clanging, Peg banging away at the sink, the water in the copper washtub bubbling, the crackling fire and the servants' bustling shouts, I hoped they heard me. The reason for my return to the dark and noisy kitchen was to prepare a remedy for my cousin. He recovered fairly well, but I wanted to do what I could to speed up the process. Rosie was cooking Sarah's invalid broth, while I had copied a recipe from Elliot's medical herbal book.

"Cayenne pepper!" I repeated.

Peg turned from the sink and shrugged. I tapped Rosie on the shoulder, but she harrumphed at me. The old girl had reminded me of a rhinoceros upon first meeting her, and that impression was still solid. After no luck rummaging around the kitchen shelves, I stepped out the back door into the dry goods pantry.

My searching brought success, for a tiny amber glass bottle was tucked behind a row of pickled beets. A whiff made my eyes water, so it was definitely cayenne pepper. When I re-entered the kitchen, a familiar sour face greeted me.

"What brings you here, girl?"

"Good morning, Adelaide."

I said nothing further and went about assembling the rest of the ingredients. She was too busy to stand around staring at me, so she picked up her maid's bucket and flounced out of the room.

Ginger, ground with the grater. Honey, apple cider vinegar, water, the pepper, and a bowl and spoon to mix. I measured a quarter teaspoon of the cayenne pepper, then the same dosage of the ground ginger. The pungent mixture was sweetened by a large spoonful of honey. Then an equally large spoonful of the acidic apple cider vinegar and half a teacup full of water. I dared not taste the awful mixture, but its purpose was not flavor. I placed the remedy and a large medicinal spoon on the tray, in addition to a fresh pot of tea and a bowl of the invalid broth.

The tray was lighter than the breakfast one I had carried up to Jane, so I wielded it easily out of the kitchen. As I came up the hall, my uncle was entering the house through the front door. He had regained his strength far quicker than his son and last night had ventured to the medical office to help Elliot.

"Good morning, Esther," he said, taking off his hat and great coat. "I see you are on your way upstairs. Let me not interrupt your duties."

"Good morning, sir," I returned. "How is Elliot faring?"

"Very well," he said, with more than a hint of pride. "He informed me you have assisted him this winter. I must commend you for such fortitude. I had it in mind you would be giving piano lessons, not nursing the ill."

Yes, it would have been nice to spend my days teaching music, I thought ruefully. There was little time to discuss my winter of service, for he was tired and I wanted to help Gabriel. So, we bid each other good day.

Yesterday I had cleaned and straightened Gabriel's bedchamber, so I walked into a tidy room. The trunks and items were put in order and the meager furniture wiped down. The floor was swept, surfaces washed free of dust, and a hearty fire crackled in the fireplace. I set the tray on a stool next to my cousin's bedside, then pushed back the bed-curtains.

"Ah," Gabriel yawned. "Hello there, Esther."

"Your color is improving," I said. "I have brought you a special broth my housekeeper used to make, as well as a cough remedy."

I sat down and spooned a large amount of the cayenne pepper mixture. Gabriel squirmed and coughed as he took it, but he was as obedient as could be through two more spoonfuls.

"Ugh," he spat. "That tastes awful."

"I had a feeling it might."

I handed him the broth, and he liked the onion and garlic flavors. It was a simple beef broth concoction with finely mashed and strained vegetables. When he was finished, I prepared to leave, but he asked me to stay. I took his hand, pleased to find his fingers warm. A tiny flush of pink had returned to his cheeks and his eyes were looking more clear each morning. After I'd sat down again, though, his friendly gaze sobered and he lay quietly, his fingers laced on his chest.

"I heard Henry Vallencourt's voice downstairs a few days ago."

"Yes," I said. "He arrived to inquire after your well-being."

"And what did you say?"

"That it would be a fortnight before you were well enough to see him." I paused, crossing my feet under the chair. "I am sorry not to mention it, but I thought it best."

"Oh, people think they know what's best for others, when they themselves never take the advice."

"You chide me," I said with a laugh. "Perhaps I should have brought the whole Vallencourt family upstairs?"

He looked at me crossly. "Annie doesn't take my nature seriously, either. But, anyway ..."

His voice trailed off. I had a feeling he might continue what he was going to say, and after a few moments of listening to the fire crackle he ventured an interesting question.

"The way Henry asked about me. Was it friendly?"

"To answer you directly, for you asked it directly, yes. He was concerned for your health, and wishes you a full recovery. The fact his own fiancee would not help with your nursing vexed him."

"Fiancee?" Gabriel said. "Who could he be marrying?"

"Your sister, Jane."

"Impossible! Henry Vallencourt would never marry Jane. He's far too ambitious to think of her as anything but a frivolity. And she thinks him stuffy and dull since he is only interested in business."

"Well, despite these differences, they have been engaged since the autumn, with a wedding date of April ninth."

He scoffed. "What a pair, Esther. He'll be at the office, and she'll be at the dress warehouses. One assumes they'll hardly see each other at all."

I sighed. The Henry Vallencourt Gabriel spoke of was the sort of man I'd believed he was. He was proper, he was ambitious, he was forward-thinking and successful. Jane's character had not altered since her brother's absence.

"I'm afraid," I began, "you will find Henry much changed. His father offered him the partnership at the Vallencourt Architectural Firm in December, and he declined. He has lost this ambition of which you speak."

"Rather Jane encouraged him to bury it." Gabriel shook his head. "She has captured him with her beguiling wiles. For the Henry I know, and I have known him my whole life, would never marry her."

She didn't love him, and I'd known that since Thanksgiving. Given my cousin's propensity for directness in conversation, I wasn't going to tell him. Neither would I reveal the ache I felt when I thought of Henry marrying so beneath him in temperament, character, and drive. It was far deeper than mere disappointment.

"I'm not supposed to bother about his welfare anyway," Gabriel said. "I wouldn't be surprised if he didn't care about mine. The last time we were in the same vicinity ... Well, it came to blows."

So, what Elliot had mentioned the day we walked home from church was true. Gabriel and Henry did have a violent quarrel.

"That's when I made up my mind to leave for war. I hated working at the medical office. When I told Father I'd rather starve than be a doctor, he was so angry he threw me out. I went to Henry, and I asked him to come with me. But he would have rather sat at a desk and designed buildings. When he told me he wouldn't, I ... I called him a coward. I said he was too soft to face a gun and would run away. Well, I was harsher than that, but you understand."

Someone called me a coward once. Yes, Henry, I thought. And look what had come of it.

"Before I can blink, we're tussling in the street like dogs. It was stupid, but we were boys. What do boys know?" He sighed and put a hand to his eyes. "Things said that should never have been said. I hated him for not coming and he hated me for leaving."

"I don't believe Henry feels this hatred any longer," I said. "He was firm about inviting you as a wedding guest. This divide between you has caused enough pain and regret. You both shall recover and come out better men for it."

Gabriel rubbed his brow. "Do you always think the best of everyone, Esther?"

"Do you always think the worst of those different from you?" I retorted. "The Vallencourts are reconstructing the city after a devastating fire. Their buildings provide homes and jobs for so many citizens. Is that any less notable than fighting in a war?"

I stopped. I couldn't believe I had become so riled up, but the directness felt refreshing. If only I could speak so boldly to his mother! My cousin looked deep in thought. After a moment, I put my hands on my knees and leaned forward.

"Gabriel, you fell out of Henry's graces. And he fell out of yours. But it is time to make amends. With him and with your father, too."

He sighed, and the strength he had to continue conversation was depleted. I wished him a restful afternoon, picked up the tray, and left the room. A difference of values between two different men and look how much had come of it. One had lost his ambition and the other his trust in others. Being a soldier was no more or less honorable than being an architect or mistress of a farm. It was the higher aim toward good that made the true difference.

Henry could accomplish so much as an architect, and he would never have been suited as a soldier. I still recalled with the most vivid clarity my first impression of Portland. The massive construction projects, hundreds of workers employed, and the incredible array of beautiful new buildings. I'd be honored to help rebuild a destroyed city and provide both shelter and commerce to its citizens. I, who had no home to claim as my own.

Gabriel had introduced doubt into his friend's future plans. Doubt that curtailed him from doing what he was meant to do, doubt that fooled him into thinking Jane Curtis was most suited to make him happy.

Later that afternoon, I was resting in my bedchamber when there was a knock upon the door.

"Yes?" I said, rising to my feet.

It was Adelaide. She looked none too pleased to see me.

"You're wanted in the parlor," she said sullenly. "Miss."

"Thank you, Adelaide."

She slunk off. I straightened my hair, smoothed my dress, then went downstairs. But before I had reached the bottom step, angry voices within the parlor stalled me. It was my aunt and uncle yet again. I was beginning to suspect as long as I stayed in the Curtis House I'd be forever a topic of heated discussion.

It was not my place to question and, in any case, I was weary of it. Rather than knocking, I walked right in. My presence ceased the discussion, though tension still filled the air. Aunt Curtis had her hands on her hips, and my uncle perched in the chair by the fire, fingers gripping his chin, tapping his lip impatiently. I tucked my hands behind my back, as I had done so many times before, and waited.

"Come here, Esther."

I hadn't heard that tone of voice from my uncle since the night we met. Commanding and with the intent to be obeyed. Swallowing hard, I went to him and stood by the fire.

"Let me see your hands."

My hands? After unlacing my fingers, I showed him. With my palms up, he gaped at the calloused skin, split and healed like a knotted tree. Turning my hands over, he inspected the criss-cross scratches, the redness, the swollen knuckles. A bruise by my wrist received a tender kiss. Embarrassed, I tried to loosen my fingers from his grip.

"Let me excuse my appearance, sir. I should have washed -"

"Washed?" he sputtered. "Esther, you have been working."

He said it like I had joined the ladies in the Old Port. I felt demeaned, as if everything I'd done this winter had been beneath my talents. Yet, I had not had a choice.

"Esther has been quite dutiful towards her cousins," Aunt Curtis said. She had crossed her arms over her bosom and was looking at me with a half-smirk. "I believe I have some hand-cream that is said to be a quick healer."

"This is not from four days of feeding broth to my son," Ambrose growled. "Nor is it from helping Elliot at the doctor's office."

I stayed mute, not daring to utter a word. My uncle was a powerful man with an equally powerful character. As for Aunt Curtis, her opinion couldn't have been clearer had it been etched into her skin. Ambrose placed my hands together as if I was praying, and held them closed with his warm fingers.

"A servant came to my bedchamber half an hour ago. She said you have been working as a maid alongside her. All winter!"

He looked horror-stricken and so distraught with emotion the first thing I wanted to do was soothe him.

"Sir," I said, "I am sorry to agitate you."

"No!" he burst out. "Never apologize to me again, Esther. You have done nothing wrong, not one day since you arrived. I wanted to give you a home here. For you to bear this cruelty with incredible grace is ..."

He couldn't go on. He held my hands against his lips as if he wanted to be attached to me forever. I was speechless. Never had I seen this tenderness in him, nor such sorrowful penitence.

Aunt Curtis was as stone-faced and immobile as a mountain. She watched us with a malevolent look, no more remorseful than a predator with its prey. Ambrose dropped my hands and stood up. He took his handkerchief out and daubed his eyes, then addressed his wife with firm calmness.

"I am going to the lawyer, Lucia. You and Jane are to be removed from the inheritance and dropped from my will. Not a single penny of mine will ever be yours again."

"You can't possibly mean that, Ambrose," Aunt Curtis said. "You promised me that money a long time ago."

"I was a fool then, and I'd be a fool now to let you have it."

"You – you leave me nothing to live on? What, shall I be a pauper with a doctor for a husband? And what of your own daughter, Jane? She is to be married!"

"You get nothing that I do not personally give to you, Lucia. Jane will receive a meager allowance until she has found an occupation to prove to me that she can be useful." Ambrose pointed to the parlor door. "Neither your presence nor your input is required any longer. Good day."

She stared at him, then at me. For the first time, I felt pity for her. Whatever reason she had justified to herself for her behavior eroded, and there was nothing remaining but to obey her husband and live with the consequences. But she held her head even higher than before as she turned and strode from the room. I felt such a strange mixture of emotions as I watched her leave. Mercy, fear, curiosity. She had caused me so much grief and misery, but it was over. She couldn't hurt me again.

My uncle's shoulders heaved in a great sigh. He smiled sadly, and when he spoke his voice was soft and kindly.

"Esther, go upstairs and pack your things. I am sorry you have been separated from your sister for so long. I am taking you to the Vallencourts to see her."

Lara! My entire being suddenly flooded with light. It was almost unbearable, the joy I felt. I couldn't help my unexpected gasp or the sob that escaped my throat. Lara. How her beautiful smile and golden cheeriness had lit up my dark days. I'd be with her soon. But then a question emerged in my mind.

"Sir, I cannot leave. Gabriel still needs my care."

"Yes, he has not fully recovered. After I leave you at the Vallencourts, I will go to the medical office and relieve Elliot of his duties. He can come home and help his brother. He will also bring Annie."

"Oh, sir!" I smiled broadly. "Let her have my old bedchamber, right beside him. Thank you for this kindness."

"I owe him that much," my uncle said soberly. "To you, I owe so much more. I saw the way you looked at my wife. For as long as I am here, I promise you will never feel anything but love in this house."

I tried to thank him, but my throat was so full I couldn't. So I went to him and wrapped my arms about him, feeling his comforting strength. I didn't know how to tell him how grateful I was.

And I didn't need to.

28

I flew about my bedchamber packing dresses and belongings. I found Lara's old trunk under the bed. I hardly noticed the shabbiness of the luggage or the plainness of my gray wool dress. I would see Lara, and it didn't matter if I showed up in a rag-bag.

There was a brisk knock on the door. "Miss?"

"Come in," I said as I picked up my sheet music folio. Oh, and I might even get to play the Vallencourt piano. It was as if the world was opening like a bud.

Mr. Jakes was at the door, followed by a stable-boy. The latter picked up my trunk and the former my carpet-bag, holding it out before him like it stank of rotten eggs. My uncle met us at the foot of the stairs, where we bundled into our outer things for the February cold. Then out into the carriage. It felt strange to be back in a moving conveyance, for I had been walking for months. Ambrose squeezed my hand, and we smiled at one another. He started drawing funny pictures on the frosty windows, and I laughed.

As we pulled from the carriageway, I couldn't help a glance up to the third floor. There was the little window of the servant's room where

I'd stayed. Weeks of gazing through its thick panes, feeling loneliness and despair. But then we turned onto High Street and more pleasant thoughts with it.

The drive seemed longer than December, so eager was I to see Lara once more. At last the huge dark shape of the Vallencourt mansion and its wide stone steps came into view.

"It is good to see you happy," my uncle remarked. "Consider this a late Christmas present. Or a birthday present, depending on the day of course."

I cocked my head, puzzled for a moment. My aunt had known my birthday, for it was one of the first things she ever said to me. Perhaps my uncle had forgotten.

"It is the tenth of May," I said. "My mother's favorite month, for that is when the lilacs bloom."

He stared at me as if I'd given him an electric shock. But then the look passed and he smiled once more.

"Remarkable," he murmured. "Quite remarkable."

I had little idea of what he was thinking and was too excited to ponder it further. The carriage pulled all the way up the cleared Vallencourt carriageway. Mr. Murton halted the horses and then jumped down off of his perch to remove the trunk. My faithful carpet-bag was at my feet, so I reached down to retrieve it.

"Well, Esther," my uncle said, "I must request you send my best wishes to your sister. I am not going in, for I have important personal business to attend to."

"Yes, sir," I said. "I understand."

"You do understand. But there is much still to know."

He again looked at me with openness and tenderness. It was like the day at church when we'd stood in the carriage yard and I'd thought he might tell me something private. But he did not then, and he did not now.

I gave him a farewell kiss on the cheek, and the driver opened the door for me. I stepped down, then turned back to wave my uncle goodbye as the carriage pulled away. When I crossed over to the grand front doors, I discovered they were opened and the Vallencourt butler was peering down at me.

"Good afternoon, sir," I said and stepped up into the house.

The Christmas decorations were gone, but the home's splendid ornamentation could never be dimmed. It was the finest marriage between architecture and decoration. But I had hardly time to admire the plaster wall paintings or intricate wood carvings, for I had reached the parlor door and opened it.

"Esther!"

I dropped my carpet-bag and enveloped my sweet sister in my arms. It was even better than our happy reunion at Christmas, for I had come to stay, and I wouldn't leave her. The most wondrous feeling of relief spread through me, lifting me so high I could float up to the painted ceiling. I'd kept my promise to Mother. Lara had been safe and sound in the most beautiful surroundings.

"So good to have you here at last!" Lara exclaimed.

She broke apart from me, clutching my hands. She looked so well and healthy, dressed in a pretty light green breakfast gown, her golden hair curled about her shoulders and ringed with lovely pearl combs.

Her winter companion stood from the sofa, smiling at us. Alexandra also looked lovely, her auburn hair glowing beneath the gas lamps, her bright blue eyes a kindly welcome. I curtseyed to her.

"I thank you kindly for being a friend to my sister, Miss Alexandra. May I wish you joy and happiness with Elliot. He has done little but speak of you all winter."

She stepped forward and gave me a sweet little embrace. "We are so glad to have you here, Miss Perry. But I believe rather it is Elliot who has been speaking of you."

She went over to a small lady's desk in the corner of the room.

"We have received so many letters from him," Lara explained. "He has stopped by many times as well, to tell us how you have helped him at the medical office. I'm frankly astonished, Esther. But I knew you were so capable."

Alexandra returned with two letters, which she handed to me. "We all here know of the great sacrifices you have made. You are to be commended for your amazing service to the patients."

I took one of the letters. It was in Elliot's hand, but it was a testimonial from one of the patients I'd tended. In astonishment, I read the praise for my work. The second letter was written directly from Elliot, going on and on about the care I'd given to the mysterious girl.

"There are a dozen more like it," Lara said. "You'd never guess who was the most interested?"

"Who?" I said.

She tucked her hands behind her back and gave me a mischievous smile. She was about to answer when a door in the hallway banged open and agitated voices filled the front foyer.

"Who could that be?" Lara asked.

"It - it sounds like Henry," Alexandra said.

She hurried to the parlor door, looked out, then turned back to us with great surprise. We quickly joined her, and the scene that met our eyes was almost not to be believed.

It was Jane! I almost didn't recognize her. Her black hair was askew, her eyes red-rimmed, and her lips pursed in a determined line. All of her well-bred composure had vanished and she was stomping up the hallway like a draft horse.

Behind her, standing rather nonchalantly in the drawing room doorway, was Henry Vallencourt. He leaned against the wall, his arms crossed casually on his chest, smirking as if this was all a private joke.

The Vallencourt housekeeper bustled from the dining room out into the foyer. One look at Jane and she snapped to attention, planting herself next to the front door.

"Fetch me a carriage!" Jane shouted.

"It cannot be done, Miss Curtis," Henry said. "Mother and Father have taken the carriage out today."

She grimaced even more, if she could manage it. "Then send for my family carriage! At once!"

"I'm sorry, Jane," I said from the parlor doorway, though it made me a sudden target of her wrathful stare. "Your father has use of it today."

She stopped at the front door. The housekeeper was ready with her cloak and bonnet. Jane was breathing so hard I thought her necklace might break. Her hands were balled into white-knuckled fists, and she glared at the door as if it was red fabric before a bull. Henry left his spot by the doorway and started up the hall.

"Well Miss Curtis, it seems you must walk home. It is only a short excursion."

She whirled, her voice as low and chilling as a snake. "It seems, Mr. Vallencourt, that your good standing in the city is tarnished. For, when this news reaches the Portland newspapers and all of your acquaintances, they will not be kind."

What news? I was so surprised by the scene between them I was transfixed at my position. Neither Alexandra or Lara had moved a muscle, either. We were like the silent chorus forced to watch a Greek tragedy unfold.

Henry stopped by the staircase balustrade. "These threats will not persuade me to change my mind. Indeed, your conduct in our own acquaintance has displayed nothing that would induce me to continue it. You are no longer welcome here and must leave. Good day."

His dismissal would have crumpled me. But Jane was too proud to be bested, even by one of the most powerful men in the city. Without even putting on her bonnet and gloves, she opened the door and let herself out of the house. The door slammed behind her.

Nobody moved, and I hardly dared breathe. Henry reached into his waistcoat and took out his pocket-watch. The last time I'd seen him do that he was displeased. But today, he smiled and put it back in his pocket.

His sister was the first to find her voice again. She slowly approached him as she might a skittish pony and, in a sweet nurturing tone, asked if he was quite well.

"Oh, yes, Alexandra," he said. "I am well. Thank you for inquiring. I do wish to welcome Miss Perry to our home."

"Thank you, sir," I said uneasily. I still hadn't moved from the doorway.

"Well." He cleared his throat. "I have much business to take care of this afternoon. If you'll excuse me. I will see you ladies at supper."

And with that, he started up the stairs. All three of us stared at each other in astonishment. I couldn't explain what had happened any more than Lara or Alexandra could. But it was clear one thing had occurred:

There would be a wedding on April ninth. But it would not be a double wedding!

"My goodness, that was quite exciting," Lara said. "Usually life here is rather formal and, dare I say, a bit dull."

"Lara," I scolded, but Alexandra chuckled.

"Yes, it can be. Yet if my brother says he is well, then we must trust him to be so. Miss Lara, take your sister up to your chamber. She may need a rest from her travels."

"Thank you, Alexandra," I said.

"All right, Esther," Lara said. "Go get your little shabby bag and come upstairs with me."

"Oh, and Miss Perry," Alexandra said. "There is also a surprise for you!"

"A surprise?"

Lara giggled. "You'll see. Come!"

Once I'd fetched my carpet-bag, Lara ushered me right to the staircase and we climbed to the second floor. Servants walked by us, dressed finer than the Curtis House. It was amusing to recognize the difference between parlor maids, housemaids, chamber-maids, manservants, and valets. So many to take care of a home as grand as this!

Lara chatted about her winter tutoring in French, Latin, mathematics, and drawing. But I was enthralled by the central chandelier hanging from the upper third floor and whooshing down like a globed waterfall to the foyer below. I leaned over the banister, delighted to take it all in. The second floor landing was the same as the Curtis House, open to the first floor below and the third floor above.

Lara's bedroom was on the right side of the landing, the first door we came to. If we were in the Curtis House, we'd be at Jane's room. A little brass key hung on a ribbon over the door-knob, which my sister took and stuck into the little lock.

"Welcome to my room," she announced.

It was as stunning as the rest of the home. There was a huge carved mahogany canopy bed draped with fresh linens, sumptuous tapestry curtains adorning the enormous windows, a fine floral rug, and objects of exceptional art and design. The fireplace was ringed by a sculpted marble mantel, and by the far window was a lady's desk and chair. The room was as big as the Curtis parlor, and three times as grand. My old shabby trunk sat at the foot of the bed. I laughed, for it was as out of place as a pigeon in a flock of doves.

"I see you have not wanted for anything this winter, Lara. What a beautiful room."

"It's quite a change from the farm," she admitted. She showed me an entire line of small bottles and jars along a shelf. "I've been working on my toilette articles." She took the top off of a jar and let me smell the pretty rose scent.

"It's lovely," I said.

"I guess the engagement is broken between Jane and Henry," she said. "I was never quite sure he cared for her, but a double wedding would have been fun."

"It would have," I admitted. "However, I did hear Jane and Aunt Curtis speaking to one another at Thanksgiving about the engagement. Unfortunately, I think my cousin's motives for marriage were purely financial."

"It's not hard to see why," Lara said. "She would have become mistress of this house. 'Most any girl I know would love to be. How have things been at the Curtis home with our uppity relatives?"

I laughed. "Lara, I won't have you lump Elliot in with his mother and sister. He is such a good man, and Alexandra so kind. They'll be a wonderful match."

"And to have this mysterious Gabriel arrive!" Lara sat down on the edge of the bed, swinging her dangling feet. "He was gone for so many years. I wished I was with you when we heard Uncle Curtis had brought him home."

"I'm afraid any excitement was short-lived. He has been ill, and I have been taking care of him." I paused. "He has the same illness Mother did."

"Oh, goodness." Her face fell. "Well, he couldn't be in more capable hands. I bet you made Sarah's broth."

"I did, and it seems to be helping." I sat beside her, playing with one of her golden curls. "But Dr. Curtis will relieve Elliot at the medical office, and so Elliot will care for his brother."

"You should have seen Henry when he heard Gabriel had come home. He paced up and down like a madman and didn't eat for two days. I've never seen anyone so distressed in my life."

"They were the best of friends," I explained, "but Gabriel told me they had a violent quarrel before parting."

She sighed. "Oh, if only I'd been there with you to partake of all of these goings-on. You have been privy to so much information, while I have been stuck studying."

I chuckled and put my arm about her, resting my head on her shoulder. "It has not been all fun and games, I assure you."

"You must have other secrets to reveal. Do tell!"

Her manner was so eager and her interest so sincere, I laughed. Long months of not being able to tell her anything, of not being able to free myself of my condition. Now to be earnestly questioned with little negative consequence? It was extraordinary. With every passing day, I felt a lifting of burdens. I held her hand.

"I have so much to tell, Lara, it would be quite the shock."

She recoiled ever so slightly from my grip. Then she looked at my fingers and sat up. In much the same manner as Ambrose Curtis, she gazed at my hands in horror.

"My goodness, Esther. What have you been doing? Washing clothes all winter?"

"Aunt Curtis put me to work," I said. "As a servant. Well, less than a servant, for she didn't pay me. I've been her maid since you left for the Vallencourts."

"What? Can she even do that?"

"How could I have prevented her?" I asked. "You and Ambrose were gone. I was not to speak of it to anyone without serious consequence."

A look of realization lit up her face. "That's why you acted so strangely at the Christmas party! I thought you didn't want to see me!"

"Oh, Lara," I said, my heart full. "I wanted to see you. My one hope was that you were enjoying yourself here. I'm so glad that you have."

"I have had a good time, but I can't believe you have been treated like this. Now that our uncle has returned, he helped you, didn't he?"

"Yes, of course," I smiled. "He was kept ignorant of his wife's dealings."

"Why you, Esther? I don't understand. Why was she so cruel?"

"If I knew that, I would tell you." I sighed. "As such, I have never questioned my life more since I came to the Curtis House."

"You took care of your cousin and were an excellent nurse at the medical office." She shook her head. "Esther, I could never do what you did. I could never be so good and so patient. You ... you inspire me."

Tears came to my eyes and I kissed her hand. All I'd wanted was to be with my sister again. Where she was, was my home.

She was silent for a moment, then her eyes brightened. "Well, I'll never call you dreary again."

I chuckled. "Thank you."

The clock on the marble chimed four times. Lara gave me one last squeeze and then hopped off the bed.

"It's time for dinner. We must reveal the surprise!"

No surprise could compare to being with Lara again, in these incredibly rich surroundings. She opened a door by the fireplace, revealing a huge closet bursting with dresses, shoes, gloves, reticules, bonnets, hats, stockings, shawls, and every other feminine accoutrement imaginable.

She pulled out a deep blue satin dress and hung it on a hook on the wall.

"Alexandra and I had it made for you. I wanted to give it to you at Christmas, but Aunt Curtis told me I should wait. Tonight, you can forget all your troubles."

I walked over to the dress, catching its gleam in the candlelight. It shimmered like a ballgown, delicate lace and beading winding its way around the bodice and sleeves. I had never worn anything like it in my life.

My heart crept from its hidden room and overflowed. I sank to the floor beneath the dress, weeping like a child.

"Esther?"

I lifted my head from my hands, tears streaming down my cheeks. I had wanted to be with my family, to never have to say good-bye to the things I held dearest. Lara embraced me and I smelled her sweet golden hair. She quietly held me as my pain and loneliness sweep up from within me. At last I broke away.

"I'm sorry, Lara. I'm sorry."

"You have nothing to apologize for!"

She gaped at me, astonished I'd even think of such a thing. She reached over and took a handkerchief from a table, handing it to me. I daubed my eyes.

"I wanted to keep us together," I confessed. "I promised Mother I wouldn't let you go."

To my surprise, she sat back and laughed. "Oh, Esther! I don't mean to poke fun at you, dear. But you must know we would have been separated at some point. You cannot come with me on my honeymoon!"

The idea struck me as absurd, and I wiped the last of the tears from my eyes.

"No, I suppose that would be silly. But I promised Mother in her final moments that I would always be there for you."

"You kept your promise." She reached for my fingers. "Look at how hard you've worked, Esther."

I closed my scratched fingers over my calloused palms. "This house, this dress. If only Mother could see me."

"She does. I know she does. If she didn't, we wouldn't be together."

Lara kissed my cheek. Yes, Mother would be proud of what I had done. At last Lara and I were together again. It was what I'd worked so hard for, what had kept me going through the dreary weeks. It wasn't wanting my farm back.

It was wanting to be with the people I loved.

29

My first Vallencourt dinner was exquisite, despite its absent party. Mr. and Mrs. Vallencourt had arrived home that afternoon, but Henry took the carriage out afterward, with no mention of his destination and no word of when he'd return. Of course, the entire topic of conversation revolved around his broken engagement. Mrs. Vallencourt was the most upset, for it had been her great desire to see her son and Miss Curtis united. Indeed, as I quietly listened to her disappointment, I wondered if it wasn't more of a forced match orchestrated by the two mothers rather than anything done on the part of their children.

Mr. Vallencourt, however, held a different opinion about the end of the double-wedding plans. Whether his son married or not was of little consequence next to his decisions about his career.

"Well, this new development in Henry's situation is quite interesting," he said. "But I believed you, my dear, that he might settle down once he was married. He had better find another soon, for I can't run the firm myself forever. What are sons for, anyway?"

Lara giggled. Yes, what were sons for? Obviously for different reasons than daughters.

"Leonard," his wife began, but he shushed her and raised his glass.

"A toast for Henry. May he find everlasting matrimony with a woman more suited to his taste and temperament."

We raised our glasses along with him. I hoped Henry would recover his ambition, but it would take time. Perhaps he was as confused as I had been about what he wanted to do, without the pressure from friend or family obligations. He carried a far greater responsibility in the city, and so must treat it with its due respect and caution. After Lara had sipped, she turned to Mr. Vallencourt.

"Sir, I think we must also have a toast for Esther. She has overcome so many burdens this winter, and I for one feel ashamed not to have relieved her."

Mr. Vallencourt looked at me. "Pray tell us, Miss Perry. We will still toast to you, but it would help us to know."

My distinct aversion to being put on the spot almost prevented me from talking about my servitude. Yet, it was what I would have done a scarce week ago. I could speak of it freely without negative consequence. Aunt Curtis had silenced me for so long, and it was time to claim my voice again.

So, I took a drink of water and then began. I told the story of my winter, from the morning I had met with Aunt Curtis to discuss my new position until when my uncle brought his son home. I told it as truthfully as I could. I didn't paint my aunt or cousin with undue harshness, nor Adelaide or even Mrs. Keswick. I made sure to praise Elliot on more than one occasion, which caused his fiancee to blush happily. I did not mention Annie, but I spoke of the medical office and my duties there. My audience sat, transfixed. Both my sister and Alexandra dabbed their eyes once or twice. I had lived it and not known the full extent of how sorrowful it had been, and my breath would catch when I relayed some of the more painful parts. But I continued my narrative until I felt I had given it due length with many details revealed.

When I had finished, a strange silence descended upon the dinner party guests. I felt I'd spoken out of turn, or perhaps revealed too much or not been civil towards those who had shaped my life this winter. The Vallencourts still had no reason to think of me as merely a farm girl. Then Mrs. Vallencourt raised her glass.

"To Miss Perry. Who has shown such sacrifice and kindness in the face of despair. Let us remember how powerful inner strength can be, when we face our own difficulties."

"Hear hear," Mr. Vallencourt added. "I once said this young woman had a steady head on her shoulders. I commend you, and may I be so bold as to say you have altered our definition of good breeding. For you, Miss Esther, are quite a lady."

The toast was made and they all nodded to me. For the first time since arriving in Portland, I sat at a table of people who looked at me with equal esteem. Without even seeking it, I had gained the Vallencourts' admiration. Yes, this is what I wanted. To be amongst the kindness and affability of those worthy enough to possess it. I'd never felt more beautiful or more contented in my life.

I had originally thought I might play a song on their lovely piano, but I was quite tired. After excusing myself, I made my way back to Lara's bedchamber. Lara soon joined me and we spent a quiet evening before the fire, watching it snow outside the window and chatting amiably.

"It's too bad Henry wasn't there to join us tonight and hear of your troubles," Lara said. She began taking the combs and ribbons out of her hair. "And you could have thanked him as well."

"For what?"

"The dress, of course."

I looked at its beautiful beading and exquisite form hanging on the wall. "I thought you and Alexandra had it designed."

"Yes, we did," she said. "But it was his idea and he insisted upon it."

The warmth that spread through me upon hearing this was not only attributed to the hearty fire.

"Gabriel and I spoke about their friendship. He used to be ambitious and strove for an architecture career with great energy."

Lara ran her fingers through her hair. "His father was so upset when

Henry said he'd not take the partnership. The whole house was in an uproar. Then all of Mr. Vallencourt's business friends tried to change his mind. But he refused. I wonder if that isn't the reason he broke off the engagement."

"Yes, most likely. He could have done much good in the city."

"To hear him talk, he said his father forced the profession on him."

"Perhaps." I yawned and reluctantly stood up, stretching. "Goodnight Lara. I am so glad to have come."

"Me, too, Esther."

We embraced and it wasn't long before I was sound asleep in the warm bed. The next morning, I awoke to see two heavily laden breakfast trays ready with hot foods. It almost brought tears to my eyes, for I was so appreciative of the time and effort that had gone into preparing them. Over buttered bread, fresh biscuits and apple butter, I told Lara about my kitchen duties. She nearly choked on her tea.

"You couldn't even use the main staircase?"

"No." I shook my head and wiped my mouth with the napkin. "It's forbidden to servants."

"Speaking of forbidden," Lara said with a smile, "you got to see the inside of the mysterious locked bedchamber!"

"Oh, it is nothing to speak of. It had been unused for so long that it had fallen into neglect. The first thing I did was clean."

She poured me a second cup of tea and one for herself. "And our cousin, Gabriel? What is he like?"

"He's a lot like his father," I said. "Brusque and surly at first, but quite amiable once you become better acquainted with him. I do hope he starts to regain his trust in others. His wife, Annie, resembles you so much, Lara. She is just as sweet, too."

"I should like to meet them, once his health has improved." She sipped her tea. "Mother was not open towards meeting new people, either. She had a hard time trusting Father, but after learning of the debt it is easy to see why."

"Why, Lara," I said, "that is the first time I've heard you speak plainly about our parents. I hope you have not become bitter towards them."

"Not at all." She shook her head. "It wasn't accurate of me to blindly judge anyone's character, positive or negative. Each of us is composed of many ingredients."

"Yes," I sighed. "We truly are."

There was a knock on the door, so I went to answer it. Mrs. Vallencourt stood out on the landing.

"Good morning, Esther," she greeted cheerfully. "I have received word from the Casco Bay Law Office that Mr. Ambrose Curtis is arriving shortly and would like a private conversation with you. Please ready yourself for his arrival."

"Yes, ma'am," I said and closed the door. "Lara, our uncle is coming."

"Oh, good," she said. "You're not going to meet him in that gray wool dress, are you?"

"I like it, Lara. Its cut and color suit me."

She rolled her eyes, then stopped, her hand to her mouth. "I'm sorry, Esther. I haven't been very kind to you and your preferences. Wear what you wish."

I chuckled. "Thank you. If you have a rather modest dress of a solid color, I'd consent to wearing it."

"All right."

She rummaged in the closet and pulled out a lovely daydress of my specifications. It was pine green with an ivory lace collar. When I put it on, it suited me perfectly, and Lara helped me fix my hair. As a final touch, she slid Sarah's comb over my dark strands, pronouncing it quite beautiful.

"You're right, Esther," she admitted. "Something fancier would not have suited your temperament."

I stepped out onto the landing and was coming downstairs when the door blew open and the butler let in my uncle. He took off his snowy hat and scarf, then looked up at me.

"Ah, Esther," he said. "I am so glad to see you well. I thought we might speak in the parlor this morning. There is something I must tell you."

He spoke seriously, and I had no idea what he might tell me. But seeing him made me feel at ease, so I took his arm and we entered the parlor together. The room was empty, save for a housemaid who had finished lighting the fire. Upon seeing us, she gave a respectful curtsey and then left.

"That was me," I said as we settled ourselves upon the sofa. "It was my job each morning to light the fires and clean the fireplace."

Ambrose adjusted his trousers, seemingly deep in thought. I waited for him to speak, but he did not, so I decided to tell him of the dinner.

"Lara and Alexandra had the dress made for me especially. Then at dinner, Lara encouraged me to speak of my time at service, so I told my story. As you can imagine, it was received with astonishment. But I was more surprised to witness the end of the engagement between Mr. Henry Vallencourt and Jane."

"Yes," he said. "When I arrived home last night, it was plain what had occurred. Well, she hadn't been worthy enough for him. When she refused to care for her brother, I could see how selfish she had become. Henry made the right decision."

He reached up and loosened his cravat, then leaned forward, his elbows on his legs and his fingers at his lips. When he at last spoke again, his voice was low and strained.

"If only I had made the same decision as Henry Vallencourt, so much could have been prevented." He sighed. "There are not many who could have borne what you did this winter, Esther. But I can think of one woman who could have."

He turned to me, and picked up my hand. I felt his warmth trickle through my fingers. He kissed the back of my hand tenderly, like he had the night we met.

"Your mother," he said, so softly I could barely hear him. "Phoebe."

I didn't know what to say. I listened to the sound of his breathing and noticed he was in tears.

"Sir."

He lifted his head. His dark eyes and lashes were wet. "You have her strength, and you have her kind heart and steady nature. I'd never thought a daughter of hers could be so like her. It has humbled me. For I have made errors of judgment and affection that have caused both me and the ones I love indescribable agony. But I feel today is the right time, and I can at last tell you."

"Tell me what, sir?"

And his answer could not have been more unexpected.

"Who you truly are."

30

The Vallencourt parlor was quiet, the cozy fire crackling in the fireplace. I sat quite still, my hands in my lap. I did not know what Ambrose would tell me, yet I felt no fear. Only a sense of patient waiting, the deepest faith that the truth would be revealed in time.

He took a deep breath, his eyes distant and pained. As if every image he relived in his mind was of a long-ago sorrow. When he at last began, his voice was so quiet and vulnerable he sounded like a child.

"I have kept the story of your past hidden from you, and I don't expect you to understand or to forgive me for the sins I've committed. Yet, I hope in time you will come to see the reasons behind what I have done. More importantly, what I have not done."

"Sir," I murmured. "Please do not fear my reaction. You have helped me more than you'll ever know. May that comfort ease your struggle."

He reached up and smoothed my hair from my face. I'd never seen a man look at me the way he did, like an artist admiring his own masterwork.

"When I look at you, all of my memories come back to me. When I hear you speak, I am once again a young man. There is so much to tell.

Perhaps the best way is to start at the beginning."

He inhaled once more, looking down at his clasped hands.

"My father was a successful physician in Bangor. Starting from a young age of twelve or thirteen, I was apprenticed to him. He taught me his trade, and over the years I accompanied him on some of his house cases. One late night, when I was eighteen, we were summoned to the house of Bangor's former mayor, Philip Sullivan. A common cold had begun to develop into influenza, and he was quite ill when Father and I arrived."

Philip Sullivan. A memory stirred from my first carriage ride to Portland. Aunt Curtis had said her father's name was Philip Sullivan.

"The girl who answered the door was the most beautiful I'd ever seen. She had lovely golden hair and blue eyes. I was smitten upon first seeing her, and thought her name of Lucia the most lovely I'd heard. She was Mr. Sullivan's eldest daughter, and I told my father the following morning I would marry her."

Aunt Curtis. That's how their acquaintance had begun. My uncle continued, his voice low.

"My father was happy for me, as the Sullivans were still a prominent family with established connections. Each day I was eager to go to the house so I could see Lucia. But she was not Mr. Sullivan's only daughter, as you are well aware."

"Yes, sir," I said. "My mother. Phoebe."

He was trembling, slowly rubbing his fingers together. "She was not in town when I first met Lucia, but within a week we had also become acquainted. She was as different from her sister as the sun and the moon. Where Lucia was proud, she was humble. Lucia was interested in society and social aspects. Phoebe was quiet and steady, seemingly unconcerned for anyone's view but her own."

He stopped, grimacing. "Oh, it is easy to sit here as a man of over forty and speak plainly. But I was young, Esther. Younger than you are now, and thrice the fool. I only had eyes for Lucia. We were married in June 1845."

The gulf of differences between my mother and her sister was apparent upon my first acquaintance with my aunt. I could well imagine Lucia as a young woman, for her personality was mirrored in her daughter, Jane. My own mother, never a beauty or blessed with social charm, stood by as witness to the match.

"And we were happy, as newlyweds are," he said, his voice heavy with bitterness. "It was a fine summer. We rented quarters near the Sullivan house so I could continue to administer medicine to her father. As the weeks wore on, I discovered a kinship with Phoebe in the medical aspect. She was as good a nurse as I was a doctor. We shared the common capacity for healing the ill. Our acquaintance improved."

I thought of my mother before the war and before the years of sorrow. It was easy to imagine her as a capable young lady, living in a grand house and caring for her ill father, while a handsome young doctor came to call upon them. How sad that she had not the strength to survive her own illness.

"In September, my wife went to Portland to stay with her close friend Mabel Vallencourt, who had been recently married. She asked me to look after her father, so I visited the Sullivans each day."

He leaned forward on the sofa, his head in his hands. He was fighting his feelings, rushing to the surface in such unbelievable torment.

"I was in Phoebe's company daily. At first, our acquaintance was only casual. But within a short time I realized I was counting the hours until I saw her face again. She had such fine character, such kindness and goodness. Lucia's beauty suddenly seemed hollow, her social vanity a false reason to hold my affection. It was Phoebe who captured me, totally and without any effort to gain my attachment."

My mind had gone blank, as if it was a stretched canvas and my uncle its artist, painting broad angry swaths. But nothing prepared me for what he was to say.

"I was in love with her, Esther. Oh, and it broke me from inside. I tried to stay away or invent some excuse to leave town, but I couldn't. I was drawn to her so strongly and inexplicably that it tormented me to be in the same room with her. It was not a fleeting fancy like with Lucia, but something so strong I couldn't even obey divine law anymore."

When he at last looked at me again, his eyes blazed with such startling passion I was taken aback. Every ounce of feeling rippled through his body.

"Her father recovered enough to attend to a business matter one afternoon. Phoebe and I were alone together. Not the threats of sin or hell or the even the shattering of my vows could keep me from being with her."

His passion dissipated, replaced by a hard and bitter agony. "And it was then that I realized what I had done. For she loved me, too."

He took a handkerchief from his jacket and held it to his eyes. I quietly moved closer to him, laying a soothing hand upon his shoulder. Mother, I never knew. What she had felt. For a man who could never be hers.

"Lucia ... returned two days later. I was the most miserable creature alive. Struggling to keep up this proper facade of happiness I was supposed to feel. I didn't know what to do. Work consumed me and I admit I welcomed the distraction. As the weeks wore on, I became a shell of my former self."

He was breathing so hard he unbuttoned his jacket. A grim smile played at his mouth.

"But my suffering was little compared to what it would become. I remember the day Phoebe came to the medical office. I was so elated to see her. I could scarcely comprehend she had come! My joy was so complete, my relief so palpable. Yet she had not come to be with me, nor to relieve my agony."

At once, I recognized the pained, tormented look in his eyes as the same way he had regarded me on the landing the night we met. When he had turned from Gabriel's bedchamber door and our eyes had locked.

"Phoebe had come to tell me ... that I would be a father."

He reached out and took my hand, but I hardly felt it. He held up his palm and put mine against his skin. Then, without knowing that I was, I looked for myself in his face. As if he was a mirror and I was studying my own features. And noticed, for the first time, how we resembled one another. His dark eyes were like my dark eyes. His hair, black as an oak at night, was like my hair.

"Yes, Esther." He nodded. "Yes."

An incredible rush of feeling engulfed me, as if I had been groping in the dark my whole life and had at last found a light. The stray pieces came together as if magnetized. So fast and so sudden, and yet I was not frightened or dismissive. I welcomed this new knowledge from the man sitting beside me who had shared it.

I was his daughter.

He covered my hands with his and held them cupped inside his warmth.

"Yes, now you know. But the story of who you are does not end there. For, as you can well imagine, Phoebe and I were thrust into a new hell. Lucia, her father, my father. It tore our two families apart."

His voice was dull with the remembered ache of the long-ago pain.

"And it tore me apart from your mother. I was never to see her again, and she was banished from her own home."

His simple description of their parting made me grieve for them. I felt wrong, for they had committed the highest of sins against his marriage ... but he was now my dearest flesh and blood. I struggled to try and fault him for his wrongs, but I found I could not. I could only sit and listen, spellbound and sorrowful, to the pain he had suffered losing my mother.

"She had nowhere to go." He dabbed his eyes again. "I couldn't help her, either. I was kept in the dark as to her whereabouts. It was only months later that I found out the Reverend Perry had taken her in."

"My grandfather," I breathed.

"Yes." Ambrose nodded. "He had two sons, if I recall."

I smiled ruefully. "William ... and George."

George Perry. The man who my entire life up until a few moments ago had been my father.

"I was never closely acquainted with him," Ambrose said quietly. "I do not know how he came to marry your mother. But he is Lara's father, I do know. She resembles the Reverend Perry a great deal. The same hair and eye color."

"She was her father's favorite. His little golden angel, he said." At Ambrose's concerned look, I shrugged my shoulders. "Oh, he regarded me well enough. He spent more time at the Sloop Tavern than at home. I tended the farm and ... I was happy to do so."

I thought of the man who had raised me as the person that he was and not a father whose traits I'd inherited. He wasn't my relation. I'd thought I was more like my mother, but I could now see that it was only half of the heritage I'd grown up with.

"Esther," he said softly. "I wish I could have helped you. Lucia discovered she was to have our first child, so any thought of running away or of taking my own life - both of which I heavily considered - couldn't occur. We moved to Portland, and I lost all contact with your mother and your grandfather as well."

I nodded. My real parents could not be together. I could almost not bear thinking of Mother holding her heart so tightly locked in her chest for years. Unable to speak of it to anyone, unable to reach out for another's sympathy. She had lost the love of her life in such a horrid way.

"I wish she had told me," I said at last. "I understand why she didn't, but I still wish she had. I might have been able to help her. She could have reconciled with Lucia and not lost her whole family."

Those years of letting Father run up debts and then the war years with him gone. She had been so broken-hearted. Family obligations, a marriage vow broken. My poor mother finding no refuge save a kindly minister.

"It was our choice to do the right thing," Ambrose said. "The day she came to the office, I said we could leave together. But your mother was a better person than I, stronger than I was. She said we had loved falsely, and it would be a deeper sin to not tell her own sister. I barely remember the first months in Portland, for I was quickly establishing my own medical practice. I wasn't even present at my wife's side the following

June, when she gave birth to Jane."

The more my father spoke, the more I realized how I was alike to him. I, too, sought solace in work when the pain I felt threatened to swallow me. It was hard enough this winter taking care of Lara, but to have my own family to look after. Jane and Elliot ...

"And Gabriel," I said aloud. "I thought Gabriel was the eldest."

"Yes," Ambrose said. "He is. The story of your true parents is told, but there is one last piece that you must know. Wait here."

With that, he stood from the sofa and went to the parlor doorway, summoning a servant. I stayed where I was, my hands in my lap, feeling both relaxed and nervous at the same time. I thought of Gabriel then, his playful brusqueness, his direct questions, his rebellious nature, his distrust in others. He was Ambrose's son, of that I was sure. They resembled one another both in appearance and temperament.

And, as I thought of my cousin, I heard a slight cough, and Ambrose was bringing him into the parlor! He was here! I leapt to my feet and went over to him, both elated and concerned, since he was still pale. But his smile was broad, and he clasped me about the neck.

"Sir," I said to Ambrose, "you should not have brought him. Gabriel, you are too ill. You must be in bed."

"Forgive me, Esther," my father said, "but it was imperative."

"Then have the cook make up his medicine." As I began telling Ambrose of the recipe, Gabriel made a face.

"Oh, let me alone, Esther. I'll be fine for one afternoon."

"And you," I said, my hands on my hips, "are far too young to be such a curmudgeon."

"You see the way she speaks to me?" Gabriel laughed. "Ordering me to do this and that. I told her when we met she'd not do me any good. And she doesn't!"

Ambrose stood before us, his arms crossed over his chest, grinning as widely as a boy. I had no idea why he was enjoying our sparring exchange, for I didn't. Gabriel brought out a strange side to me and had since the moment we'd met. I felt more playful and also more inclined to tell him what to do, like a clucking mother hen.

"I still think you need some remedy while you're here," I said.

"All right. Fetch me a hot water bottle and some castor oil. Seems you won't rest easy until you do, I suppose."

"Castor oil does not help a cough," I muttered, but Ambrose summoned one of the housemaids and I asked for the items from the kitchen. Once they'd been brought and the dosage administered to its reluctant patient, I made him comfortable in the chair with extra pillows and a blanket.

"That's enough, Esther." I continued to plump his pillows until he playfully smacked my hand away. "I said enough. Goodness, you're worse than Annie."

"I have seen this illness take its worst course," I said. "You will be fortunate to live through it."

"With you around, I think not."

Both Ambrose and I laughed out loud. It was hard to take my cousin seriously, with such a determined attitude towards surliness. I couldn't help but be amused by it.

"Now that we are assembled," Ambrose said, "Esther, I would like you to come sit beside me. I told Gabriel this morning before we arrived about your mother and I. So, he knows that you are my daughter."

Gabriel stuck his tongue out and made a funny face. I snickered.

"Quite gentlemanly." Ambrose chuckled. "However, there is something I must tell you both. I'm not even sure how to tell you, so I'll do what I can. But first, let me ask you a question, Gabriel."

"Yes, Father."

"What is your birthday?"

"You know when my birthday is," he said, but at Ambrose's insistent look, rolled his eyes. "May tenth."

A lightning rod of feeling shot up my spine and my heart began to beat faster. Ambrose turned to me.

"And what is your birthday, Esther?"

My throat was so dry I could hardly answer him. "May tenth."

Gabriel stared at me for a long moment. But then his thick brows drew together and he looked at Ambrose. "Father, what are you saying?"

"Phoebe and I were Esther's parents," he said. "And we are your parents, too."

His mouth dropped open. I, too, mirrored the surprise in such completeness that the room disappeared, and it was only Gabriel and I staring at one another. We were brother and sister, but in the most intimate way two siblings could be attached.

We were twins.

"Good God in heaven!" Gabriel blurted. "I was going to say this can't be true, but I look at you and I feel it. It's so strong."

"It is." I shook my head, disbelief and belief jumbled together in my heart. "You are my brother. My twin brother."

"No wonder we bring out each other's best sides," he laughed. "I can't help ribbing you, Esther. It's too much fun."

My mind alternated between blank and frenzied. "Yes, and I am not able to take it seriously, which is hardly in my nature at all. You bring out a good side to me, and I feel like I belong when I'm with you. It is so different than with any other."

Ambrose smiled. "It was funny watching you two interact with each other. Like a brother and a sister. I don't think anyone will be able to understand the connection that two separated at birth could feel. I'm sorry you grew up apart, but now you have been reunited. You can spend the rest of your lives knowing that not only do you have another sibling, but that sibling is your twin."

"Well, there it is," Gabriel scoffed. "You're stuck with me, Esther."

But he couldn't hide his grumpy play-acting for longer than a moment, and we were soon both laughing again. Yet, as our mirth died down, a nagging question arose in my mind. I addressed my father with my inquiry.

"Sir, you said you didn't have contact with my mother. How did Gabriel come to live with you, and I did not?"

"You're right, I didn't see your mother. But Lucia found out two infants had been born. She brought Gabriel home to us. I ... I didn't know he was a twin. Esther, I'm sorry but I never knew you existed."

I smiled ruefully, but for my Aunt Curtis I felt a stab of anger. She hadn't merely brought Gabriel. She had taken him from his real mother. She had taken him from me. I struggled with my feelings, as I had struggled from the moment we met. She had known about me and never told my father.

But Ambrose's sin against her and her marriage was horrific, and it had twisted her into a wrathful spite. Which she then exercised over me to perfection.

Everything she had said or done suddenly became clear. Why she was so cruel to me, why I was treated the way I had been. I felt quietly calmed, as if a box had clicked shut and its contents were at last secure.

"We have been parted ships for years. But we are together, and we can begin again." He paused, then looked at Gabriel. "To you, my son, I owe an apology for my silence and my grief. Every time I looked at you, I saw Phoebe. I was a fool for pushing you to do something you didn't want to. I should have given you the space and the freedom to be your own person."

My father began to weep, and I rubbed his shoulder. "I was so afraid of losing you, Gabriel. I had lost your mother, and it almost killed me. I'd have rather plunged into the icy ocean waters than go through that again. I'm sorry I never told you of her."

Gabriel had the blanket pressed against his face, sobbing quietly. He'd never known his real mother, and had instead been raised by a tyrant for a father, who was so grief-stricken and unhappy that he controlled and pushed away the boy he loved the most.

"Forgiveness is a delicate thing," I said quietly.

I went to Gabriel and helped him to his feet. While supporting my brother, who was my exact height, I beckoned Ambrose over. The three of us embraced. I knelt against Ambrose's soft wool jacket, breathing in his rich leathery scent. Gabriel wrapped his arms about me. Small stone walls inside me, ones I'd erected from hurt and isolation, were being taken down, and I felt a rush like cool, clear water.

Forgiveness was delicate and it took time. But if I could at last lay to rest the inner turmoil I had suffered, then I welcomed it.

I welcomed peace with all my being.

31

I had found my new family. It was the most comforting feeling to look into the eyes of my father and brother, and to receive their warm love in return. At last I belonged here, in this city, with those I loved by my side.

Ambrose then stepped back from Gabriel and I, reaching within his jacket. He produced a plain envelope bulging with its contents.

"There is still yet one more thing I must reveal to both of you. However, it requires an audience."

He strode over to the door, summoned a servant, and asked her to fetch every other member of the household down to the parlor. Gabriel and I smiled at one another, but I also felt fearful apprehension. What would Henry Vallencourt think of me? How would he regard me? The story of my birth was not respectable for someone of his status. I could lose his good graces and also diminish my newfound position of respect within his family. I had just found out about myself ... couldn't it wait?

"Uncle!" Lara exclaimed as I heard her footsteps skipping down the main staircase.

My sister's cheery greeting lifted my spirits a little. The Vallencourts could peer down upon me, but Lara never would. She was followed by Alexandra, and then Mr. and Mrs. Vallencourt arrived. As I greeted them and the parlor became louder with the commotion of their shock over seeing Gabriel, I began to feel quite nervous. Henry hadn't been seen for two days.

"You're right, Esther," Gabriel was saying. "How extraordinary that your sister should look so similar to Annie!"

"Annie is your wife?" Lara said with a laugh. "You have been much talked about, you know. Esther and I were at a loss to explain your mysterious room!"

Gabriel chuckled. "Talks like her, too!"

Then suddenly, he was there in the parlor doorway. Henry Vallencourt, dressed informally in a simple white shirt and gray waistcoat, his sleeves rolled up and his jaw stubbled beneath his sleepy gaze. It appeared he'd been summoned from bed, and to me had never looked more handsome. But his exhaustion vanished when he beheld the familiar occupant in the chair.

"Gabriel," he said gravely. "I thought you unable to leave your sickbed."

But before a conversation, whether pleasant or strained, could begin between them, my father stepped in and brandished the fat envelope.

"I apologize for being abrupt, but I have a matter of business to commence. First things first, however. Mabel and Leonard -" he said, gesturing to Henry's parents - "are aware of the unusual circumstances I have revealed to Esther and Gabriel this morning. But Lara, Miss Alexandra, and Henry have not yet been informed. This will come as a great shock, but let me be clear that every word I speak is true. Seat yourselves, if you would."

Mr. and Mrs. Vallencourt sat upon the sofa, looking remarkably placid. Lara, Alexandra, and I sat near one another, while Henry took the chair closest to Gabriel. It gave me a slight hope that things may be mended, for at least they were not regarding each other with anger.

"There is no easy way to explain this," Ambrose admitted quietly, "so I will come out and say it. Esther and Gabriel are twin brother and sister."

The commotion earlier couldn't compare to the instant barrage of surprised voices. Lara, as I would have guessed, looked the most amazed and instantly bombarded my father with questions. Mrs. Vallencourt appeared quite composed, and Mr. Vallencourt laughed hysterically as if the funniest joke had been uttered. Both Ambrose and Gabriel spent a busy quarter-hour answering everybody's inquiries, and Alexandra kept repeating her observation that my brother and I resembled one another. I remained silent, smiling and nodding at their astonished looks. Henry, too, was mute, studying the carpet pattern as if he was about to take a test on it. He looked intensely bothered by this news, and not in a good way.

Well, the great blow had dropped and gradually the room died down, until it was only Lara chatting with Gabriel about our mother. He listened intently, without a sound, while she spoke of the mother he'd never known. And he was visibly moved to tears while she sorrowfully told of our mother's last moments.

Gabriel looked at me. "She never forgot about me, did she?"

I shook my head. "No. But I wish she had told me. I might have tried to find you, and part of our broken family would have been reconciled."

Everyone in the room was silent for a moment, those in the Vallencourt household privately thanking God that their family had always been together. It was an incredible privilege.

At last, Ambrose rose again and addressed us with his envelope. "I thank you all for your open hearts and minds towards this new development in the Curtis family. Esther, Gabriel and myself feel grateful for your kindness. In light of this new information, however, I have made some legal changes. Let me show two documents Esther and Gabriel have probably never seen before."

He opened the envelope and reached inside. He pulled out two old, faded and yellowed pieces of paper, which he displayed on a low marble tea table in the center of the parlor. All about the room could be heard little gasps. I was shocked to silence.

Two birth certificates. Listing Phoebe Sullivan as the mother and Ambrose Curtis as the father. Both listing May 10th, 1846 as the date of birth. My original birth name was Esther Curtis, which made me smile.

But the most interesting part of both documents was the birth-times. I was a full eight minutes older than my brother. Ambrose drew everyone's attention to this fact.

"Yes, Esther is the eldest of the two siblings. It also makes her the eldest of all of my children, since my daughter Jane was born in June of 1846. When Gabriel was two months of age, I opened a trust fund at Portland Savings and Loan Bank. Since that time, I have steadily deposited a portion of my monthly earnings. The amount is now eighty thousand dollars."

Nobody in the room was prepared to hear such a sum. It was so astronomically large as not to be believed. Eighty thousand dollars was the largest amount of money I'd ever heard of in my life. It was twice the debt of Perry Farm!

Ambrose then reached inside the envelope again and pulled out several papers clipped together. Holding them against his chest like a shield, he slowly walked over to where I sat, waiting numbly in the chair. I felt like I had the day I found out about the farm debt. The amount of money blocked out all other thoughts.

My father gently knelt down in front of me.

"Esther, your birth certificate was mailed from Mr. Silas Greene in Bayview. This trust fund, an inheritance, was to be given to my eldest child upon their twenty-third birthday or upon their wedding day, whichever came first. This morning, I went to the Casco Bay Law Office and made my changes." He took a deep breath. "You, Esther, are the recipient. On May tenth of this year, 1869, it will be your twenty-third birthday."

I stared at him, my mouth open. He placed the papers in my lap, and then reached for my hands, clasping them inside his warmth.

"The entire amount is yours."

I tried to look into his warm dark eyes, but the happiness was too great a joy. I began to weep. Ambrose kissed my hands.

"It is my deepest honor to bestow this gift upon the most worthy of young women. You will never want for anything ever again."

I leaned forward and placed my forehead on our hands, sobbing. I was so overwhelmed. I barely heard the applause from the others in the room. My legs were watery as my father helped me to my feet, and then kissed my forehead. Mrs. Vallencourt fetched a pen from the lady's desk and handed it to me. I knelt before the table, the documents shaking beneath my trembling fingers, and signed my name as sole benefactor.

There was another round of applause from those present, my father's the loudest of all. Lara handed me a handkerchief, rubbing my back, and I stood to embrace her. As I smelled her sweet hair and heard her congratulatory whispers, it was as comforting as walking up the carriageway towards my home. Having arrived at last to the place I was most content and happy.

When I finally dried my eyes and my heart quieted its joyous pounding, I took a deep breath, and looked about the room. Gabriel was smirking from his chair, buried under his blankets, and looking amused by this change of fortune. I laughed out loud.

"Gabriel, are you wishing you were the eldest?"

"I'll never hear the end of it," he said loudly, and the whole room chuckled. "One more reason for you to order me around."

I shook my head. "No. I only want what's best for you, so I'm giving you half. You don't have to scrape by any more. Start a new life for yourself and Annie."

He scoffed at first, as I knew he would. But when he saw I was serious, he bowed his head and mumbled his gratitude. I went to him and clasped his hand in mine. It felt like we were emerging from our ordeals together.

"Oh, Esther, I am so happy for you!" Lara exclaimed. "You have forty thousand dollars. You can buy back Perry Farm."

I could, and the thought had been present since Ambrose had announced the fortune was bestowed upon me. I gave my brother's hand one last squeeze, looking over at Henry. He was leaning back in his seat, his hands at his lips, pensive and serious. I could buy Perry Farm. But was it what I wanted?

I crossed the room and walked over to my sister. "Oh, Lara, I could return to Bayview. I cannot deny how deeply I miss the farm, and I shall always miss it. It was our childhood home, and I wanted it to be mine."

She bit her lip, her eyes filling with tears. I held out my hand and took her little fingers.

"Lara, now I want something better. I want to be with the people I love and my family is here, in Portland." I paused, my heart so full I could barely speak. "Dearest, thank you for helping me get through these tough times. For you, I bestow half of my share. You will receive twenty thousand dollars, to do what you will."

The applause from the rest of the group burst forth, but it was nothing compared to my sister's look of beautiful joy. She leapt up into my arms, thanking me over and over again.

"I love you so dearly," she wept.

"I love you, too. You were right, Lara." I smoothed her golden hair. "How could I be dreary as long as we're together."

It was the greatest blessing to not only care for my sister, but to raise her life to its utmost happiness. I could see her marrying a horse farmer and enjoying her womanly years from the saddle. Whenever I pictured her, I thought of her riding. I couldn't believe I could make her dreams come true.

When at last we parted, I looked at Alexandra. She returned my gaze with a look of surprise and started to raise her hands, but I stopped her.

"There is no need to refuse, Alexandra. My gift is for both you and Elliot, for no-one was kinder or more welcoming to me this winter. I bestow upon you five thousand dollars, to expand the doctor's office and hire more assistance."

"Oh, thank you, Esther." She stood and kissed me upon the cheek. "I can speak for both Elliot and myself when we say how grateful we are."

"It is your kindness that makes it such a pleasure to help. As Elliot said to me once - good things all around, eh?"

She nodded, and the others in the room chuckled. Yes, good things all around. I would help my family, and I, too, would be helped in return. As I returned to the chair and took my seat, I thought of Jane. Ambrose had said that he would remove financial stability from his wife and daughter, but I could afford to be generous. An hour ago, I had a handful of coins to my name. My fortune was not only great, but more than enough to share. I had fifteen thousand dollars. But I felt richer than any bank amount, in the love and mutual camaraderie I shared with the people in this room.

Pleasant conversation struck up, everyone talking about the inheritance. Gabriel brought his father to tears when he said he'd use the money to build a hospital in Richmond, and might even try his hand at the medical profession again. Lara made joke after joke about how many lady's toilette articles she'd have to sell now that she was so poor, which made Alexandra giggle until her cheeks turned pink. Mrs. Vallencourt made plans for a celebration party to be held on May tenth, and Mr. Vallencourt commended Ambrose on his fine diligence towards saving so much money. But there was one person who did not participate in the conversation, and, indeed, had not said a word all morning.

Henry.

He had smiled once or twice, but that was all. I had thought of financially assisting him in a future profession. But it would have drawn attention to his lack of one, so I hadn't said anything. To hurt his pride on so deep a level would have been injurious.

The clock on the mantel struck eleven, and the housekeeper entered the parlor to inform us luncheon was ready. We all stood and made our way into the dining room. Lara immediately sought and commanded my attention on our way across the hall. Though I wanted to speak to Henry privately, it was not to be.

Ambrose was the last to join our party at the dinner table, but Henry's seat was still absent. My father then relayed the disappointing message that Henry was not to accompany us and had retired to his room.

I kept up a good conversation during our meal, especially keeping an eye on my brother's appetite, but in truth I was quite crushed. I felt like Henry truly had shunned me, that the illicit story of my past was too great an obstacle for his regard.

When at last the final plate was cleared, Ambrose invited both myself and Lara to return to the house. I was not to see Henry before our parting, and now I had the prospect of facing Aunt Curtis and Jane.

It was not the first time I had returned to the Curtis House feeling both dread and relief.

32

I expected Mr. Jakes to meet us at his usual post at the front door, but I was wholly gladdened to see Annie greet us. She had recovered enough to come to the house and be reunited with her husband. We had barely entered the front hall before Gabriel flew into his wife's arms. Their exuberant affection caused Lara and I to laugh out loud.

"Why, this must be Lara Perry!" Annie stared at her. "Your sister is right. We look so much alike we could be sisters!"

"You're not going to believe this, Annie," Lara said, "but it so happens we are!"

The poor girl couldn't have been more astonished. There was much to explain and many happy hours of acquaintance to be made, but Gabriel's rest was highly necessary. So Annie and Lara helped him upstairs with all the fuss and bother of two caring women, while Ambrose and I stood for a moment in the front hall. When they had at last reached his bedchamber door, he turned to me.

"Esther," he said quietly.

"Yes, sir."

"Last night, I informed my wife and daughter of everything that was said in the Vallencourt parlor. Tomorrow morning, Lucia and Jane are leaving on a train for New York City."

"Oh, sir," I said. "I am deeply sorry."

"Please. There is no reason to apologize. Lucia did request a private discussion with you in the parlor. I shall have her sent for."

I nodded, biting my lip. What would she say to me? It was like the morning she had told me I was to be a servant, my head swirling with questions. It was a true shame this revelation of my past had caused such dissolution between her and Ambrose.

After a parting embrace from my father, I went into the empty parlor. So many memories of this room, enough for me to feel a strange but welcome homecoming. The cold mornings I'd knelt before the fire with sooty fingers, coaxing a fresh blaze. The first time Henry had spoken to me, standing by the piano. Watching Elliot and Alexandra dance together, such dedication to the steps. When Ambrose had come home and I'd made him comfortable in his wingback chair. I even thought of Adelaide and her brisk furniture polishing. I'd created a new life for myself here, and it settled so deeply within me.

I could face her. I could do this. Was it any harder than the burdens I'd overcome? Was her control over me so absolute that she must be master to my emotions, too?

No. I was my own person, complete in and of myself.

After sitting on the sofa for a few minutes, listening to the clock on the mantel and the snapping fire, the parlor door opened and my aunt entered.

She was clothed as plainly as I'd ever seen her, in an ordinary day-dress of dark blue cotton. A lace fichu was tied about her shoulders, and her frosted blond hair was simply styled. There was not a jewel around her neck, on her fingers, or adorning her garments. Her homely appearance called attention to her facial features, and she resembled my mother more than I ever thought she had. They had the same shape to the eyes, the same cheekbones.

I rose from the sofa and gave a light bow. "Do be seated please, Aunt

Curtis. I am ready to hear what you would like to discuss."

She didn't sit. "You must be pleased by this sudden reversal of circumstance."

"I am," I admitted. I seated myself again on the sofa, arranging my green wool dress. "But not so that I may exercise the power that comes with it. If my inheritance is to bring happiness, then it must be used responsibly."

"What happiness is there to be found for all parties?" she said. "I am forced to rely upon former acquaintances for my welfare, and my daughter's situation has become similarly low."

Her tone was as brusque and crisp as ever. I took a deep breath.

"My share of the fortune, after I have bestowed parts of it upon others, is fifteen thousand dollars."

I paused, watching her reaction. But her grim mouth never moved, nor did the coldness in her eyes dissipate.

"It is more than enough for my own welfare. I would like to give you and Jane enough to cover living expenses for six months, so that you may have ample time to establish a new life."

"I will not take charity," she quipped. "Especially not from you."

I was prepared for her refusal. Indeed, if she had accepted my initial offer, I might have been wary.

"Then I will place the amount of one thousand dollars in a separate trust fund, to be distributed in your name six months after I receive the money, along with any interest it has accrued in the meantime. The date you receive it will be February 10th, 1870."

"And if I refuse this gesture?"

"You won't," I said simply. "It is not charity, but an expression of my gratitude. For there was one action on your part that I am sincerely grateful for."

She crossed her arms. "What are you speaking of?"

"On her deathbed, my mother requested that her obituary be printed in the *Portland Press Herald*. There is no probable way that Ambrose would have read that edition of the newspaper. But you did. You told your husband about my mother's death, and you made the travel arrangements to come to Bayview. None of the blessings Lara or I have received would be ours without it."

She was silent, and we regarded each other for a long moment. Suddenly, she looked down and her lip trembled. With her thumb, she twisted her wedding ring, glowing with a burnished luster in the firelight.

At last she looked at me once more. For the first time there was no coldness, no harshness, no ice. Her look was almost ... motherly.

"I raised your brother, Esther. And no matter how hard I tried to hate Phoebe, I could never hate Gabriel. He has become my son. When he was believed dead, it was devastating. A mother should never lose her child." She breathed, her eyes mournful. "I made Phoebe feel that hurt. She took my love, so I took her boy."

My throat was so full I couldn't speak. My aunt's words, her broken voice. So many years of sorrow.

"You look like him." Her eyes passed over my features. "Like your brother. You are a good nurse, too, like Ambrose is a good doctor. You have such unearthly patience with the sick. It is your family's profession."

"And Gabriel will recover," I said. "You need not worry for him."

She took a deep breath and slowly let it out. "It's not true, that time is supposed to heal pain. It's not true."

I nodded, looking down at my hands in my lap. The scratches were starting to heal and the bruises fading.

"My mother hid her pain. She never spoke of her family or of her son. I wish she would have told me. It will take a long time for me to understand her silence. I feel like she lied to me my whole life."

The corner of her mouth lifted in a grim smile. "I look at you and Lara, and I remember how Phoebe and I once were. She hid her heart inside her lies, as I have."

She stopped. She was a shattered and broken-hearted woman, who had thought she'd done everything right. She had beauty, she had money, she had a handsome new husband. And his blindness had cost her a lifetime of happiness. I didn't know how I'd feel if Henry had agreed to be mine, only to cast his eyes to Lara. It was an unimaginable loss.

I stood and walked slowly over to her. I extended my hand, without an idea of whether she would accept it or not.

Yet, she did. As I clasped her fingers, I felt the true delicateness of our mutual forgiveness. It was like the opening note of a piano sonata, with the promise of a full song to unfold. A beginning.

It would be a long time, and perhaps she'd never stop seeing her pain in me. I could live with that. Our years of silence had come to an end.

We had both lived at the heart of a lie.

33

"So, Annie, what are you going to do with your new fortune?"

Annie tapped her finger against her chin. "Well, Miss Lara, Gabriel has mentioned that hospital he'd like to have built. Of course, we have been living in a home not up to a woman's standards. Not even a man could live there!"

Lara giggled. "It will be so nice for you to have a home. As for me, I'm going to go against all convention."

"Lara," I began, but she leaned over and put her hand on my knee.

"No, Esther, you cannot stop me. I'm going to open that saddle and tack merchant store I said I would."

Annie stared at her as if she'd just announced she'd join a rodeo. I laughed, clearly remembering Lara joking about such a proposition on our first ride to Portland. But this time, Aunt Curtis wasn't present to admonish her. She and Jane had left last Monday morning, bound for the first train south to New York City.

With their absence, my life had settled and rooted like an oak tree. I took breakfast in my room with Lara and Annie each morning, administered medicines to my recovering brother, and enjoyed Elliot's company when he stopped by.

But the deepest pleasure of all was the newfound love I felt for my father. Ambrose and I read to each other by the parlor fire at night, and I played piano for him, too. Having never known such contentment in my life, it was like an ever full wellspring I drew from every hour.

"You should see my sister in a saddle," I said to Annie, still chuckling. "Lara is never happier than when her feet are in the stirrups."

"My grandfather owned a large horse farm in Virginia. He taught me to ride when I was a wee thing."

"Sometimes," Lara confessed, her voice low, "I even ride Western saddle. Don't tell Esther!"

"I'm right here," I said. "I can hear you!"

The two golden-haired ladies laughed. With Gabriel on the mend and the winter days melting into spring, there was much to enjoy. I'd miss Gabriel and Annie when they departed after the birthday celebration on May tenth, but their own lives could begin anew. I'd never left Maine in my life, and of course had been invited to stay with them in Virginia once they became settled. Lara had plans to move into Gabriel's bedchamber and give it her own feminine touch.

"What about you, Esther?" Annie asked. "Where will you live?"

I looked up at the parlor walls, at the scrolling golden wallpaper, the gilded-edged portraits, the gray winter light upon the polished mahogany furniture.

"Here. I have fallen in love with this home. My father will also stay, and I as his companion as long as he needs me. I would like to teach piano. Elliot and Alexandra may join us after they marry."

Then, almost as if on cue, the front door opened. The three of us rose to our feet in time to see Miss Alexandra Vallencourt enter through the parlor doorway, still wearing her traveling cloak and bonnet. Her cheeks were bright pink, and she rubbed her mittened hands together.

"My goodness, it's cold out!"

Lara giggled. "Nice to see you this morning, Alexandra. You look like you just strolled on over here!"

"We did," said a pleasant male voice.

My heart slammed so hard in my chest it was difficult to breathe, and I dropped to the sofa. The front door swept shut and Henry Vallencourt came into the parlor behind his sister, stomping his feet and brushing down the snow from his jacket. I forced myself to keep my gaze steady and calm, for inside I may as well have been a winter storm.

"You walked?" Annie gasped. "What, was not a driver available?"

"It was his idea." Alexandra untied her bonnet and removed it, showing her pretty auburn hair. "Good morning to you all."

"Yes, I confess I wanted to come by foot." Henry had pulled off his scarf and gloves, handing them to Mr. Jakes. His attire was simple and handsome, a fitted dark gray suit and matching waistcoat. "It has been mentioned in the past the walk is ten minutes. We have definitely determined the distance to be far shorter than we ever thought possible."

"Well, perhaps a little too long in February," Alexandra gently corrected.

His smile to her was so warm I felt myself relaxing. But I was quickly brought to attention again.

"Miss Perry?"

All three ladies turned their curious blue-eyed gazes to me as I humbly rose from the sofa and bowed my head.

"Yes, sir."

"I have received word from your father that Gabriel is well, and has requested to see me. Please take me to him."

I nodded. "Yes, of course."

Pleading silently to my nerves to calm themselves, I lifted the skirt of my navy wool dress and steadily walked over to the parlor door. Henry excused himself to the rest of our party and joined me out in the front hall. I dared not look at him. I hardly dared to breathe. My mind had become as white and blank as fresh fallen snow. I wanted to make conversation, but couldn't think of anything to say. Not even with my aunt had I felt so flustered and nervous.

We were not even halfway up the stairs before a chorus of giggles came from the parlor. My cheeks flamed, and I tripped on my own gown. Luckily, I was able to remedy my clumsiness, but felt like a fool all the same.

"You were correct about the walk," he said quietly from behind me. "It is quite brisk and refreshing."

"Yes," was all I could think of to say.

Good heavens, I truly was no more than the mute rustic he'd met at our first dinner. Finally, I inwardly gave up on appearing from any higher station than I'd come from. I was Esther from Perry Farm, and no Vallencourt invitation or newfound financial status could change it. I was simply ... me.

We reached the landing and turned right, continuing up the three steps to the second floor. At the first door, a door that had been such a part of my life at the Curtis House, I stopped and turned about, keeping my gaze firmly fixed anywhere but his face.

"Thank you," Henry said.

I nodded, my mouth too dry to say anything. He was standing so close I noticed the intricate stitching on his waistcoat and smelled his woodsy outdoor scent. For a moment, I thought he might say something else.

But his mind was preoccupied with his errand. So, he turned the knob and went into the little hallway separating Gabriel's bedchamber from mine. Gabriel's door was open, and from my position on the landing I could see his room looked bright and cozy. The window curtains were pushed back to let in the daylight, and a hearty fire crackled.

"Ah, Henry! You have come."

I wanted to move from the doorway, for I was not invited to listen. But it would have brought me such vexation if they should quarrel once more, so I forced myself to stay where I was. Neither my brother or Henry could see me from where I stood, but I could clearly hear their voices.

"Good afternoon, Gabriel. You look much improved over a week's time."

"Sit! Bring up a chair."

I was pleased to hear how hearty and well Gabriel sounded. He was making a full recovery, which brought such relief my breath caught. I heard the sound of scraping chair legs, then a creak as Henry settled.

"It is thanks to Esther, as you well know," Gabriel continued. "I'd be taking up too much space in a pine box without her."

Henry chuckled. "I have been acquainted with twins, and they are supposed to have a remarkable bond. It seems none other could have cured you."

"I couldn't do it on my own."

I smiled, knowing Gabriel would never admit his appreciation to me.

"She also cured me of something else," my brother added, his tone more serious. "Judgment. I've been a bigger fool than ... well, a half-built fence has more sense than I did. Henry, I do apologize for what I said to you that night. You were like a brother to me, and it was wrong. I was more wrong than I've ever been in my life."

The pause after he'd said this remorseful speech seemed far too long, and I held my breath. Would Henry accept it? He had shown no indication at the Vallencourt mansion he forgave my brother for his youthful anger.

At last, I heard Henry sigh. When he spoke, his voice was so quiet I had to lean forward. But my patience was well-rewarded.

"And I must offer my apology as well. I've also been foolish, but in the ways of integrity. I let pride get in the way of honor."

I inhaled so deeply my corset laces dug into my back, and then let it out as quietly as I could. The mutual apologies had been made. It was time for them to begin anew.

Henry's chair scraped along the floor and the bed creaked. It sounded like they were both rising to their feet. A moment later, I heard them clap each other on the back. An embrace of truce. The bed creaked again as my brother laid down. He coughed slightly, nowhere near the severity of his former illness.

"So, you're a free man, Henry Vallencourt. No bride and no obligations."

Henry laughed. "Oh, I am, am I? Is a Vallencourt ever truly free?"

"Of course," Gabriel snorted. "But I hope you search inside and dig up the man I used to know. Because he was as honorable and upright as they come."

"I'll see what I can do, Gabriel. Your share of the inheritance will pay for a life of freedom for yourself, to be sure."

"It's astonishing how generous Esther has been." Gabriel sighed. "She's even giving my mother and sister a thousand dollars to start a new life. I'd have kicked them to the cobblestones. She's a better person than me."

I blushed, twisting my hands together. Better enjoy the praise as a silent observer, I thought. It also made me realize how little time I would spend with my brother before he left for Virginia.

It was a fine thing that Henry and Gabriel had reconciled. They could begin their friendship again as men, and not the judgmental and prideful boys they'd once been.

I walked downstairs and returned to a pleasant conversation in the parlor. Alexandra had offered the positions of bridesmaids to Annie, Lara, and myself.

"Oh, please let the dress color be blue," my sister said. "We all have the prettiest blue eyes. Well, save Esther of course, and she'd look lovely in the color as well."

"Yes," I said, for I was wearing a dress of deep navy. "I think it a fine color, should you select it."

"Blue it is." Alexandra smiled.

"Oh, and Esther," my sister added. "I have decided to write to Mr. Hodges and request that I may purchase Sarge."

I stared at her. "Lara!"

"I take it you approve." She grinned. "I'll write to him directly."

"That is wonderful," I said. "I should think he'd sell him if you offered a fair asking price."

"Fair is nothing to Mr. Hodges. Of course he'll be greedy." Lara said it with such certainty it caused the rest of us to giggle. "But I'll get my horse back."

Annie chuckled. "I don't know where that bluntness comes from. But my husband sure has it."

"That he does," Lara said, then turned to me. "Will you please play a song for us?"

"What a fine idea," Alexandra agreed. "I loved hearing you play, and it's been such a long time."

My heart glowed with the warmth of my company. Though it had been several weeks since the end of my service, I still felt a thrill when I saw my sheet music folio on the stand. I could indulge my passion for music whenever I wished.

I stood and went over to the piano. I picked up the folio and began rifling through the different pieces. I could play Chopin or perhaps Liszt. Some of the Bach pieces were cheerful and not too lengthy.

"Any requests?" I said.

"The *Pathetique Sonata*."

It was Henry. I abruptly looked up, almost dropping the folio. It trembled in my hands, the sheet music fluttering. He was standing just inside the parlor doorway, his jacket slung across his arm, his demeanor as relaxed and pleasant as I'd ever seen him. Alexandra gestured to an empty chair.

"So lovely to have you join us, Henry. Esther was about to play. Do be seated."

He walked slowly into the room and approached the chair. But instead of sitting down, he placed his jacket over the back of the chair and shook his head.

"No, but thank you for offering."

I stood frozen next to the piano bench, the folio balanced on my hands, struggling to find words to say something. Anything, really. But I couldn't take my eyes off of him. My heart felt full once again, but this time it was not with an aching sorrow. Lara looked at me, then looked at Henry. Abruptly, she turned to Annie and blurted:

"Annie, won't you come upstairs with me? I would like to tell Gabriel all about my merchant idea."

Silence. Henry placed his hands on the back of the chair, but still did not take his seat. Alexandra suddenly looked at her brother, gave a courteous smile, and got to her feet.

"Yes," she said to Annie. "I should like to see your husband as well. He has recovered, has he not?"

I blushed. Annie smirked, for she at last understood and didn't need any more coaxing before she also rose from the sofa. Almost before I knew what was happening, the three ladies had resumed their conversation about blue bridesmaid gowns on their way across the parlor and over to the doorway. Their voices echoed in the front hall, then a chorus of giggles and the sound of light footsteps on the main staircase.

Henry and I were alone.

I didn't know what to do. I didn't know what to say. My mind was as blank and quiet as the ivory keys on the piano. He took a step towards me, hands easing into his trouser pockets, as comfortable and relaxed as could be.

"Will you play for me?"

Oh, yes. I would play for you. Only for you. I stared down at the folio in my hands as if seeing it for the first time. With clumsy fingers, I gently took the sonata sheet music pages. He slowly leaned down and pulled out the bench. I tucked the pages on the stand, gently closed the folio and placed it on top of the piano. Lifting my skirts, I slid onto the bench and seated myself. My feet slipped from beneath my dress and found the pedals. Pressing first the left pedal and then the right, in my little dance of greeting.

Henry stepped behind me, and I could hear him breathing, feel his warmth pressing against my back. My heart's pounding began to ease, like the tide calming after a storm. His warm fingers slid over my shoulders.

I closed my eyes, put my hands on the keys, and began the song. And with each note, I felt more and more full, as if pure sunlight was pouring into my empty body. He hummed the melody behind me, his voice a rich and mellow tenor. The music drifted and swelled, and with each note I felt myself becoming more complete. Like a painting receiving its final brushes of colored light. At last, the artist could stand back from her masterpiece and feel the joyous, finished contentment of a creative endeavor. The final measure, and those last harmonious notes lingered in the air between Henry and I, his voice and my music together.

He leaned down and placed his warm cheek against my temple, his breath on my shoulder.

"It was beautiful, Esther."

It was. A moment almost magical in its expression. He came around to the side of the bench, and seated himself beside me as if he wished to play a duet. He on the lower keys and me on the higher. I remembered the day I'd thought of the differences between us as the notes on a piano. He had been out of my range ...

I put my left hand on the middle C major chord, and he closed his right hand over my fingers. Shyly, I looked at him, my shoulder against his arm, his handsome face so close to mine. His eyes were dark and warm, and a smile tugged at his lips.

"There is something I must tell you."

I nodded, breathing as steadily as I could as he laced his fingers with mine.

"Last night, I met with my father. He renewed his offer of partnership at the architectural firm, and I have accepted it. I accompany him to the office on Monday."

His voice was quiet and content, the pronouncement of a man who had aligned his inner passions with his outer actions. It was how I'd longed for him to speak since the night in the Vallencourt library.

"I am ... deeply proud of you," I whispered.

He looked down at our hands. "Thank you. I want to help rebuild this city."

My nervousness quietly vanished, as greenery covers soil. At last, I could look at him as a man of character and worth, able to occupy the position he had desired and was born for. I allowed my affection for him then, deep and true, to overwhelm me in the best sense.

"You have made me realize how greatly it meant to me. I am sorry you lost your home, but I hope you have become happy here."

"I have, sir."

He pressed his lips to my hand. "How could I not want to be a better man with such grace and kindness as you have shown. Say you will be by my side. Dearest Esther."

My heart opened and washed warm light all around the inside of me. All the cold winds I'd felt vanished into an exquisite silence.

"Henry," I said aloud.

To say it. To feel each note of his name like a beloved sonata. I closed my eyes, and he kissed me. Words vanished and I felt nothing but a lovely melody, a quiet insistent symphony. It was a new song.

The song of us.

34

On April 9th, 1869, in the city of Portland, Maine, there was a double wedding.

All who attended pronounced the bridesmaids especially exquisite in their light blue georgette gowns. At last, the Curtis and Vallencourt families were united, as had been the long desired outcome for both parties. It was widely thought a fortuitous match for the new Mrs. Vallencourt, since a rumor that she was the grand-daughter of a former Bangor mayor put to rest any gossip about her rural upbringing. Indeed, in a remarkable fashion considering the Vallencourts' prominence, the lady was immediately accepted into the highest of social circles, and her exquisite manners soothed any quizzical brows or negative misgivings.

Henry Vallencourt exhibited an extraordinary gesture of benevolence by bringing his bride's old housekeeper, Sarah Wicklow, to come and live with them. There was not a dry eye in the household when this happy reunion occurred. Lara Perry, the bride's sister, was especially delighted that Sarah had brought a certain equine who was made as comfortable as possible in the family stables.

As for the city itself, Portland gained the Latin motto of "Resurgam"

- for it rose from the ashes of the dreadful 1866 fire - and a new symbol, in the form of a phoenix. A city is made by its citizens, and Portland could boast no better examples than those who worked at the Vallencourt Architectural Firm on Fore Street or the talented doctors at the medical office on Federal Street.

Two years later in 1871, the city's most prominent physician and his youngest son were involved in a committee to build Maine General Hospital. Those who have visited its facilities pronounce them quite clean and comfortable. The same thing can be said for the hospital in Richmond, Virginia, built by another member of this talented medical family.

If you perchance come and visit Portland, do walk along Middle Street and take a moment to admire the amazing buildings constructed during the great city-wide rebuilding. The Curtis House at the corner of Spring and High Streets still commands a lovely view of Portland Harbor from its uppermost windows. You can also visit the beautiful mansion on Danforth Street, walk up its wide stone steps and pass through its large front doors to the magnificent front hall. The first door on the left will lead you into the parlor.

There you will see a gorgeous piano, where the illustrious mistress played hour after contented hour, filling her stunning home with music.

Beethoven's *Pathetique Sonata* was said to be her favorite.

The End

Made in the USA
Charleston, SC
28 November 2015